Praise for Maximum Velocity

"Those glorious golden age sci-fi pulp magazines have now been reincarnated."

Midwest Book Review, review of *Space Pirates.*

"Reading this book has reminded me of all the reasons I love Sci-Fi."

Pauline Creeden, author of *The Prodigal Life*,
review of *Space Battles.*

MAXIMUM VELOCITY

The Best of Full Throttle Space Tales

MAXIMUM VELOCITY

The Best of Full Throttle Space Tales

Edited by David Lee Summers,
Carol Hightshoe, Dayton Ward,
Jennifer Brozek, and
Bryan Thomas Schmidt

WordFire Press
Colorado Springs, Colorado

MAXIMUM VELOCITY: THE BEST OF THE FULL THROTTLE SPACE TALES

Originally compiled by Hadrosaur Productions 2016

Individual story copyrights and first publication information:

Additional copyright information on page 379

ISBN: 978-1-61475-529-6

Cover design by Janet McDonald

Cover artwork images by Adobe Stock

Edited by David Lee Summers, Carol Hightshoe, Dayton Ward, Jennifer Brozek, and Bryan Thomas Schmidt

Kevin J. Anderson, Art Director

Book Design by RuneWright, LLC
www.RuneWright.com

Published by
WordFire Press, an imprint of
WordFire, Inc.
PO Box 1840
Monument CO 80132

Kevin J. Anderson & Rebecca Moesta, Publishers

WordFire Press Trade Paperback Edition August 2017
Printed in the USA
wordfirepress.com

CONTENTS

Part I: Space Pirates **1**

On the Eve of the Last Great Ratings War 3

Space Pirate Cookies 27

Earth-Saturn Transit 53

Part II: Space Sirens **77**

Outpost 6 79

Hijacking the Legacy 99

Rebel Moon 113

Part III: Space Grunts **127**

Price of Command 129

Finders Keepers 147

Granny's Grunts 175

Part IV: Space Horrors **189**

Last Man Standing 191

Into the Abyss 221

Listening 241

Part V: Space Tramps **261**

Backup 263

The Frigate Lieutenant's Woman 279

Oh Give Me Land, Lots of Land, Under Starry Skies Above 295

Part VI: Space Battles **325**

The Thirteens 327

The Joystick War 345

Guard Dog 367

Additional Copyright Information 379

About the Editors 381

Other WordFire Press Anthologies 383

Introduction

Accelerating to Maximum Velocity

David Lee Summers

Welcome to *Maximum Velocity*, an anthology which collects the best stories from a run of six books known collectively as the Full-Throttle Space Tales Series, published between 2008 and 2012. My name is David Lee Summers and I'm joined by editors Carol Hightshoe, Dayton Ward, Jennifer Brozek, and Bryan Thomas Schmidt. We'll be your hosts on this series of adventures set in the distant future. As you prepare for this ride, I hope you'll allow me a moment to reflect on the journey so far.

In 2007, David Boop approached me on behalf of his publisher, David Rozansky, about editing an anthology of fun, action-charged tales about space pirates. I put out a call and started collecting stories. David, David, and I met later that year at MileHiCon in Denver, Colorado along with some other editors and authors—most of whom, fortunately, were not named David. Over dinner we came to realize that we could tell action-charged stories about many types of people. We made plans to collect anthologies about women in space, soldiers in space, vampires in space, and more.

Over the next five years, our team of editors collected six anthologies. *Space Pirates* was the first followed by *Space Sirens* edited by Carol Hightshoe, which told stories of strong women exploring the stars. Dayton Ward, well known for his *Star Trek* tie-in work was tapped to edit an anthology about line soldiers fighting among the stars called *Space Grunts*. I returned to edit the series' fourth volume about the monsters and scary things one might find while exploring the cosmos called *Space Horrors*. Jennifer Brozek, already a well-regarded editor in her own right and who went on to garner a Hugo nomination, suggested an anthology about vagabonds travelling the spaceways called *Space Tramps*. Last but not least, Bryan Thomas Schmidt, who has also since garnered a Hugo nomination for his editorial work, collected *Space Battles*.

As time went on, the original publisher of the Full-Throttle Space Tales decided to move away from publishing fiction and the anthologies were taken out of print. Despite that, those of us who had put so much time and love into this series felt there was too much good material to allow it to languish, so we decided to collect the very best of the Full-Throttle Space Tales and present them under one cover.

Selecting the best of a good set of stories, especially ones you're attached to is never easy. Our process was to give each of our anthologies to the next editor in line and let them pick their favorite stories. So Carol Hightshoe selected her favorite stories from *Space Pirates*, Dayton Ward selected his favorites from *Space Sirens*, and so on. The upshot is that each story in this volume has been vetted not just by one editor, but at least two. Even though most of the editors had stories in these collections, none of them nominated their own. Once the selections were made, the original editors went back and worked with the authors to polish the stories and really make them shine for this volume. Each story is preceded by a new introduction by its editor.

Okay, that's the pre-flight talk. Make sure those tray tables and seats are in the upright position for takeoff, because it's time to open the throttle and accelerate to maximum velocity!

Part I:
Space Pirates

Edited by David Lee Summers

On the Eve of the Last Great Ratings War

by David Boop

Introduction to "On the Eve of the Last Great Ratings War"

I suspect all of us who have owned pets have found ourselves wondering what they think about. What's more, animals have long been bred to perform specialized tasks for humans. As we go into space and as we improve our genetic engineering skills, I can easily imagine scientists creating smarter dogs and cats, bred to do the dirty jobs that humans don't want to do. Of course, any time someone has to do those dirty jobs, they will rebel and piracy has long been a means to express that rebellion.

Those ideas alone had the potential for a great story, but David Boop added a look at our ability to become celebrities through reality television and the internet. In the process, he snuck some social commentary into a story that has both action and humor.

I first met David Boop at a writer's workshop at the Opus Fantasy Arts Festival in Denver, Colorado. I saw a lot of promise in David at that early meeting and he has gone on to do great things. Turn the page to find out what happens on the eve of the last great ratings war.

"Do you have the signal, Nip?"

"It's coming, sir. And sir? Please stop calling me 'Nip.'"

"I will *consider* not calling you Nip when you have the signal."

The young Feigatos was agitated. Yellow fur creased on his brow as declawed fingers raked over the keyboard. "It's coming. When have I let you down?"

"Let me think. The F'jorian Nebula," the Captain responded, finger poised on his chin.

"That wasn't my—"

"And den dere was da Beteene job," Demmy, the first mate, said in a loud whisper. His whiskers brushed against his gray fur as he scratched his nose.

"Oh, and don't forget that incident on M34 run," said Doc Likimous, his smooth, nearly translucent skin making him seem alien even next to his fellow Feigatos.

The Captain grinned. The men were just giving the kit some well-intentioned ribbing, but he knew their hacker would lose focus if they cut too deep. "Okay, crew. Let the cat do his job." To his hacker, he asked, "You will break us in, will you not, Nip?" He placed his large gloved paw on the shoulder of his hyperspace fidelity stream expert. "This is far from your first HyFi hack. Should be no trouble at all."

"No, Captain, not at all."

Nip placed his paws behind his head in triumph as the bridge of the star-vessel *Nolean* lit up with the holographic image of the Hu'nax Imperial Network logo—a giant fist blazoned in reds and blacks. A pleasant female voice emanated from the floating logo:

"H.I.N. presents the Imperial Transport Channel. Your stream will begin shortly."

The Captain was pleased. His lips curled into a ferocious smile and white teeth stood out against the orange fur that covered his feline head and muscular body. He looked every bit the predator his ancestors were, complemented with the latest in modern gunmetal-gray armor and two oversized boarding blasters.

He walked over to his captain's chair and sat down. The carved baobab wood offset the metal and plastics of the bridge, which made him feel more at home there than anywhere in the galaxy. He drug a claw against a replaceable plank embedded in the armrest, feeling the curl of the shaving under his nail. Of all the ships he had stolen for his personal use, this was his favorite. He even named it after his first love.

The cat pirate cut an imposing figure on the bridge of the *Stalker*-class attack vessel; the ship as fine a balance of style and function as its commander. Its double-wedge shape allowed it unparalleled agility in both real and hyperspace. Gun ports filled its concave sides, ready for close combat maneuvers.

"Good job, Nip. Let us see if our prey's stream is up yet."

Nip cursed under his breath at the Captain's pet name for him. His padded fingers tapped keys sternly. "Got it."

The holographic image changed from the H.I.N. logo to that of another ship's bridge. It was large and luxurious and implied the power and prestige befitting a transport vessel in service to the Imperium. The Hu'nax commander sat in his chair, just starting his testimonial. The Captain sighed. He hated this most about monitoring the network: broadcast ego trips.

"Well, yes, the mantle of command does wear heavily on this crown sometimes, but when the Emperor calls you, you respond."

The first mate shook his head. "Who is dis waste of bandwidth?"

"Nip, run a hyki on this guy."

Nip sampled the Hu'nax commander's retinal pattern and pulled up his bio page. Fresh from the academy with mediocre marks across the board, the Captain had seen scarier lint between his toes.

"Gentlecats, we have a company man here!"

The crew laughed. Any nearly hairless ape-descendant this green was considered a "company man." Recent graduates knew nothing about ship combat that hadn't come from their officer's manual and were easy pickings … usually.

The Captain paged his boarding crew. Azalin, his Mũssex squad leader, answered. Slanted red eyes looked at the Captain down a brown-furred nose.

Yess, Captain? Azalin projected.

Like the rest of his crew, the Captain had overridden his reflex to lick his lips every time he saw Azzie. Only a few centuries ago, Feigatos considered Mũssex prey. Despite years of genetic manipulation, most Feigatos wouldn't pass up a chance at a Mũssex meal. Azzie had changed that thanks to his telepathic abilities, a rarity amongst his kind. Azzie had convinced the Captain that their interests ran parallel and, in turn, the Captain had spared the rodent-like thief's life. Since the hodgepodge crew of the *Nolean* was already an assortment of misfits, the Mũssex fit right in.

"Looks like a company man, but do be careful anyway."

Azzie thought, *I alwayss am.*

True to the Captain's faith in him, the Mũssex had always been first through the hatch, his diminutive size and faster-than-Hu'nax reflexes made him nearly impossible to get a lock on. Azzie broke through gauntlets like sour milk through a kitten.

The Captain turned back to the projection.

"I was chosen specially for this assignment by the general himself. He saw my demo reel at graduation and said I was just the guy he was looking for. He liked my persona, my ease in front of the hy-cam."

The Captain guffawed, "Is there a Hu'nax that doesn't go into the academy hoping to be a military celebrity? I would bet a week's rations that the general has never heard his name. People that high up rarely deal directly with their underlings."

"They won't tell me what I'm hauling, but I'm sure it's pretty important. I was given a special instructional stream on tactics to fend off those lousy Feigato pirates."

The Captain stroked the hairs under his chin and voiced his thoughts out loud, "It is like this hork is inviting me to attack. Does he truly think that he can make a name for himself by taking me out?"

"He's an arrogant bastard, dat's fer sure, Captain." Demmy gave the projection a two-claw salute.

"How long until he is in range, Harra?"

The *Nolean*'s navigator scanned the data displayed at her station. She purred out his answer, while never taking her eyes off the monitor. "The transport will be passing us in four hundred point thirty-five seconds, Captain."

Their ship was attached to large piece of celestial matter rotating in the outer ring of a gas planet. A secondary gas giant lay relatively close, causing a flux in the hyperspace lane. The combined gravitational pull forced ships to leave hyperspace and recalculate. Transports had to put up with this or avoid the system altogether. However, since it was fastest route, ships dealt with the 3.28 seconds delay as they readjusted their coordinates.

The Captain knew about the prime ambush spot for years, but he never used it. He hoped the Empire would think it was their little secret, so he passed up small- and medium-sized transports. One day, he believed, they'd send something succulent through here, and it would be worth all the small meals he'd given up.

Finally, the rumor that a special shipment would be passing through this very area came within earshot of the Captain, a meal so secret that its contents were known only to the Emperor's closest advisors. Taking it would be a huge blow to the Imperium and could give the Captain the biggest ratings jump of his pirating career.

"Do you smell it, Demmy? This could be the one. The haul we need to draw the Emperor out."

"Aye, Captain. Dis could make you a serious contender; one da people would take notice of."

"Nip? How large is the feed?"

"It's going out to 218 systems; that's over half. There are some 35 trillion beings tuned in to this HyFi network, currently."

The Captain pounded his right fist against his armrest. "Bast's balls! Primetime! I cannot imagine a better set-up."

Doc walked up beside his leader and said, "Set-up is right. You can't tell me this doesn't stink of a trap, right?"

The Captain leapt up and looked into his closest advisor's eyes, questioning their intent. He saw nothing but sincerity within the ice blue gaze. He turned away, unfazed by Doc's concern.

"No, it is the real deal. It is too perfect." The Captain walked between stations, checking and rechecking readings. The crew could see his predator's instinct at work. "Every trap the Imperium has set for us pirates has always had a flaw. One that is noticeable, exploitable. Even after all this time, they still can't set the perfect trap." He shook his head violently, which caused his black-tipped ears to blur. "No, this is no trap. I would have had a whisper of something like that on the solar winds, Doc. I just think our time has finally come."

Likimous looked down in silence for a moment, and then recited, "'In the fields of observation chance favors only the prepared mind.' Pasteur."

"What's dat supposed to mean?" said Demmy who, after finishing his own set of double-checks, had grown agitated.

"It means that only by looking deeper can you see the truth."

The Captain slapped his ship's surgeon on the back. "Nothing to worry about, Doc. By this time tomorrow, we will be in the running for control of this galaxy and you will have worried for nothing."

Nip looked up from his HyFi rig. "You really believe that, Captain?"

"Aye, I do, Nip. As it was written, so shall it be."

The crew joined in, as the Captain recited the ancient code, "They that control the ratings, control the galaxy!"

They all knew the tale of old Earth, though some would discredit it as myth. Rebels had taken to the airwaves to fight the evil corporations that ran the world. Their pirate broadcasts had garnered sympathy and woken a people lulled into being sheep by entertainment and commercials.

"Yes, Nip. Ever since the Hu'nax first took the world back from their evil overlords, the motto has stood. You would not remember the tales handed down to us from the first generation of *genimals*. Humans, for that was what they were called back then, had kinder hearts and insatiable curiosity. Their single-world government, the Hu'nax Confederacy, ran pure in those first centuries. They worked hard to explore the galaxy, yet like most people with ultimate power, they started thinking themselves gods."

Doc took over the narration, "The Hu'nax created genimals for exploration in harsher regions of space, thus helping their control to expand quickly. The Feigatos, the Mũssex, and the Perresímos; each a race imbued with skills to weather specific environments, however, our ancestral instincts were still locked deep within our DNA."

"Despite genetic conditioning, safeguards wore off da longer we were in space," Demmy added, "Da Perresímos turned on da Feigatos, da Feigatos on da Mũssex, and all turned on da Hu'nax. Dey had colonized a thousand worlds, but couldn't control dem once war erupted."

The Captain continued, "Aye, and while further genetic manipulations lessened the effect, the damage was done. The Hu'nax reigned in control of their worlds with force and, in time, became as brutal an overseer as their predecessors had been."

"So, the Feigatos became pirates."

"Aye, Nip, in hopes of recreating the balance that once existed."

"And that's why you let the mous … er, Azzie, live?"

The Captain let the accidental racial slur slide because of Nip's age, barely over a kit that he was. It was okay for the Mũssex to call each other "mouse" or "rat," same as Feigatos calling themselves "cats," but interspecies slurs were not allowed on his watch. "That and others. How can we run a galaxy if we are slaves to our own instincts? If we are truly to rule as benevolent leaders, we need be masters of ourselves. I will not have a cat on my ship who is not. Working with Azzie tests that and, so far, it has worked to our advantage."

The bridge crew busied themselves for the impending assault. Nip made sure his hack stayed clean and untraceable. He double-checked the feeds for all broadcast locations: anti-grav cams with the boarding crew, the bridge cam, and the outside wide-angle cams for battle sequences. The viewers had to switch between feeds and Nip needed all shots to be perfect. If this went down the way the Captain wanted, Nip was sure they'd generate enough support to force the Emperor into a ratings battle.

When that happened, the Captain could finally get his name back; the one he'd sacrificed the day he went pirate.

Harra called out, "Forty-two point three five seconds to gravity well."

"We have deployed the hyperspace mines, as planned?" asked the Captain.

Demmy nodded, "Dey'll go off half a second after dat bloated pig of a ship drops out of hyperspace. Its engines will be useless fer an hour."

That pleased the Captain. Everything was going as expected. Yet Doc's fears echoed in his mind. He'd covered every contingency, hadn't he? All save for one. There was always one weak link in the plan. He leaned over to the com again. He hated to do this so close to "go time," but there was too much at stake to risk loose ends.

"Master-of-arms? Take Azalin into custody, quickly. Lock him up, now."

Outrage swept through his crew. Nip opened his mouth to protest, but was silenced by a look from the Captain. Even Demmy, who had been Azzie's biggest detractor at the first, was shocked. "Are ya sure dat's necessary, Captain?"

"Are you questioning me, First Mate?"

Demmy didn't like it, but he knew better than to try to countermand a direct order.

They watched on the antigrav hy-cams as Master Jaggit relieved Azzie of his weapons and escorted him to the brig. He went without any hostility. It was done in 15.25 seconds. The Captain loved how efficient his crew had become.

Harra counted, "5, 4, 3, 2, 1. Transport dropping out of hyperspace. Mines detonated. The ship is trapped in real space, Captain."

"Power up the engines, Harra. Demmy, release the clamps. Let us go harpoon a whale."

The *Nolean* rumbled as she peeled off her rock. Her engines came to life and the pirates flew in quickly for their first attack run. Nip transposed the Hu'nax logo with that of the ship's—a lion skull crossed with two femurs. The interruption would cause millions of beings to stay glued to their projectors in anticipation of the impending battle. People loved watching chaos and the Captain couldn't be happier.

"Launch the EM harpoon!"

"Aye, Captain!" called the gunnery sergeant. He targeted the transport's array and fired the large pointed missile. As a spearhead, the missile contained enough harmonics to break through any imperial force shield leaving behind a path in its wake that the *Nolean* could follow, reducing stress to her own shield generators.

That specialized a weapon had cost the Captain three times what the *Nolean* was worth, but like the gravity well, the Captain knew one day it would come in handy.

The missile pierced the force field and embedded in the side of the white vessel. Lights all over the ship dimmed and the crew saw a frightened look on the Hu'nax commander's fleshy face as he lost power throughout his ship. His last streamed words were directed point blank at the cam.

"Help me! I'm under attack by pir—"

The Captain took over the stream.

"Greetings, citizens of the Hu'nax Empire. I am the Captain of the *Nolean* and today I invite you to watch as I steal a crown jewel right from under your Emperor's nose. Like you, I have *no* idea what form the treasure takes, but I believe we are going to have fun regardless." He winked at the cam. "If you look at the sidebar to your right, you will be able to click on the background of this mission, including vidcaps of secret meetings I arranged to gather this intel. Also, down below, my HyFi expert has created searchable hykis on most of the crew, including their astrology signs, blood types, and what they will be listening to as we gut the Empire's transport.

"Finally, ladies, click on my image anytime to go to my dating profile on HySpace to find out my turn-ons, turn-offs and what I like to do on a first date.

"Remember, this is not *just* a rebellion. It *is* entertainment!"

The Captain looked over to Nip, who acted as his producer now. The kit gave a thumbs-up. "Looking good, Captain! I'm registering a record number of hits on all links."

The sound of detonations against the *Nolean*'s force shield caused the Captain to raise an eyebrow. "What is this, First Mate? How do they still have weapons?"

Demmy scanned a monitor. "Looks like dis is a newer version of da H234 Transport, Captain. Dey have a secondary power supply, shielded against IM attack. It seems limited to life-support and defense."

"A new ship? One with a shielded secondary power supply? You would almost think it was designed to fend off pirates, eh, Demmy?"

The mock surprise was evident and Demmy laughed and tried to emulate the Captain's tone, "Aye, Captain. Dis could make dings tough on us pirates. What ever shall we do?"

"Harra! Take us into combat positioning. Gunny, let's take out those missile launchers." The Captain smiled for his cam. "Well, this is a treat! I was worried you might get bored with us just docking and boarding the transport, but now you will get to see some actual ship-to-ship combat. Demmy will explain."

"Danke, Captain." Demmy's smile was nervous. He wasn't as used to being front and center as the Captain. Nip had given him enough lessons to get him this far, but no one had illusions about Demmy becoming a star. "We'll have da advantage, despite da transport being larger and containing a higher volume of weapons. Da *Nolean* was designed for dis exact ding. Scroll to your left and you see da stats of our baby. For da uninitiated, space combat works not just up and down, or forward and backwards. No, in the vacuum of space you have a whole sphere to move within. Da *Nolean*, being an attack craft, can swiftly move at any angle, allowing it to twist and turn like a fish in pond. Da M234 Transport couldn't move with our agility even if deir engines weren't down."

"Thank you, First Mate Demmy. For you dwelling-makers out there, Demmy's wife hosts a decorating stream on everything from redesigning your brood's room to adding atmosphere to your planet's moons. Click on 'Colony Living with Salania' on TTC: The Terraforming Channel from the drop-down marked 'links.'"

"Captain? Weapons are disabled. We're free to dock."

"Thank you, Harra."

While the crew prepared to board, Nip spliced in Harra's testimonial he'd shot earlier in the day. She had a natural sexiness in front of the camera, some of which came from her half-Siamese ancestry, and Nip tried not to drool on the hy-cam when he filmed her.

"The Captain found me, like he does most of the crew; dwellingless, hungry and dirt poor. I'd been a HyFi star for about ten point two-three seconds. I still don't know what all happened. I'd followed the plan to perfection starting with being a runner-up on a star-maker program." Harra ticked off items on her fingers. *"Then I released my 'stolen' sex-stream to decent reviews. Cut an*

album that went trillium on first stream. Went off and had an affair with that member of the Imperium. I should have been big, yet somehow it all came crashing down. Maybe I should have taken those singing lessons, after all?"

The shot cut to the master-of-arms and the boarding crew outside the hatch of the Hu'nax vessel. Jaggit was a ragged veteran of too many firefights. There were bald patches where blaster fire had scorched his fur. If there was ever more of a pirate's pirate, the galaxy hadn't found him yet.

He addressed the audience. "This here hatch blowin' be brought to you by Foster's Body Armor. When the shit really hits the fan, have your ass in a Foster's can!" He turned and the name "Foster's" was prominently displayed in digital glory across his buttocks. It glowed blue so viewers at home could click on it to go to the retailer's site.

The Captain hated the product endorsement deals some of the crew had started making. However, he paid them so little he couldn't help but support these side ventures. "Well said, Master Jaggit. However, if we could, for the moment, focus on the other kind of booty, I would be ever so grateful."

Jaggit looked a little embarrassed, but not disheartened. It was a gift of the Captain's to reprimand without destroying confidence. "Sure thing, Cap'n. Fellas? Let's blow this pig!"

The explosion looked far more spectacular than it actually was. Nip had added a few extra bangs and flashes using his FX generator, plus laid down a score that accented the impending firefight. Blaster bolts came spirally out of the detonation smoke. The *Nolean*'s crew returned fire, laying down a wall of suppression. Jaggit dove through first, clearing the smoke and rolling forward into a crouch. He used a shoulder-mounted blaster with Heads-Up Display implants within his eyes. With lightning skill, he painted each of the front line defenders and took them out. He took a couple shots to his right arm, but the damage hardly threw off his aim. The rest of the boarding party joined the fray having been relayed the targeting intel. The Captain slipped an eye patch over his left eye. It had similar HUD features, which allowed him to monitor ship information in real time.

Antigrav cams buzzed around under Nip's control. He had to dodge the Hu'nax's own cams, even though they were all but useless without their network feed. Nip went in close to some of the soldiers, capturing retinal scans and pulling up hykis on each. He was noticing a trend within the intelligence he gathered. There wasn't a single officer or grunt that was more than six months out of the academy. They were all company men.

Nip turned on his own cam. "Captain? I think we've got a problem."

"Little busy right now, Nip. Can it wait?" The defenders retreated down a corridor and tried to set up a secondary defense. Klaxons bleated in the background. *Classic*, the Captain thought.

"Maybe, but I don't think so. I'm starting to get the same feeling Doc did. Something's not right here."

"Hold on. We are about to toss a grenade." There was a loud boom. That, plus the alarms made Nip difficult to hear. "Say again?"

"I said, I THINK IT'S A TRAP!" A stray bolt took out one of the antigrav cams near the Captain. "Captain? *Captain!*" Nip switched to a second cam where the reverse angle was better. He could see the whole party and everyone was all right. White teeth gleamed through the smoke as it thinned.

"Thanks to the sacrifice of your cam, Nip, we broke through the line. We have taken the corridor. Jaggit and Likimous are leading a group to the bridge to secure things there. I'm taking some cats to the hold to see if this was all worth the effort." He waved to the prone bodies. "I do not relish the death of these young, brave men. They are pawns, used and discarded by an uncaring empire. If any of the families are watching right now, I honor their sacrifice."

The Captain bowed his head and Nip brought up respectful music and images gathered of the dead. Nip put thoughts of a trap behind him. The Captain knew what he was doing.

"What was it you wanted to say, Nip?"

"Nothing, Captain. Nothing."

Nip's antigrav cams split with the groups. Jaggit had no problem securing the bridge. The commander practically gave the master-at-arms welcome gifts when his team arrived. The Captain, meanwhile, was working with his group to break the security code on the hold. Blasting was not an option when the cargo was unknown. His code breaker was bent over the panel furiously trying to descramble its secret.

"Not to rush you, my dear, but we have eaten up fifteen minutes of our hour, and you know me … I hate to have things come down to the wire."

Her actual name was Amis, but "Yeti" would have better matched her look and temperament. Her round body was covered with starched white hair that stuck straight out at all angles.

"With all due respect, Captain, don't you tell me my job. I'm not the Nip. I don't need prodding! And don't give me that, 'My Dear' crap. I'll have you up on harassment charges in two point one four seconds."

The Captain raised his paws in surrender as Amis stood up triumphantly.

"There!" she said. She turned to face the opening door, weapon drawn.

Amis's head blossomed red as blaster fire hit her flat face. The Captain's reflexes barely saved him from the next barrage, though he felt his armor take a sting or two in the back. Another of his cats fell, his paw never making it all the way to his gun belt. The Captain scrambled on all fours, spun onto his back and fired as he slid down the corridor.

Dog soldiers poured from the hold. Snarling, howling. Their jowls drooling with saliva they flung left and right as they mowed down the *Nolean*'s boarding party.

The Captain saw the shape of things, so he threw down his blasters and held up his hands. Nobody left in his group to mend even if the Doc wasn't with the other group. In a way he was glad Likimous wasn't here. He didn't want to see the cat's smug look at being right.

The Hu'nax Imperium must have finally made a secret deal with the Perresímos, and it had worked.

One soldier, gray with low-hanging jowls, looked at a hovering cam and tapped a button on his arm. The cam went dead, as did all the others on the *Nolean*.

O O O

The Hu'nax logo once again spun in the air above the HyFi hacker. They'd overridden Nip's security protocols with surprising ease. Their encryption was years beyond anything the youth had encountered. Nip wasn't sure he could retake the signal from where he sat at the bridge. The dog soldiers hadn't made it that far, taking the ship a level at a time. The bridge crew could be the last free cats on board. At least the Imperium hadn't started broadcasting executions … yet.

"I can't reach anyone: the Captain, Jaggit. We're on our own, Demmy."

"How many we talkin' about, Nip?"

"There was a squad, maybe twenty, that took out the Captain's team, but I'll bet there is more than that."

"We'll be preparin' to repel invaders, then."

Nip was even more alarmed. "The Captain said if a boarding like this should happen we were to make a run for it. Save what crew remained."

"Aye, he did say dat, didn't he?" Demmy let his words hang, waiting to see what their hacker would do.

"But, we don't do that, do we? Never leave a cat behind … if you can help it."

"Aye, kittiebuck. Dat'll be the stuff." He addressed the bridge. "Harra? Arm the crew. Gunny, let's see if we can target that jammer onboard and toast it." To the rest he said, "Okay, let's go get the Captain back."

That might be presumptuouss, at this point, projected Azzie.

O O O

The Captain had been taken to the transport commander's office. Per his orders, Demmy, Jaggit and the rest of the crew had surrendered without another loss of life. When his time came, the Captain would know intimately how much blood would be on his hands, and he didn't want any more.

Behind the desk, instead of the Hu'nax officer, sat a Perresímos Sergeant Commander. He was lean and muscular and apparently in charge of the situation. Short brown and tan hair covered most of his body yet his snout was jet black. When he smiled, black gums outlined bright-white, razor-sharp teeth.

"So, the all-so slippery captain of the *Nolean* has finally been brought to his knees. This makes the alliance worth it, if for nothing else."

He waited on the Captain to retort, but found none coming. The sergeant got up, walked over to the bound Feigatos, and got directly in the Captain's face. Breath, like dead meat, made the Captain's eyes water. "Aw, not so glib now, are you? Where are your fancy cams now? Where are your product endorsements?"

"Where is your master? Why is he not behind you, holding your leash?"

The backhand was hard, but it could have been harder. The Captain's best guess was that the prisoners were not to be roughed up too much. Visible damage might gain a sympathy vote at the execution.

The sergeant returned to the desk. "You Feigatos, you really think you're saving the galaxy? How arrogant! Maybe the galaxy has never needed saving. Maybe what it most needs is to evolve."

The inside of the Captain's cheek had been cut with the blow. He spat blood on the carpet. "And how do you think that will happen? Through compliance? Through becoming slaves again?"

"It comes from within, Captain. Or should I call you …"

"Stop! Do not use that name. I do not care how you got it, but if you grant me any boon, do not say that name."

The sergeant's laugh had a howl-like resonance to it, "Hawoo! Does a name hold so much meaning to you? If you want a consideration, why not ask for the lives of your crew? Or a quick death? But to waste your energy on a name? Ridiculous!"

The Captain chuckled along with the soldier. "I am sure it is something you could never understand. You have given away your freedom. For a Feigatos pirate captain, identity is everything. We sacrifice our names and only by returning balance to the galaxy are we allowed to reclaim it."

A serious look passed over his adversary's face. "You truly believe you're right, don't you? You'd rather die a nameless death? Has it ever occurred to you that balance could come just by joining with the Hu'nax? They aren't what they once were. There are those in power that seek change. The Perresímos will have a voice once your rebellion is squashed. For the first time, the negotiations put us on almost equal ground to the Hu'nax."

The Captain gave his adversary a half-smile. "Do you think they'll honor that? You are a fool."

"No! You're the fool! You lost good cats today. Cats that might have lived to see a new era of equality and prosperity."

In a voice just about a whisper, the Captain said, "Do not call us cats."

The Perresímos leaned forward, cocking an ear toward his prisoner, "I'm sorry, could you repeat that?"

"I said, 'Do not call us CATS!'"

Straightening up, he grinned, "Fine! Instead, I will call you the late crew of the *Nolean*." He snapped and two dog soldiers came in and dragged the Captain away.

O O O

The exchange had left a bad taste in the Sergeant Commander's maw. It bothered him and even ripping into the soft flesh of the cat pirate would not cleanse it. Instead, he decided to distract himself from it by talking to the fool Hu'nax commander of the transport. He entered through the still-open door and addressed the sergeant who had returned to his seat.

"Um, my ship should be operational again in about twenty minutes."

The dog soldier tilted his head to the side. "Whose ship?"

"Sorry, sir. Your ship should be ready in nineteen point five."

"Good."

"Um, can I ask how you did it?"

The Perresímos appraised the weak Hu'nax and wondered why he had to play the role of servant to this thing. He placed his paws on the table, interlocked fingers on top. "Did what?"

"How did you take them out so quickly?"

The sergeant motioned to the chair recently vacated by the cat and the Hu'nax sat.

Irony, thought the soldier.

"This ship has several features you were not aware of. We designed it with the strict intent of capturing pirates."

"You designed it? You mean as part of the alliance?"

"Yes. Who better to outsmart a cat pirate than a dog?"

He chuckled and the commander chuckled along uncomfortably. "Yes, but like what? How is it different?"

"This transport is like two ships in one. It has a completely separate mainframe that can control every aspect of the ship. The bridge, should it be knocked out as it was, is unnecessary and only there for show. This allows us to run our new hyperspace jammer. They're blind to the network and each other. They have no way to communicate with each other."

Righteous indignation grew in the Hu'nax commander. "Why was I not briefed on any of this?"

The sergeant leaned forward and addressed the man in the same way he addressed the cat, "Because you are as unnecessary as the bridge you sit on."

O O O

"Hey," a Perresímos soldier called to his flank, "There's something in here!"

They had entered the detention bloc aboard the *Nolean.* The soldiers had met surprisingly little resistance as they took the ship level by level.

"Why if it isn't a widdle mousey? Hello widdle mousey. Were the big bad cats gonna eat you?"

Azzie cowered in the corner. The two dog soldiers laughed and continued their taunting.

"I'll never understand why the Hu'nax didn't make these things able to talk. Weren't they supposed to be for underground exploration? I'd think they'd have wanted them to report in."

"Oh, they can think and hype in reports and stuff," said the other, "I think the Hu'nax found them too disgusting to talk to."

Oh, we can talk fine, thank you. We just prefer talking to intelligent speciess only.

The soldiers looked around for the source of the voice and finally turned to find a heavily armed rodent smirking at them. They fell with little noise.

Azzie left his never-locked cell and made his way from the *Nolean* to the Imperium transport. His covert skills allowed him to move with ease within the shadows. He occasionally had to cling to the ceiling as dog soldiers passed underneath him, but the creatures rarely looked up. The Perresímos were rumored to have an excellent sense of smell, but with all the smoke and overwhelming "catness" of the ship, Azzie doubted they would ever discern him.

He was already behind schedule, having taken extra time to convince Nip that the best thing the bridge crew could do was hunker down and wait.

Do you understand now? Azzie had thought after explaining.

"The Captain was planning on taking the transport all along?"

It'ss not an actual transport, but made to look like one. But yess, he'd heard about a new pirate killer being developed. He didn't know about the Perresímoss deal. He cussed so loudly I still have a headache.

"Locking you up was an extra precaution?"

Yess. That way we'd be able to coordinate our attack without use of hyperspace frequencies. Now, I have to go take the secondary bridge.

"Wait! What does he need me to do?"

Break that encryption. Without it, we'll never be able to take the ship on cam.

"But this thing is light years ahead of me!"

No, it'ss not. That'ss why the Captain chose you. He saw in you infinite ability. Now that you know who developed it, thiss should be a piece of cheese to you.

The hacker hadn't looked at the problem that way. He was still thinking it was Hu'nax designed. He went back to work and left the rescue to Azzie.

The concentration of soldiers made the going slower in the transport, so Azzie took to the air ducts. He found the secondary bridge and listened in.

"An escort vessel! Why is the Emperor sending an escort vessel?"

He could see a brown and tan Perresímos below through a vent. The dog didn't look happy. He was talking to someone through

HyFi but the other's words were unclear. Their implication was.

"This wasn't part of the deal. We'd bring the pirates in and announce the alliance to the whole galaxy. That would make the eventual merger of our two races go smoother."

More words then, "Yes, sir. I understand." The Perresímos sounded defeated, but angry.

"What is it, Sergeant?" asked a dog soldier.

"This mission should have been the beginning of something grand, our first joint operation, but now it's going to look like the Hu'nax planned everything and used us as tools. I smell a rat!"

Not me, Azzie thought to himself, but checked his armpits anyway.

O O O

The Captain was fuming. Doc tried to comfort him as best he could. "They say 'One must be a god to be able to tell successes from failures without making a mistake.' You couldn't have known what would happen, Captain. It was un …"

"The thing is, I did know."

"What?"

"I knew all along it was a trap. I just thought I had prepared enough. It was the Perresímos I was not prepared for. Had I known, I would not have been so cavalier."

Jaggit pointed toward the brig's door where a guest had arrived. "Ya might get yer chance to fix that, Cap'n, after all."

The sergeant dismissed the guards from in front of the Captain's cell. He paced back and forth a bit.

"Something on your mind?" asked the Captain.

"What if you're right? What if the purpose of this whole alliance is to get us back under the control of the Hu'nax?"

"Yeah, an escort battleship does not sound all that friendly, especially when you have already got things well under control."

The Perresímos's jaw hung loose.

"I have my sources." The Captain motioned up to the ceiling where Azzie had just arrived via the vent. He dropped to the floor, gun at the ready, but not directly pointing at the sergeant.

It took some doing to convince the Captain that the best hope for the galaxy iss a meeting of the mindss, so to speak. Azzie laughed at his own pun. It came out like a snicker.

"They can …"

"Yeah, Azzie and his whole race have their own language, but only a few can project thoughts. When I rescued him, it was the beginning of something bigger. Something you could be a part of."

"What? A part of what?" The soldier didn't look convinced.

A gleam reflected in the Captain's eye.

"Piracy."

"Hawoo! I'm not like you!" He waved the idea off. "I'm used to following orders. I can't think independently like you do."

The Captain sat back on the cell bench, legs crossed. He waved a paw around nonchalantly. "You almost beat me, you know. You and your people. This ship you designed? Brilliant. Let us face facts. You had to think like a pirate to best a pirate. It will not be as hard as you think to use that instinct for some better purpose."

Azzie unlocked the cell, keeping his red eyes on the Perresímos as he did it, but the soldier made no effort to stop him. The Captain walked up to the dog soldier, placed a paw on either shoulder and said, "I had planned to steal this ship from the beginning, but I think there is a better captain for it."

"I-I couldn't."

"There is a fully loaded attack vessel on its way here. Do you not see the invisible leash? Snap it!"

The sergeant looked inward, as though a million scenarios played out in his mind. When he brought his head up again, it was slow and deliberate and a shine appeared his eyes that had started to grow. It looked a lot, to the Captain, like a pirate's gleam.

"Let's take that ship!"

O O O

"Nip! The code is …"

"Already got it, Captain."

The Captain ran onto the bridge just as the Hu'nax logo from the galaxy-wide stream changed to that of another bridge. Unlike the earlier Imperium transport, this vessel was clearly a war craft. Digital charts floated in the air around an older and hardened Hu'nax. Decorations adorned his lapels showcasing years of service. One was clearly a purple Emmy, the highest honor in the Hu'nax military. The Captain didn't need a hyki to know who this person was and what his appearance on the hyfi network meant.

"Oh my, *the* General himself. This is an honor."

"I'm ready to tap in whenever," Nip said.

The Captain shook his head. "No, let us see what he has to say. Make sure the *Sirius* is getting the feed, though."

"*Sirius*? As in da dog star?" said Demmy, not believing his ears.

"Hey! Cut him some slack. He *is* new to the pirating game."

The General addressed his cam. He was comfortable there, like a seasoned pro. His silver hair was cut neatly and a salt-n-pepper Van Dyke fit perfectly in the center of his chiseled chin. His gestures accented his words, making him not only a great military strategist, but an experienced celebrity, as well. The Captain knew the General had been out of the spotlight awhile, not as long as the Emperor mind you. Despite this, his performance was flawless.

"The Imperium apologizes for the interruption of your program. What you just saw was part of a long-term plan we put in motion years ago to end this pirate nuisance. You may have caught a glimpse of a few brave Perresímos warriors there in that last segment."

He spun in his chair to give the audience a close view of his smile. His hy-cam2 was adjusted with warmer tones to make him seem friendlier.

"Have no fear. The Perresímos have decided, after years of hostile negotiations, to come back to the fold. They have graciously thrown their full support behind our quest for peace in the galaxy. They, like you viewers at home, know that only through acceptance of the Hu'nax Imperium's rule, can this terrible fighting come to an end."

The General returned to address hy-cam1.

"There will be no peace through acts of piracy. There is no victory in committing crimes. When my fully armed attack vessel reaches the coordinates, I will personally oversee the captured pirate crew's execution, which will be covered on all Imperium networks. Commentary will be provided by only the most authoritative of panelists. And even the Emperor himself will broadcast a

pre-recorded message for his people. We will send a message to the whole galaxy that the Emperor will never engage in a ratings war with such feline scum."

"Now, Nip."

Nip pushed a button and the Captain appeared split screen with the General.

"Feline scum, huh? Only my mother, Bast rest her soul, could call me that!"

"What? What is the meaning of this? How'd you escape?"

"General, that is a trade secret and we never reveal trade secrets. Right, crew?"

The crew laughed and Nip added a window in the corner with the Perresímos sergeant's stream.

"General? May I introduce Captain … er, what is your name again?"

"Mochar."

"Captain Mochar of the newly rechristened *Sirius*."

"Mochar! How dare you! We placed our full trust in you and your team and you turn on us?"

"I didn't like what you were feeding me, General. A dog can eat only so much shit before he starves."

The General turned beet-red. *"Where is my captain and crew of that transport? What have you done with them?"*

"Bring up the feed, Nip." said the Captain.

Another pop-up appeared in the corner. A dozen men sat huddled together, naked. In the front, the transport's former commander rocked back and forth like a disobedient child, a spiked collar around his neck.

"You betrayed us, General," Captain Mochar challenged. "The whole Hu'nax Imperium betrayed us. And for that you'll find not one, but two opponents when you arrive. I have already sent word to the Perresímos high council. We will no longer heel to your command."

Azzie stepped up beside the Captain. "Oh, and Azzie here says make it three as the Mũssex do not like you much either."

The General's mouth hung open for three point seven-eight seconds. Nip put a hang-time counter in the corner of the screen. When he regained his composure, he shouted, "*Abort. Turnabout!*"

"Too late, sir! We're already caught in the gravity well. Dropping out of hyperspace now."

The Captain asked, "Nip? How are the ratings?"

Nip's eyes were wide. "I don't think there is an intelligent being in the cosmos not tuned in right now, Captain."

"Then let us give them their money's worth. Harra! Assume attack position epsilon. Gunny, is the EM harpoon reloaded?"

"Yes, Captain!"

"I am assuming they are prepared for it, so be ready to back it up with a couple of missiles. Azzie! Get your boarding team ready. This will not be like the transport. I want everyone packing grenade launchers … and Demmy?"

"Yes, sir?"

"Send a hype to my agent. I am going to need some vidblog appearances lined up after today."

The older cat laughed and saluted. "Aye, sir. Dat be certainly true!"

The Captain looked to the com. "Captain Mochar, shall we gut this swine?"

"Ready on your lead, Captain."

"Excellent!"

Doc leaned over to Nip and whispered, "The truest test of fame is to have a crazy person imagine he's you."

Nip snorted as he tried to keep the laughter in. He regained composure with a raised eyebrow from his Captain.

The Feigatos leader gave his crew one last look before nodding his pleasure.

He stared forward at the target coming into range and spoke the word he'd waited most of his life to say,

"Primetime!"

David Boop is a Denver-based speculative fiction author. He's also an award-winning essayist, and screenwriter. Before turning to fiction, David worked as a DJ, film critic, journalist, and actor. As Editor-in-Chief at *IntraDenver.net*, David's team was on the ground at Columbine making them the first *internet only* newspaper to cover such an event. That year, they won an award for excellence from the Colorado Press Association for their design and coverage.

His debut novel, the sci-fi/noir She Murdered Me with Science, is back in print from WordFire Press after a six-year hiatus. In 2017, he edited the weird western anthology, Straight Outta Tombstone, for Baen. While also known for weird western series The Drowned Horse Chronicle, he's published across several genres including horror, fantasy, and media tie-ins for Predator, The Green Hornet, The Black Bat and Veronica Mars. His RPG work includes Flash Gordon, Rippers Resurrected and Deadlands: Noir for Savage Worlds.

He's a single dad, Summa Cum Laude creative writing graduate, part-time temp worker and believer. His hobbies include film noir, anime, the Blues and Mayan History. You can find out more on his fanpage, facebook.com/dboop.updates or Twitter @david_boop.

Space Pirate Cookies

by C.J. Henderson

Introduction to "Space Pirate Cookies"

I don't think an anthology of space pirate stories would be complete without at least one robotic parrot standing on a starship captain's shoulder. Leave it to C.J. Henderson to give us that image, then turn it into something utterly unexpected. Like David Boop, I met C.J. at the Opus Fantasy Arts Festival in Denver. Unlike David, C.J. was already a veteran writer at the time, having written stories for Batman, The Punisher, and Neil Gaiman's Lady Justice. I was floored and honored when C.J. Henderson said he wanted to write stories for the works I edited.

Much like the robot parrot in the early pages of the story, the titular space pirate cookies aren't quite what you expect. C.J. introduces us to the crew of the Roosevelt, humanity's first ship to explore the stars. The problem is, the stars are already well explored by numerous other alien species and they don't much care for humans, who are the new kids on the block. With tongue thoroughly in cheek, C.J. reminds us what it's like to be on the receiving end of prejudice, especially when that prejudice is just one part of an elaborate and terrifying plot.

◁ ▷

"Dignity does not consist in possessing honours, but in deserving them."

—Aristotle

"Avast, ye filthy swabs, fire at will—blow their cringing hides to the red flames of Perdition!"

The snarling character exhorting his men onward to gleeful murder was certainly a colorful sort. From the button-down cuffs and epaulets of his woolen frock coat to the tricorne hat he wore jammed under his bubble-shaped space helmet, he gave new meaning to words such as "curious" and "outlandish." Or perhaps "goofy." Especially if one considered his diamond eye patch, blood-streaked cutlass, or the robot parrot sitting on his shoulder.

"Awk—*buzz/ klik*—pieces of nine, pieces of nine—*zzzkt*"

The wholesale slaughter of innocents raced across the decks of the bizarre, seemingly wooden, apparently wind-driven spaceships, until finally a blood-soaked member of the pirate crew, the internal organs of several alien species hanging from his uplifted fist bellowed, "They're beaten, Captain, sir."

"Of course they are," the peg-legged, eye-patched master of the human buccaneers pointed at the cringing members of a variety of other species huddled pitifully at his feet, shouting drunkenly at the top of his lungs, "Because we're from Earth, and we fights dirty!"

Pulling a pistol from his pink silk sash, the drooling, comic opera pirate captain first scratched his posterior with its muzzle, then turned and jammed it against the head of what appeared to be a Lupnicki courtesan and pulled the trigger, scattering her brains across the deck of his ship. As his human crew laughed at such a morbid entertainment, the captain took a bow, then belched, the noise of it echoing inside his helmet so severely it bugged out his rheumy eyes—or at least, the visible one.

"Captain, sir," a wildly excited voice sounded off to the right, dragging all attention in its direction. "We *found* 'em!"

And, as all breaths were held in rapt curiosity as to which "'ems" had been found, two of the largest buccaneers, one a bare-chested black human with sharpened teeth, the other a pig wearing a vest, Hawaiian skirt and a graduation mortarboard, dragged an overflowing chest into sight as the captain exclaimed with a vulgar glee, *"Space Pirate Cookies!"*

And then, pirates from all over the ship rallied around the treat-laden chest, grabbing boxes of cookies, smacking one another in the head so as to steal each other's bottles of milk, and spitting voluminous amounts of crumbs as they sang:

"Space Pirate Cookies—
There is no better treat—
Nothin' we like better to eat—
So blippin', krippin sweet.
"Space Pirate Cookies—
All filled with blood and cream—
Every bite's a dream—
You can hear the ingredients scream!"

At that point, the gingerbread, shortcake-stuffed buccaneers began indiscriminately raping and murdering their captives as well as one another, dunking handfuls of cookies in blood and brains, and swallowing them whole while continuing to warble on about the joys of rapine slaughter and dessert treats until finally a harsh and disgruntled voice cried out, "Turn that crap off!"

The voice making the demand was a deep and rumbling one, issuing forth from the lower diaphragm of Chief Gunnery Officer Rockland Vespucci, more commonly known as Rocky, of the good ship *Roosevelt* out of Earth. Standing a strapping 6'2"—when he could stand that was—Vespucci was considered quite a charismatic individual, well ... among members of his own species, anyway. And, of course, when he was sober. At the moment of his outburst, he was certainly among members of his own species, but he was just as certainly by no means sober. Neither were the other members of the *Roosevelt*'s crew gathered around him, however, which is, really, what nearly started the Earth's first intergalactic war in the first place.

"Hey, didn't you hear the man," echoed Machinist First Mate Li Qui Kon, better known to top notch wire-and-screw jockeys everywhere as Noodles, "cut that feed or we'll show you a belligerence that will shake your miserable Pan-Galactic League of Suns to its butter-side-downed core!"

"Give in to the inevitable," squeaked the bartender, a mountain of a being with a tiny voice so wildly disproportionate to its size it caused even creatures of its own race to blink in confusion. "It's just a commercial. See, look, it's already back to the show."

The bartender was indeed correct—the Coronian singing star, Nell Char Yllier, was already back on the screen, warbling something about forgetting one's troubles and being happy, surrounded by a half dozen female dancers doing their best to look bubbly and carefree despite their tightly-binding costumes. So wonderful were her tones, and so dazzling the steps of her strapped and restrained troupe that the sailors were almost ready to turn down the thermostat on their tempers and go back to the well-revered, age-old nautical pastime of complaining about something rather than doing something about it when the bartender made his fatal mistake.

In truth, the fellow could not really be blamed for his error. If the sailors in question had been Golblacians, or Fogelites, or Embrians (well, if they had been Embrians, there would not have been anything to worry about in the first place—but back to the point) he would have known what to do. The veteran suds-and-sours jockey had stood his station for several decades, and knew the flare-to-violence levels of every race from Andrewns to Zyganirs. But, the upstart human race came from that far end of the galaxy into which most reputable species did not bother to venture. They were too new, too unpredictably odd. And so it was, in an attempt to facilitate their arrival back at a place of pleasant, wallet-emptying drunkenness, he uttered those fateful words that began the entire incident that would come to be known as Darkest Black Glibsday;

"Look, how about a round on the house?"

And that, that tiniest of mistakes, was the beginning of it all.

O O O

"Damn aliens," muttered Rocky, holding his throbbing head while sliding down a wall outside the bar. His voice a mumbling slur decipherable only to those of equal inebriation, he added, "No damn respect. Tramp all over a guy's … ummmm, ah … dignity. Yeah, that's it. It ain't right."

"You, you, ah yeah, you ..." Noodles attempted to answer, directing his index finger aloft, at first shaking it to help make his point, then holding it steady because the motion of its waving back and forth had begun to make him seasick, "you know it, pal."

"Always puttin' down humans, juss, juss be ... because they've had their damn club for, for what, what—how long?"

"A thousand hundred million and six years." Rocky eyed Noodles for a moment after his outburst, then replied, "I thought it was seven."

"Must've been a leap year."

Both sailors nodded to each other, continuing their monumentally slow slide down the wall they had chosen to help prop up, neither speaking again until they felt cold, alien concrete beneath them. Settling in, their near-numb fingers feeling about to make certain they could not fall off the sidewalk, the two took deep breaths, sighing in relief over having made it to their seats without injury. Then, feeling secure, the pair settled in to venting their righteous fury at the Pan-Galactic League of Suns and all its members.

This captured their limited ability to focus for some time. Normally the pair had quite a high tolerance for the liquid stimulants of other planets. Indeed, the *Roosevelt* had made port at some seventy-eight different worlds, and Rocky and Noodles had tied one on with a vengeance on seventy-five of them. But, Fadilson was a new world to those plying the spaceways out from the Sol System, and thus possessed some gray areas.

For instance, no planet in the League was known to possess a higher oxygen concentrate to its atmosphere than Fadilson. This fact was made known to the men and women of the *Roosevelt* before disembarking, of course, but was happily ignored as irrelevant by swabbies and officers alike. The place also was known for the odd fact it had a house of worship and a tavern on every street, no matter how large or small the town. Temples had not interested the swabbies all that much, but after finding out the planet's one other interesting geographic fact, they had decided to find every bistro, lounge and cocktail-building establishment in town.

Alone and in bunches, the crew had managed to make great progress, uncovering many interesting cabarets such as Tibric's

Treacherous Taproom, the Sum Zero Saloon and Noodles' personal favorite, the Alehouse of the Gods. Of course, that was mainly because the bartender was a robot and machinists are notorious fans of artificial life forms, especially the kind employed at the Alehouse, which could not only mix every drink in the known universe—from a Thurmian Gargleblaster to a HeyDiddleDiddle-on-the-Rocks—but which could do so while shelling peanuts, washing up the dirty glasses and reciting Vogon poetry for those not buying what it felt was sufficient quantities of intoxicants.

All had seemed well, and the *Roosevelt*'s crew was by and large having a fine time, until that is, they came across that which was to change the course of human destiny—the phenomenon known as Space Pirate Cookies. The treats were a new product, one released in between shore leaves for the sailors of the *Roosevelt.* By themselves they seemed innocuous enough little dunkables, and to be fair it was not the cookies that had put the crew out of sorts. It was the advertising used to make them a household word from one end of the galaxy to the other which humanity-at-large found so completely off-putting.

Space Pirate Cookies came in a mind-boggling vast variety of flavors—they would have to. The snack pastries that came in the cute, human-shapes the galaxy was growing to adore—but for all the wrong reasons—had to be appealing to the one hundred and eighty-five different races officially registered as protectorates of the Pan-Galactic League of Suns, as well as to the five founding races, of course. And that was simply to be able to capture a decent slice of the galactic market share.

As cookies went, they were tasty enough. Not as creamy as the Feezba Chip Pouts of Breniki 7, or as crumblicious as those mouth-watering bursts of joy, the wondrous Velpin Grooblie Drops, nor did they even approach the delectable chewiness of the Archway Mouthful of Frogs, still they had their audience, and that, once again, was because of their advertising.

Space Pirate Cookies were "okay," taste-wise, but the trillions of beings who were doing their bit for intergalactic consumerism were doing so for one reason—they loved the commercials. The adverts had funny songs, colorful characters, and they pandered to the latest racist impulse sweeping the galaxy—mistrusting, fearing and generally hating those upstarts from Earth.

Now, do understand, humanity had not acted at all inappropriately when its first starships penetrated the outer confines of the Sol System, ready to explore the vast and foreboding unknown, only to find a cosmos awaiting them as neatly explored and subdivided as an English country garden. They were disappointed, of course—no great expeditions filled with peril, no staggering challenges laden with fabulous adventure awaited them. It was a surprise, to say the least.

Moreover, those who had labored and trained all their days to be the new Magellan or Columbus found instead that fate had relegated them to being more the new Ralph Kramden or Willy Loman—bus drivers and traveling salesmen rather than explorers. All races ran up against this obstacle when first they met the League, but humanity confused the Pan-Galactics because never before had a species ever seemed so, well … disappointed. Reaching the League meant an end to disease and hunger. Promise not to make war on any member or protected race, and access to the wealth of the galaxy's scientific knowledge was bestowed freely—at, of course, carefully regulated and competitive prices.

Earth had received instructions on how to repair all the damage it had done to itself, as well as cheap, renewable energy sources, cures for most ailments, directional transmitters for talking to God (it confused humanity to no end that when asked what the one true faith was He seemed to favor the Libertarians) and well, just all manner of wonders. What they lost, however, was that indefinable quality of self-determination, the chance to find these things for themselves. Willing to take the goodies, especially considering that there was no, in any way, shape or form, sensible alternative, still it meant the party was over. All had been delivered, wrapped in a tidy pink bow. There was no more.

And so, as they sat staggered and blinded, drunker than a charred and steaming Benjamin Franklin when he belched, "I tied a key to the end of a string and did *what*?"

Rocky and Noodles fell into a sorry, self-pitying depression of epic proportions. Both had left home to explore the cosmos, to be the men with the first sets of eyes to see vast and amazing unknowns, to fight great battles, to live lives of excitement and challenge. Sadly, to date, their greatest challenge had been to find a snack with the light and salty corn-goodness of Fritos ten million light years from Earth. It was not the kind of test-your-limits-to-the-utmost challenge either of them had had in mind when enlisting.

"I'm tellin' ya, Noodles …"

"What?"

"Did you want somethin', little buddy?"

"What?" Scratching his head, a gesture that took most of his available energy, the machinist said, "You said you were telling me something …"

"Was it important?"

"I don't know," answered Noodles, his tone one so over-reachingly depressed that the sound of it caused a nest of nearby rodents to question the meaning of it all and then ultimately take their lives rather than face the all-encompassing despair that had taken root in their souls. "But then, is *anything* important anymore?"

And, with hearing those words, Rocky was struck with a wild and impossible scheme one would have thought too insane even for him. Sitting forward so quickly he actually bounced his eyeballs off their protective membranes, causing himself a moment of temporary blindness, the gunner coughed up three taverns' worth of assorted liquors, the remains of two meals, and a claim stub he had been searching for all weekend. Wiping his mouth on his sleeve, an action he was hoping would not damage the fabric, he blurted, "Noodles, all them Space Pirate Cookie rats do is make fun of humans, right?" When the machinist nodded in agreement, practically passing out from the exertion, his pal continued. "It ain't bad enough we get into space and find the whole place is just one big Levittown, but these guys, I mean … those guys, I mean, I just wanta …"

Rocky made unconscious motions of strangling some living thing, his eyes shining with a light bright enough to guarantee he found such an idea splendid. As he did so, his mind played for him the seemingly relentless advertisements for Space Pirate Cookies he had been forced to endure since making port. The videos showed the men of Earth as savage monsters, as vicious thugs bereft of morals, honor, common sense, or even acceptable table manners. Their implication was that all humans were rapacious, murdering thieves and that the universe was better off without them. And, to be fair to the gunnery officer's mounting temper, he would not have been nearly as incensed if he had not noticed a marked change in the non-human population of the town.

The natural prejudice many of Earth felt the member races of the League harbored against humanity was in full evidence. Everywhere the sailors went, beings from all races were ready to point fingers, jabber about fearing the eventual hauling of their keels now that Earthers had arrived, and laughing hysterically at their supposed wit. In the first ten or twelve taverns they visited, the swabbies were able to keep their wits about them. But, as the juice of the grape, the wheat and the chocolate-and-caffeined caramel beans worked its usual magic, self-control had begun to evaporate. Once Rocky had reached the sidewalk, it had been boiled into non-existence.

"So," asked Noodles quietly, the aroma of his buddy's eruption prodding the machinist on toward his own Vesuvian impersonation, "what is it you wanta do?"

Noodles' response to his question gave the gunnery officer's mind a reason to focus. What did he want to do? Obviously, he thought, from the delight his hands were having pretending to choke the life out of something, mayhem would have to be involved with any future actions designed to brighten his mood. But, what kind of mayhem? Against what or whom? And on what kind of scale? And, as his rage and frustration worked together to find answers that, although not intelligent or even remotely logical might still give some sort of "6" to the "3+3=" rattling about within his head, suddenly a smile, one both peaceful and sinister spread across Rocky's face.

"Noodles," he said, the wild gleam in his eyes suggesting nothing but trouble, "I know exactly what I want to do."

"It doesn't involve more drinking, does it?"

"Nope," answered the gunner. Struggling to push his way back up the wall, "I think we've downed just the right amount."

"For what?"

"We, little buddy," announced Rocky, back on his feet, his hand extended toward his friend to help him regain his own, "are going for a ride."

Swallowing a deep breath, Noodles took his friend's hand, then grunted and wheezed his own way to an almost upright position, asking, "Where?"

"To wherever the hell it is they make those damn Space Pirate Cookies."

Feeling a greatly unwanted wave of sobriety racing for his pickled brain cells, the machinist blanched, staggering back several steps to where he could hold onto the wall for support. Coughing with choked surprise, he finally was able to get control of himself sufficiently to say, "Wait a minute, wait just a minute. The only way we could find them would be with the ship's computers. And, if we found them, the only way we could reach them would be with the ship. And, and, and … ah … the captain would, I mean, I'm thinking, ah … he would never let us …"

And then, Noodles' eyes cleared so rapidly the force of them opening in surprise knocked the machinist backward, bouncing his head off the wall against which he had so recently been resting. Stunned by what he had just realized, he shouted;

"You, you—you mean, you want to steal the *Roosevelt*! Steal her, and take her out of orbit, and then, take her out and find these cookie-makers and use the power of the United Earth Navy to blast them into chocolate chips! Yes—that's what you're saying—right?"

"Yeah," answered Rocky, grinning like an ape that had finally figured out the difference between a salad fork and a dessert spoon. "You want'a?"

"Did the Buddha drink Mint Juleps?"

And thus the whole mindless tragedy began.

O O O

Captain Alexander Benjamin Valance was not a happy man. For one thing, he had fallen asleep with his legs and arms in a tangle so overwhelmingly complete that all four of his appendages had been almost completely without blood since he had stumbled into his bunk. For another, at two years, eight months, fifteen days out from Earth, he had put up with the wacky, infantile and just plain brainless stunts of his crew longer than any reasonable man should have been asked to tolerate.

He had suffered the endless nonsense of their infighting over whom the *Roosevelt* had been named for—Franklin or Theodore. He had bailed them out when they had shaved the sacred monkeys of Templeworld. He had made the appropriate excuses and restitutions when they had conned the guards of the Pen'dwaker Holding Facility into allowing them to transform the prison into a gambling den (for a mere 18.3% of the gross) for their Intergalactic Crap Shoot of the Millennium tournament. He had even found a way to smooth things over when they had sponsored their infamous inter-species mixer where they introduced the debutante daughters of the leading politicians of the Pan-Galactic League of Suns to the bears, cows, pigs and chimps they were transporting to the Inter-Galaxy Zoo on Chamre XI.

Indeed, it was his weariness of riding herd on the compliment of 400 of Earth's sharpest minds and broadest backs that had caused him to do something he had often dreamed longingly about, but not once acted upon during all of his two years, eight months, and fifteen days at the helm of Earth's mightiest warship. For once, after making port on Fadilson, Valance had decided he could use a little shore leave himself.

"Captain … what are you doing here?"

Yes, for once he had walked down the gangplank with the rest of the first wave heading offship with no thought more foremost in his mind than getting thoroughly and utterly polluted. Trained to explore the stars, prepared to take the greatest of risks, to dare the spectacular, brave the unthinkable, he had been the first to take a ship in the Great Dark, and thus the first human being to find out the game was completely and utterly over.

"This is my bunk, you know," mumbled the groggy Valance. "I do sleep here."

As sick of a military career without a trace of military action within it, no new peoples to meet, no trade routes to open, no tensions to either alleviate or to put down with a vengeance as any being could be, the captain had finally given in and taken solace within the bottle, the stop-gap solution to naval despair since the first aquanauts anywhere had piled into a canoe with beers and spears and set off to finally see just what the hell was around the bend.

"Bu—" the ensign stopped in mid-conjunction, the mixture of trepidation, terror and relief to be found on his face completely unreadable to the vastly hung-over captain of the *Roosevelt*.

"Did you want something, Sailor?"

The man stood shaking in Valance's doorway, unable to answer. After only a few seconds, however, despite the crushing weight of his hangover, the captain's well-trained senses began to pick up clues as to what was going on. The ensign working at gathering his wits before him was excited beyond any reasonable point—which meant something unreasonable had happened. The lad also was obviously afraid of something.

The back of Valance's mind rebelled at such a thought. Young to be a captain, especially of the Earth's first Dreadnought class starship, still he was a cool and competent commander, one who felt in his heart of hearts that the only thing his crew had any legitimate right to fear was him. Part of his mind immediately moved to dismiss such self-centered thinking, but then he stopped himself, realizing that was exactly what was going on.

"Sailor," muttered Valance, holding one hand over his eyes to keep them from spilling out and rolling about on the floor, "what's going on?"

"We did a bad thing, Captain."

And with those words, Alexander Benjamin Valance removed his hand from his eyes, fixing his gaze upon the hapless ensign. Throwing himself to his feet with an effort which made the labors of Sisyphus appear to be nothing more than a game of shuffleboard, the captain quickly worked his way past the nerve-tingling pain of his sleeping limbs, around his need for fresh air, a shower and something in his stomach with a lesser alcohol content than rocket fuel. Steeling himself for whatever horrible truth he was about to learn, his mind raced in a thousand directions at once. What, oh what, had Vespucci and Kon done this time?

"How bad?"

As the ensign started to speak, Valance felt the need to sit down. As he continued, the captain felt the need to lie down. By the time the junior officer finished, Valance was contemplating ritual suicide. Deciding the high command would turn to voodoo to reanimate his carcass just so they could disembowel him themselves, however, he chose against hari kari. Not, that is, that he had decided against bloodshed—he just saw no immediate need for it to be his own.

O O O

"Captain on the—*Captain*?!" The yeoman who had begun to automatically announce Valance's presence realized what she had done, did a double-take, then shouted, "Captain on the bridge! The *real* captain, you monkeys!"

Rocky turned to see Valance's formidable presence filling the doorway. Holding his head, still suffering from the night before, the gunnery officer said weakly, "Captain, sir … huh … we, ah um well …"

"I take it you didn't know I was on board when you decided to take your little jaunt. Is that what you're trying to tell me as you continue to sit in *my* chair, Mr. Rockland?"

"Ah, yeah," responded Rocky, still seated. "Actually, it was, sir."

As Valance continued to stare at the gunner, from the sidelines Noodles made hand motions indicating that perhaps his friend should maybe get out of the captain's chair, perhaps salute, or at least try to quit passing gas. Noticing the machinist's animated pantomimes, he asked, "Geezzzzit, Noodles, what'ya want?"

"He's trying to suggest that it might be a good idea if you got the hell *out* of my chair, you peanut-brained imbecile!"

Somehow catching the meaning of the captain's more direct suggestion, Rocky tumbled forward out of the ship's command center, crashing against the equally hungover navigator. Valance debated having his seat fumigated, but decided on just letting the air purification system deal with the remains of the gunner's bad evening. Despite what all the ensign had told him, the captain needed to hear what had happened from the source.

"Tell it, Rockland. And don't leave out any of the good parts."

Honest and heartfelt apology cascaded from every pore as the gunnery officer explained how their current situation had come to pass. He related the entire crew's outrage over both the Space Pirate Cookie advertisements as well as the greatly heightened edge of discomfort said ads had created. Privately Valance understood his crew's irritation over these points, having experienced them himself the day before, but he kept the information from showing as even a sympathetic glint in his eye. Instead, he merely snarled, "Yes, go on."

Rocky did. In short order, despite his brain's continual refusal to remove the floating stars and polka dots from before his eyes, or to stop his teeth from itching, the gunnery officer told the whole, embarrassing tale. He sketched out his and Noodles' talk on the sidewalk, and then their subsequent trip back inside the tavern to gather together all the available *Roosevelt* crewmen they could find. He told of how their idea had gone over like an offer of ice cream in Hell, how every swabbie they could find, and even a few of the locals, rallied to the idea of stealing the ship, finding the location of the Space Pirate Cookie factory, and then sending it to that place where offers of ice cream were looked upon so favorably.

When the captain asked how they were able to countermand the *Roosevelt*'s layers of security codes, to pilot the ship without his executive clearances, and to reach deep space (like any spacer, he had known they were in the Great Dark from the moment he awoke) without Earth Command Authorization Releases, Noodles took over the explanations, getting an able assist from Technician Second Class Thorner and Quartermaster Harris. Remembering immediately how that pair had engineered the replacement of the Grand High Exalted Poobah of the Pan-Galactic League of Sun's acceptance broadcast for his new term in office with Richard M. Nixon's "I am not a crook" speech, he pushed the machinist to skip the details. After all, how they got to the Great Dark really was not all that important. What they had done since they got there, however, that was a different story.

"Well, sir," hemmed Rocky, getting ready to throw in a few dozen haws in the proper places, "drunk as we was, we got pretty single-minded. Since these cookie makers are a company, it wasn't all that hard to get a fix on them."

"Any normal person would never have been able to get a swing at their vector," added Thorner. "With the ship's access to trade lines, though, we were able to nail it pretty quick."

"I'll be certain to mention such in your next efficiency rating," answered Valance drolly. Getting back to Rocky, with eyes steely and hard, he said, "So you and your hyenas managed to steal the ship and get her into the Deep. I imagine we're on a full speed charge toward wherever the buccaneer bakers are located—correct?"

"Aye, sir."

"And just out of curiosity, you slackjaws couldn't have kept this information a secret, could you? I mean, it wouldn't be possible for us to just turn around and get the blazes back to Fadilson without anyone knowing about your little escapade, would it?"

"I'm afraid not, sir."

"No, no, of course not," agreed Valance with an angry sarcasm. "But indulge me, Lieutenant, just *why* can't we do so?"

"Well, sir," stumbled Rocky, suddenly wishing he had taken his mother's advice and joined the priesthood, "you see, after we got on-course for the cookie factory, we thought maybe we should make an announcement about it ..."

"Certainly," growled the captain. "What could be more natural?"

"So we sent one out, ah, over the official bands...."

"Of course you did."

"And basically, well ... in the name of the Earth ... ah, we declared war on the Space Pirate Cookie Company."

Silence filled the room with a noticeable pressure. The captain stared at Rocky for a long moment, unmoving. Unblinking. Then finally, with all present subconsciously holding their breath to the point of bursting, Valance reacted. Breaking off eye contact with the gunner, he tilted his head downward, looking at nothing specifically, and then began to laugh.

At first it was a simple one-note noise, as akin to humming as anything else. But, after only a handful of seconds, it expanded, becoming a loud and raucous thing, one so jocular and merry one could not help but join in. All across the bridge, semi-sober sailors began to chuckle, then guffaw, eventually falling into the knee-slapping helpless state of full-blown hysterics that had seized Valance.

"You declared war on a cookie factory?" The captain had to choke his question out in between bursts of merriment.

Caught in much the same dilemma, Rocky answered, "Yes, sir. Full scale."

"You announced this over the spaceways, of course?"

"Oh yes, sir, Captain. Full intent. Full disclosure. Full speed ahead."

"And the League," answered Valance, his revelry tapering off just a touch, "and Earth High Command, they've made their positions clear—yes?"

"Oh, yes sir," howled Rocky, only seeing the humorous side of his answer, "they both pretty much want us dead."

"In fact," interrupted Noodles, chiming in as if actually in a hurry to get hung along with his pal, "the League is still on hold."

All laughter stopped at that point as completely as if each of the merry-makers had been slapped in the face with a wet porcupine. His mood crystallizing into a thing severe and frightening to behold, the captain snarled, "You've had the League on hold all this time? Are you all out of your goddamned—"

"Sir," shouted Thorner, the large man's booming voice refocusing everyone's attention on their far-from-finished hangovers, "the League demanded to talk to you, refusing to believe you weren't on board. We sent Brodsky to check your cabin so we could tell them with cleanslate assurance you weren't on board—that we did this all on our own."

"But that, um …" added Harris, the first to recognize the irony of their situation, "that didn't … work out for us, sir."

"Ya think," growled Valance. The captain lowered his vision once more, his mind racing desperately. He had to speak with the League, had to find a way out for his crew, and for the Earth. His head throbbing, eyes burning, bones melting, he gave the high sign to communications officer Feng to patch him through to the League connection. Making an audible gulp, the young woman depressed the correct switch, and the face of the Grand High

Exalted Poobah of the Pan-Galactic League of Suns appeared on the forward monitor.

"Captain Valance," the Telrecian known as Merli Acirde said coolly, "I'm told you are not presently aboard the *Roosevelt*. Pray tell, from where are you transmitting?"

"Good to see you again, too, your Poobahship. If you don't mind, I think I can explain this whole mess so everyone can just go back about their business."

"Correct me if I'm wrong," answered the Grand High Exalted One, "but I believe I am already in possession of the facts. Your drunken crew, from your warship, with you on board, sent out a legal and binding confirmation of hostilities against member citizens of the Pan-Galactic League of Suns. Is that not the case?"

Valance froze his first, second, and even his third responses within his throat. He knew he was playing a high stakes game, and that more than his own safety or satisfaction had to be considered. He also, however, was suffering from a hangover so stupefying he actually needed to remind himself to breathe every so often. Feeling he had regained a fraction of his self-control, he began. "It wasn't a serious confirmation, your Bigness. The boys, they've just—"

"Please, Captain, allow me to 'slice to the pursuit,' as you humans say. I have a speech to prepare for tonight's annual League dinner, so allow me to be brief. You and yours have committed the highest of crimes. Whatever your infantile reasons, the fact is you have given me clear justification to release the Pan-Galactic armada to pursue, hunt down, and blow your ship out of the deep. After that, it will track a course to your home system and obliterate every mote of human effluence."

"You, you," stammered Rocky, his eyes wide as saucers, "we was just on a tear. You can't do that."

"Ahhhh, Mr. Rockland, how glad I am to see you amidst the doomed." Preening like a coyote that had just eradicated the last roadrunner from the surface of its world, the Grand High Exalted Poobah of the Pan-Galactic League of Suns added: "And since you seem to have forgotten with whom you are dealing, I shall remind you. I am the combined will and final voice of civilized space. I can do whatever I want. I might not be 'a crook,' Mr. Rockland, but I'm a very patient, and vengeful being, and if there are gods in any heavens, they will arrange that the news of your destruction be brought to me during dessert so that they both might be made all the sweeter."

And with those words, the main bridge monitor went black. The crew of the *Roosevelt* present within command remained silent, all waiting for Valance's orders. To a man, despite their varying degrees of alcohol-induced suffering, each one of them despaired their actions. They had not only doomed their home world and all the planets, satellites and asteroid settlements it controlled, but worse, they had disappointed their captain. After a terribly long silence, Valance broke the hideous quiet, asking, "What's our heading?"

"Ah, actually, sir," answered Noodles, "we're still headed for the Space Pirate Cookie factory at full tear."

"Good." As those around him gave their captain a quizzical stare, not certain what he was up to, Valance pulled down a great, cleansing breath through his nostrils, exhaled, pulled down another, then announced over the ship's speakers: "Men, I'm not going to bother with accusations or recriminations. Quite frankly, at this point I don't care what got us here. To be perfectly honest, I'm as sick as every one of you over how Earth has been treated ever since we got out here. In fact, I believe our pal the Poobah's been waiting for something like this since long before our boys Milhoused him."

Rocky and Noodles grinned at each other, both as pleased as if they had just won a lifetime supply of bacon—thick-sliced and Canadian.

As the rest of the crew began to perk up around them as well, Valance barked: "All right, these spudboys want to start some shit, I say, bring it on. If they think the human race is a dog they can simply tell to roll over and play dead, I say we go Perryrhodanic on their asses and show these silk-breeched Betties how we do things on our side of the tracks. How about it, men of the *Roosevelt,* who's for blowing the living hell out a cookie factory?!"

And with those words, and a great deal of unrestrained cheering, the finest ship in the great Earth exploration fleet went to Top Turbo Thrust and sailed forth toward destiny.

O O O

"For the last time, you four, are you absolutely certain you want to do this?"

Valance stared at the almost sober quartet before him, trying not to let his inordinate pride show through. If any of them were to realize how he felt at that moment, he knew there would be no talking them out of their suggestion. As they all assured the captain they were as determined as ever, Thorner stepped forward, offering, "Look, Captain sir, it just makes sense. We're the ones that got this all started."

"Hey," shouted Rocky, "you and Harris were just the first apes me and Noodles come across. If anyone gets the credit for endangering all of humanity, it's gotta be us."

As the four began arguing over how little each of the others had contributed to the coming destruction of the human race, Valance barked an "at ease" at them, then said, "All right, we'll play it your way. We're just a hair out from the asteroid complex where they make these damn cookies, so let's make certain we all understand each other. You four are going to take a dropship in, get inside and blow the place. That will keep the armada coming this way, looking for the *Roosevelt.*"

The sailors all nodded, hands unconsciously checking their side arms. Knowing time was precious, Valance wrapped things up quickly, saying, "In the meantime, the rest of the crew and I will doublelight it back to Earth. With the League blocking all transmissions, the only way we can warn them is in person."

"Five minutes to drop." As the five all looked at Yeoman Feng's image on the console, the captain affirmed her message was received and understood, then turned back to the sailors before him. Pursing his lips for a moment, knowing he had time for only the shortest of goodbyes to the men before him whom, in all likelihood, he would never see again, he said, "Gentlemen, it's been a pure, goddamned honor."

As Valance's hand shot upward, Rocky, Noodles, Harris and Thorner all snapped to attention, getting their own hands to their helmets a split-second before the captain's reached his forehead.

Valance saluted, his men returned it, then they turned and piled into their dropship. As they did so, Valance pointed toward the skull and crossbones freshly painted on its bow, calling out, "Nice touch."

"They wanted pirates," answered Harris, "we'll give them a few."

And, in only minutes the *Roosevelt* was but an echoing speck fading from sight. At the helm, Thorner moved them with all due haste toward the bakery complex hidden in the asteroids ahead. The instant they were far enough away from the *Roosevelt* for minimum safety, the Dreadnought's great protonic engines roared and the ship disappeared down a parabolic chuckhole toward home. Wordlessly, the quartet inside the extremely recently renamed good dropship *Bucket O'Blood* moved into the asteroid belt, drifting in toward the already visible complex.

The cookie factories, warehouses and staging areas were enormous, some of the massive ovens covering hundreds of acres. Landing in the shadows of several Brobdingnagian syrup towers, the assault team gathered their explosives, record cameras and infiltration tools and exited the *Bucket O'Blood*, then headed for what appeared to be a little-used side entrance to what they hoped was the main administration building. Even before landing, the swabbies had agreed that destroying the lair of the company's "suits" would best achieve their goals. Or, as Thorner had put it, "It's not like we've got anything against the bakers."

"You try one of their Little Taste of Andromedas?"

The others had smiled at the tech's dry humor, Harris noting that it was not half as dry as the cookies in question, a bon mot which brought a needed chuckle to them all. After that, however, their mission had become a strictly business affair. Twenty minutes after the tiny spot of humor, the quartet had made their way inside what indeed turned out to be the administrative headquarters of the Space Pirate Cookie Corporation.

As the team moved upward through the building, they were struck with the ease of their passage. True, they had been forced to duck and cover several times as various office types hurried down one hallway or another, but for the most part their journey from the outside to the main offices of the company proceeded without interruption.

"I'm thinking," said Harris, "fun as it's been playing pirate, if we do actually kill anyone, it would be like admitting these cookie bastards were right about Earth. You know what I mean?"

Indeed, all of his fellows knew exactly what he meant. The same notion had been plaguing the rest of the swabbies since they had launched from the *Roosevelt.*

Making a nasty face, Rocky said, "Don't you just hate guys who take all the fun out of everything?"

The others chuckled, but realizing their time to act was tight, Thorner offered, "Look, we have to do something. So, why don't we just march in on their meeting, tell them to clear out, and then blow up their damn corporate HQ without hurting anyone or even burning up any of their damn cookies. If Earth's gotta go, let's help her go with some class."

Everyone agreed, all except Harris who asked if they could not, please, let the Little Tastes of Andromeda burn. After that, knowing they were but a doorknob's turn away from making their room reservations for Valhalla, the quartet entered the main offices of SPC/Co., only to find the surprise of their lives.

"Humans," cried out one of the aliens joyously around the conspicuously large table taking up most of the meeting room. "Is this perfect or what?"

"Come in, brothers, come in," shouted another, one attired in such a shiny, multi-layered garment it had to be assumed he was the biggest of the wigs present. "'Tis fitting indeed for humans to be here at our moment of triumph."

"Ah, yeah," said Rocky. "But, er … which moment was that again?"

"The moment when we bring the repressive, stagnating dictatorship of the accursed Pan-Galactic League of Suns to its collective knees." As many around the table thumped and whistled at what they obviously approved as a fine sentiment, Noodles asked, "Huh, I know why we might want to do such a thing, but that would mainly be because of you guys. No offense, but, why would you want to do it?"

"Because," snarled the obvious ringleader, "the League has been lying to everyone for millennia. The galaxy hasn't been completely explored—shaz'bot, most of it is still unknown!"

"What?" The word echoed from one swabbie to another.

"It's true," said an alien garbed in only slightly less shiny layers, obviously a vice-president. "I used to be an aide to that Telrecian bastard, Merli Acirde. "The five 'great' races have been conning every new species they've found since forever. They pull their patented 'here's some goodies' bit with every slogbrain that pulls itself up out of the ooze, then intimidates them into just becoming another consumer outlet. Stay home, put your feet up, let us take care of you."

"You mean," said Rocky, his voice as filled with wonder as his heart was throbbing with hope, "there's still worlds to find out there?"

"There's a million of them—a billion," shouted the vice president. "And we're all going to have our crack at them as soon as we bring down the League."

"Nifty," answered Thorner. "How you gonna do that?"

"We member races of the resistance, we built SPC/Co for one reason. Sorry about picking on the Earth and all, but you play to your audience, you know?" As the sailors all agreed the fellow had a point, the alien continued, telling them, "The Space Pirate Cookies that were sent to the League's big five homeworlds were filled with a responsive nano-explosive. When our grand high exalted Pooh-Bah gives his speech in a few minutes, his voice will resonate with the nanites built into each cookie. Even ones digested six months ago will have left enough traces behind to ensure anyone who's eaten one will be blown to smithereens. Acirde will no sooner begin his speech when he along with billions of the oppressors will die—and then, the galaxy will be free to find its own destiny once more!"

As the alien VP panted from the exertion of his speech, smiling with a decidedly wild-eyed glee, the swabbies looked at each other. They knew they and every other human was safe, that only beings from the Pan-Galactic's big five, and perhaps a few snack-hungry tourists to their worlds would be affected. If they were to simply congratulate the corporate revolutionaries around the table and sit back and wait, their troubles, as well as Earth's, were over.

All they had to do was approve the deaths of billions. Something the grand high exalted Pooh-Bah, Merli Acirde, was happy to allow. As the men of the *Roosevelt* looked around the room, noting just how many guards were actually stationed within its confines, Thorner muttered;

"Hey, Mikey-boy, you had your cameras rolling the whole time?"

"As per procedure," answered Harris. "Think maybe I should send out a broadcast?"

"You know," said Noodles, his fingers casually slipping the binding clasp on his sidearm, "that's probably a good idea."

"Okay, boys," added Rocky in a tone as serious as a barium enema, "let's show these half-wits what it really means to be a goddamned human being."

And then, pistols were freed, triggers were pulled, and bodily fluids yellow, green and vermillion ran across the decks of corporate piracy.

O O O

"That's certainly an exciting story, Captain Valance."

The *Galaxy Today* reporter gushed, her excitement over being close to the first actual hero the known universe had seen in ages causing her reproductive juices to bubble with the excitement of the Trevi Fountain. As she beamed and Valance continued to spin the story he and his men had cooked up, said men turned from the monitor broadcasting the captain's interview to one another, clinking their bottles and glasses one against the other.

"Well, gentlemen, I think we pulled this one outta the fire rather nicely."

To point out that Rocky had somehow become the undisputed master of understatement would have been as uselessly redundant as sending a gallon of unleaded to the heart of the sun. But then, he could be excused, considering the circumstances. Quartermaster Harris's broadcast had been instantly picked up by the League's armada, which had responded in a traditional manner by homing in on the signal, then sending in a thousand League Marines to "pacify" the situation.

The soldiers, having seen the images being sent from the SPC/Co. boardroom targeted the corporate officers and their minions, arriving just in time to save the four humans who, to be fair, had made excellent use of the element of surprise, but who had also run out of time. Merli Acirde was stopped before he could broadcast his speech, and was also immediately stripped of his rank and put into confinement pending an investigation.

Now, it was true everyone paying the slightest attention knew the League was merely playing for time, trying to maintain their position as Kings of the Mountain. And, again to be fair, everyone with any reasonable understanding of how such games were played, knew that the League's iron grasp on the affairs of the galaxy might have been relaxed, but that they would by no means be swept away by events.

"Still," mused Noodles, reaching for a ninth, frosty cold Woodchuck Ale, "it's nice to know that we shook things up a little."

"A little?" Thorner spat a swallow of his Great Balls o'Firepower cocktail across the table, then shouted, "We struck away the chains shackling the oppressed of the universe!"

"We also worked it so the captain came out a hero, taught the galaxy what it means to screw with the human race, and kept ourselves alive long enough to enjoy it all," said Harris. His feet on the table, hands behind his head and seven inches of a nicely-fired Avo Uvezian hand-rolled clenched firmly between his teeth, he added, "Not bad for a bunch of upstarts from the armpit of the universe, eh?"

"Not bad at all," agreed Noodles. "This means we're all going to get to do what we signed up to do in the first place—explore the Cosmos. Be the first beings to set foot on strange, new worlds. To seek out new life, and new civilizations …"

"To boldly go," shouted Thorner, his eyes filled with glee, "where no space pirates have gone before!"

All raised their drinks, saluted one another, then drank deeply once more. Noting Rocky's unusual silence, Noodles asked him the reason.

Looking a bit sheepish, the gunner answered, "It's nothin', really. We liberated all those cookies before we left the factory—right?" When all agreed, Rocky said, "Well, I've just been tryin' a bunch of 'em. And, interestin' enough, you know what I found?" When the others inquired, he told them, "These Little Drops of Andromeda, they really ain't that bad."

All three of the gunnery officer's shipmates made quite caustic responses, but Rocky heard none of it for as they shouted their jibes the great protonic engines of the *Roosevelt* were brought on-line, and the finest ship in the great Earth exploration fleet went to Top Turbo Thrust and finally sailed forth, as it had been aching to since it was commissioned, to boldly search for drinks where no man had gotten drunk before.

CJ Henderson was the creator of both the Teddy London occult detective series and the Piers Knight supernatural investigator series. He wrote some 70 books, including such diverse titles as *The Encyclopedia of Science Fiction Movies, Black Sabbath: the Ozzy Osbourne Years,* and *Baby's First Mythos,* as well as thousands of short stories, comics and miscellaneous non-fiction pieces. In the wonderful world of comics he wrote everything from Batman and the Punisher to Archie and Cherry Pop-Tart.

Earth-Saturn Transit

by W.A. Hoffman

Introduction to "Earth-Saturn Transit"

In addition to editing and writing science fiction, I'm an astronomer who has operated telescopes at Kitt Peak National Observatory for most of the past decade. My love of science makes me something of a sucker for a good, hard science fiction story and "Earth-Saturn Transit" delivers just that. W.A. Hoffman imagines a plausible way for one ship to attack and raid another in space while giving us a good look at Saturn that almost makes us believe she's visited herself.

Hard science fiction isn't just physics, though. It's understanding how people will evolve and change in the environments humans will find themselves in. This story shows us a complex human society and doesn't forget that even today, love is not a clear-cut emotion defined by the sexes of the people involved. In a society where humans take new forms to adapt to new environments, love is likely to take new forms as well.

◁ ▷

I floated on the rec deck, one foot hooked in the netting and my eyes on a wide-view projector I had linked to an external camera. Saturn filled the room: bands of blue and peach from floor to ceiling, glistening rings spreading from the exercise equipment to the pantry. Wheeling specks and clots of debris from an exploded gas tanker passed by and messed with my view of the great planet. They made it real and not some orbital camera ad image I could have seen on Earth.

I would have preferred a better view. Our ship, the *Mantis*, drifted in that tanker's debris field, though; lying in wait for a passing outbound Martian ship that would use Saturn to slingshot it away to really distant wonders. We weren't here to provide me with pretty scenery. My wants and needs weren't very important in the big picture: they never were.

We had drifted here, in freefall and the illusion of freedom, all wrapped up in the laws of gravity and physics, for thirty-two standard days; and we would keep drifting here until the Nav's calculations said the door, or window, for this outbound route had closed, or shifted, or whatever they did. I would continue to drift in the rec deck netting, just another lump of the *Mantis*'s mass, put in motion by my ambition and trapped by my contract, until we caught one of those ships and they needed me to board it and subdue its crew; because that was what I did: that was my job for the last two years and the next eight.

I didn't know a lot about Saturn. I was pretty sure I knew more of my mother's Neo-Pagan crap than I did real science. My mother had called Saturn the great taskmaster, the planet of karma. It caused delay and taught discipline in whatever sign of the zodiac it rested in when you were born—on Earth—or that it passed through—relative to Earth. I wondered what the astrologers tried to say about its meaning if you were in orbit around it. My mother hadn't gotten into that part of her faith: the part that dealt with the human race going into space. She had been a devout Gaia worshipper. Mankind wasn't supposed to go into space. That was just a way poor misguided souls attempted to escape our karmic duty to our Mother.

Though my mother and her people were full of crap, I was beginning to think they were right about Saturn being the great bringer of delay. Since I came near it, my life had crawled to a halt and I had too much time to think thoughts I didn't care for. In the past standard month, the boredom had only been broken by the occasional piece of debris moving at a different relative velocity to the rest of the cloud—or more importantly, us. I had had to suit up and join Dozi in making repairs twice. I was starting to think Saturn was going to hit us with a big one somehow, and teach me why man should leave space to the Gods.

A tone sounded, signaling the coming hour and a shift change. A moment later, Quinn and Faun flowed out of the companionway from the upper decks. Quinn hovered at the doorway, one finger on a hold, and looked at me as if I were something the recycler had spit out.

I flicked off the projector and pushed my way to the edge of the netting. "I'm leaving, Princess," I said with my best I'm-a-stupid-ape smile.

Her cupid lips twitched in a grimace, and she pushed off to the galley, leaving Faun hovering in the doorway behind her.

I didn't watch him; I watched her. She was the only woman onboard, and the view was worth making her mad again and getting another lecture from the captain. Quinn's legs were sheathed by a thin pair of ship's tights. They were long and sleek and seemed to take forever to reach her nicely rounded rump. Her hairless scalp was covered by a complex pattern of metallic ink that glowed softly in the lights. The tat work framed her face and flowed down her neck, giving the illusion of her having hair, just like the billowing shirt it disappeared into gave the illusion of her having a bust. I felt an urge to run my fingers through real hair and cup real breasts—not that Quinn's breasts weren't real, just that there wasn't enough of them for me to think she might be a legal adult. All the Collie women are that way: petite and thin, as if the giant space colonies they come from lack the room to house full-sized women.

She knew I was looking at her, just as I knew Faun was looking at me. She hated the Eart ape looking at her. The Eart ape hated the Loonie boy looking at him. I figured the Loonie boy hated knowing the Collie princess was seeing him looking and not getting looked at: connecting us all in one big anti-social circle jerk of lust and unhappiness. But that was how things went on the *Mantis*. Space ships are full of people who hate other people, but who've let their ambition drive them into being locked up in little boxes with other people who hate people for months or years at a time.

I had tried, sincerely even, to make friends when I had been brought on board. I had thought it would be like the army; but in the army, we had all been soldiers together. Here, I was a dirty Eart contractor and they were all officers. I was barely human in their eyes, or maybe it was that I was human and they now thought they were something more: the next step in evolution. I would have thought that funny, if it didn't piss me off so much.

The one time I had tried to flirt with Quinn the Colony princess, she had looked at me as if I were a dog trying to hump her leg. It still stung. I wondered if she treated me like a dog because she didn't know how to separate pets from people in her mind. Maybe she hadn't been around animals. I doubted it, though. From what she said, her family had money, and I had seen lots of pictures of the happy Colonists in their space stations playing with dogs in their parks.

So I watched her prep a soup pouch—one long leg hooked over a hold, and her body twisted at an interesting angle—and asked. "Quinn, did you ever have a dog?"

She turned her head to give me a quizzical grimace. I thought the look was more for my asking the question than what I asked.

"You know," I said with a grin. "A dog. Small hairy thing. Four legs. Barks. It's a pet."

"Yes," she said, and pushed back to the companionway with her soup and coffee pouches, as if talking to me about her pet would dirty her memory of the animal.

I shook my head and gave her my ape smile again.

Faun the Loonie still watched me from the doorway. He only moved enough to let her pass.

The Colonists are stuck up rich bastards: the ones who escaped Earth before the big melt and the holy wars. They live in beautiful stations designed to mimic Earth at Her best. I didn't like them, but I could understand them. The Loonies I wasn't too sure about. They had settled Luna before the Earth-orbit colonies were even constructed. They had taken to living in space as if they could force their own evolution. They are second only to the Mercs in body-alteration, bio-net implanting, and abandoning Earth-grav living conditions. I doubted Faun could walk in a full G, but he flowed through Zero-G like water.

The Collies are distant because they're snobs, the Loonies are distant because they're weird. Androgynous little bastards: male or female, age ten or a hundred and twenty-five, they all look like they're maybe sixteen. They live in their Loonie Suits: smart-cloth, self-contained EV units that fit them like a second skin and can protect them from just about anything except a heavy projectile weapon or more than a week in hard vacuum. If the *Mantis* suddenly blew up, Faun would live and the rest of us would die. I understood what a good idea that was, especially when we were floating in a little metal can in a debris cloud at thousands of miles per hour; but I couldn't see how anyone could stand being covered from head to toe in skin-tight mesh—and that was just the parts I could see. I didn't even want to think about the waste-management systems the suit had: they had to be inserted.

Faun's suit was gray and silver and he always kept the mask on, so being around him was like being around a robot or a real space alien. I couldn't see his eyes, read his expression, or even his body language; and he didn't talk unless he needed to, and when he did it was in this distant monotone. I only knew he saw something about me that he liked because there are certain things that a man can just feel, and I felt them whenever he turned his silver-masked face my way.

"Did you have a dog?" I asked him, and tried in vain to meet his gaze. Sometimes if the light was just right, I could actually see his eyes through the mesh. The light wasn't right.

"I had rats," he said. "My brother had a monkey. Dogs don't do well in space. Cats do better."

"Hairless cats, I bet," I sighed, and wondered if I should get something to eat before retreating to my quarters.

"No," he said. "Cats should have fur."

I frowned at him, and wondered if he was serious.

Our engineer, Dozi, dropped down the companionway and shouldered his thick Venetian body past Faun. He paused—one massive, long arm easily stopping and reversing his mass with a twist of his wrist—and turned to glare at me from beneath a heavy brow that just looked wrong without a thick black caterpillar of hair.

But like all good spacers, he was depilated. I was the only ape with hair onboard.

"Quit talking to the girl, ape," Dozi growled.

I saluted him with my middle finger in a gesture even the high and mighty spacemen still understand—especially ones like Dozi, who spent a lot of his time with a custom-made Merc love doll.

Faun gave a little noise. I thought it might have been a snort of laughter, but the idea was so odd I wasn't sure if I should believe it.

Dozi grumbled and moved on to the galley. He talked a lot, but he would never actually come after me; despite his looking like a gorilla, he didn't have any combat training; and despite my only learning to maneuver in Zero-G two years ago, I did.

Captain Jacobs pushed out of the companionway. He had come down head first, and quickly righted himself relative to Faun and me once he found us near the doorway.

I nodded respectfully. "Captain."

He put a look of fatherly disapproval on his blandly handsome Collie face. "Quinn says you were bothering her again. Now we've had this discussion before, Rowan."

I gave him the pleasantly bland look I had always given officers. "I'm sorry, sir. I forgot myself."

"If it happens again, there will need to be consequences," he said, and moved off to the galley.

I kept my mouth shut and my thoughts off my face and nodded politely before pushing up the companionway.

I was surprised to feel a hand on my arm, and I looked over as I reached the sleep deck. Faun was hovering beside me in the narrow space.

"Do you hate him?" he whispered.

"The captain?" I mouthed.

He nodded.

"Hate's a strong word. I don't like to think I care that much," I said carefully, and glanced up and down. It looked as if we were alone, and the doors around us to the cabins were heavily soundproofed. "And it's not like it matters. He can make me the sorriest man alive with a thought."

"What if he could not use the control chip?" Faun asked.

I wished I could see his eyes. "What do you mean?"

There was movement below, and suddenly Dozi was filling the companionway beneath our feet. He smirked up at us in a way that said he thought Faun saw something in me too.

Faun shot up the companionway and out of sight onto the bridge. I pushed sideways to the door to my cabin and slipped into its privacy with a sigh of relief. The little space wasn't wide enough for me to stretch out if I strung my sleep-netting horizontally, and if I put my feet on the floor I could touch the ceiling with the flat of my hands; but it was all I had and I was lucky to have it.

What the hell had Faun been talking about? I had been told when it was implanted that the contractor chip in the base of my skull would kill me if it was tampered with. Of course, it makes sense to tell a man who has just found out he will be a slave for the next ten years—and maybe longer—something like that. Otherwise, all of us stupid Earthers who signed labor contracts, came up the well, and then found out just how bad our lives were going to be, would rebel—and then who would they have to man the mines, do station construction, and the rest of their dirty, dangerous jobs?

I was dozing when the alert claxon went off. It was the one for an approaching ship. I made sure the rush of bodies going up had passed before I followed them to the bridge. The other five members of the *Mantis*'s crew were rushing around, happy they finally had something to do. I went to drift in the corner, out of the way so that no one would tell me to leave.

Dozi and Quinn crammed his bulky Ven body and her dainty Col one into the same station, strapped and jacked themselves in, and combined their knowledge of Martian ship engineering and Venetian drone technology to confirm we did have a transport in our trap. They gauged her make, model, cargo-tonnage, drives, and maneuvering capacity; and compared that info with our drones floating along the edges of the ten thousand cubic kilometers of wreckage to determine which of the drones were in the best position to be activated and used during our attack. The Martian would only pass through the thin upper section of the debris—luckily most of our drones were there.

Our Mercan navigator, Akira, twitched in his couch, as if all the feeds entering his neck and head were shocking his atrophied body. He displayed projections of all the scenarios that could develop based on the data Dozi and Quinn were feeding him. The screens filled again and again with different trajectory paths of the drones, the Martian, and us. Faun perched at his console, monitoring the prey's transmissions and glancing at the screens. The captain floated in the middle of the domed room, upright with his arms crossed, like a statue, using his wireless connection to the ship to constantly adjust the images as he sorted and analyzed them.

Decisions were made, and the drones readied to do their jobs. When the Martian reached the proper point—in about ten hours—two of the robotic units would accelerate from their hiding places and explode cones of projectiles into the current trajectory of the Martian ship. Our prey wouldn't encounter the tiny steel pellets for thirty-nine hours after the release at their current velocity; but if the Martians were too stupid to change course—toward our planned trajectory—the pellets would tear them to pieces. Of course, they could just turn away; heading up above the plane of Saturn's orbit, but that would throw them off their slingshot and make it impossible for them to reach their destination. It could even kill them if their margins for life support were too narrow.

The rest of the drones would be spread out to form a transceiver net to attempt to block the Martian's transmissions. Nothing moved now, though. We had to wait in silence until our prey came closer. I slipped off the bridge and retreated to my cabin, a calmer pill, and another Twentieth-century espionage novel.

I returned to the bridge when I heard the alarms sound again. The Martian had reached the point of no return in the trap, and the drones were activated. Now we would wait to see how they changed course, before we left our position in the cloaking flak cloud that we had spread to hide us in the debris and fell into Saturn's gravity well behind our prey. I went below and exercised.

Hours later, there was another alarm, this one signaling that we would soon begin to move. I hurried to the bridge. The Martian had changed course in the desired direction. Akira gave a whoop of happiness and sputtered an unintelligible stream of Mercan as he fired the maneuvering thrusters and the *Mantis* began to accelerate. I shook my head at his enthusiasm; the ship's movement was enough to make me slowly drift toward the floor. Back on Earth, no amount of telling me about space travel had prepared me for how very slow everything seems to happen in space. I had thought it would all be like the multi-G-force rush of escaping Earth's gravity. My heart had been crushed in my chest and I had felt free as the clouds receded behind us and we rocketed into space. I was an idiot: just a dumb Eart ape like they all thought.

Now that the Martian could see us, we began to wait for their hail. I brought my reading pad up from my cabin and drifted in the corner. I liked to listen to the transmissions: it let me know how difficult my job was going to be. Sometimes the Martians were pretty calm about the whole thing—the other nations had been preying on their shipping for over two decades—but sometimes they were really angry and took it personally. I had had to kill a couple of those.

The transceiver chimed less than an hour later. Faun opened the channel, and the bridge was filled with angry Martian ranting. The speaker was so mad the usual sing-song quality of their language was lost. He just spit it out in little bursts. The translator slowly parsed the message into Collie. The gist of it was that we were insane and in violation of a treaty.

"What treaty?" Dozi roared.

The captain shook his head and looked to Faun, who was paging through a news site and sending a message to the Venetian Admiralty. We were out here preying on the Martians under their license.

"There is a treaty," Faun said with a shrug, and posted it up on a floating screen.

"Not for me!" Dozi ranted. "Not after all those bastards have done. They bombed Novo Kiev. They burned out the Chelnov Colony. They collected everyone on Odessa and took them to the mines on Triton. We Venetians would never sign a treaty. There's no peace beyond the Belt!"

He sounded odd, as if he had rehearsed his little speech.

"Everybody signed it," Faun said emotionlessly. "The Republic of Venus, the Federation of Luna, the United Colonies, Mercury, and even the United Nations of Earth."

I read the screen. Mars had finally agreed to a treaty that could maybe end the decades of warfare beyond the asteroid belt. They agreed to cease hostilities within the Belt; and grant Venus, Mercury, Luna, and the Colonies the right to maintain any cities or stations they had already established on or around the moons of the outer planets; and allow for the peaceful expansion and exploration of what remained of the solar system. There had been peace talks about this since before I was born, and now it had happened, nineteen standard days ago, while we were maintaining transceiver silence.

A text transmission came in and Faun posted it to a screen. The Venetian Admiralty wanted to know what the hell we were still doing out here. They had issued a recall of the privateers weeks ago. The crew of the *Mantis* was out of a job, and I wasn't sure what it meant for me.

"We have to break off," Quinn said.

"Why?" Dozi yelled. "You believe this farce?"

I looked around. Akira's round little face was contorted in a grin, but it was hard to tell if that was from the news or the constant stroke all of the hardware in his head seemed to cause him. Quinn looked as shocked as she sounded, but Dozi still seemed a little too blustery, even for him. The captain appeared truly surprised. Faun was unreadable as always, but he seemed very still and I could see his gaze was roaming around the room like mine. There was a moment .when our eyes might have met, and he turned his head quickly.

"Akira, change course," the captain said with a sigh.

"But Captain," Dozi said. "What are we going to do?"

"Find new jobs," the captain said, and drifted to the companionway.

Behind his back, Dozi glanced toward Faun and Akira as if he were looking for support. "But Captain, this isn't going to last. The damn Martians will break the treaty, they always do. They don't want anyone else out here."

The captain stopped and turned. "So what are you suggesting, Dozi? That we become pirates? Are you insane?"

Dozi bit his thick lip and shrugged. "I'm just saying.... It won't last. And if we walk away now, then it'll be harder to get back in."

"Change is hard," the captain said in the patronizing voice he usually only used on me. "You'll adapt. We all have lives to return to." He turned away and lowered himself down the companionway.

I didn't think our Ven engineer agreed with him, and maybe Dozi wasn't the only one. He was looking at Faun and Akira again. Faun tensed and I thought he might say something.

"You're crazy," Quinn said with a smirk. "Piracy is impossible. Where will you dock? Where will you buy thruster fuel? Drones? Air? Food? Once they find out who you are—and they will—your accounts would be frozen. And if you get caught—and you will—you'll get your brain altered and spend the rest of your life making processors ... and liking it. You'll be so happy. You won't even know you're a mindless drone."

"That's an outbound ship," Dozi said, drifting over to get in her face, his voice lowering in volume as he closed. "The Consortium stations will buy cargo off anyone, no questions asked. The drones will keep the Martians from calling for help, the ape can kill them, and we'll wipe their systems. They won't know we did it."

I shook my head, but no one was watching. He was crazy.

"The drones aren't foolproof," Quinn scoffed. "And Ven Ad already knows we're out here!"

"It doesn't matter!" Dozi yelled, but I could see he knew she was right. "What are we supposed to do now?"

"Go be a pirate. Run for the rest of your life," Quinn said.

"Lots people run now," Akira said. He didn't speak often, not intelligibly, and definitely not Collie. "More run now after this." He pointed a stubby arm at the floating screen with the treaty information. "New colonies way out. I hear trans."

"Shut up, you retarded dwarf!" Quinn said. "You would be happy flying around for the rest of your life. Some of us just do this for the money." She gave one last scowl at the others and darted down the companionway.

I moved, and three sets of eyes were immediately on me. The two that I could read were speculative and a little fearful.

"You should ask the captain what happens to you," Faun said. I couldn't read anything in his tone.

I wanted to ask Faun what the hell he was up to, not the captain. I could feel something in the air: it was the tingle I got before a battle. But like a good soldier, I did as he suggested and slipped down the companionway to the captain's door and pressed the buzzer.

The captain looked surprised to see me, and distracted. He let me stand in the doorway and returned to sitting at his desk—he had the only cabin large enough for a desk. There was enough acceleration that my bare feet felt natural resting on the floor. I thought his butt probably felt pretty natural on its stool. It reminded me of the army and I found myself standing at attention.

"What can I do for you, Rowan?" he asked.

"What happens to me, sir?" I asked. "When you quit privateering?"

He frowned, and there was as much annoyance in it as confusion. He probably thought I was the least of his problems. "What are you worried about?"

"Whether I'll be sold," I answered quickly, because I had finally figured that out. Either he would sell me, or I would be forced to go and live in the colonies as his pet ape and do chores or Gods-only-knew-what.

He frowned again, this time with what I read as sincere thought. "Well, Rowan, I'll be returning to Asimov Colony. I can't see where I'll have need of your services there." He looked a little guilty. "But don't worry, I'll find you a good home."

"I would appreciate that, sir," I said. "I don't want to end up in a mine."

He nodded, but his eyes dodged away. I smiled pleasantly and left him. The door closed quickly behind me.

I had to wait a couple hours before Faun got off duty and returned to his cabin. He grabbed my shirt and pulled me inside as soon as he opened the door and found me standing there. His cabin was the same size as mine, and full of personal storage cartons on one side, so we were forced to stand almost chest-to-chest with the sleep netting crowding us. With his feet on the floor, he barely stood as high as my shoulder. The angle was good though: I could see his eyes—at least enough to know where to focus.

"He will sell you to the highest bidder," he said quietly.

"Yeah, I got that," I said. "What are you doing?"

"You are his insurance policy against us," he said.

I could see that, too. I nodded. "So you'll disable my control chip so he can't make my head explode, and I'll help you out. Then what?"

"Not disable," he sighed. "The chip will self-destruct if tampered with. I can relieve him of the control codes, though; and transfer them to me."

That made me mad. I couldn't say exactly why.

"So why tell me at all?" I growled, and backed him to the wall. "Just flip the damn switch and give the orders."

"Non, non," he said quickly, and rattled off something in Lunite. He shook his head. He was breathing heavily and his fists were clenched, and even with such unusually strong signs from him, I couldn't tell why. Was he excited because I had him backed to the wall, or scared?

"What do I get out of the new regime?" I asked.

"You will be part of the crew and not a contractor," he said earnestly. "The contract will be voided."

"I'll still be your slave," I snapped. "And what duties will you expect?"

"Non," he said with a lot of head shaking. "I would never …"

I stood back. "No, no, not with the dirty Eart ape. You just dream about it, but you would never stoop that low."

He slumped dejectedly. I had hit home. It just fueled my rage.

I leaned in to brace my hands on either side of his shoulders. I could see his scared eyes. "Tell you what, if you want me to work for you, you're going to have to prove you can work for me. You want me to help with your little mutiny, when it's over, you strip that suit off and I do what I please."

He gasped, the intake of air sucking his mask into a little *O* of surprise over his mouth. *"Non,"* he breathed it back out softly and peered up at me. "Your profile.... You identify as hetero."

I snorted. "Back where I come from, you don't exactly qualify as male."

"Get out!" His hands hit my chest and slammed me back into the boxes. "Never! Maybe you are as stupid as Dozi says!"

He slammed the door open, and I let him shove me out into the companionway.

I hovered there until the acceleration made me start to sink, and then I grabbed the ladder. The rage was gone. It was always like that. Somebody said something that pinched some nerve and off I went and I spent the rest of my life regretting it. And now I was going to do it in a mine: being expendable and sharing bunks, toilets, hard labor, unsafe conditions, chemical castration, and beatings, with hundreds of other stupid Earts who couldn't make a good decision to save their lives.

Faun didn't respond when I buzzed his door. I ate and worked out, trying to avoid the rest of the crew, who luckily seemed to be trying to avoid one another too. Then I sat in my doorway and read, with my feet dangling in the companionway, and waited for Faun to emerge.

It took four hours, and even though I had spent more of that time rehearsing than reading, the words still stuck in my throat when he looked at me.

"Wait," I managed as he darted down the companionway.

He reversed at the bottom, and came back up to hover with a hand on the ladder so that our heads were even. "What?"

"I'm sorry," I said, and hoped that even though he spent his life hiding his face, his whole race didn't, and he could at least interpret other people's expressions. I wasn't trying to hide anything. I was a sorry idiot.

"Where I was raised ..." I said. I didn't want to get into discussing my mother's commune, but I couldn't exactly avoid it: it was the only excuse I had. "Men were men and women, women, and ... men were supposed to worship the Goddess in all her forms, including women, and, um ... men just didn't ... It was sacrilege. And ... I know ... that's not how things are out here, and I should not be ..."

"You don't have to explain," he said, and looked away. "All the religions on Earth have prohibitions against it."

"Yeah," I sighed. "Well, I don't like to think I'm a member of any religion, I've been fighting that my whole life, but … it's stuck in my head, I guess. So … it just … that and being owned by anyone, anymore. That's what really … bothered me, and the other, I was just … being an ass to mention it, and …"

He looked at me again. "It won't be like that," he whispered. "I swear."

"I want to believe you, but … it's hard for me to trust a person when I can't look them in the eye."

He took a deep breath.

A shadow fell over us and we looked up. Quinn was dropping so fast she nearly collided with him.

"Get out of the way!" she snapped. "What are you idiots doing?"

"I'm reading," I said.

Faun was already gone, going up the ladder instead of down.

I retreated to my room, leaving the door cracked so I could see when Quinn came back up. When she did, and disappeared into her cabin, I slipped out and went to the bridge. Faun was perched on the edge of a console, talking quietly with Akira. The rest of the bridge was empty.

"Akira is in on it," Faun said quietly. "The captain is in his cabin, asleep. Quinn is …"

"In her cabin," I said. "You have the whole ship bugged?"

He shrugged.

"Dozi?" I asked.

"With us," he said.

"Can we really find a safe port if we do this?" I asked. I looked to Akira: he never bothered to hide whatever he was thinking.

Faun did something with his wrist controls and pulled off his mask and hood with a swift motion.

I blinked in surprise. He was pretty. There was still something masculine about him, but if he wore a dress and a wig it would have been hard to tell. His bald scalp was covered in subtle tat work. His big gray eyes were almost as pale as his blue-tinged skin, but they met mine solidly and I found that reassuring.

"Thanks," I muttered.

"There are safe ports for outlaws and refuges," Faun said. "There are people out here who want something different and do not like being owned and controlled, either. We will never be able to go back inside the Belt. And if we are caught, we will be rehabilitated."

I nodded. "I'm in. Can you make the code changes for the chip whenever?"

He shook his head. "There will be an alarm on his private circuit when I make the change."

I sighed. "How fast can you do it? And you're sure, right? You don't know how damn bad that thing hurts, and more than a few seconds and I start losing motor functions and IQ … permanently."

"I have been thinking that my switching the codes will be the signal," he said solemnly, his eyes steady on mine. "I can do it, and I do know. I had my bio-net disrupted by feedback once. I was in the hospital for a month."

I believed him, and relief flowed through me. "So when?"

He pointed at a small set of screens showing our trajectory. They didn't match the ones floating overhead. According to this information we were still in pursuit of the Martian. We were less than eight hours out.

"We need whatever she is carrying," Faun said. "We will need money. Akira needs to decelerate soon. The captain will figure it out then."

I was amazed at how much they were hiding. "Did you know about the treaty?" I asked. "And … how long have you been working on …"

He smiled grimly. "Yes, and we were planning this before then."

"Damn," I said sincerely. "So, when it happens … You want him dead? And what about Quinn?"

Akira chortled, but Faun didn't seem pleased with the question.

"It would be easier if they died," Faun said reluctantly.

I thought about it and didn't find any reluctance. I shrugged. "I don't have a problem with that. So, Akira needs to flip the ship, and you need to change the codes, and … we have a party. You have a plan?"

Faun looked to Akira and I could tell they were considering it: telepathy through their computer feeds: no words, just data.

"We need to act soon," Faun told me. "I have summoned Dozi." He replaced his hood and mask.

I realized I had forgotten an important bit of information. "You're going to be captain, right?" I asked Faun.

He nodded. "Dozi was not happy, but Akira sides with me, and …" He looked at me.

"I side with you," I assured him. "It'll probably take all three of us to keep that Ven bastard in line."

Faun sighed. *"Oui."*

The captain emerged from the companionway, holding a flechette gun. "I'm not stupid, Faun, but Dozi is," he said smugly. "Did you really think this would work?"

I expected the pain of the control chip firing. Every muscle in my body tensed for it. It didn't come.

The captain's eyes widened as he looked from me to Faun. "I am impressed you managed to hack the codes. I was told that was impossible. But it doesn't …"

I was moving.

Out of the corner of my eye I saw Faun throw himself on top of Akira. His suit shined silver, as if he were suddenly encased in chrome.

The captain had been aiming at Faun. He took precious seconds—for him—to adjust the angle of the barrel toward me. It was a stupid thing. The cone of razors the flechette pistol fired would have torn me to shreds without his re-aiming, but he had probably never fired one. He was thinking all the wrong thoughts: trying to act on logic and not instinct. The army had beaten the logic out of me when it came to a fight. If you had to think about it, you were dead.

I hit him hard and he fired wide. I heard the little blades pinging off exposed metal on the far side of the room as I drove us into a wall. I got a handhold on a beam with my left and began to pound with my right. He was already stunned from hitting the ceiling.

"Stop!" Faun yelled from below. "We need his head!"

I didn't need to continue anyway: the captain was unconscious.

I whirled and snatched the pistol that had drifted from his grasp. I pumped another capsule into the chamber as I reversed to kick straight down toward the companionway. I found Dozi and Quinn fighting on the rec deck. The woman had been holding back on everyone: she had had some combat training, and she had scored twice on the big Ven with a little blade. Blood followed him in slow trails as he threw himself around the room trying to avoid her. I stood in the doorway, guessed my angle, and fired at a point where I thought she wouldn't be able to avoid the cone of death even if she saw it coming. I didn't really care if I hit Dozi or not: it made things easier.

They both dodged: Dozi just enough; Quinn, not quite. The blades shredded the flesh of her legs, and she screamed and writhed in the middle of the room. I dove at her and got a good handful of shirt. I hooked my other hand in the netting to swing her around, aiming her head into a wall. She went limp on impact.

I turned and found Dozi swearing at me and Faun standing in the doorway.

"You okay? Akira?" I asked Faun.

The silver head nodded.

I floated there, still holding Quinn's limp body, and watched the blood drift around as I tried to calm my breathing.

"We did it," Faun said. "We're free."

I didn't know what he thought he needed to be free of, or Dozi, or Akira. I didn't feel free. I felt as chained to the physics of my life as I had ever been, just like the drifting blood was at the mercy of the actions that released it.

"I suppose I have to clean this mess up," I sighed.

"No," Faun said. "We need things from their bio-nets, and … their eyes for the biometrics, and … I will see to it."

"Good," I said. I didn't want any part of that, or anything for that matter. "I'll be in my cabin for a while. Wake me when we catch the Martian."

His hand fell on my arm as I began to pass him. "Thank you."

"You're welcome," I said. Beyond him, I saw Dozi trying to look at one of his wounds. He was still cursing. "If you need any other help …"

"I will signal you," Faun said quietly.

I felt a tone in my head. It was like I heard something my ears didn't. I thought I had felt it before when they tested the chips, but I hadn't felt it since.

I jerked away from him and squawked, "What was that?"

"I am sorry," he said, and I could hear the alarm in his voice. "It is just a chip feature. The captain never …"

"No, he never," I snapped.

"All right, all right," Faun said soothingly. "I will not use it. I am sorry. We all have … It is part of our bio-nets. We signal one another all the time …"

"Okay, okay, I get that," I said, and I did. I knew he meant it. I just didn't like it. "Just … I need to be alone."

I retreated to my cabin and closed and locked the door. I often felt exhausted after the excitement of a fight, but this was different. This was the way I used to feel on Yule morning when I didn't get the present I wanted. I didn't feel cheated, just disappointed. I took a sleeper pill. Thinking about it wasn't going to help. It never did.

Faun came to get me sometime later, no chime in my head, just the one at my door.

"We are close," he said quietly.

"How are things?" I asked as I shoved the sleep out of my head.

"We got what we needed. The bodies are gone. Dozi is … behaving," he sighed quietly.

"You go ahead and do that thing in my head if it's an emergency," I said.

He nodded and led me up to the bridge.

We were a couple hours from intercept, and the Martian was trying to defend herself. Our scoop was in, and Akira would be using maneuvering thrusters to bring us into grapple range. Dozi was suited and at the drone station and Faun was at his usual communications console. I suited up in my armored EV, pulled a temp couch from the wall, and strapped myself in.

For the next two hours, Akira engaged in a game of cat and mouse with velocity, Saturn's gravity, and fuel conservation, as he brought us ever closer to the evading ship. She was trying every trick we had seen the Martians use: from ejecting debris to burning her fuel in an attempt to decelerate enough that we would be forced to pass her. Akira almost rammed her instead. Dozi swore a lot at this, but managed to grapple the Martian with lines. We swung out and around relative to our prey, and dragged her with us until both ships ended up ninety degrees off their original orientations. Even though the lines were anchored at reinforced frame points, and the *Mantis* was designed for it, she groaned and complained at the sudden strain; and my heart tried to crawl up my throat as I thought about the sheer stupidity of what we were doing when nothing but vacuum waited outside our thin hull.

Dozi finished grappling with our arm while Akira finished matching our trajectory. Then it was my turn. I dropped to the maintenance deck, feeling three sets of eyes on me as I went. I checked my gear and pulled up a wire-frame schematic of the Martian to float in the corner of my faceplate as I waited for the airlock to cycle. Then there was just the suit between me and nothing, and Saturn filled the universe. His rings were almost too bright to look at, and they seemed so close that I could just thrust to the end of my tether and walk on them.

I floated there in awe. Not because what I saw was pretty, but because it reached inside my chest and head and gripped me and shook until I remembered why I had wanted to come to space: until I remembered all my boyhood dreams: until I remembered just how amazing life was—all of it. Every step I had ever taken was worthwhile if it had brought me to this. I wasn't a victim of fate and bad choices. I had wanted this, and now I had it. I howled with joy and no one heard me and I didn't care. Saturn heard me.

"Rowan?" Faun's voice came through the speaker. "You're not moving, and …"

I wasn't sure what the suit sensors had told him of my heart rate and breathing. I stifled a laugh and toggled the mike. "I'm fine. Just … had to look. It's amazing."

"There's damage?" Dozi yelled. "I can't see it with the drones."

"No, Saturn," I said.

"What the …" Dozi's voice suddenly cut out.

"Are you okay?" Faun asked calmly.

"Yeah," I said. "It doesn't look the same as it does on the screens. Don't worry your pretty head. I'm moving now."

"No hurry," he said.

"You're lying." I chuckled as I turned away from Saturn's splendor and toward the Martian.

Our prey was named the *Quonyang*, and she was three times the mass of our *Mantis*. Even with cargo ballutes, I wasn't sure how we were going to empty her, but the logistics were Faun's problem, not mine. The ships nestled side by side like a mother whale and her baby, haloed by the sun. My facemask was nearly black trying to compensate for the direct solar light, and I began to maneuver down to get the ships completely between me and the rays before I approached an entry.

Her crew blew her outer airlock doors with explosives. I watched one door wheel up and over the *Mantis*. It would have broken every bone in my body if it had struck me. It was pretty to watch as it eclipsed the sun and tumbled into the void. I silently thanked Saturn for holding my attention and Dozi for destroying the external Martian cameras with one of our drones. Not being able to see my approach, the desperate crew had timed their sabotage to correspond with when I should have arrived at their airlocks if I hadn't been floating there staring like an idiot at the wonders of the universe.

In the ten ships I had boarded, I had only seen them prepare to destroy their ship to stop me twice. Most of the Martian crews realized we just wanted the cargo: they fought, but not so that they committed suicide. These guys either had enough to fear back home that they thought this cargo was worth dying for, or they thought we were going to kill them. Which made sense, since we weren't privateers of one government preying on another's shipping anymore, but pirates. Who knew what we would do? Desperate men do crazy things.

I thought of all the crazy things desperate Martians might try as I considered the schematic. After blowing their airlocks, they had to be expecting a decompression somewhere, so I assumed they were suited up. It also meant they had explosives and were insane enough to use them. The whole ship was probably booby-trapped.

Faun's voice was like my conscience again. "Rowan?"

I knew my crewmates had seen the airlock doors go. "I'm trying to figure out how to avoid booby-traps," I said.

"Dozi says to cut into the hold," Faun said.

"All right." It sounded good to me. The bastards couldn't rig their entire hull and we didn't need them, just the cargo.

I maneuvered over, clamped myself down, and began to carefully cut a hole with a vacuum torch into their hull. No air escaped as I broke through. Once again I was reminded of how slowly things seemed to move in space as I cut a hole large enough to look through. I moved around and kept one eye on my progress and another on Saturn. I might as well enjoy the view while I was out here. I might as well do a lot of things.

I sent my crew a picture with the suit camera of the cartons I saw inside.

"Pharmaceuticals," Faun said after they had deciphered the Martian characters.

I could hear Dozi and Akira whooping in the background. We had hit the mother lode.

"I told the Martians we just want the cargo, and they have said they will do nothing to stop us," Faun said.

I didn't fully believe that, and I doubted he did either. I stayed wary as I began to cut a much larger hole in the hull.

There was a tone in my head. I shoved off from their hull and reeled myself back up my tether to our airlock in silence.

I felt more vulnerable standing in the lock in the bulky suit boarding my own ship than I had ever felt boarding one of the Martians. I wasn't afraid for myself, though. I was worried about Faun.

I readied a crowbar and a flechette pistol as the lock cycled. I couldn't see anyone through the interior window but it wasn't as if I had a field of view, between my faceplate and the little port. No one was in the inner bay. I shoved off up the companionway, thankful Akira had us at Zero-G again.

They were all on the bridge, and I understood why Faun had signaled: Dozi was armed with a Taser and standing between him and Akira. Dozi couldn't hurt Faun due to the Loonie suit, but without Akira I doubted we were going to fly anywhere, at least not well. They were all arguing.

Dozi seemed really surprised at my sudden entry: enough that he aimed the useless Taser at a fully-suited man and gave Akira the opportunity to spray him with a canister of gas. Then I was on the Ven engineer. We didn't wrestle long; whatever Akira had hit him with was potent.

I rotated around Dozi's choking and writhing body until I could see the others. Faun's suit was opaque and Akira's couch was encapsulated in an emergency dome. One of them had triggered the bridge hatch so the gas wouldn't get into the rest of the ship.

I toggled my suit mike. "He going to die?"

Akira and Faun nodded.

"We need his head?" I asked.

Another set of nods.

I cursed to myself. I really wanted to hit Dozi with the crowbar a few times.

It took an hour for Dozi to finally stop twitching and Faun to force-cycle the bridge's air through the cleaner. Faun and Akira were communicating through their bio-nets during that time, but I was out of the loop. It gave me time to think: about Saturn, and how much the Martian's cargo might be worth, about how I could use my share of that to get my chip removed and make some changes I hadn't considered even wanting before, like getting a bio-net, and adapting to … space, my way.

Now that all the people who had problems with our new course had been accounted for, Faun was free to leave Akira with the ship and help me tackle unloading the Martian. Even if we had thought the little Mercan wanted to betray us, he needed us as much as we needed him.

"You will need to learn the drones," Faun said as he donned a normal EV suit on top of his skin-tight one.

"I was thinking there's a lot of stuff I need to do," I said.

"Such as?" he asked through the suit channel as we stepped into the airlock.

"Get laid," I said with a grin he couldn't see. Even though we were right next to one another in the lock, with the suits on we were just voices.

"There might be women where we end up," he said quietly.

"I don't think I need to wait that long," I said, and realized that hadn't sounded quite right. "Maybe I don't need a woman," I added. "Maybe I need to just see what's in front of me, and appreciate it."

The outer door opened and I stepped out to the vista of Saturn once again. I pulled him with me.

W.A. Hoffman believes a geek is someone who can tell you everything about the propulsion system of the space ship in their favorite TV series, a nerd is someone who knows how and why the same propulsion system violates the laws of physics, and a dork is someone able and willing to explain the difference. Hoffman prides herself on being all three. She's spent her life daydreaming and absorbing movies, art, and the written word on any conceivable subject. Every few years she reaches critical mass and weaves the voices in her head with the endless supply of useless facts to create fiction. Dedicated to independent publishing and artistic freedom, she established her own publishing company, Alien Perspective, in 2001. Her published works include numerous short stories and the novels *Love & Benjamins*, *Blood is Thicker than Water*, and the Raised by Wolves buccaneer series: *Brethren*, *Matelots*, *Treasure*, and *Wolves*. For more information about her or her other works, please visit alienperspective.com.

Part II:
Space Sirens

Edited by Carol Hightshoe

Outpost 6

by Julia Phillips

Introduction to "Outpost 6"

When you hear the term "Space Sirens" a number of different images might come to mind. Some of them might involve the "World's Oldest Profession" and some might involve variations of the sirens from the Odyssey. In "Outpost 6" there are references to both of these types of sirens—even if they aren't the true focus of the story.

Doctor Nyssa Robbins is a woman running away from a bad break-up and takes a job as a "frontier" doctor on Outpost 6. It is a typical mining town in all respects and Doctor Robbins soon has her hands full with a cave-in and a handsome Sheriff.

When I first read "Outpost 6," I was drawn to the character of Doctor Nyssa Robbins. A woman who comes across as a real person. The world of Outpost 6 may be on a distant world, but it could also be here on Earth. Real people and real situations made this a great story and I was honored to include it in Space Sirens.

◁ ▷

Nyssa passed the time sleeping as much as possible. These transport ships tried to pass themselves off as luxury liners, equipped with everything a person could want. Except fresh air, sunshine, private bathrooms, good meals, entertainment that was actually entertaining, and a place to escape from single men. The last one was the one that pissed her off the most. Wasn't that the whole stupid reason she was on this ship in the first place?

Never drink on a broken heart, an empty stomach, and next to a newly constructed Outpost Recruiting office. When Nyssa walked in with a medical degree, three years of Level 1 Trauma experience, and a new academic degree in xenobiology, the recruiter nearly needed the young doctor's care. And when she said she wanted to go as far away as possible, he took her at her word with no dispensation for her state of sobriety.

Well, five weeks on a ship had sobered her up in more ways than one. Every day she got further away from her life, her friends and family, her ex; well, okay, that was a plus, but the only one at the moment.

Nyssa rolled out of bed and got dressed. If the ship stayed on schedule, this would be her last breakfast of dried eggs and powered milk. The ship was supposed to land on Cybele at mid-afternoon local time, which was about 3:00 in the morning in her Chicago world. The clock on the ship had been adjusting gradually since they left, so there would be no jetlag once she got there. One hundred fifty years of space travel and "spacelag" still hadn't caught on as a term. She took one last look in the mirror to check that her light brown hair wasn't sticking up anywhere out of her ponytail and she left her cabin.

The posters along the hallways were both informative and annoying. There were maps of town, lists of public services, restaurants and hotels for travelers conducting business. All of them had the official seal of the Outpost Research Institute, ORI, the agency supposedly in charge of the exploration and construction of each new outpost created in the name of Science. Between construction jobs and opportunities for bilking rich dreamers, the whole project was degenerating to the name of Commerce.

This was the newest Outpost, a mere thirty years away from the day the first settlers arrived on the only habitable planet in the Argo Navis solar system, an impressive 40 light year distance from home. The fourth planet away from the sun Puppis, Cybele was a slightly cool but temperate ecosystem, pristine until development by the

ORI. Now it had a growing capital city in New Atlanta, mining operations for export, ocean and ground transportation systems, and it was the first Outpost to share a permanent location with another species. The Idolums, a Greek name meaning "ghost" and given to them since they had refused to share anything of substance about their origins, were basically human, except for a pale red/orange skin color and a second set of arms with the elongated torso required to support them. As someone who came from a busy trauma room, a second set of arms didn't seem like a bad thing to have.

She walked into the cafeteria and grabbed a tray. She couldn't stand the sight of this food anymore, so she sort of squinted at it, only looking enough to hit the plate. She'd managed to make a few friends on her trip. She'd carefully integrated into their little group to keep herself protected as much as possible from the rest of the passengers. They were already at the same table they'd claimed their second day on board.

Blythe Gibbons was about her age with an infectious smile and bright eyes. She was on her way to an exclusive hotel/restaurant in New Atlanta to become the executive day chef. Clara Drew was trying desperately to get her 2-year-old daughter Eva to eat something, but Eva was clearly as done with this food as everyone else. Clara had not seen her husband since just after Eva was born. The ORI had offered the young geologist a king's ransom, and he'd gone off to work on the expanding train network on Cybele, waiting until he was sure the place was civilized enough for his young family to join him.

Nelia Efrain looked sympathetically at the young mother, knowing what it was like to raise a child alone. As a young widow, she'd raised her son, Vincente, alone. Now she was moving to Outpost 6 to be near him. His job as the new head of the Amycus Mining Company gave him the means to care for her.

Nyssa sat in the purposefully empty chair. "Blythe, it is borderline cruel to subject us to this food. You should just march back into that kitchen and throw the chef in the freezer."

Blythe laughed. "Don't land me in the brig on our last day." She pushed the eggs around on her plate. "Although I have thought about it."

Clara shifted Eva on her lap. "Just say your prayers of thanks that it's over and be glad we're not headed straight back to Earth like the crew."

"It's just eggs," Nelia sighed. "The three of you are acting as though it were poison."

"Have you tried them today?" Nyssa asked, seeing no evidence on the woman's plate of the yellow goo.

Nelia straightened in her chair. The carriage and demeanor of her fifty-five years gave her gravitas and authority, in spite of her tiny frame. "Food is food, and there are plenty who have none to complain about."

The three younger women looked down at their plates, reminded of the hardships many endured during the Great Drought and the coastal blight that followed just two generations ago.

Nelia continued, "Though if we gave them this, I think they'd say no thank you."

A chorus of stifled snickers began the rest of the breakfast conversation, as the excitement of finally arriving at their destination began to show on their faces.

O O O

Nyssa looked out the window of her cabin onto the rugged landscape north of town. Railcar tracks snaked their way into valleys where they would deliver supplies and equipment and bring back raw materials and precious metals. It was the latter that was responsible for the sudden boom in traffic to the newest outpost.

New Atlanta was little more than a gathering place with a spaceport. The city was placed much like the original cradle of civilization on Earth. It was near the sea which was fed by a decent sized river. The band of moderate temperatures made for a long growing season with the ocean helping to create a regular rain cycle. Tracks were installed to go into the mountains as well as single lines branching out toward small farming and ranching communities that were springing up to provide central supplies and communications with the capital city and only spaceport.

Nyssa had waited a little while to leave the ship, letting the worst of the crowd get off. As the new head of pretty much everything medical on this planet, the Institute had sent her well-supplied with drugs, replacement medical equipment, and anything else she might need. There had been a small portion of the shipping container left available to transport her personal belongings.

Finally, she grabbed her bags and headed for the dock, passing Clara and Eva in the passageway.

"I won't forget," Clara said. "I'll bring Eva in for a check-up by the end of the month. What do I do if I need you before then?"

"I'm supposed to run the only hospital in town." Nyssa shrugged. "I hope I'm not too hard to find."

O O O

The air smelled like a mixture of sea salt and industrial oil, but it still seemed like the freshest air she'd ever breathed. Nyssa looked down the platform, watching the reunion of Clara with her husband. They were both glowing in their smiles: a happy start to their new adventure.

"Dr. Robbins."

Nyssa turned around. Never had two people resembled their photograph as much as these two did. She'd had little else to do during the trip than study the literature of Outpost 6, and the Governor and his wife were on every page. Now, the corpulent pair was smiling at her; looking like Santa and Mrs. Claus in the off-season. "Governor Lange, Mrs. Lange, I wasn't expecting you to pick me up at the port."

"Nonsense, dear," Mrs. Lange said, laying a motherly hand on Nyssa's arm. "Territory governor doesn't take up that much time around here."

Governor Lange looked slightly perturbed at the aspersion on his duty schedule, but turned a genuinely smug grin at Nyssa. "It's not every day, or every territory, that gets their own xenobiologist on staff. There's little more than a country doctor position here."

"Sounds perfect," Nyssa smiled through her exhaustion. Being planetside again was making her sleepy. The oxygen content was definitely lighter than it was on ship.

Mrs. Lange looked at her sympathetically. "You must be exhausted, dear. We'll take you right over to your new home."

"It's next to your office, but not attached," he assured her. "You should have a little privacy in your time off."

"Thank you, but I'm waiting on the supply container to come off the ship. They let me pack my personal things in it, since there was room."

"Peony, why don't you take the good doctor along with you? I'll get Thomas and we'll bring that container to you in a bit." He leaned closer to Nyssa and spoke in a loud whisper. "They don't empty the cargo bay until all of the passengers have gathered their cabin personal effects. They say there's less mix-up, but I just think they're lazy." He pulled his jacket down tight, a feat of little difficulty, and strode with official purpose toward the dock office.

"This way, Dr. Robbins," Peony said and led Nyssa with single-minded determination toward town.

O O O

Nyssa was stunned with her new practice. It was simple and functional, designed with four examination rooms, a reception area and a convertible emergency room with six additional gurneys and equipment hook-ups to serve as a mock hospital. She had two administration clerks and three nurses, plus two nurse practitioners on her staff. The one thing that was disturbing was the lack of patients.

"Melanie," Nyssa asked her receptionist. "Do I have any appointments?"

"No."

Nyssa waited a moment before prompting. "Do you know why?"

"Because we haven't had a doctor on staff for two months. Minor stuff has been routed to the port because most of the ships have staff doctors. They'll come back; they always do."

"Come back? How often do you change doctors around here?"

"You'll be my fourth."

"And how long have you worked here?"

"Almost a year."

"A year?" The first trails of real doubt began to run through her mind. "Why so many doctors?"

Melanie shrugged. "I don't know. It's not like we're ever that busy."

On cue the door opened and two women entered the clinic. Nyssa smiled at Blythe, but quickly frowned to see Blythe limping, showing the universal limp of a turned ankle.

"Should I ask what happened?" Nyssa quipped.

"Bad turn on the dance floor," she said, wincing as she worked her way up onto the examination bed.

"Why were you dancing?" Nyssa asked, noticing that both of them were overdressed for this early in the evening. Make-up and fancy clothes and shoes did not fit what she'd seen of the town on her way from the port.

"She was trying to get used to the work," the other woman offered. "I'm Sidra."

"Nyssa Robbins, nice to meet you." Returning her attention to Blythe, "Does this new job involve dancing chefs?"

"The chef job fell through," Blythe answered, wincing as Nyssa began checking her ankle. "The manager hired me, but he left without telling the owner and she hired someone else. She felt really bad and promised she wouldn't leave me without a job."

"Well, I don't think you broke it, but your dancing career is going to have to wait. Let's get this scanned and then I'll get you wrapped up." She stopped. "Melanie, where is my scanner?"

She pointed down the hall. "Third room on the left."

Nyssa noticed something on the bottom of Blythe's shoe. "I think I see what caused your problem. You stepped on a lime. Someone should keep the kitchen floor a little cleaner."

Sidra grumbled. "Someone should tell Max to wipe off the bar."

"You were dancing on the bar?"

Blythe shrugged, embarrassed. "You know this really hurts."

"I'll get you fixed up. I promise."

O O O

Nyssa walked back up to the front desk. "Melanie, what kind of 'restaurant' has girls up on the bar?"

"Frankie's."

"Frankie's?"

"There are two ways to work at Frankie's. Be thankful she was on the bar."

Nyssa blinked in disbelief. "You're pretty casual about it."

"Business is business, and Frankie owns about half of this town and a piece of most of the rest." Melanie shook her head. "You're at an Outpost now; get used to being on the edge."

"All I know is my friend signed up for a job to be a professional chef, not … a professional."

"Things change, honey," a woman said from the lobby area. "You have to change with them."

"I'm sorry, but you are …?"

"I'm Frankie."

Nyssa stared dumbfounded. The woman was nothing like she expected. Her graying hair was cut in an impressive style and her nails were perfectly business manicured. Her clothes were tailored and obviously designer. She looked like she could have just walked out of a hospital board meeting. "So you run the …"

"House with the great reputation."

"Ah."

Blythe came out of the exam room on crutches with Sidra beside her. "Hi, Frankie," she said shyly. "I'm sorry…."

"Don't worry about it," Frankie said gently. "Half of life is figuring out what you're not good at. Now Sidra will help you back to your room and we'll talk later."

Blythe nodded, looked back at Nyssa. "I'll see you, soon. Thanks for the pills." She adjusted her crutches and hobbled out the door.

"Is she a friend of yours?"

"We were on the same ship. She said she had a chef's job here."

"Yes, well, there's a reason my manager isn't my manager anymore. Not telling me about Blythe was the least of the things he wasn't telling me." Frankie looked reassuringly at Nyssa. "People come and go through here. She'll get back in the kitchen. In the meantime, I'll see she has a job … out front at my other place. Too many chefs and I'll have more fights in the kitchen than I do at the bar."

"You have another place?"

"She was hired to work at Athene's. That's my classy oceanfront establishment and that's where I want my best chefs. Frankie's crowd is … a little less discerning in their taste."

"I'll remember that," Nyssa nodded, finding Frankie's honesty refreshing.

"The trick, sweetie, is diversification. I am a business woman. I run businesses that provide services: laundromats, restaurants, computer access ports, hotels (of the sleeping variety), and a port machine shop. Not to mention, I'm the mayor of this town."

"Oh, I wish I'd seen that election."

"It was a landslide. And just so you know, I own the beauty shop, too." She smiled at her. "You should stop by for a visit one day."

Nyssa suddenly became conscious of her dowdy appearance next to the working girls. "Thanks."

"And … uh … stop by the club for supper. The least I can do for the new doc is buy her dinner. Maybe I'll even find where that Key to the City went. They only issue us one."

Gov. Lange puffed his way into the clinic. "This way, Thomas."

A man backed in through the double door at the front of the clinic, pulling an anti-grav sled with the ORI container on it, and followed by two armed deputies.

Thomas looked up at Nyssa and smiled and she knew she was in trouble. Broad shouldered and blue eyed with a smile that was kind and reassuring, he was not the type of person she expected to see in a far off place like this. Damn it.

Gov. Lange made the introduction. "Dr. Robbins, let me introduce our sheriff, Thomas Carlyle. Thomas, meet Dr. Nyssa Robbins, our saving grace."

"It's a pleasure, ma'am."

Nyssa forced a smile. She hated to be ma'amed. "Were the deputies necessary?"

"Just a precaution. We get a lot of strangers through town and the ORI sent special instructions to take care of you."

"How thoughtful," Nyssa muttered. Now she had to worry about getting killed in her sleep. She could have stayed in Chicago for that. "Can you move that on through the swinging doors? I'll sort and catalog it later."

Thomas signaled the deputies and they moved the sled to the back. He turned back to the group and saw Frankie.

"You're getting skinny again, Tommy," she chided. "You need to come by a little more often."

"Yes, Mayor Sands. I've been busy."

"Too busy for me? Half the people you arrest come from my place. You could save yourself time if you were already there."

"Yes, ma'am," Thomas nodded. Turning to Nyssa, he added, "My office is just down the street and I live around the corner. If you need anything while you're getting settled, just let me know."

"Thank you, I will," Nyssa nodded. Of course, the handsome sheriff was her neighbor, because that was just her luck.

He all but tipped his hat as he and the deputies returned to duty.

"He's a good man," Frankie said, once Thomas was out of earshot. "You could do worse."

"Done worse. That's how I got here."

"Well, I got here on the first ship thirty-two years ago, along with Thomas's mother. She didn't know she was pregnant when she came on board and we barely made it down before he arrived. He's the first born on this planet and I think that makes him kind of special." She gave Nyssa a sly smile. "Give him a chance. I'll bet you a round for the house that you'll think so too."

O O O

There were no other patients that afternoon, so Nyssa took her suitcases and boxes out of the shipping container and began to make her small house into something she could call hers. The kitchen and living areas were downstairs and the two bedrooms and bath were upstairs, not a bad amount of space to call her own. Once her clothes were put away and a few pictures placed on the walls, she took an inventory of the kitchen.

The cabinets were full of basic staples, but the refrigerator was almost empty. A loaf of bread and some milk were all that were inside, along with a note from Peony Lange saying they would go shopping at the market when she was settled. Nyssa grabbed a pot from the cabinet and started to draw water into it to boil some noodles when strains of music floated in through the open window. She opened her back door and stepped out onto the small deck.

The music came from across the street and, in the near dark, she recognized Thomas. He wasn't kidding when he said he lived around the corner. She watched him from the shadow of her door. Denim shirt and damp hair, jeans and bare feet, he sat on the bench, strumming on an old guitar. The moon was half-full, and the streetlights were dim here; he looked amazing.

"Doc, you are in so much trouble," Nyssa muttered, forcing herself to close the door and go upstairs.

O O O

Nyssa sat bolt upright in bed. The house trembled in the throes of an earthquake. Outpost 6 was not supposed to have tectonic instability. So much for truth in advertising. The rumbling subsided and Nyssa sat in the quiet gloom. A few moments later, she heard the glass she'd left on the nightstand begin to rattle as the first aftershock hit. It seemed to roll longer than the earthquake itself, until she reminded herself that she'd slept through part of it. The aftershock dissipated, but the growing noise outside told her there were people hurt, so she got dressed and grabbed her gear.

She'd never actually seen bedlam before, but she imagined it was pretty close to the scene in front of her. She opened up the clinic and started laying out extra supplies in easy reach of the emergency beds. Her staff arrived a few minutes behind her and a few minutes before the crowd.

Half of the people seemed surprised to see the clinic even open, let alone a doctor on duty. The wounded generally consisted of people who'd been battered and bruised by falling objects, requiring little more than a stitch here and a bandage there. The worst case she saw was one man who'd been too close to a window that had blown in. She spent nearly half an hour removing the small shards and as she was pulling out the last piece, Thomas came running into the clinic.

"Grab your bag, Doc. We have to go."

"Where?" Nyssa asked, complying with his request before she'd even registered it.

"The quake cracked a beam in the mine. The entrance collapsed and there are people inside."

O O O

Nyssa's teeth ached after the ride to the mine on Thomas's skiff. The contraption was old but she would have sworn he deliberately flew over the worst patches of ground, except he hadn't even looked at the road. His eyes seemed to be on the hills and he had no care how he arrived there.

There was a crowd of men arguing in front of the mine. As Nyssa and Thomas approached, the leaders became defined as two men and one Idolum, all yelling too loud to hear any opinion but their own. A loud whistle from Thomas got their attention.

"Any word?" Thomas asked the first man.

"Nothing yet," he replied. "You must be the new doctor," he said, noticing Nyssa. "You flew in with my mom."

Nyssa smiled. "You must be Vincente."

"Sorry about the welcome."

"How many were inside, Damek?" Thomas asked the Idolum.

"Two crews were inside," he replied in a thick accent. "The deeper one never made it out. At least twenty."

"What about the access tunnels?" Thomas addressed the second man.

"No way to tell if they are intact. We can't send anyone down until the aftershocks stop." He looked over at Nyssa. "Gideon Drew. Clara says hi."

Thomas snapped. "Can we focus on how we're going to get them out?"

"My crews are bracing the entrance so we can start moving the rocks out, but it's going to be a few more hours," Gideon defended.

Nyssa looked up at the sealed mine opening and wondered how far the tunnels had collapsed. These situations didn't usually seem to end well, but she had briefed herself on the structure of the mines on Cybele and if the miners weren't already crushed, the next likely cause of death might be preventable. "Are the air pumps running?"

The Idolum looked at her as though she'd just asked the dumbest question ever uttered. "All equipment is set on a tremor switch. Everything shuts down."

"Then you need to restart the pumps. Buy us time to get in there."

Damek used his height advantage to try to intimidate her. "You have no authority here."

Nyssa leveled him with a look that could cut glass. "The ORI says I'm the head doctor on this post. Basically, your mine just became my hospital, which means I'm in charge. Now, will starting the generators blow anything up?"

"No," he replied icily.

"Then start them. Reduce the oxygen if you have to, but start them."

The foreman crossed both sets of arms and glared, but then complied with her request.

A member of Gideon's crew yelled for him to come over and someone stepped beside Vincente, showing him a readout on a screen. Thomas stepped back closer to Nyssa. "I hate standing around."

Vincente looked up from the printout. "We've got an idea on the blockage. The miners have to be in tunnel three or four or they'd be able to reach the backside of the rocks at the door." He headed up to tell Gideon and left them standing in front of Thomas's skiff.

Thomas seemed to mutter to himself for a moment, and then he looked at Nyssa. "I think I can get us inside, but it may be kind of rough. You'll get dirty."

"I'm way too tired to properly yell at you for that, so I'll say I'm not afraid of dirt and if you can get us in there, do it."

Thomas moved quietly back toward his skiff and Nyssa followed his lead. They got into the skiff and left.

O O O

The skiff came to a stop a little ways up the mountain and about forty degrees around the base from the entrance to the mine. Thomas grabbed the two cases of gear Nyssa packed and took off up the hill, cutting through the dark without care. Nyssa caught up and nearly ran him over. He'd set the gear down and was pulling vines and overgrowth away from a hole into the mountain. He pulled a lantern from his bag and led the way inside.

The space opened up a little inside. Nyssa wandered forward marveling at the reflective ores in the walls. "What is this place?"

"An airshaft from a cave that collapsed years ago. It's small, but you might fit."

"Thanks, I think," Nyssa replied. "If you knew about this shaft, why didn't you just tell them at the front?"

"Because this will only get someone in," he returned testily. "The entrance will still have to be cleared to get everyone out. They need to work up front."

"All of them?"

"All of them," Thomas snapped harshly, then retreated to a more contrite position. "It takes everyone's work when the entrance collapses. You have nothing to do until they bring you patients, but you can go to the men. See them as patients before you see them as bodies. Or maybe they didn't clarify that you're also the chief coroner."

The ORI had made that point clear to her, but she didn't see the benefit of confirming it now. "Fine. Where are my patients?"

Thomas held the lantern over a hole in the floor. It was about two feet across and continued well beyond the reach of the light. "Down there."

"Why am I seeing visions of a white rabbit?" Nyssa muttered. "Where does this come out?"

"About thirty feet into tunnel four."

"What if the miners are in tunnel three?"

"They cross. You should be able to get around." He wrapped a rope around Nyssa's waist and clipped it tight, and then he began speaking very quickly. "Don't worry; I can talk you through it. Just keep your feet and your wits and you'll be fine."

"Are you okay?" Nyssa asked.

"I'm claustrophobic."

Nyssa peered down into the abyss. "Well, I'm afraid of heights, so this should be fun. How *did* you know about this place?"

"How do you think I got claustrophobic?"

"Right." Nyssa gathered as much gear and supplies as she could and started filling her pack. "How far down is it?"

"Not more than fifty feet. If you stay on this side, you should be able to find some toeholds. This shaft was cut a little bigger for an emergency exit."

"Emergency exit for whom?" she fussed, noting the narrow size. "The canary?"

"That's why they don't let guys like me into the mines. We plug up the tunnels."

Nyssa's heart raced as she stepped to the edge of the hole. She was required to be certified in climbing in order to keep her Rescuer Status on the Trauma Board, but climbing in the simulation unit was nothing like this. "You're not going to let go, are you?"

"Not a bit."

"I'll release the rope when I get down. Lower as much of my gear as you can before you go."

"I'm not leaving."

"You're crawling out of your skin, I can see it. Get outside. Go back to the entrance …"

"I'm not leaving you in here alone. I won't do it to someone else."

The resolve behind that declaration was strong and Nyssa made no further comment. "Wish me luck."

"Luck."

There was a twinkle in his eyes she swore wasn't there before. She leaned back a little on the ropes and Thomas braced his feet against rocks on the floor. With a little moving around of her foot, Nyssa found the first toehold Thomas had mentioned and then, exploiting the small size of the hole for bracing, she used them to climb all the way down.

The darkness was a help. She found not knowing where she was did wonders for not worrying how far she had to fall. She concentrated on one toehold at a time, and they were spaced very well. Her rhythm was so set by the time she reached the tunnel she nearly fell when it opened up.

Thomas felt the jerk on the rope. "Are you okay?"

"It's definitely less than fifty feet," she yelled up, releasing the rope from around her. "I'm clear," Nyssa called. She heard the metal clip on the rope bounce around as Thomas pulled the rope away.

She dug her flashlight out of her pocket and turned it on. The tunnel was devoid of any people but the debris was dense. Loose rocks and abandoned equipment littered the way toward the tunnel junction. A thud behind her told her the rest of her equipment had arrived.

"How's it look?" Thomas's voice echoed into the tunnel.

"Not bad. You can tell them tunnel four is holding all the way to the junction. The miners have to be in tunnel three and that's where I'm going."

"I'll use the short wave on the skiff and then I'll be right back."

"Okay, but make sure …"

Another ripple ran through the earth. Much more minor than before, it was still a jarring feeling when standing on solid rock. The dust obscured Nyssa's view of the tunnel and she grabbed a folded bandage and tried to breathe through it. As quickly as it came, it dissipated.

"Nyssa, hold tight. I'll get you out of there."

"Forget it. Just go back and tell them to get that entrance cleared. We're going to need to get out of here fast."

There was silence for a moment, and just when Nyssa thought he'd already left, he spoke up. "I'll go use the short wave, but I'm still not leaving you in that hole."

"Then stay near the entrance and breathe steady. I'll be right back." Nyssa gathered the remaining cases and hurried down the tunnel, avoiding the tools and rocks, and cut left in the direction of tunnel three.

O O O

Rocks had fallen across the tunnel, but not all the way to the top. The Idolum had been true to his grudging word and Nyssa felt the air moving from the tunnel to the central hub. "Is anyone here?"

A raspy voice echoed out from the tunnel. "Where else would we be?"

"Home with your families, if you had any sense."

A few laughs from the other side of the rock at least confirmed there were other survivors. Trying to hold her flashlight, her gear and climb up the rocks without breaking her own leg was nearly impossible, but the pile was fairly stable. Once she passed over the top of the rocks, she was able to set her supply case down and use both hands to steady herself while she worked her way to the floor.

She took her flashlight and aimed it at the ceiling. The soft glow was gentler to the men who had spent the last couple of hours in the pitch black, but it still let her survey the tunnel. There were at least two dozen men sitting on the floor, looking like they were on a break.

"Not the way I like to meet people," Nyssa stated, her psychology lectures swimming laps in her head, "But I'm Dr. Robbins and can I say you really know how to throw a welcome party."

An older man's voice chuckled, "Happy to oblige."

"Good," Nyssa said, "Because I need your help to triage. Is anyone bleeding? Got an obvious broken bone?"

"Yes," said a voice near her feet. "It's my leg."

Nyssa leaned down and moved the flashlight over his legs. One was definitely misshapen, giving confirmation of a broken tibia. "Congratulations, it's a fracture." She began rummaging around in her pack for some of the pain killer sprays she'd thrown in. As long as it was a sealed break, there was nothing to do but keep him calm and prevent anything further from happening. "Anyone else got something for me?"

O O O

Nyssa patted the last man on the shoulder, having checked and hydrated all of them. "Okay, they should be here soon. Does anyone need anything?" She leaned down next to an old codger named Quincy with a moderate cut across his humeral artery.

Adjusting his bandage and sling, she asked, "Are you okay?"

"With a pretty young doctor here, it's the best cave-in I've had."

"Best? How many have you been in?"

"This is my … Hey, Bernie, how many is this?"

"Three for me," answered another miner of about the same age. "Happens when the Siren's hungry."

"The Siren?"

"Local legend," Ezekiel said, an especially dour miner who'd escaped with just a few cuts. "The tectonics in this mine are stable, but every five or ten years, a tremor hits and the tunnels collapse. Inside, the Siren claims her price in human souls."

"Lovely," Nyssa said sarcastically, taking a seat next to Quincy. "Well, I say not on my watch."

The men laughed, but the joke was cut short by a jarring sensation that rumbled through the floor, giving the impression of an impertinently stamped foot. Utter silence hung in the air, only to be broken by the slightest hint of an echo. A couple of moments passed and voices became discernable. Nyssa and a few of the ambulatory miners crawled back up the rocks to yell out into the tunnel.

Gideon and Vincente were the first to run up to the stone wall. Gideon gawked when he saw Nyssa looking over the top. "How did you get down here?"

"Found a short cut," she said, unsure of how much trouble she might put Thomas into. "Everyone is alive and stable, but can you get us out of here?" Nyssa looked up and saw Damek staring at her. She could have sworn she saw him smiling.

O O O

Her hospital was full. The miners and crew with simple injuries had been checked out and sent home. Quincy and his cut arm were resting on a gurney, as was the young miner Solomon with the broken, and now set, leg.

Frankie had some of her girls bring over food and coffee for the rescue workers, the miners and the medical staff. Everything was finally beginning to settle down, just in time for the sun to rise.

"This will tide you over," Frankie said, bringing Nyssa a cup of coffee. "I've got Blythe running the night crew for some eggs and pancakes in another hour."

"Do you always do so much?"

"I take good care of my town." Frankie looked down at her expensive casual loafers. "We don't always get such a happy ending."

Nyssa wanted to ask, but something in Frankie's demeanor didn't let her form the words.

"Did the miners mention the Siren?"

Nyssa nodded.

"She did a number on us about ten years after we landed and got settled." Frankie's voice became more melancholy with each word she uttered. "Tunnel seven used to be straight back from the entrance. They hit a really rich vein of the purest silver outside of a lab. A quake hit at late-afternoon, when both the day and night crews were in place. The tunnel split and cracked and … all that could be done was the recovery work." She took a ragged breath and tried to snap out of it. "That was the night Thomas lost his father. If he acts strangely, just be kind to him, because the Siren wasn't."

"Frankie," Nyssa said, "Personifying a natural disaster isn't logical."

Frankie smiled, a bit of the spark coming back into her eyes. "Trust me, sweetie, you're going to find that logic doesn't apply around here."

"Logic never applies without sleep." Nyssa grinned. "Which I'm looking forward to getting soon."

"You earned it, Doc," Thomas said from the front door of the clinic.

"We earned it," she corrected, feeling a sudden need to play comforter. Frankie was really going to be in trouble for sharing with her. "You knew where to go."

"And you knew what to do. We're going to make a good team."

He smiled at Nyssa and all she could think was how good the idea sounded. Before she could say anything else, Thomas nodded to them and walked back outside. Frankie analyzed her with a look, and then patted her on the arm and walked over to cheer up Nyssa's patients.

Nyssa surveyed the ward of wounded, then took her coffee cup and walked out onto the front porch. She looked at the town and beyond into the mountains, toward the now quiet mine. The sun was rising on her second day on Outpost 6. Welcome home.

Julia Phillips has lived most of her life in Longmont, Colorado. The research skills she learned earning her B.S. in Biology have come in handy researching all aspects of the history and myth she uses for her stories.

Screenplay work has been the dominant occupier of her time for last few years, but she hopes to have a new addition to her *Miranda, Queen of Argyll* series before too long. The rarified air of Colorado keeps her working on new and different projects all the time.

Hijacking the *Legacy*

by David Lee Summers

Introduction to "Hijacking the *Legacy*"

David Lee Summers included one of my stories in Space Pirates—the first of the Full-Throttle Space Tales anthologies, so when he sent me "Hijacking the Legacy," I have to admit I was already slightly biased toward including it. Plus, David is an author who always delivers a good tale. I wasn't disappointed.

"Hijacking the Legacy" is the story of Suki Mori—a young lady who finds herself as the guest of the privateer Ellison Firebrandt. A young lady, who wants nothing more than to go home, so she uses her technical skills to take control of the space vessel Legacy. She then finds herself in worse trouble than she bargained for.

While the stories selected as the best stories were selected by one of the other editors, Dayton Ward, I would have put "Hijacking the Legacy" on my short list as well.

◁ ▷

Suki Mori stood before a door not marked on any plan of the privateer vessel *Legacy* she'd found on the computer. At a casual glance, one might think the space was an extra fuel cell or a backup oxygen supply. However, only standard utility power lines and ventilation shafts fed the space—and there was a door.

The ship's captain, Ellison Firebrandt, rescued her from the clutches of a drug lord on the planet Prospero a month earlier. From there, they traveled to Earth, dropped off a passenger and picked up a load of cargo from one of Firebrandt's contacts. They were now traversing the galaxy and there was little to do aboard the ship other than read and study the contents of the ship's computer. While studying the ship's plans, she came across the mysterious room. She also discovered several databases that contained codes and passwords—encrypted, but she was very good with puzzles and was pretty sure she had broken the encryption.

She pulled a paper from her pocket that contained several codes, her first choice circled. Typing it in, she smiled when the door slid aside. "Lights," she said as she cautiously stepped inside. Low-level lights came on and Suki looked around at a room full of shipping containers—not very exciting for a secret room. As she moved farther in, she caught sight of a glow from behind one of the containers. A few more steps and she noticed several transparent stasis boxes, like those museums and universities used for transporting fragile items in a controlled atmosphere. Suspended in the boxes were paintings—very good paintings.

Suki's parents were scientists and she had been raised on an asteroid. She didn't know much about art, but she had seen holograms of many of Earth's great masterworks. As she looked around, she thought she recognized a painting by Van Gogh and another by Rembrandt. The signatures on the paintings confirmed her suspicions. Continuing along the row of paintings she came across one that caused her to gasp. She put her hand to her chest and felt her heart pounding. The serene face and the hint of a smile were unmistakable, even to someone who knew little about art. It was the Mona Lisa.

"Ah, now there's a compelling siren," came a voice from behind her. "What songs she would have sung if she hadn't been frozen in time."

Suki whirled around and nearly fell back into the stasis boxes. She found herself looking into Ellison Firebrandt's gray eyes. His head was cocked to the side and his fists were on his hips. His lopsided smile conveyed a mixture of admiration and annoyance. "I thought Roberts and Computer were the only ones who could decrypt the code for this room," said the captain referring to his first mate and drone-like computer specialist.

"Is that ... is that really ...?" Suki couldn't quite find the words, but she pointed at the Mona Lisa.

"It is." Firebrandt took her hand and led her from the room. "She, along with many of these other works, were on a transport going to Nouveau Paris on Alpha Coma Berenices." He sighed and shook his head. "They were created on Earth and that's where they belong, not out among the colonies."

Suki chewed her lower lip. She remembered hearing that many valuable paintings—including the Mona Lisa—had been stolen from a cargo ship. She never dreamed Ellison Firebrandt had done the deed. "But we were just on Earth," she said. "Why didn't you leave the paintings then?"

Firebrandt commanded the lights off, closed the door, and entered a new code. "It's not that simple," explained the captain. "If I gave them back to the Louvre, they would just ship them back to the museum they originally sold the paintings to. Most of the other contacts I have are ... shall we say a bit unsavory. They would take the paintings, but again, there's no guarantee they would stay on Earth, nor that they would be available for public viewing. I have to give them to the right person."

Suki looked at the door. "Still, it doesn't seem right for them to be shut up in your hold like that."

"I know," said Firebrandt.

"So, what do we do now?"

"Now?" The captain freed his long red hair from the ponytail he normally kept it in while on duty. "Now, it's time for dinner. I just prepared two lovely roast quail that I acquired with our earnings on Earth and I thought you might like to join me."

"That sounds delightful," said Suki. As they walked away from the hold, she looked back at the closed door and pondered the paintings on the other side. Turning her attention forward, she followed the captain through the other holds and up a ladder to the deck above.

A few minutes later they reached the captain's cabin. Inside, candles on the table illuminated the room in a soft light. Ellison Firebrandt had paneled his cabin in wood, an expensive luxury, but it gave the room a home-like feeling—or like it belonged aboard a ship at sea rather than aboard a space vessel. She sat at the table and watched Firebrandt as he scurried about the cabin, removing the quail from his small oven, setting them on plates, and spooning a cherry sauce over them.

Captain Ellison Firebrandt compelled her. He was handsome and, in many ways, very sensitive. She looked up at his Letter of Marque, hanging in a frame on the wall. He saw himself as a soldier fighting for Earth and yet it was clearly illegal, even by Earth laws, for him to possess the paintings she had found in the hold.

Just as the captain placed a plate in front of her, the intercom chimed. Placing the other plate at his own place, he answered the call. "This is the captain. Go ahead."

"This is Roberts," came the voice of the first officer from the command deck. "We came out of jump and found ourselves right on top of a freighter bound for New Earth. We've jammed their signals. Shall we pursue?"

"Yes," answered Firebrandt. "How long until she's in range?"

"About thirty minutes," answered Roberts.

"I'll be up shortly." The captain sat down and indicated Suki should eat. He tore into his own quail like a man famished. About halfway through, he remembered to pour some wine for Suki. He didn't drink any, preferring water.

"What happens when we catch the freighter?" asked Suki, pretty sure she knew the answer.

"A lot depends on what they're carrying, but New Earth has not been on the best of terms with the home world lately. We're under orders to take any ships we come across."

"I understand." Suki took small bites, attempting to savor the quail but having a difficult time really appreciating the fine job the captain had done preparing the meal.

After a few minutes, Firebrandt stood and placed his plate in the sanitizer. He blew out the candles and looked at Suki. "I'm sorry about the timing," he said. "Stay here. You'll be safest in this cabin." With that, he strode through the door.

Suki sighed and pushed the plate away.

Raised on an asteroid and having lived on a planet for the previous three years, Suki wasn't sure what to expect from a space battle. She cleared away her plate with the half-eaten quail and moved the candles to shelves and secured them. She activated the holographic display at the center of the table and brought up the scene being displayed in the primary holo tank on the command deck.

She could just make out the black, Erdonium hull of the New Earth freighter, illuminated by the gentle blue glow of the Erdon-Quinn engine at the ship's stern. As time passed, Suki could tell they were getting closer to freighter. About a half-hour after the captain left, high-energy pulses flew from the *Legacy* toward the other ship. They struck the freighter's engine which flared a bright blue for a moment then went black. From numbers displayed in the hologram, Suki could tell the ship continued forward. It still had momentum, but could no longer change its course or speed.

It took another two hours for *Legacy* to catch up with the freighter and lock on after the engines had been disabled. During that time, Suki browsed the captain's library and wondered what he was doing up on the command deck. She imagined he must be plotting strategy and keeping an eye on the ship's functions. Still, it was nothing like the action she had seen in pirate holograms she'd watched as a little girl. There, a pirate ship would catch and dock with another ship in a matter of minutes if not less. She barely felt the gentle bump indicating *Legacy* had docked with its prey.

After another hour, the silence in the cabin grew truly oppressive. In spite of the captain's admonition to remain in the cabin until he returned, Suki decided to see what was happening. She found the door locked. "What? Doesn't he trust me?" she growled.

Suki stormed back to the holographic display and called up databases containing passwords and door codes throughout the ship. After a few minutes, she found the code for the captain's door. Applying the encryption algorithm she'd developed, she stepped to the door and punched in the code. The door slid aside.

Suki peered around the doorframe into the corridor. With no sign of fighting, she crept down the corridor toward the ship's bow. The ship was eerily quiet. She could just make out the soft whooshing noises of water pumps and the air circulation system. Three of *Legacy*'s crewmembers stepped past, pushing anti-gravity sleds. The last one in line nodded to her and smiled. She continued until she reached the airlock. The door was open and she could look into the other ship. There were two people on the deck, just on the other side. One lay in a pool of blood, his head at an odd angle—almost severed from his neck. Next to the man was a woman with a gaping, black hole in her chest. Further along the corridor, more bodies were scattered, some with bloody sword wounds, others with cauterized holes blasted through them. One was completely missing a head; another's intestines lay exposed and glistening. Suki fell to her hands and knees and vomited the lovely quail dinner onto the deck.

One of *Legacy*'s crewmembers stepped around the corner and helped Suki to her feet. She recognized the crewmember as Nicole Lowry. "Easy there," said Lowry. "What are you doing out and about, wandering the decks? This isn't a good place for passengers."

Suki looked at Lowry, her eyes wide, and wondered what part the woman had played in the carnage she had just seen.

Lowry sighed and helped Suki find a place to sit away from the airlock. Then, she activated her wrist comm and contacted the captain. "Sir, I think we have a problem."

Ellison Firebrandt appeared a few minutes later. "Quite a haul," he said as he escorted Suki back toward her cabin. "They were carrying weapons for a ground invasion. It seems Earth was right. New Earth was planning to invade some other colonies." Suki heard the words, but didn't completely register what the captain was saying. In the past few weeks, Suki had been abducted by a drug cartel, rescued by a privateer who carried valuable paintings in his hold, and was now overwhelmed by the sight of the bodies she had seen on the ship from New Earth. It was all too much. "I'll be back to check on you later," said Firebrandt as he opened the door to her cabin.

Suki nodded, thinking it was time to make a change in the way her life was going.

O O O

Firebrandt did return a few hours later, expressing pleasure at the haul but also concern for Suki. "We are a privateer vessel," he said gently. "We fight for Earth like any other soldiers. We do our best to minimize losses on our side … and theirs."

"I know all that," she said quietly. "It's just that the difference between knowing and experiencing is more than I'd imagined." She turned and took his hands in hers. "I'd like to go home. I'd like to go back to my parents and spend a little time rethinking my life—maybe with the credits I earned on Prospero, I could get into a university on Earth."

Firebrandt took a deep breath and let it out slowly. He looked down and then sniffed, as though fighting back tears. Finally, he looked up. "We're a long ways from the home solar system and the asteroid where your parents are," he said. "We have to push on and deliver the cargo we're carrying. We can take you back when we return to the home system."

"So, does that make me a prisoner?" Suki narrowed her gaze. "You did lock me in your cabin during the battle."

Firebrandt sighed. "I locked others out. The battle could have gone badly. I knew you could get out any time you wanted." The last sentence sounded like an afterthought to Suki.

"I want to go home now," she said forcefully.

"I'm sorry," said Firebrandt tenderly. "We can't just yet." He closed his eyes and then opened them again. "Soon." He stepped forward, took her chin gently in his hand, and looked into her eyes. "I'll see you tomorrow. We can talk more then." He bent down and kissed her gently on the forehead, then turned and left the cabin.

Suki fell back on the bed, unhappy. If the course were carefully planned, *Legacy* could be back at Earth in just a few jumps. It wouldn't take long and the captain could refuel with the money he earned from the arms he just captured. She didn't understand why he felt he had to press on, unless she was also a spoil of war.

She began thinking about *Legacy*'s schematics. The ship had many automated functions, which would allow a single person to fly it, if needed. She lay on the bed for a little while and tried to go to sleep. Still awake an hour later, she sat up, stepped over to the holographic console, and checked the location of the ship's compliment. As she suspected, most were in their cabins after the raid. Only the man known as Computer occupied the command deck as they moved away from the sacked freighter.

She spent an hour poring over charts and found a way back to Earth. It required *Legacy* turn back on its original course and make for a jump point to Epsilon Indi. Two more jumps after that and they would arrive in Earth's solar system, near the asteroid belt. *Legacy* would be low on fuel but Firebrandt could refuel the ship at the science station her parents called home and be back on his way.

Continuing her search of the ship's database gave Suki the codes to the chips implanted in Computer's brain. She sat back and took stock of her plan. For a moment, she thought it would be better to forget the whole thing and just go back to bed. Surely Firebrandt and Roberts would stop her before she made it very far. Despite that, she thought Firebrandt's fondness for her might cause him to relent and take her home once he saw her determination. With that thought in mind, she wrote a short program that would command the ship to travel the course she had plotted. Then, she activated the code that locked all crewmembers into their cabins. "See how you like that, Captain Firebrandt," she said to herself with a sneer.

Finally, Suki sent a short, sharp burst of information through the chips in Computer's brain. With that, she went forward to the command deck. Carefully peering around the doorframe, she saw a pale, thin man slumped over his station. She stepped over and checked Computer's pulse. Satisfied he was just unconscious, she grabbed his wrists and yanked him unceremoniously out of his chair. From there, she dragged him to a storage room just outside the command deck and locked the door.

Returning to the command deck, Suki closed and locked the door behind her and then stepped up to the ship's wheel console and activated the program that would take her home. The holographic tank at the front of the command deck displayed the ship's new course. Thrusters fired and the ship vibrated as it turned back toward the jump point for Epsilon Indi. She found a chair and sat down, monitoring the information in the holographic tank and stealing glances back toward the command deck's main door. She hoped the ship would make its first jump before Firebrandt retook the bridge. By then, she hoped they'd be committed to the course and the captain would have no choice but to take her home.

However, she wasn't that lucky. About thirty minutes from the jump point, the door to the command deck flew open and Firebrandt and Roberts strode in with hepler pistols drawn. They scanned the deck and the captain's shoulders sank. A moment later, Suki found herself looking down the barrel of Roberts' pistol.

"Drop your weapon," ordered the captain.

"But, sir," protested Roberts. "She hijacked the ship. That's mutiny."

"I know," said Firebrandt, his voice catching. He looked around at the men and women behind him. "Assume your stations. Find out where we are and get us back on course." He reached out and took Suki's arm. "Now I need to figure out what to do with you."

"Captain," called Lowry from the forward sensor station. "We have a problem."

"This is the Cruiser *New New Jersey*," came a voice from the intercom. "You will stand down and prepare to be boarded."

Roberts spat a string of curses and turned around to face Firebrandt and Suki. "It's a New Earth Cruiser, no doubt responding to the distress signal from the ship we attacked." He put his hand on his hepler pistol and Suki could see the muscle in his jaw tensing and untensing, as though the first mate would like nothing better than to shoot her on the spot. Looking up at Firebrandt's scowl, she could tell the captain was tempted to allow Roberts to do so.

"Analysis," ordered the captain.

"They outgun us twenty to one," said Roberts. "There's no way we can fight."

"And they're right on top of us," said Lowry. "We have nowhere to run."

Suki looked down at her feet. She had been overwhelmed by the reality that Firebrandt was a privateer, that he killed people in the line of duty. However, the last thing she wanted was for him to be captured. She felt a lump in her throat and knew she was responsible. Looking up at the hologram, she saw the New Earth ship almost on them. Turning to Firebrandt she whispered, "I got us into this; I'll get us out … somehow."

O O O

When the boarding party from *New New Jersey* stormed the *Legacy*'s command deck, they found Firebrandt holding Suki's arm and Roberts' weapon drawn. They had no doubt she was their prisoner. The marines escorted the *Legacy*'s crew to *New New Jersey*'s brig and took Suki to the bridge. One of the marines escorting her saluted the man sitting in the command seat.

The commander, sporting a blond crewcut and wearing a crisp tan uniform, stood. "I am Captain William R. Stewart." He looked her up and down with a smirk. "You're a prisoner of the pirates?" he asked.

"I just want to go home," said Suki, tiredly.

"And where would home be, little lady?" asked the captain.

"My mother's the chief mineralogist on Ceres," explained Suki. "My dad's a chemist."

"Well, New Earth isn't on the best of terms with the home world," Captain Stewart said as though trying to couch complex politics in terms a child could understand. "We'll take you back to New Earth and from there we can let the diplomats work things out. In the meantime, you can have my quarters," he said magnanimously. He nodded to the marines. As they escorted Suki off the bridge, she heard the helmsman report they were approaching the stranded freighter.

The marines led Suki down one deck to a small cabin. Looking around, it was clear Captain William R. Stewart of *New New Jersey* wasn't a reader. He had a few holos about military history, but nothing else. A photo on the captain's desk showed a bleach-blonde with an ample bosom in a bikini. It was signed, "To Billy Bob with Love."

"Give me a break," Suki muttered as she found the controls to the captain's command console. Apparently, Captain "Billy Bob" Stewart wasn't *completely* stupid and didn't leave her access to everything, but she could view sensor telemetry and monitor communications. She followed *New New Jersey*'s progress as they approached the freighter and deployed a rescue party.

After watching the start of the rescue operations, Suki decided to take a peek into the corridor. Even though she was a "guest," one of the marine escorts stood guard outside the captain's quarters. She returned to the command console and found she could call up the ship's schematics. *New New Jersey* was about twice the size of *Legacy* and came equipped with shuttles that could carry the marines down to a planet for an attack. Better yet, the shuttles had sufficient capacity to return the crew of *Legacy* to their own ship.

Suki started looking through the captain's desk drawers. She found a data pad and grinned as she turned it on. The captain, afraid he would forget his passwords, had saved them, but either because his mind was on the capture of *Legacy* and the rescue operation, or simply not thinking of Suki as a threat, he had not ordered the pad removed.

It didn't take long for Suki to find her way into *New New Jersey*'s secure files. A search of the crew manifest told her much of the technical crew had gone aboard the freighter, helping repair the damage done by *Legacy*. Captain Stewart and his command crew were on the bridge. One guard was stationed outside of the captain's quarters and three more were stationed outside the brig.

Continuing her perusal of the ship's computer, she found the captain's audio logs. A plan began to form and it didn't take long for Suki to find three audio files that would serve her purpose. Knowing she didn't have much time, she went into action.

First, she enabled the security protocols that locked down the bridge and disabled communications and weapons. She then piped three audio snippets from Captain Stewart through the rest of the ship: "This is the captain." "We have a situation in the airlock." "All security forces report on the double."

With that, she chanced a peek outside the cabin. Her guard retreated down the hall. Suki grabbed the captain's data pad and ran the other direction, toward the brig. There she noticed the guards had left their posts, trusting shields and automated defenses to keep the prisoners secure until they returned. She entered the brig where she was met by the scowling faces of *Legacy*'s crew.

She stepped up to the cell that held Firebrandt and looked him in the eye. "You rescued me from the drug cartel on Prospero," she said. "Now it's my turn to return the favor." She typed in a code and opened Firebrandt's cell.

"You'll go to prison for helping us," said Firebrandt, stepping out.

"We wouldn't be here if it wasn't for her," growled Roberts from the adjoining cell.

"I know." Suki turned around and entered the code, opening his cell. "It's your choice. Take me with you or leave me here. I'm willing to face my fate whatever you choose."

"Very well," said Firebrandt. "Release the rest of the crew and lead us to the shuttles."

O O O

Two days later, *Legacy* had successfully outrun *New New Jersey* and jumped to the next star system on its original course. Suki found herself in the ship's mess facing Firebrandt, Roberts, Lowry, Computer and the rest of the crew.

"Ms. Suki Mori," Firebrandt began, "you stand accused of hijacking *Legacy* and of mutiny against her captain." Suki could hear the strain in Firebrandt's voice. Anger tightened his neck muscles while red-rimmed eyes betrayed sadness. "Because this vessel is a duly appointed privateer, the crew must vote on the charges against you. Do you understand?"

Suki nodded, her shoulders squared.

Firebrandt stood and moved around the desk so he faced the crew. "Does anyone dispute the facts in this case?"

Heads shook in unison.

"Does anyone wish to speak on behalf of Ms. Mori?"

Suki tried to find words to speak for herself, but couldn't. She saw Nicole Lowry open her mouth and then close it again. Finally, the first mate, Carter Roberts stood. "I'm not happy about being locked in my cabin or in the brig of a New Earth vessel, but Suki Mori showed us what a damn good pirate she was by hijacking this ship out from under us. I think she's learned her lesson and she has skills we can use." He rubbed his hand over his bald head and then turned to face the crew. "What say you all?"

Members of the crew looked from one to the other. Finally, Nicole Lowry raised her thumb. Computer and Roberts followed. Soon, the rest of the crew gave a thumbs-up.

Firebrandt nodded. "Very well," he said, his voice tight. Suki couldn't tell if he was happy because she was to be spared or disappointed because she wouldn't be punished for betraying him. He turned and looked her in the eye. "Suki, you are a siren who has captivated this crew, myself included. I just hope you won't lead us to disaster."

"I'll do everything I can to earn your trust back, Captain Firebrandt," said Suki solemnly. "All I wanted to do was go home. I just didn't realize I was there already."

David Lee Summers is an author, editor, and astronomer living in Southern New Mexico. He edited the science fiction and fantasy magazines *Hadrosaur Tales* and *Tales of the Talisman* for ten years each along with the anthologies *A Kepler's Dozen*, *Space Pirates*, and *Space Horrors*. He's also the author of ten novels including *Owl Dance* and *The Astronomer's Crypt*. His short fiction has appeared in such venues as *Cemetery Dance* and *Realms of Fantasy* Magazines. When not working with the written word, David operates telescopes at Kitt Peak National Observatory. Learn more about David at davidleesummers.com.

Rebel Moon

by Carol Hightshoe

Introduction to "Rebel Moon"

As an author and an editor, I'm always a little hesitant to add my own stories into anthologies I'm editing. That being said, David Rozansky, the publisher for Flying Pen Press did encourage us to include our own stories in the original collections.

"Rebel Moon" started life as a Star Trek story I wrote for the Strange New Worlds contests. After several rewrites, to remove the serial numbers (so to speak)—I sent the story to David Boop, the wonderful person behind the Full-Throttle Space Tales series, to read and critique and to also get a second opinion on whether I should include it. He had some good comments and suggestions and I happily edited and did another rewrite before adding it to the anthology. Then when Dayton Ward selected it as one of the best of Space Sirens, to say I was thrilled would be a serious understatement.

In "Rebel Moon" we meet Selaynia—a covert operations agent who has had enough of the games the agency she works for plays and wants out. She is strong-willed with a telepathic wolf companion. Between them, they are considered to be one of the best teams the Confederation has—and the agency isn't going to let them leave without a fight.

◁ ▷

Selaynia paused as she stepped off the shuttle and onto the landing deck of the Melpomene mining station. This was the largest of the nine moons orbiting Aganippe and had become the primary home for the refugees leaving what was left of the Centauri Alliance. Even the Confederation had been known to avoid the Corycian System with its unpredictable plasma storms that hindered travel as well as the three asteroid belts. Those hazards were what made it the perfect place for planning a rebellion and that was why she was here.

Before the Alliance's surrender, she had been sent to Wyvern as a defector, carrying information on Alliance defense strategies. Despite the misinformation included in what she had given them, the Confederation had still managed to defeat the Alliance. Now, after several months trapped on that tropical planet, she was here on a lifeless moon. One of nine used as mining stations around Aganippe.

:*Melpomene,* Shadowmist's voice echoed in her head. :*The Muse of Tragedy. Seems an appropriate place to organize a rebellion.*

"At least they didn't pick Thalia, the Muse of Comedy, as the primary base," she said. "Come on let's blend in and then find Commander Mallory."

:*There are too many minds to try and cloud here. I cannot focus on that and still be able to sense what is going on.*

She rested her hand on the wolf's head and scratched his ears. "Don't worry about it. I doubt it will really matter if anyone remembers seeing us here."

The wolf looked up at her, then licked her hand.

"Come on furball—see if you can locate Commander Mallory in this swarm of minds."

The wolf growled then nipped at her hand. :*I hate that nickname.*

"I know."

Selaynia followed the large silver-tipped black wolf and grinned as people in the corridor moved quickly out of his way. They didn't seem to care if they bumped into or even knocked over someone else, as long as they were able to move away from her companion. One or two paused long enough to look at her and she knew they would definitely remember her long silver hair and gray eyes. Most of the time, Shadowmist was able to create a psychic fog that caused most people to not notice them—that was one of the reasons she was as good at her job as she was. Actually, Shadowmist was the primary reason she was as good at her job as she was. His telepathic abilities often provided her with information and warnings in addition to being able to protect her from being observed. While most of the Alliance knew the Canthralian Wolves were telepathic; because of the isolationist attitude of the planet, no one really understood how powerful they were. She doubted there was anyone on Canthralas itself who actually knew how powerful the wolves were.

She stopped in the middle of the corridor, her right hand going to the dagger on her left arm. There had been a tingle in her mind, another telepath trying to scan her. She glanced at Shadowmist who had also stopped, his ears pricked forward and his stance rigid.

:*I felt it too,* he sent.

"Great," she whispered. "Canthralian, Rhiashian or someone else?" Despite their bond, she had never been able to project her thoughts to Shadowmist unless she also spoke them.

:*I couldn't tell. It was very powerful, but too brief to read.*

Selaynia frowned. It really didn't matter which of the telepathic races it was—any of them could be trouble. Her grip on the dagger tightened. She trusted the older style weapon more than she trusted the energy pistol she carried. Most of the current personal shield technology would stop directed energy weapons, but not a properly handled physical weapon. Besides, she just preferred it. The dagger was in her hand and she assumed a defensive stance as Shadowmist's howl echoed in the corridor. The other people pressed against the walls. Most covering their ears as they stared at her and the wolf.

"Shadow!"

The wolf didn't answer her. She tried to relax and touch his mind and found only silence. Even the familiar wolf song that was always in her mind was gone. Someone had dropped a psychic shield over her partner.

She grabbed the nearest person in what was once an Alliance uniform. "Where's Commander Mallory's office?"

"Two levels up; end of Alpha corridor."

"Show me!" She pushed him in front of her. "Now!"

She slapped Shadowmist as she followed the man. The wolf stopped howling and she heard him following her.

Selaynia paused and slipped her dagger back into its sheath as she looked at the door she had been "escorted" to. "Anything?"

:*I am still blocked.*

"Damn." She reached for the door buzzer.

:*Danger!*

Selaynia spun around, both of her daggers flying and passing through one of the large Rhiash warriors standing in the now deserted corridor as she dove to the side. Shadowmist was leaping at the smaller Rhiash female and Selaynia grinned as the wolf passed through her. They were only illusions—exceptional ones, but still illusions. The last thing she wanted at this time was to be fighting a Rhiash Triad. The females had strong telepathic abilities, which they used to cloud their opponents' minds while the males were outstanding warriors. Despite their humanoid appearance, they were tougher and had fewer pain receptors, which allowed them to continue fighting past the point where most humans would quit. The females were the exact opposite of the males, almost ethereal in their appearance. The one thing that truly distinguished the Rhiash from other humanoid species was their resemblance to felines: particularly their eyes and ears.

"Always the actress, aren't you," the female Rhiash said as if Shadowmist had not just proven she wasn't real. "The Confederation sends their thanks for providing them with the location of this little operation."

The two warriors maintained their positions next to the female. Selaynia clenched her fists tightly as she realized she would have to play this little scenario out before she would get to see Commander Mallory. "I don't know what you're talking about," she said.

"Really? My counterpart on Wyvern said you were good. Of course, it is easy to be good when you have a telepathic companion who can read the thoughts and emotions of others then pass that information to you. That is the reason she made sure you got the message to come here. She knew you would be able to lead us here. Now, stand away from that door."

Selaynia shook her head. "I don't think so." She took a deep breath then smiled. "Enough!" She turned her back on the Rhiash and faced the door. "This has all the earmarks of a telepathic game and I don't want to play."

She winced as a sharp stabbing pain hit her head and she glanced back to see the Rhiash vanish.

"I was warned you would see through my little game quickly," a man said as he stepped through the door. "I see that warning was correct."

Selaynia took a step back as she studied the man exiting the office. He was tall with an almost imperious air about him. His dark hair was neatly trimmed and his amber eyes were bright, but cautious as they studied her.

"Commander." She nodded her head slightly. "I guess I should take your suspicions as a compliment to my acting skills. My *defection* was that convincing, I take it?"

"It was. You understand I had to be sure."

She nodded. "If you're convinced, I would appreciate being shown to quarters. It was a bumpy ride getting here, and it will take me a few hours to get rid of the headache your telepath gave me. And, by the way, where is the person who gave it to me?"

Mallory gestured behind him and another man stepped out of the office accompanied by a small silver wolf.

"Jaharel?" Selaynia took another step back as the breath seemed to stop in her throat.

"Selaynia?" He stared at her.

He was exactly as she remembered him. The dark gray hair that was a match for his gray eyes; the athletic build and chiseled face. Surprisingly, he also didn't seem to have aged any in the ten years since she had last seen him.

Shadowmist gave a short bark as the other wolf trotted over to him and they touched noses.

"I … We thought you were dead," Jaharel said.

"The clan elders exiled me for helping the Alliance stop the raiders, so I left."

"Jaharel," Mallory interrupted. "If you would, please escort our guest to quarters in section five-alpha." He held his hand out. "David Mallory."

"Selaynia."

"Glad to have you here. Go, get some rest and I'll explain things in the morning."

O O O

"Good morning." Mallory looked up as Selaynia entered his office the next morning.

She ignored the greeting and dropped into one of the chairs, then waited.

Mallory only raised an eyebrow. "Again, thank you for coming."

"Get to the point, Commander. I've had time to think about the implications of Jaharel being here and I don't think I'm going to like what you are going to ask us to do."

"I doubt you will either, but it has to be asked." He paused and his gaze moved to Shadowmist for a moment then back to her.

"While telepaths have occasionally appeared among different races, there were less than a handful of races for whom telepathic abilities are common."

Selaynia leaned forward in chair. "Were?"

"During the last days, before the Alliance was forced to surrender, the Rhiash targeted those worlds. The only known telepaths left are the Rhiash and the Canthralian Wolves."

Selaynia rested her hand on Shadowmist's head as he whined softly. "They destroyed the other telepathic races?" Her hand tightened on the wolf's fur.

"We're pretty sure some individuals escaped, but their numbers will be extremely small. While we're hoping some of those are able to make their way here, that is not the primary concern at this time." He paused and his gaze darted between her and Shadowmist. "You know how strong the telepathic gifts of the Canthralian Wolves are; now imagine those gifts being combined with the telepathic powers of the Rhiash females."

Selaynia dropped her head for a moment then took a deep breath as Shadowmist placed his head on her knee. "Do you understand what it is you are asking us to do?"

"I understand it may be difficult ..."

"Difficult?" Selaynia interrupted him, before he could say anything else. "Difficult. If you know anything about Canthralas, you know it will be damn near impossible. I tried once to get the clans and packs to band together to stop a group that was taking pups from our world. Because of my actions and involvement with the outsiders that helped me, I was exiled from my home.

"Humans have a phrase, *Lone Wolf*, which is used to describe someone who acts on his own, outside the normal constraints of society. Canthralas is a planet of *Lone Wolves*, at least as far as outsiders are concerned. Within the family units, they are fiercely protective, but they will *not* get involved in anything outside their clans."

"But the Rhiash are taking the wolves from the planet—doesn't that protective attitude extend to them?"

Selaynia shook her head. "I doubt the Rhiash have taken bonded wolves from any of the clans. A bonded wolf will die before the bond with their partner is broken. If they want to develop the strong telepathic talents, they will be taking the pups and bonding with them." She took another breath and paused for several seconds her gaze focused on Shadowmist's ears as she continued to play with the fur on his neck. "It is doubtful the clans will unite and that is the only way they will be able to protect the unbonded ones."

"But surely they realize the wolves are one of your greatest resources."

Selaynia's head snapped up as Shadowmist started growling. "They are not a resource! They are sentient beings—as intelligent as you or I. They are our partners; not something to be exploited!"

"Yet, the Canthralians are allowing them to be exploited." Mallory's voice was soft and Selaynia thought she caught the hint of a smile at the corners of his eyes. "As I understand it, there are packs of unbonded wolves living in various areas; perhaps it is them you should ask for help in fighting the Rhiash who are stealing their children."

Selaynia pursed her lips together, laughed softly and nodded her head. "You do understand; better than I would have suspected. That is probably the best way to proceed."

"I was one of those who helped to stop the last set of raiders. I did learn a thing or two about the Canthralians at that time. And

Jaharel has made it a point to continue my education since he came here." He stood and held out his hand.

Selaynia grinned as she stood and grasped the offered hand. "Very well. Whenever Jaharel is ready to leave, so are we."

"I asked him and Smokeshadow to wait at the landing bay." He reached down and pressed a small button on the desk. "Mr. Stevens, can you please escort Selaynia and Shadowmist to the landing bay," Mallory said when a young man opened the door.

"Yes, sir. If you'll follow me." He turned and left the room without waiting.

O O O

Selaynia paused at the door to the hanger. Jaharel was standing with his back to her. Smokeshadow was under the shuttle and raised her head as Shadowmist barked once in greeting.

Why did it have to be Jaharel? she thought. The history between them was not easily forgotten even with the years and distance involved.

Shadowmist had started past her to touch noses with Smokeshadow, but stopped and trotted back to her, his nose touching her hand.

:*There is something he is hiding. Smokeshadow is helping him to shield his mind. I don't understand.*

Selaynia swallowed hard as Jaharel turned then dropped his gaze to the floor. It had been quick, but not quick enough to hide the pain she saw in his silver-gray eyes.

She closed her eyes for a moment and dropped her head slightly. "Don't worry about it," she whispered. *Touched by wolf song*, she thought.

She and Jaharel would have been mated prior to her being bonded to Shadowmist and her getting involved with the Alliance if the clan elders hadn't intervened by saying she had been touched by wolf song. Even before she had bonded with Shadowmist, she had a special relationship with all of the wolves. Even those who had partners would sometimes speak to her and come to her when they needed something. There were times she could almost hear the song that echoed through their voices, even when they weren't speaking to her. It was a part of her soul.

It was the wolf song that had driven her to stop the raiders, even before the Alliance arrived. She could hear the pain and loss in the song and she needed to do something about it. She looked down at Shadowmist, who was looking up at her with his golden brown eyes. She could almost hear the song; even here—with so much distance between her and Canthralas, she could almost hear it.

"You ready?" Jaharel's voice interrupted her thoughts and she felt the song drift away.

She nodded and entered the shuttle for the long trip to Canthralas.

O O O

"Well?"

"Well what?" She turned to Jaharel as he exited the shuttle. She shivered as she felt a tingle in her mind. There was something at the edge of her thoughts, something trying to touch her memories. The feeling was replaced by the sound of wolf song in her mind.

"Have you truly become an outsider?"

"What?" Her breath caught in her throat as she stared at him.

"You have ignored me during this trip despite our being trapped together. We are of the same clan. We were to be mated." He dropped his gaze to the floor. "Now you ignore me."

"I am exiled from the clan and the elders forbade our mating. It has been ten years since I left Grey Shadows. You said you thought me dead. Did you not find another?"

"No."

He looked up and Selaynia saw something flicker in his eyes. Was it hope or was it fear? She wasn't sure.

"The elders never told us you were exiled. After your family completed the mourning rituals, I left and ran with Silver Dawn's pack. That was when I bonded to Smokeshadow." He reached up and ran his hand through his dark silver hair.

"You ran with one of the packs. No one has done that for many generations."

"Just as no one has been touched by wolf song." He took her hands in his, gripping them tightly, and smiled. "Selaynia, I knew what I was risking by asking the Alliance for aid in protecting the young ones." He paused and took a quick breath. "I asked for you to be the one to go with me back to Canthralas."

"You what?" She felt her chest tighten and she took a long deep breath as she tried to calm her emotions. *What's happening to my control,* she thought. She was good at her job because of Shadowmist's help and her control. She never let her emotions show, she was always restrained and calm. And, with Shadowmist's help she was able to blend into any group she chose. *Why am I losing all of that—now?*

:*Because you want to,* Shadowmist's voice whispered in her mind.

There it was. He was right. She wanted to lose herself in the memories and in the possibilities of the future. But, now was not the time. She took another deep breath and slowly pulled her hands away from Jaharel.

"First, let's figure out what we are going to do about the Rhiash who are stealing the young ones. Then you and I will talk."

He nodded and Selaynia felt a sharp pain in her heart at the way his eyes darkened. She reached up and placed her hand against his cheek. "No howls of sorrow—not at this time."

He turned slightly and kissed the palm of her hand. "No howls of sorrow," he whispered.

"Did you have something in mind regarding the Rhiash?"

"I have run with Silver Dawn's pack. They are the dominant pack and Silver Dawn has influence over the others because of this. You have been touched by wolf song. I propose you call a gathering."

"A gathering hasn't occurred …"

"… for many generations. It has been at least as long as it has been since there was one who ran with the packs and one who was touched by wolf song." He paused then grabbed her hands again. "Selaynia; the elders may have told you you were exiled, but they never made the formal declaration."

"That may be true, but they know the truth of the situation—as do I."

He released her hand and took a step back. "I believe the best place to try and call the packs is the Mist Peaks. It is just outside

Silver Dawn's territory and not controlled by any of the others."

"And only a short hike from here," she said.

"There is that." He laughed and gestured to a narrow path leading into the hills.

O O O

Selaynia watched as the twin moons rose; their light muted by the mist that shrouded these peaks. It was a scene she had missed seeing for the last ten years. She closed her eyes and opened her mind; not just to the bond she and Shadowmist shared, but also to the faint echo of wolf song she could feel at the edge of her thoughts. The wolf song that had once been so strong in her mind was now only a faint whisper. Had the Rhiash diminished the wolves to this point, or was something blocking the song. Her gaze went to Smokeshadow who stood next to Jaharel. The female wolf had not tried to touch her mind and Shadowmist had told her that other than the initial greeting at Mallory's office, she had ignored him as well.

Selaynia glanced down at Shadowmist then froze as the wolf song grew stronger. She let the song fill her mind and throat as she howled. She let herself be pulled deeper into the song as answering howls echoed through the area. The wolves had come to her call. She gasped as the wolf song intensified and she felt the packs probing her memories.

Several minutes later, she relaxed as her mind was released and a large white male left the gathered packs and approached her slowly. Selaynia held out the back of her hand for the elder wolf to sniff. "Silver Dawn," she said bowing her head slightly.

:*The images you have shown us are very distressing.* He paused and glanced at Jaharel.

Several of the other pack leaders moved up to stand behind Silver Dawn. Selaynia blinked several times as Shadowmist also moved to stand with the elder wolf. "What?" she whispered.

:*However, we have also read deception in your mind. You yourself have worked with these Rhiash; assisting them in their war against those you once called your friends. Now you come to us, using your gift to call the packs to you;*

even as the Rhiash accompanying you have called for her warriors to attack us.

"What? No!"

Selaynia spun around to see Jaharel's appearance shift into the same illusionary Rhiash female she had faced on Melpomene. Her daggers were in her hand and she lunged for the Rhiash as several energy beams streaked down at the gathered wolves.

Selaynia hesitated as Smokeshadow jumped toward her, the wolf's teeth catching her right wrist and biting down hard. The dagger she was holding dropped to the ground and she found herself falling, the weight of the wolf slamming her against the rocks.

Smokeshadow continued to hold her wrist in her teeth as Selaynia tried to push her arm against the wolf hoping to force her mouth open. *:I'm sorry,* she heard Smokeshadow whisper in her mind.

Selaynia reached for the wolf with her free hand twisting to apply pressure to either side of the jaw hinge. She wasn't able to put much force on the pressure point, but combined with pushing her other arm she was able to force the wolf's mouth open. She jerked her arm forward quickly, ignoring the pain as Smokeshadow's teeth still ripped into her flesh. Her uninjured hand slid down and grabbed the wolf's throat, stopping, at least temporarily, her next attack. It was enough time for her to draw her energy pistol.

"Do you hear the howls?" the Rhiash asked. "The pain as they lay dying?"

Selaynia jabbed her thumb quickly into Smokeshadow's throat, causing the wolf to jerk away from her. That small movement showed her where the Rhiash was and she fired the energy pistol.

Smokeshadow's howl as well as several others filled her ears and her mind as she fell into darkness.

O O O

Selaynia awoke to Shadowmist gently licking her cheek. "What happened?" Her voice cracked and she started coughing as she tried to force herself into a sitting position. She stopped as she saw she was still on the landing deck of Melpomene. The bodies of two other wolves, Smokeshadow and Silver Dawn, lay nearby as well as that of Jaharel.

:*You never thought to ask how he knew to ask for you?* Despite the accusatory question, there was only compassion in the wolf's voice.

"He was working for the Rhiash," Mallory said from the doorway. "We suspected, but couldn't prove anything." He stepped forward and held out his hand. "He came to us with the story about the Rhiash taking the pups." He paused. "However, no one has ever seen them with one."

"It's possible he was lying about that. But why?"

:*In order to return to Canthralas and do just what he claimed he was here to stop.* Smokeshadow's voice whispered.

Selaynia spun around to see the female wolf was standing, her head lowered and eyes clouded with grief.

:*After you left Canthralas, he did run with Silver Dawn's pack for a time. But, the grief of losing you was too much. He blamed the Alliance for that. He and I were bonded, but Silver Dawn and others could sense what he was becoming. Silver Dawn was able to hide his own presence and came with us a few years ago when Jaharel left Canthralas and sought out the Rhiash. He was the one who helped them find ways to defeat the other telepathic races. However, when he attempted to lead them to Canthralas, Silver Dawn and I were able to prevent him from finding the planet. This caused him to be accused of treachery by the Rhiash and he fled to this place. He learned you were still alive and hoped to use you to return to Canthralas so he could accomplish what you saw him doing.*

"It was all an illusion?" Selaynia looked over at Jaharel's body.

:*Yes,* Shadowmist said.

"But …"

:*It was necessary.*

:*It was my idea to make you think he was a Rhiash,* Shadowmist said. :*It was the only way to ensure you acted when the opportunity came.*

Selaynia nodded then looked down at the damage to her right wrist. "It wasn't all an illusion."

:*I'm sorry.*

She walked slowly over to Silver Dawn's body. "I don't understand how you are still alive." She turned back to Smokeshadow. "You and Jaharel were bonded."

The wolf hesitated and Shadowmist rubbed his muzzle against hers. :*Silver Dawn shielded me. He took the backlash from the destruction of the bond.*

"You need to get some rest; as do the four feets," Mallory said.

Selaynia nodded. She paused as she looked down into Shadowmist's golden brown eyes. She had known the telepathic gifts of her friend were strong, but had never suspected they would be this powerful. Shadowmist only gave her a canine grin as he and Smokeshadow bobbed their heads toward the door. They were right—she needed to get some rest. Tomorrow, they had a rebellion to start planning.

A native Texan, **Carol Hightshoe** found her way to her current home in Colorado by way of a five-year detour in The Nederlands—courtesy of her husband Tim and the US Air Force. She has been published in various anthologies and magazines including *Creature Fantastic*, *PanGaia* Magazine, *Stories of Strength*, *Baen's Universe*, *Tales of the Talisman* and *A Kepler's Dozen*. Her novels include: *Call of Chaos*, *Chaos Embraced*, *The Road into Chaos*, and *Chaos Challenged*. In addition to her own writing, she is the editor and publisher of the online e-zines: *The Lorelei Signal* and *Sorcerous Signals* as well as running her own micro-press, WolfSinger Publications.

Part III:
Space Grunts

Edited by Dayton Ward

PRICE OF COMMAND

by Irene Radford and Bob Brown

Introduction to "Price of Command"

One of the things I wanted to do with Space Grunts was provide a variety of perspectives, from combatants to observers, and from the generals and their "big picture" perspective to the grunts in the trenches with only the war that's right in front of them. Sprinkled in and around those "points of interest," I wanted whatever other engaging viewpoints I could find.

I was immediately drawn to Irene and Bob's conversational, occasionally disjointed approach to offering us Corporal Jimmy Seaforth's point of view of Captain Katie Talbot, a character Irene created for a trilogy of novels she'd previously written. With short, choppy sentences and a verbal shorthand Irene trusts us to understand as we go, "Price of Command," reads like a story recounted by a trooper sitting in a hooch or standing around a fire, enjoying a bit of downtime with his buddies.

We don't need to have read Irene's other novels to gain an appreciation of Captain Talbot as viewed by Seaforth, but this story certainly makes us want to go and find those books. It's a perfect counterbalance to several of the other stories in the anthology that provide more traditional, action-oriented military SF themes.

◁ ▷

The most beautiful woman in the galaxy, and she's our boss," Sergeant George Lolopolinski grumbled.

We called him Jolly behind his back in the 8th Division of His Majesty's Galactic Marine Corps.

Me? Jimmy Seaforth, I'm just a Corporal communications grunt. I set up the equipment so that our guys in the field can link to the brass who are safely ensconced behind shields and plasma cannons on the big ships in orbit.

In this case, the brass is Captain Kathleen Marie Talbot of His Majesty's Galactic Navy. One point eight meters of legs and tits with flaming red hair cropped space-short and green eyes that could burn holes through you.

The way our Captain Katie fills out her uniform blouse makes a man think of long, frosty nights dirtside in front of a fire with a bottle of wine and a warm blanket.

"Who was the idiot who invented the no-fraternization rule?" Jolly continued his litany of complaint.

Did I mention that we gave him the nickname because it was the exact opposite of his personality? Like calling a man who stood two and half meters tall "Shorty."

"I'm sure the Emperor gets around the rule." I jabbed Jolly in the ribs to shut him up. When Captain Katie briefed the troops, you stood tall and kept your eyes forward. God, sometimes I wish I was shorter.

Jolly hadn't been on Captain Katie's last campaign. I ran the comms board when the second fleet got caught in a trap behind enemy lines. First salvo took out most of the brass. Captain, then Lieutenant Commander, Katie was the only officer left with any brains. Single handedly she regrouped the remnants of the fleet, and not only got us home, but took a couple of destroyers with us. Since then, she, or better we, have more confirmed reptilian kills than the entire fleet had in the previous two years.

The lizards don't take prisoners. Neither do we, frankly. Rumor has it they eat carrion, and our amino acids work just fine in their digestive systems.

We've taken our licks too. Got caught groundside on the bad side of a full brigade when our bombardment ship got "engine trouble." We limped back to the capital on minimal supplies and barely enough fuel for life support let alone any kind of speed. We were a mess.

The Emperor toasted and celebrated Our Katie for three weeks. She put enough meat back on her skinny frame to fill out her uniform. Then His Majesty jumped her two grades over her field rank and gave her command of a light cruiser and a job: clean out a nest of pirates once and for all.

We don't need a second front against pirates within our own space. Fighting the lizards at the edge of our territory was bad enough.

Who better than Our Katie to take on the pirates?

Captain Kathleen Marie Talbot fixed Jolly with a stern gaze. He kept his spine at full salute, but I watched his muscles sort of melt into subservience.

"Troops, our orders are to take out the smuggler's headquarters that occupies the island continent on the equator. The O'Hara brothers have been a thorn in the side of peaceful and civilized commerce for too long. We've got to shut them down, but the brass wants them alive and talking. When the compound is secure, you Corporal Seaforth, will clone the communications, then destroy the equipment. Obliterate it down to melted elements. I don't want so much as a molecule left salvageable. Do you understand, Corporal?"

"Yes, sir!" I snapped a salute.

"And you, Sergeant Lolopolinski," she paused as she inspected his uniform for the smallest crease or mote of dust.

"Yes, sir!" He, too, saluted.

Captain Katie grunted her approval of his appearance, grudgingly. If I read her expression right, she wanted to assign this man elsewhere, like the battlefront on the rim of civilization. But he was the best sniper in the crew, and the most doggedly determined to get his job done so he could go back to lying in his rack and grumbling about how ill-treated he was by the brass.

See that's the advantage of being a grunt like us. We can talk and grumble among ourselves. Our Katie had no one to talk to.

"Your job, Sergeant, is to protect Corporal Seaforth at all cost. He is to return alive with the pirate communications clone intact.

Those communications come directly to me by his hand. Do you understand, Sergeant?"

"Sir, yes, sir!" He reverted to basic training salute protocol in his trembling awe of our captain.

She jerked her head once in an abbreviated nod and moved on to finalize plans with Major D'Jarra. He'd worked side by side with Our Katie during that long hard haul from battlefield disaster to home. Since the captain had to stay aboard ship, the only other officer I trusted on this mission was D'Jarra.

Maybe he was the only officer *she* trusted to complete this mission properly. Otherwise, why not send a raw lieutenant who needed the experience?

Those of us who survived Our Katie's war were a tight knit group. We'd learned how each other thinks. We'd learned our weaknesses and strengths. And we trusted each other with our lives and our souls.

Jolly would never understand that level of trust because he hadn't earned it.

Then we all paraded in front of our captain as we took our assigned places onboard the transport. I hated ship to dirt transports. Not a glamorous officers' shuttle. Nu-uh. Not by a long shot.

Each one of us wore fully inflated gel armor between the layers of khaki and camouflage. We all carried full packs and weapons. I had the added burden of another twenty kilos of communications gear. Everything I needed to set up a field array and copy the pirates' logs of calls to and from the base.

As I passed Our Katie, toward the end of the line, I saw something in her eyes that said more than her rigid posture and jutting chin.

"Do me proud, Jimmy," she whispered.

"Aye, aye, Captain."

She quirked me a half smile. "I expect nothing less than the best from you, Jimmy. But next time you pick a bar fight just to lose your sergeant's stripe, let me know ahead of time."

"Yes, sir."

"We both know you are better than some screw up grunt. I trust you to get this job done *properly.*"

We both nodded once. Then the press of people behind me pushed me through the hatch and out of her line of sight.

She'd meant more than she said. I knew it. See, being a comms tech is more than knowing the electronics and how to jury rig fried circuits. It's knowing how to read between the lines to make sure the message gets to the right person, not necessarily the one whose name is on the address label. It's reading in spirals to crack a code. And it's watching body language as the message is being spoken, or written.

And it's knowing how to keep my mouth shut.

Our Katie trusted me to do something special. I just didn't know what yet.

I angled, pushed, and jabbed my elbows in a few ribs to grab a position on the outer edge of the transport egg, a big black, windowless vessel. The brass says this is so they can put more mass into the shielding against space radiation and enemy fire.

Uncomfortable at best, I had to perch my skinny butt on a fifteen-centimeter-wide bench. My pack tried to pull me backward. The comm equipment rested on the deck between my knees. With a bulkhead to lean against on one side, I found it easier to balance everything and rest my shoulder against something more solid than Lolopolinski.

By the time we touched down dirtside three hours later we were all so uncomfortable we itched to shoot someone. Anyone who got in our way.

Maybe the Brass factored that in when designing the eggs.

At first sign of touchdown, the troops around me stood as one, shuffling and grumbling and arming their weapons. I almost didn't hear D'Jarra's parting words. "We want these people alive, especially the three O'Hara brothers!"

That made me pause long enough to lose track of Lolopolinski in the crush to get out of the claustrophobic egg.

In civilized space the only good pirate is a dead pirate. Out on the battle front you count as an ally anyone who doesn't shoot first. Behind the lines you look more closely at the niceties of legal and illegal.

We'd all heard about the three O'Hara brothers and their exploits. Smart. These guys were always three jumps ahead of the law with tech and brains. Sometimes they had already sold their stolen cargo and moved on before a crime was even discovered. If they didn't steal from everybody, even those who had little or nothing to steal, they might have become folk heroes to the poor, displaced, and downtrodden.

But they stole from anybody and stepped on those who got in the way.

So why did the brass want these guys alive? Not just so they could bring them to trial and make an example to all lawbreakers I was betting.

Something was up and Captain Katie expected me to figure it out.

"Bet that *take 'em alive* order is from our bleeding heart princess," Jolly muttered. "Her daddy's a planetary governor and bought her commission. She doesn't really know what pirates are like. I say we shoot *'em* all dead and call it self-defense."

I rolled my eyes. "If you only knew the truth, Jolly."

See, on those long nights of standing watch while running dark and silent trying to escape the enemy, Our Katie and I talked a bit. I think I'm the only person she allowed herself to talk to. Probably because neither of us knew if we'd survive to remember those heart-to-hearts.

A planetary governor adopted her when she was seven. After that she had a pretty good life of fine schools and debutante balls. Then she graduated top of her class at the Academy and started a roller-coaster career aimed at the top.

Before that Cinderella life the previous governor had gone power-mad and crazy, outlawed her family just to get his hands on their little shipping business. Katie escaped the raid on the family home. She had no idea if her mom or brothers survived. Never any mention of a father. Her adopted dad found her alone and starving in a prison cell.

After that, she didn't sleep much, always afraid of the nightmares.

"Hey, I read the news. I know the truth. I can look at the captain objectively," Jolly insisted. "If she's not the Emperor's mistress, then every reporter in the capital got the wrong story."

I kept my mouth shut. Better that than ending up planting a fist in his jaw and getting busted down another pay grade. Besides, my life might depend upon this lout's goodwill. I'd gladly lay down my life for Our Katie. I wasn't too keen on throwing it away for the likes of Jolly's temper.

We fanned out from the transport, creeping through scrub with not enough cover to hide a good shit. The refractive threads woven into our uniforms would make energy from lights and sensors slide around us. In twilight and darkness we were invisible to the walled compound ten klicks away.

Patrolling snipers were another matter. They'd see us and shoot us down fast, if we didn't see and shoot them first. The first line of troops had silencers on their blasters.

"This is creepy," Jolly whispered five klicks in. A sheen of sweat covered his face. The night was warm, tropically humid, not hot enough to make Jolly look like a quivering mass of jelly.

"Yeah, we should have seen someone by now."

An eerie silence pressed down on us worse than the humidity. Not even birds or insects called through the darkness.

"Watch out for booby traps." The whispered warning came through our helmet comms. I dropped my face plate as an added precaution. Made me hotter, but I'd rather lose a kilo of water weight in sweat than get shrapnel in the face.

Jolly and I both jerked our attention to our feet and the three-meter circle around us. "Fifteen centimeters left," Jolly whispered. His big hand shot out to stop me from stepping around a clump of prickly plants.

My heart skipped two beats and my breath caught in my throat. A braid of grasses looked almost normal. But it was a braid, not a twist. The faceplate got my night vision to follow the braid from end to end across my path. The ground looked a little too compact, like it had been tamped down with a boot or a shovel.

A trip wire.

Jolly raised his hand in overt signal. At the same time he spoke quietly into his helmet mic. The entire line came to a shuffling halt.

Seconds later, D'Jarra trotted along, coming up behind us.

"Good catch, Sergeant." He patted Jolly's shoulder. Then he spoke into his own helmet mic, alerting all of us what to watch for.

Two bomb squad geeks came along and began scanning the trap.

They shook their heads, put away their gadgets and began carefully digging around the mine. "Old fashioned explosives on a trip wire," one of them said. "Never seen anything this devious outside of training."

"Simple, effective, and below our detection equipment. We can only see them with our eyes. Be careful out there, troops." D'Jarra left the geeks to clear out the trap and signaled us all forward. We moved slower, more careful, afraid that each step might be our last.

By the time the eight-meter-high plascrete wall came into view, the geeks had cleaned out eighty traps and dawn made hints of showing up on the long horizon. I don't know how many hours had passed during our cautious trek.

At least nobody got hurt. We'd found all the traps.

Too easy. It was all too easy. Real pirates should have started shooting before this. Maybe they weren't real pirates.

I remembered Captain Katie's story, how her family had been framed and outlawed. And she wanted these guys alive.

She'd never told me her last name from before her adoption.

Nor had she told me anything about the year-long siege of an enemy jump point that ended up in her ship and crew being blown to smithereens seconds after she piloted away an emergency shuttle with a VIP passenger.

At least that was the official story. Her silence on the topic told me there was more.

She knew how to keep her mouth shut better than I did. Her ghosts made her lonelier than mine made me. I could talk about mine to the troops in my squad, to a sergeant, to a shrink if I had to.

Our Katie had reasons not to talk to anyone. Reasons beyond her elevated rank.

"I'm just a grunt. I'm not supposed to think," I said to myself. In fifteen years of service I've made sergeant four times. One time I kept the rank for a whole two months. Then I decided I didn't want the responsibility for thinking too much. I didn't like the reduced circle of people I could talk to.

I couldn't imagine how Captain Katie dealt with thinking for a crew of six hundred and interpreting orders from officers higher up. She had no one to talk to and hash out the nuances of orders and counter orders and politics in the military and the government.

"Remember that you're just a grunt and you might stay alive," Jolly reminded me.

Oops, I must not have turned off my helmet mic. See, that's why I like my two stripes better than three. The lower I stay in the ranks, the shorter my fall when I screw up.

But Our Katie saw me as more than a grunt. She needed me to figure something out. Something that had to do with this eerie silence.

Almost as if the compound was deserted. The booby traps just made their defenses look good.

Which meant that the closer we got to that godawful wall, the more clever those traps would get.

The ground rolled and bucked. Crackling pain ripped through my head as a wall of noise crashed around us.

My ears went numb. My knees folded. My teeth chattered. The sweat on my face froze.

Then Jolly's weight landed on top of me, pinning me in my cramped crouch. My knees screamed at the double burden. I wondered if my spine got permanently bent in the shape of my double pack. I really needed to straighten up before everything crumbled to bone and cartilage stew.

He had orders to protect me. Did he have to cripple me in the process?

Then bits and pieces of dirt and grass and gore rained down on us. A big gob of somebody landed on my faceplate. It oozed and ran, smearing along its horrible path.

I could barely see well enough to aim my damn weapon, let alone bring it to bear.

Jolly pushed my head down, pressing it into the dirt. Only the gory faceplate kept enough space between me and suffocation.

I heard gibbering wails all up and down the line. The comms in my helmet exploded through my deadened hearing with commands, counter orders, screams of pain, and shouts for medics.

"Shut the fuck up!" D'Jarra shouted.

Blessed silence reigned except for the lingering chiming of my eardrums.

"Everyone, on your feet and open your eyes," the lieutenant settled everyone by the sheer force of training and our respect for him. He deployed people where they needed to be.

"You okay, Jimmy?" D'Jarra's voice came through on a private frequency.

"I think so, sir." I checked my joints one by one as Jolly helped me stand. A bit stiff and bruised. Nothing broken. The blood and mess came from someone else.

I swallowed my gag reflex and turned my back on the center of activity fifteen meters to my left, at the far end of the line.

Over the years I'd seen enough crap to accept it as the price of being a grunt, with a bit of sadness for the dead and maimed. I thanked whatever god listened that it wasn't me, but I didn't puke my guts up like a couple of greenhorns down the line.

The price of being a grunt is never knowing who was going to get lucky enough to retire with a pension. The benefit of staying a grunt was being able to slap backs and rejoice when we got lucky, then together lift a glass in salute to our fallen comrades.

"I'm sending a geek with gadgets to walk in front of you, Jimmy. You've got to get into the compound and do your thing."

"You thinking what I'm thinking, sir?"

"That this place is deserted? Yeah, I'm thinking we got a leak and they got word of our coming two, maybe three days ago. A day ahead of us entering the system and sensor range."

Before he finished talking a geek trotted along the back of the line until he found me. Without a word he scanned the ground in a three meter circle with both his gadgets and his eyes.

I cleaned off my face plate as best I could with water from my canteen and clean grass I broke off from the clump I'd been lying on. By the time the geek nodded for me to proceed, I could almost see where I was putting my feet.

We'd hardly gone ten paces when the geek stopped and held both arms out to his side.

You can bet I froze with one foot still half in the air, not willing to put it down again until the all clear.

"Got one." The geek pointed to a spot three centimeters from where my foot was poised.

By the time I found a safe place to step I was shaking all over. This was getting too intense. If I got blown up, who was going to figure out what Our Katie wanted me to find? Sure, there were two other comms specialists in the platoons. Sure, any one of them could clone the data and return it to headquarters.

But I was the one Captain Kathleen Marie Talbot had ordered to do her proud.

The low-tech mines we could only spot with our eyes got more frequent and closer together, in clusters. The geek spotted the pattern to them at almost the same moment as Jolly.

Me, I was too damn busy watching where to walk to pay attention to the fact that every tenth step I had a mine either in front of me or to my left.

After that, with the geeks in front, the rest of us lined up behind them and walked slowly but safely up to the wall. Then we had to figure out how to get over it or through it. I could have stood on Jolly's shoulders and barely brushed my fingertips against the coils of razor wire on top.

D'Jarra sent two teams of five to the right and left with orders to watch their step.

Jolly scratched his head a moment, walked up to the gate and pushed it open. All the locks and cross bars were on the inside and none of them engaged.

We didn't exactly waltz into the compound. Still too many opportunities for traps. One guy nearly got a concussion from a sword on a swing arm triggered when he opened the door of a storage room. That one surprised me. The gel armor in the overlapping neck flaps of his helmet and uniform would have stopped the blade. Maybe he'd walk away with a bruise, but he'd walk away.

What was the purpose of that?

"Nothing here but ghosts," Jolly muttered. "Creepier than the silent jungle."

"Yeah." I'd scouted a couple of ghost ships in my day. I'd rather face a full platoon of starving lizards than a ghost ship after the lizards had finished with it. Or a ghost compound.

A door swung and creaked in the wind that came up suddenly. I think I jumped a full meter, almost into Jolly's arms. That same wind rustled through litter and snaked up my pants legs, chilling the sweat that coated my body.

Not funny.

"This reminds me of weeks of running dark and silent behind enemy lines," I said very quietly, afraid of stirring up a few of my own ghosts. Or some of Captain Katie's.

Damn what did she mean for me to do? She should have trusted an officer, not a screw-up grunt.

But she trusted me. I had to see this through.

Jolly led me cautiously around the interior courtyard, opening doors with his blaster aimed to take out anyone or anything that moved inside. I followed in his footsteps. A deep sense of gloom settled heavily in my gut. Somehow I knew I wasn't gonna make it out of this one.

But if I was gonna die here, I'd go out with my mission complete. Our Katie trusted me to do that.

Maybe that was what I saw in her eyes: the loss of a friend from those long days and nights of running silent and dark. The only friend she could talk to.

With that thought I straightened my shoulders and took the next fateful step, and the one after that until Jolly found a corridor that led inward. He opened three more doors along the hallway. They revealed rooms where people lived and left in a hurry. I smelled rotting food from abandoned meals. We saw clothing strewn about and checked it for traps. Then I found a lonely teddy bear, so threadbare I couldn't be sure it originally had green fur, the same color as Our Katie's eyes.

The stuffed toy got to me. A child had lived here and left that beloved companion behind. I tucked the worn-out bear into a pocket on the side of my pack. Don't know why. Just seemed like that bear needed a home. Maybe it would bring me luck, or a little companionship in my final moments. Someone to talk to.

Then we stumbled into the communications room. No windows, two points of access, one from the corridor, one from a different courtyard at the back of the compound. Jolly checked it all out before motioning me in.

I settled at the central board and began to do my job. Step one: examine everything closely, looking for more traps. I found three in the first three minutes. Simple stuff a child could find if they looked.

Captain Katie trusted me to look.

I dismantled the systems that would fry every chip in the board the second I powered it up.

The fourth trap was more subtle. That one would send high powered shocks through the interface screen the moment I touched it.

Another scan with both my eyes and my gadgets—some of them not exactly legal but effective.

Nothing.

Maybe the pirates didn't have time for anything more complex since they left in such a hurry.

Maybe. I didn't trust them. So I went over it all again. Sure enough I found a fifth trap, a duplicate of the third in a different spot. This one was trickier because it was a remote, stuck underneath the auxiliary chair across the room.

Eventually I found all ten traps. Then I took a deep breath, touched the bear for luck and powered up.

So far, so good. Data burst across the screen built into the desktop. It came fast and furious, scrolling faster than I could read. I caught words and phrases. A lot of voice traffic to dealers on unallied worlds. More pirates. The O'Hara brothers were efficient and tidy. They'd logged every message with time, date, and place of origin. The brass was gonna love that, names and address of smugglers and fences all over the galaxy.

My cloning equipment caught it all.

Then we got to the really good stuff, encoded texts both incoming and outgoing. I found a pause button. My equipment stopped. I followed the scroll down to the last message. Incoming, seventy-two hours before. No address, just the initials KMO.

About the time the *Champion* entered the jump point.

That was the leak Captain Katie wanted me to find. I knew that all three of the pirate brothers had the same initials, they were broadcast on every wanted poster in the Empire. Kameron Marcus O'Hara, Konner Michael O'Hara, Kimmer Martin O'Hara.

Kathleen Marie? No. Couldn't be. Not Our Katie.

Her family was framed and outlawed when she was seven. She lost touch with them. They abandoned her just like the O'Haras abandoned this compound.

Cold with dread I reached to activate the message but not the cloning.

Then I spotted an anomaly on the screen. If I tried to open that message, something would blow from inside. Just the message, or me?

My sweat smelled rank with fear and indecision. I was just a grunt. I didn't have the smarts or the training to make this deep a decision.

Our Katie trusted me to find the anomaly and understand it.

I looked up to see if Jolly could give me any inspiration. He leaned against the doorframe, just outside the room, keeping a wary eye on that inner courtyard, as if he expected bogies out there.

"The price of being a grunt is depending on someone else making my decisions," I said quietly to the ghosts in the compound and in my head. "Captain Kathleen Marie Talbot knows more than I do and she trusts me to do the right thing." I owed her my life and my soul.

I owed her respect and obedience.

I owed her friendship.

"I'll do you proud, Captain."

I set my equipment to clone all the text up to that last message. Then I shut it down. A less wary tech wouldn't have stopped. Anyone but me wouldn't have found all eleven traps.

Cool calm settled on my shoulders. Two more deep breaths and I wouldn't have to worry about thinking too much anymore.

I activated the message.

Blue crackles exploded all across the screen, burning my fingers, traveling up my arm to my heart. My entire body jerked in painful spasms.

My vision narrowed and grew dark. No fear. Acceptance. In a minute the pain would go away and I'd be free of having to make decisions.

The troops would lift a glass in my honor and talk about me, some good, some bad. But they'd talk out their grief and fear and pain.

Just before my body closed down I saw the words flash across the screen, "Get out now. Katie." Then it dissolved in a miasma of fracturing pixels.

I smiled to myself. I saved Our Katie's butt this time. We were even.

That thought lasted through hours and hours of unconsciousness. Typical grunt screw up. I couldn't even die for Our Katie.

I woke up in MedBay Central as the head of my bed raised from flat to half that. I had huge bandages where my hand used to be. The room blurred and spun. I think I caught images of enough arcane equipment to support two dozen lives artificially. I heard it grind and groan, beep to itself, and drip chemicals into me.

"Sign this." Captain Katie thrust a plassheet on a board under my nose.

"So there really are angels in heaven," I replied.

She snorted. "Fat chance that I'll ever make angel, let alone get into heaven."

"What is this?" My words didn't slur. I didn't feel any pain. I didn't feel much at all except curiosity.

"That's a five-year contract to serve as my personal ensign. If you're careful, I won't promote you to lieutenant before then."

"Um, I'm just a grunt. A screw-up grunt."

"But you're my grunt. And now you're my ensign." She pushed the board closer to my chest.

"Um …" I held up my useless right hand, the one I'd fried saving her butt. "Can't sign. I'd rather that was my discharge. I'm not officer material."

"Yes you are. Use your other hand or make an X with the stylus in your mouth." She yanked her personal mini stylus off her earring and folded the fingers of my left hand around it.

"Can't feel my hand," I lied. "I'm too drugged to know what I'm doing. I can't serve with only one hand."

"Electronic nerve blockers for the pain. Your mind is clear." She guided my hand to the plassheet.

"If you authorized very expensive and experimental ENBs, then I assume you authorized the medics to re-grow my hand." Part of me rejoiced that My Katie loved me enough to do that for me. I had a chance to live and serve. To be her friend again. Another part of me cursed that she denied me my right to retire on full disability pension with a bonus for going down on enemy soil during a combat mission.

"Got it in one. Now sign your contract."

Ah, but I knew My Katie well. I read the damn thing first.

Sure enough, by making me her personal ensign—translate as slave—she put a huge gag clause in the contract.

I thrust the sheet back at her. "I'm just a grunt and you don't have to buy my silence. I'm your friend."

"Captains aren't allowed friends. Besides, that clause is so higher ups can't make you talk about me. Think of this promotion as a reward."

"Why? Why'd you do it?" I set the stylus in place to sign my full name, James Aloysius Seaforth, then stopped before beginning the awkward scrawl.

"The price of command. I had to complete the mission or kiss my career goodbye."

"But they are your family," I agreed. "The service is my family, the troops are my brothers and sisters. I don't really know if I'd go that far to save them. What's going on in your head and your heart?"

"Run silent, run dark," she said quietly, evoking all kinds of memories in me.

I finished signing my life over to her.

"And thanks, Jimmy, for bringing Murphy back to me. He's seen me through a lot of rough and lonely times. But the price of command is making hard and lonely decisions. I left Murphy with my niece during that year I was supposed to be besieging an enemy jump point. Now he's yours." She tucked the green threadbare teddy beneath the sheet next to me.

"Captain."

"Yes, Jimmy."

"I think the price of command is too high for the likes of me."

"That's what Murphy is for. To ease you into the job." She nodded and left me alone with only a silent teddy bear for company.

Irene Radford has been writing stories ever since she figured out what a pencil was for. Editing grew out of her love of the craft of writing.

A member of an endangered species—a native Oregonian who lives in Oregon—she and her husband make their home in Welches, Oregon where deer, bears, coyotes, hawks, owls, and woodpeckers feed regularly on their back deck.

A museum trained historian, Irene has spent many hours prowling pioneer cemeteries deepening her connections to the past. Raised in a military family she grew up all over the US and learned early on that books are friends that don't get left behind with a move. Her interests and reading range from ancient history, to spiritual meditations, to space stations, and a whole lot in between.

Mostly Irene writes fantasy and historical fantasy including the best-selling *Dragon Nimbus* Series and the masterwork *Merlin's Descendants* series. In other lifetimes she writes urban fantasy as P.R. Frost or Phyllis Ames, and space opera as C.F. Bentley. Lately she ventured into Steampunk as Julia Verne St. John.

If you wish information on the latest releases from Ms Radford, under any of her pen names, you can subscribe to her newsletter at ireneradford.net.

Bob Brown lives in Washington State with 32 chickens, two pugs, one dog, three cats and his wife of innumerable years. He is the author of numerous short stories, the children's book, *The Dragon, the Damsel, and the Knight* and the co-author of "The Lost Enforcer," with Irene Radford, a noted fantasy writer.

Brown has received numerous awards from the Northwest Society for Professional Journalists for his Northwest Public Radio work. He also operates a small family farm dedicated to providing a place for his grandchildren to run and is the owner of B Cubed Press.

Finders Keepers

by Scott Pearson

Introduction to "Finders Keepers"

You can't have a military science fiction anthology without some futuristic soldiers taking on an implacable alien foe, right? When I was assembling Space Grunts, I had several great stories fitting this bill, providing a healthy dose of action to go with some of the smaller, even quieter stories I'd selected for the book.

Scott's story channels a lot of that vibe many of us feel when we first hear the term "military science fiction" being bandied about. "Finders Keepers" provides a classic setup, with a compelling human character pitted against an unknown alien adversary for control of the ship and her crew, the rest of whom have been rendered unconscious. It's not just wall-to-wall action, though; the struggle between Corporal M.J. Robeson and the "Finder" is also a contest of wits and wills. It's a great little thriller as well as a military SF tale, made all the better by Scott's crisp writing.

Since writing "Finders Keepers," Scott has discussed giving us more stories set within the world he created for this first tale. I hope he's able to do that, one of these days. We need more Corporal Robeson.

◁ ▷

The security field shorted out with a blinding concussive wave, tossing Corporal M.J. Robeson backward, the flash overwhelming her still sensitive eyes. She hit the bulkhead shoulders first, then her head snapped back with enough force that she nearly lost consciousness. Head still spinning, she drew her smartgun, but it slipped from her hand, dangling from its coiled lanyard between handgrip and holster. She kept on her feet, blinking rapidly, hoping to regain enough sight to defend against the inevitable attack from the humanoid prisoner, but the whiteout was only slowly fading. Although Robeson's ears were ringing from the explosion, she could hear the hostile intruder's uneven footsteps lurching toward her from the brig.

Robeson swung a roundhouse punch with her left arm while she fumbled for her weapon with the other. The punch was stopped by a hand catching her firmly by the wrist. Twisting her arm beneath and around to break the hold, she opened her fist and reached for his throat. He caught her arm again and grabbed her outstretched fingers with his other hand.

Unable to retrieve her sidearm during the blind struggle, she took advantage of both of her enemy's hands being occupied. She jerked her left arm upward, creating an opening as she curled the fingers of her right hand into a half-fist. The leopard-paw punch she launched at his neck was potentially lethal, which would leave her without much information on the hostile, but if he killed her first that would be a meaningless concern. Just as Robeson's knuckles jabbed hard into his throat, she felt intense pain in her left fingers and cried out. She heard the loud pop of dislocating bones over the choking cough of the hostile.

They reeled away from each other, Robeson still blinded, just as she had been back in her quarters when all this had started. She ducked down and launched herself in the escaping prisoner's direction.

O O O

Robeson had come to slowly, a dry taste like rust in her mouth. Her stomach twisted with nausea, and her dark skin felt clammy.

Opening her eyes, she was not sure where she was. Her memory was as hazy as her vision. She lay on her back, her limp limbs sprawled out and her head rolled to the side. Blinking with great effort, she tried to focus on her surroundings.

Instead she became aware of the sound of sublight engines thrumming in the deck beneath her. That stimulated a rush of memories: she was a squad leader of the United Earth Systems Marines serving aboard the starship *Alliance*, and the ship was exploring beyond the boundaries of the Allied Colonies. She took a few deep breaths to settle her stomach. Struggling to get her numb right hand to her face, she clumsily rubbed at her eyes with unfeeling fingers. She first saw the deck of her quarters and then her right arm in the sleeve of her gray physical training uniform. Her vision continued to clear, letting her see beyond her arm to the small couch where she'd been sitting before passing out.

As control of her limbs slowly returned, she carefully sat up and was rewarded with a fresh wave of nausea. Fumbling her hand across the low table in front of the couch, she found her tablet and pulled it closer. She activated the comm function and tapped the sickbay icon.

"This is Corporal Robeson," she said, her voice ragged but growing stronger. "I need emergency assistance." There was no response. She looked closer at the tablet's screen, a little bigger than her open hand, and saw Dr. Selby collapsed on the deck in his office. "What the hell?" She signaled the bridge but got no response. That helped clear the haze like a splash of ice water.

She tapped in a security override and opened a video feed from the bridge. Everyone was down, slumped over their consoles or sprawled on the deck. Her pulse raced. She cycled through comms all over the ship, at duty stations and in personal quarters. Robeson couldn't find anyone who was conscious. Had there been some sort of shipwide life-support malfunction?

"Can't be just me." The *Alliance* had a crew of over seven hundred, plus a Marine platoon of forty-one, all together nearly eight hundred officers, enlisted, and civilian specialists. "There has to be someone else awake."

Steadying herself with one hand on the table, she eased into a crouch, testing her legs. Satisfied she wasn't going to fall back down, she got to her feet, wobbled a bit, then staggered across the small room, bracing her arms against the nearest wall as she approached her desk. There she grabbed her hand scanner and checked for biosigns. At first she saw nothing but the low, steady readings of the unconscious. But then there it was: a single active reading other than her own. Someone was moving near the computer core. *Great! They must be trying to fix whatever caused this.* But then Robeson examined the biosign more closely—and didn't recognize the species. An unknown humanoid was aboard the *Alliance*. This wasn't a malfunction; it was an invasion.

"But an invasion of one? You've got to be kidding." She adjusted the scanner to search for any biosigns matching the intruder. Nothing. The hostile was definitely alone. "Course, everyone's knocked out … most likely reinforcements are on the way, maybe even close by." Robeson rubbed her eyes again with one hand as she tried to formulate a plan. She continued talking to the empty room. "Take out the hostile first, or try to wake people up? All it has to do is run away, waste time until back-up gets here. But if I could wake Selby, he could work on more of the crew while I hunt down the hostile. Then we'd have more people ready when the second wave hits." Nodding her head at the latter idea, she went over to the couch and sat down.

After a glance at her scanner for the intruder's present location, she grabbed her tablet and tapped into various nearby comms until she saw the hostile walking along a corridor, toward the video feed. He looked male, though it was hard to tell with extraterrestrials, even if they were humanoid. He wore loose-fitting black clothing, and the short sleeves revealed heavily muscled arms. The skin looked mammalian, but its mottled color created patterns like scales on his arms and face. A frill of small ears encircled his head, and above and below them he had short hair with a spotted pattern similar to his skin. His three eyes stared almost directly at her, but Robeson had only activated one-way viewing.

Suddenly the hostile stopped, tilting his head back and forth, and pulled a hand computer from a pocket at his waist. As he looked at it, his two outer eyes widened while the one in the middle rolled around independently. He dropped it back in his pocket and walked briskly past the comm.

Robeson glanced at her scanner. The computer core was amidships, on deck seven below the dorsal island, one of four towers of scanning, communication, targeting, and weapons hardware that jutted out from the ship's hull. Her quarters were in the stern, deck twelve, just above the launch bay. The intruder was heading aft.

"So, Three Eyes is coming to check on me." Even so, waking the doctor still seemed like the right plan. The scanner showed the hostile continuing aft on deck seven. Sickbay was amidships, on deck eight. With a little luck, she could head amidships below him and get up to sickbay before he got down to the platoon living quarters.

She smiled. "And I've even got time for a few surprises."

O O O

The Finder, Secondary Grade, hurried down the corridor tilting his head from side to side. The sleeper mist was supposed to be foolproof, and it would still be hours before the command ship arrived. Now here he was alone on the Combine's new ship with an intruder who was awake. Although he hadn't been able to finish retasking the ship's computer to Combine specs, his interface unit had still been able to direct him to the location of the intruder, and he was almost there. He took another turn and soon faced the door. Never in his time as a Finder had he had to combat an intruder. He needed to resolve this situation or he would bring dishonor to his clan.

With a final tilt of his head, he amended that to "more dishonor." He had seen enough of this ship's records to know the intruders had had no previous contact with the Combine. He believed that liberations should be restricted to those who had engaged the Combine. But there were no exceptions to his directives, and he would carry out his duties. If he made Primary Grade, perhaps then he could show some discretion during liberations while still serving the Combine's needs.

He drew his stunner and tapped the panel beside the door. The door slid open, and he saw the intruder's body on the floor. Keeping the stunner focused on the alien, he took a few steps into the room, pausing as he glanced at the stunner's targeting scanner. The biosigns from the intruder were low, indicating unconsciousness. He relaxed. The intruder's apparent resistance to the mist must have only been temporary.

"Look out behind you."

The Finder spun toward the voice, raising his stunner and firing off a spread of microdarts. They bounced off the wall with metallic pings. He saw the face of an intruder watching him from the screen of one of their tablet computers, which was propped on a desk across the room. Frowning, he forced himself not to look over his shoulder at the body behind him, obviously someone the intruder had dragged in here as a decoy. He should have monitored its biosigns on the way instead of just running to its original location. Mission parameters had changed, and he had to adapt and be more suspicious.

"I want you off my ship," the intruder said.

"This a Combine ship now." He used her language. "*You* are the intruder."

She looked surprised for a moment, almost smiling as she nodded. "I get it. It's easier to hack a ship's systems if you know the language." She leaned forward, her face filling the small screen. Any trace of a smile was gone. He found her single-toned skin unsettling. "But it's not your ship while there's still a Marine on her feet."

The Finder opened his mouth as if to reply, then turned and bolted toward the door. It slid shut as he approached, and he slammed into it.

"You almost saw that coming in time," she said.

Turning back toward the tablet, he made sure not to show the pain in his eyes. "Open the door, or I'll kill your crewmate."

She shook her head at him. "Wrong play. That would really piss me off." The screen went blank.

The Finder blinked his outer eyes while the middle one stared at the tablet. The intruder had called his bluff. This was going to be challenging—which could increase the reward.

He holstered his stunner and pulled the interface unit from his pocket. He had to get this door open.

O O O

"Come on, Doc, wake up!" Robeson gave Selby another rough poke in the ribs, but even after all the stimulants she had pumped into him there was no reaction.

After she had dragged PFC Bloch into her quarters, set up her tablet, and activated one of her special security programs on the door, Robeson had checked in on her squad. Eight of them had been unconscious in their adjoining quarters, but seemed to be in no immediate danger. On her way to sickbay, she had come across dozens more crew members in the corridors, lying in awkward positions on the deck. Whatever the intruder had done, it had been widespread and fast, dropping people in their tracks.

But scanning Selby with sickbay equipment had not given her any answers, at least none that she understood. Robeson had used up her field medic training and then some, and now she only hoped she hadn't made Selby's condition worse. She ran her hands over her close-cropped hair.

"Okay, my strategy was sound, but now it's time for Plan B—stomping ass with big boots. I'll take Three Eyes alive and get some intel. First step is checking out his fancy dart gun." Robeson reviewed the scans she'd taken. She'd caught a break by startling him into firing, which had drawn her attention to the weapon.

A warning beep from her scanner interrupted her. The hostile was already out of her quarters and heading toward sickbay. "You are officially on my last nerve, mister," Robeson said with a frown. She grabbed the medikit she had laid out on the floor by Selby. Soon she'd be going one-on-one with the real intruder.

O O O

The Finder ran full-out down a corridor, needing speed more than stealth. He held his stunner at the ready as he dodged around unconscious intruders. Nearing a four-way intersection, he heard the footsteps of the active intruder approaching from the left. A second later he was past the corner and nearly face-to-face with her, already squeezing the trigger.

A full spread of microdarts sprayed from the stunner as he continued through the intersection. At least a dozen found their mark, sinking into the dark flesh of the intruder's neck and face. Her head pulled back in reaction to the impact, but instead of immediately falling unconscious, she attempted to return fire.

Surprised that she had somehow nullified the darts, but relieved she hadn't noticed her smartgun had been deactivated, he skidded to a stop and leaped toward his opponent.

O O O

As the hostile came at her, Robeson dropped her nonfunctioning smartgun. She'd set it for a low-voltage electrolaser burst, which would have knocked him out; the gun could also fire various nonlethal and lethal projectiles, including nanotech smart bullets. But he must have hacked the ship's security protocols that regulated weapons use. She cursed herself for missing that, but she was still in the game because the scanning she'd done from sickbay had indicated a variety of possible antitoxins for the darts. She'd taken all of them.

The hostile launched a flurry of blows, coming in close with fast hand work. His middle eye stared at her face while the outer eyes followed her hands. The first round of attacks was easy enough to deflect, but he was clearly well versed in hand-to-hand combat. Robeson held back, blocking slowly, hoping to trick the hostile into underestimating her. They danced around the corridor, the only sound their falling blows, breathing, and occasional sharp exhalations of pain. Robeson's Marine training had covered a variety of martial arts, and she drew from those that best-served her physique. Now that the hostile was convinced of his superiority, it was time to go on the offensive.

She sped up her blocks and put more force into her counterblows, but continued letting the hostile lead the fight. She allowed him to maneuver her close to a bulkhead, as if he was cornering her. That middle eye, which never seemed to blink, opened a bit wider. Robeson left a large opening in her defense and he fell for it, putting his whole body behind a punch. She deftly ducked and stepped aside, hearing his fist plow into the wall with a sharp crack. Robeson came in close as he cried out, grabbing his arm and spinning around to break it, adding a growling *kiai* vocalization to help her focus and to intimidate the hostile. But his elbow suddenly folded back the other way—damn unknown physiology—taking all the leverage out of her attack. He turned, kicking a shin into her waist, and she stumbled backward.

O O O

The Finder adjusted his stance as the intruder quickly rebounded, pushing off the wall. He stepped forward to meet her, unleashing a cascade of increasingly complex swings, jabs, and parries. The intruder fought well, but the Finder was a master of his clan's combat style. He did not doubt that soon the intruder would fall beneath his relentless blows. But as they circled around each other, and the intruder made increasingly disturbing sounds synchronized with her powerful attacks, the Finder did not gain the ground he expected to. Her earlier ploy, which had cost him a broken finger, had not been a lucky fluke. Not only was the intruder stronger than he had realized, she was quite fast, equaling him move for move. He was not sure when the transition occurred, but he was no longer in the offensive position. To reestablish dominance over the fight, he moved into a sequence of jabs and grabs building toward a throw to pin her to the deck.

"Gettin' fancy now, huh?" the intruder said as he stepped up his attack.

She smiled at him, her dark face covered with moisture, apparently from her exertions. She twisted sideways beyond his own range of motion, wrong-footing him, and then kicked her left heel into his right shin. As he tried to regain his balance, her left elbow came up toward his head. He could only protect his face with his injured hand. He grunted in pain as he deflected her attack.

"How's that hand feel?" she said with a wicked grin. Her right fist thudded into his chest.

He ignored the taunts, shook off her blows, and came back with both hands, but he couldn't help favoring the broken finger, and it compromised his attack. She brushed aside his maneuver with her forearm as her other hand again sped toward his chest. It landed only an openhanded cuff, but he felt the air rush out of his lungs. He tried to regain his breath, wondering why she had not applied a more direct blow … unless she was leading into a spinning kick. He quickly lifted his arms to protect his head, expecting a strike to the temple or throat.

But she had not chosen either of those targets. Completing her half spin, she watched him over her shoulder as her foot rocketed toward his lower chest. He tried to bring his arms down to block, but her leg came in underneath. Before the impact he noted that her foot was held at the perfect angle to ensure maximum energy transfer from her boot heel to his chest. He heard ribs break as he flew back from the kick, stopping suddenly as he crashed into a wall. Sliding to the floor, he saw her spin forward again, her fist coming toward him. Darkness.

O O O

Robeson observed her unconscious prisoner through the watery distortions of the security field across the brig's door. The lids of his outer eyes fluttered with each shallow breath, while the center eye remained open.

Although her computer access was limited by the hostile's sabotage, she'd been able to determine the *Alliance* was following a programmed course—to a rendezvous with his reinforcements, she assumed. She had been able to modify her smartgun to circumvent the protocols that had prevented it from firing, and it was back in its drop-leg holster. She scratched her neck and cheek where the darts had struck. Some sort of residual allergic reaction, she guessed. She made an effort to ignore the itching, along with her body's overall aches and pains, and focused on the hostile. The biomonitor beside the door indicated he would soon regain consciousness. As she squinted at him through the field, he took a deeper breath. Finally, all three eyes opened wide and he sat up hesitantly, placing a hand on his chest.

"I broke two of your ribs," Robeson said. "I gave you some pain killers, but I only have field training. I can't guarantee the meds won't have side effects."

He tilted his head from side to side, then slowly stood, keeping one hand on his broken ribs. With a slight wince he stepped closer to the field, not looking away from her gaze.

Robeson waited for a response, then shrugged. "If you help me revive the crew, we'll be lenient. You seem to have gone out of your way not to hurt us." She paused, wondering what would happen to the unconscious crew when they met the rest of the hostiles, but still got no response. "I was able to run some long-range scans. I didn't see any ships. It must be several hours at least before you get reinforcements. By then I'll have the crew up anyway, and we'll defend ourselves. With less leniency."

O O O

Although the Finder found her treatment of him generous, there was no point in speaking with her. He closed his eyes and concentrated on activating his transducer.

"I scanned your ship in the launch bay," the intruder continued, gesturing toward a computer station near the main door into the brig. "Maybe I'll just put you in binders, toss you inside, and jettison the whole thing."

That almost broke the Finder's concentration. To be found helpless in his own ship would bring great dishonor and probably a demotion. He would be forced to take duties that required more serious compromises of his personal ethics. It would be difficult to work his way back up. That couldn't happen. He had to secure this ship, no matter the sacrifice. He looked deeper within.

O O O

Robeson had found some leverage. The idea of being jettisoned from *Alliance* had rattled her prisoner. His skin seemed to flush, the mottled pattern shifting around. But he kept his eyes and mouth closed.

"I guess your superiors would come down hard on you for that."

Now the color drained from his skin and his limbs began trembling. Robeson wasn't sure if he was panicking or having some sort of seizure. She glanced at the biomonitor but didn't know what to make of the readings. As she looked back at her prisoner, the brig's security field erupted like a nova, the flash overloading her vision as the concussive disruption threw her off her feet and into the wall.

O O O

The Finder had never been forced to activate his transducer before, and it was painful beyond belief. It was spliced into his thigh bone in such a way that it did not register on most scans, and he feared the force of its electromagnetic discharge had cracked the bone. Beyond that, it had left him feeling as if he had been running for hours, his whole body numb and weak.

Still, he had to move. He lurched forward on the aching leg toward the intruder. She swung blindly at him, her eyes watering. The Finder wanted payback and grabbed her fingers. The personal indulgence cost him; even as he heard the satisfying sound of her joints dislocating, her knuckles jabbed into his throat.

He staggered under the blow, choking and coughing. The Finder needed to get control of this situation, but before he had recovered from the near-lethal punch, the intruder slammed into him. Disoriented and unable to hold his weight on the transducer leg, he fell to the deck. She tumbled down beside him while trying to protect her injured hand. He lashed out with his good leg, catching the intruder in the side of the head. She rolled away from him, screaming in pain and anger. He forced himself to his feet and, half walking, half hopping, made his way into the corridor. To avoid recapture, he might yet be forced to abandon ship.

O O O

Robeson heard the intruder leave the brig from where she lay face down on the deck. Her head throbbed with pain from the kick, and her dislocated fingers felt like they were slowly catching fire. With her eyes closed, she reached for her left hand. Her index and middle fingers stuck out backward, away from her palm. She wrapped her right hand around her index finger, and slowly and firmly pulled it out and then straightened it, feeling it slide back into place. Exhaling with some relief, she moved to the middle finger, repeating the motions. As that finger also slid into its proper location, the burning sensation lessened. That was all she could do for now.

She lay there without moving for a minute, letting the pounding in her head subside while keeping her eyes closed. Finally, it seemed the headache had dulled as much as it could for now, enough to be able to get back in the fight. She opened her eyes, saw the deck through a blurry haze, and hoped her sight wasn't permanently damaged. Rolling onto her back, she reached down for her smartgun's retention lanyard and pulled the weapon into her hand. After holstering it, she moved into a sitting position and took her scanner from her belt.

Blinking and squinting at the display, which she had to hold centimeters from her face, she saw the hostile heading toward the launch bay. "I can't let him get to his ship." Squinting at the scanner again, she saw that he was moving slowly, obviously hampered by injuries. "I'll go a different way, get in front of him."

She affixed the scanner to her waist, got unsteadily to her feet, and exited the brig. Smiling grimly, she said, "I just hope he doesn't have any more tricks up his sleeve."

O O O

The Finder limped along, leaning against the corridor wall and dragging his aching leg. He was certain now that he had hairline fractures both above and below the transducer. His throat was tender where the intruder had struck him, and his broken ribs made breathing difficult. He also had burns on his hands and face from the field overload.

Though the intruder had some sort of resistance to the sleeper mist, his command ship would be here long before the rest of the former crew regained consciousness. This ship would still be liberated, but he would receive no credit. He had hoped to become Primary soon; now he would count himself lucky if he maintained a rank of Tertiary.

He paused to get his bearings, looking up and down the corridor. Had he taken a wrong turn? He had a terrific headache, a side effect of using the transducer, and it was disorienting him. Starting forward again, he lost his balance. He caught himself on his broken leg, sending a wave of pain through his battered body. When it reached his pounding head, he almost blacked out. He took several deep breaths while standing on just his good leg, until the encroaching darkness receded from his vision. Then, clenching his jaw, he started walking again. It was time to get off this ship and hope the Liberator would show him mercy, regardless of clan.

O O O

Robeson's eyes wouldn't stop watering, and they felt like they were full of hot sand. She assumed her corneas had been burned. Even the subdued lighting of the corridors was too much, and her lids were swollen like a boxer's. But, according to the scanner, she had reached the launch bay just ahead of the intruder. She had come through the maintenance level beneath the bay, opposite where his ship was parked. She scuttled up a ladder and into the expansive bay, with its three-deck-high ceiling.

Moving toward the one-person craft, she dodged around various drop ships, fighters, and stealth vessels, some dedicated spacecraft, others able to enter atmospheres. Luckily for her sensitive eyes, the only lights in the launch bay were various warning indicators around equipment, gangways, and ladders. As she finally approached the small ship, she heard a nearby door to the corridor slide open. She spun toward the sound, aiming her smartgun at the blurry backlit shape, and fired an electrolaser burst.

O O O

The EL burst narrowly missed the Finder, flashing past into the corridor. It would have caught him square in the chest, but he had been leaning to one side, dragging his bad leg. Squinting through the brightness and the wave of static electricity that danced across his face, he saw the intruder correcting her aim.

Just a fraction of a second before the intruder fired again, he slapped the emergency tab on his belt. His scout ship powered up, the main engines giving off a short ionic pulse as they came on line. The pulse knocked the intruder off her feet, sending her second shot wild, and rolled her across the deck. He hurried forward as much as he could, frowning as he glanced around the bay. The intruder lay between him and the robotic flyer, which had infiltrated the bay and released the sleeper mist. He had powered it down manually after coming aboard but neglected to stow it in his ship.

He wondered if he should try to get the flyer, but the intruder was already firing again, a clean miss behind him as he hobbled forward. If he hadn't been in so much pain, the Finder would have smiled at her persistence. Ahead of him the hatch to his ship was opening automatically, lowering to make a short ramp. He stumbled up the ramp, falling against the edge of the open hatchway. She fired again, this time missing in front of him. The blast dispersed along the hull of his ship. She had him bracketed now.

As the Finder held onto the bulkhead to keep from falling, he reached inside and hit the touchpad to close the hatch. The ramp lifted beneath him. He slumped down the bulkhead, collapsing toward the deck. Just as he flopped to his side and the hatch was almost closed, an EL burst snaked through the narrow opening and hit his broken leg. He cried out. The transducer kept the shock from traveling through his nervous system and rendering him unconscious, but the pain was searing. The blast had also somehow caused the transducer to reactivate, and it was building up energy, and heat, inside his leg. The hatch was closed now, and he dragged himself forward to the controls. He climbed into the pilot seat as the transducer misfired. The discharge shattered his thigh bone, sending shards through his muscles and skin. He screamed at this new burst of agony. Grabbing the manual control stick, he thrust it forward, nearly falling out of the seat as the shuttle scraped across the deck plating.

O O O

Robeson had rolled onto her hands and knees to continue firing as the hostile clambered into his ship. When she heard him scream, she got to her feet and rushed for the hatch, but it was already shut. She pounded on the hull as the ship started to lift off. Friction with the deck caused it to skew to the side, pushing her backward. She had time to jump out of the way, but still got another burst from its engines as its stern swung past. Diving to the deck, she curled into a protective ball with her back to the blast. It was over quickly as the ship cleared the deck and shot down one of the starboard launch tubes, through a series of containment fields which kept the room pressurized.

"And stay out!" Robeson yelled. She lay there for a few minutes, her body aching from head to toe, her eyes on fire. Finally, she rolled onto her back. "I've got to get Selby up, I can't do this alone."

After slowly standing and stretching her battered body, she started for the door, but stopped when she noticed something on the deck. She squinted and blinked. The object was oval shaped and about a half-meter long. It had a smooth, unbroken surface except for a keypad and a few jet nozzles for maneuvering. She reached for her scanner and realized she had lost it. Glancing around, she saw it a few meters away. She retrieved it and scanned the object, concerned that it was an explosive.

Some familiar spikes caught her attention, and she sat down beside the object as she adjusted her scans to focus on those elements. The device contained some miniaturized components with energy readings similar to the *Alliance*'s jump drive, which slid the ship between normal dimensions in bursts of faster-than-light travel.

"Okay," she said. "I doubt this thing goes FtL, but I bet it can jump right through hulls." Maybe once this was aboard the intruder had been able to scan for the transponder settings that allowed small craft to pass through the containment fields. She shook her head and continued scanning the device's internal structure, discovering a hollow space inside. Whatever had filled this empty reservoir had left some residual traces, enough to set off a biohazard alert on the scanner. Robeson frowned suspiciously. Resetting the scanner for medical data, she rescanned the reservoir and then scanned herself. As the results flickered up on the screen, her frown slowly faded.

O O O

The Finder turned away from the viewer as the Combine ship approached its latest liberation. To his right, the Liberator, Primary Grade, leaned forward in her command chair. Her ear frills were flushed with excitement; even after rising all the way to Primary and getting her own ship, it was obvious that every liberation thrilled her. "Scans?"

A Secondary Scan-Tech spoke up immediately. "All scans are as the Finder predicted, Liberator. There is only one conscious intruder." He paused. "However, there is more computer activity than there should be at this stage."

The Finder cleared his throat. "I explained that, Liberator. I was not able to complete the retask before the intruder prematurely regained consciousness." When there was no immediate response he decided to press forward in his defense. "Medical has not yet determined why the sleeper mist did not function properly."

The Liberator frowned, and the Finder realized it had been a mistake to attempt to share the blame with the Med-Techs. "Consider yourself lucky you are still a Finder, Quaternary. You are dismissed."

Holding himself at attention, the Finder forced himself not to react to his demotion to the lowest grade. "I'm sorry, Liberator, but—"

"You continue to display the shortcomings of your clan. You are dismissed."

"Yes, Liberator." The Finder turned on his good leg and began his painful exit; his transducer leg was still in a field cast. Between the demotion and his clan's standing, he was not worthy of expedited surgery. His bone regeneration would have to wait until after the liberation.

As he left the control room, the Finder was uncertain which was more painful, his leg or his humiliation. But given that his next suggestion would have been to remind the Scan-Tech of the intruder's resourcefulness, he took some satisfaction that the next mistake would not rest on his shoulders. Even Liberators could be demoted.

O O O

Robeson hurried up the gangway from the secondary bridge deck onto the captain's bridge. She limped a bit, but she'd had some pain meds for all the injuries she'd accumulated over the last few hours, including a minor concussion. Selby had cleaned and dressed the series of puncture wounds from the darts, splinted the first two fingers on her left hand, and given her some drops for her eyes. The drops had helped, but further treatments would be necessary to help her eyes heal. She still wore her PTU, the gray material torn and smudged with grime and blood.

"Why haven't we launched fighters yet?" she blurted as she emerged into the subdued lighting of the captain's bridge. She hadn't thought she was shouting, but her voice seemed to echo back at her, and the bridge crew all turned from their stations to stare at her.

She came to a stop, feeling like a child barging into a roomful of grown-ups. It was only her second time on the captain's bridge since being assigned to the *Alliance*, and she found herself looking around with wide eyes. It was a relatively small, round room. An immersive monitor ran 360 degrees around the bridge, starting just a meter above the deck and wrapping across the low dome of the ceiling. When fully activated, as it was now, it simulated the bridge sitting atop the dorsal island of the ship under a glass bubble. In fact, the captain's bridge was on deck nine below the dorsal, safely within the hull.

Near the center of the bridge were three wide, curving consoles, each with three stations. One faced the bow, one to port, and one to starboard, forming a U-shaped control space. The gangway from the secondary bridge deck—which held four wings dedicated to flight, engineering, weapon, and sensor control—came up astern of the open end of the U. A walkway around the outside of the consoles provided close access to the monitor; any portion of it could be isolated and used as an auxiliary display for mission-specific information, along with any necessary touch controls on the monitor itself.

Captain Rick Harper, wearing his khaki service uniform, paced within the U of the consoles, his serious steel-gray crew cut belied by the light in his blue eyes and the smirk he wore as he glanced back at her. "Ahh, Corporal. I didn't hear you come in."

Robeson was uncertain whether the joke was supposed to put her at ease or on edge. The rest of the bridge crew still faced her, their expressions neutral. "Sorry, sir, it's just that I saw the scans—"

Harper shook his head. "The pilots are in no condition to fly yet." Walking toward her, he reached out a hand. "You've been right busy while the rest of us were having a kip." She took the captain's hand, receiving a firm handshake. "Well done. After we get through this I'll be writing up a commendation for you."

At that the bridge crew broke into brief applause, accompanied by various "Good jobs" and "Congratulations."

Robeson forgot to blink or respond for a several seconds. "Oh." Then she smiled and felt her aches ease just a bit. "I mean, thank you, sir." She glanced around at the rest of the officers as they turned back to their stations. "Thanks."

"Right," Harper said with a nod. "Now, look over here." He turned, pointing at the monitor off the port bow.

Robeson sighted along the captain's arm and spotted the Combine ship, slowly growing larger as it matched *Alliance*'s speed and course, coming to claim its prize.

He stepped around the consoles to stand close to the monitor. Robeson had heard that the captain rarely sat at the command station at the forward console when he relieved the officer of the deck, preferring to stay on his feet. Harper reached out and tapped the image of the Combine ship, and a list of specs came up in a window nearby. It was heavily armed for its size, but still would have been easily outgunned by the *Alliance* under normal conditions. But they weren't back to normal conditions yet.

Without turning his head from the monitor, Harper said, "Now then, what's this business about performing unauthorized interdimensional experiments on the doctor?"

Phrased that way it sounds really bad, Robeson thought. "Well, sir, it didn't seem that I had much choice."

"At ease, Corporal. I was just having you on."

"Oh. Of course, sir." When Robeson had scanned herself in the launch bay, she had found traces of the same biohazard she had detected in the reservoir of the hostile's device. It had to be what he'd used to knock out the crew. Since it appeared that the device could pass through bulkheads to get aboard, she guessed that it was also able to disperse its toxin in bursts through its outer covering and into a ship's ventilation system. Assuming that there must be some way to reverse the process, she had taken the device to sickbay, placed it next to Selby's unconscious body, and started pressing buttons on its control panel.

Luckily—and the doctor was quick to acknowledge the necessity of her actions—she had succeeded in getting the device to "recall" the toxin, sifting it right through the doctor's tissues as he lay within the effect of its interdimensional field. Selby had been unwilling to repeat the unknown procedure on the crew, noting that the intruder's ship had not used the technology, only the remote probe. Instead the doctor had been able to synthesize an antidote to the bioengineered toxin, albeit in small quantities. They'd been able to awaken just fourteen more people so far, and Robeson had spent most of the time running around the ship searching for key personnel. She'd found a couple pilots and their flight crews, but time and the antidote were both in short supply.

Harper turned to face her. "The chief was inspired by your Selby experiments, actually. She came up with a bit of a surprise for our visitors." Chief Engineer Liz Alinari had been one of the first people Robeson had found for Selby to awaken. Alinari had regained control of most of the ship's primary systems, including helm, in short order. In their current state, however, retreat still wouldn't have gotten them far, so Harper, thinking that the best defense was a good offense, had decided to bring the fight to the enemy. They remained on the course the intruder had programmed, but did so per Harper's orders.

"Is there anything I can do to help, sir?"

"In addition to single-handedly saving our collective bum?" Harper smiled and put a hand gently on one of her sore shoulders. "Have a seat at auxiliary, Corporal. You've earned a break."

Robeson opened her mouth to protest, but thought better of it when Harper gave her a warning look, as if sensing that she might not respond in the affirmative. "Yes, sir," she said. "Thank you, sir." She walked the short distance to the starboard console. Lieutenant Jeff "Mustang" Ford sat at the weapons station, eyes on his main display, running firing simulations. The engineering station at his left was empty. Robeson sat at auxiliary on his right and activated the panel to feel like she was doing something, but found herself just watching the captain instead.

Harper turned away from the monitor and leaned forward on the port console on his elbows, looking down at the people seated there. "Thompson?"

Lieutenant Ella Thompson looked up from her panel at the science station. She was the youngest bridge officer, her long brown hair in a loose braid down her back. "Looks like the masking signal is working. They just scanned us again without any reaction I could see. I don't think they know that we're out of bed, sir."

With a nod, Harper turned slightly toward communications. "Peniche?"

Lt. Eduardo Peniche, a former professor of linguistics from a colony world, shook his head. "No external comm traffic, Captain. And I'm afraid if I tried to hack into their internal comms, I'd set off alarms."

Chief Selshwan at navigation, one of a handful of extraterrestrials onboard, spoke up without prompting. She was an amphibious mammalian, and it was hard to read her emotions from her smooth, pale skin. "Target continues its course unaltered, a near intersection with *Alliance*. It will arrive just off the port island, at docking distance."

With a nod, Harper looked up and across to the starboard console as he walked toward the forward console.

"Do you have your target yet?"

Ford continued tapping away at his board as he replied. "It's a little tricky working off passive readings only, sir, but I think so." He tapped a few more times then spun his seat around. "I'll need to target the relative ventral of the hostile, about two-thirds of the way back from bow to stern."

Lieutenant Aamina Nejem spoke up from her helm station at the forward console. "I'll do what I can."

Meanwhile, Harper had reached the forward console, but he didn't sit at the command station. He stayed in front of the console, reaching over to activate a comm. "Harper to Alinari."

"Alinari here."

"Is our little scheme ready?"

"I just finished the final systems check. We're good to go."

Harper smiled. "It won't be long now. Harper out." He closed the channel and glanced over at Lt. Joan Winston at operations. He didn't say anything, just tilted his head.

"Looking good, sir, all things considered," she said. "Automated systems are nominal. Selby continues to revive the crew as quickly as possible. We'll even have two fighters cleared for launch in about twenty minutes."

Harper nodded then straightened up, looking around the bridge. "Right. Steady on, everyone." He circled around the console and moved toward his chair.

The bridge crew, except Ford, turned to port, watching the hostile ship on the monitor for a few seconds. Ford had tasked a portion of the monitor in front of his station to display a view from the port weapons array. Robeson glanced around as the crew turned back to their stations. When she'd been on the captain's bridge the first time, the *Alliance* had been in Mars orbit, the officer of the deck and an ensign at helm the only two people on duty, so there hadn't been any action. After watching the crew at their assigned duties for a moment, she looked back to port. The Combine ship was now coming alongside and matching *Alliance*'s speed.

"Wait for it," Harper said, holding a hand out, his index finger pointing upward. He remained standing in front of his seat.

Thompson looked up. "They're onto us, raising shields and charging weapons."

"Now, Nejem!"

Nejem changed course, turning toward the other ship and dipping *Alliance*'s bow down. Harper sat down with a bump.

Ford proceeded without further orders from Harper, firing a plasma beam low across the bow of the other ship. As the approaching ship performed an evasive maneuver away from the plasma, returning fire as it went, its bow came up. As it rolled up and away, Nejem curved in tighter toward the enemy ship, ignoring incoming energy weapon blasts, pointing *Alliance* right at the belly of the other ship, just as Ford had requested.

"Torpedo away," Ford said, almost yelling in excitement. He looked up at the monitor to watch.

The single torpedo, which Alinari had interfaced with the Combine's own device recovered from the launch bay, streaked toward its target. It had of necessity been a rush job, and the chief engineer had estimated only a fifty percent chance of success. But then the torpedo disappeared from view for a fraction of a second before reappearing within the shield radius of the other ship, hitting Ford's target dead center. There was a brief flash of impact on its hull, followed by a gush of fire from inside which was quickly extinguished by the vacuum of space. The ship seemed to shudder and drifted off course, leaving a small cloud of debris ejected by explosive decompression.

Thompson could now run active scans, and she was watching her display while tapping furiously at her board. "Direct hit. Their FtL engines are offline and power to shields has dropped by fifty percent."

The ship faltered, starting to slowly spin before stabilizing its course. Once stabilized, it resumed firing, but the shots went wide as the ship made a clumsy attempt to turn away.

Harper nodded. "I'd like to try talking to them."

"Aye, Captain," Peniche said. He worked at his board, waited, then repeated the attempt. Glancing at Harper, he said, "Their comm systems appear to be online, but they're not responding."

"Send this, all frequencies, audio and visual feed, all lingua codes." After he got the nod from Peniche, he stood back up. "This is Captain Rick Harper. You will cease firing immediately and retreat or we will disable you further."

As the ship shakily completed its turn, it stopped firing and increased to maximum sublight.

"I believe our message got through," Winston said, sharing a grin with Harper.

Harper said, "Full stop, Nejem. Let them go."

"Aye, full stop."

As the Combine ship retreated, Peniche's panel beeped. He tapped at the controls. "We're receiving a narrow-beam audio signal from the ship. It seems to be a personal signal, not from the ship's main communication grid." He looked over at Robeson. "It's for you, Corporal."

Robeson's eyebrows rose in surprise, and she looked at Harper.

Harper shrugged and turned toward Peniche. "Can you return a narrow-beam signal without their bridge knowing?"

"I can minimize the chances of the signal being picked up on their main grid, but I can't guarantee a secure link for long."

"Patch it through, please, Lieutenant." Harper nodded toward Robeson.

A voice familiar to Robeson alone came over the speakers. "You were a worthy adversary, Lieutenant Robeson. It is against our customs to share personal names outside our clans, much less with strangers, but you earned it. I am Finder Shotiah, of clan Ylosro, of the Combine ship *Dark Stealth.*"

Robeson frowned. The entire bridge crew was watching her, and it made her uncomfortable. "Under the circumstances, that doesn't mean much to me."

"I understand. But I am under my own circumstances."

"You tried to hijack my ship. What circumstances justify that?"

There was a long silence. Robeson and Harper both looked at Peniche, who indicated the channel was still open with a nod.

Shotiah finally replied. "I don't have time to explain my circumstances. Suffice to say that it was not my decision to target your ship. My voice in the Combine is diminished by my failures today, but I will tell the Ylosro you deserve free passage as a ward of our clan. I wish you safe voyage, Robeson."

"That wish is a little late."

Again there was no response. This time Peniche said, "He closed the channel."

Harper sighed and faced Robeson. "You could have been a bit more diplomatic, Corporal. He did risk contacting you directly."

"We don't really know that, sir." She felt no sympathy for her adversary, who had left her beaten and bruised as she fought for her ship. "This could just be part of a trap."

Harper turned back toward the monitor as the *Dark Stealth* continued away at sublight. "I guess we'll find out the next time we meet them."

"Captain," said Peniche. "We just received another narrow-beam communications burst on the same frequency as before." He took a moment to make some adjustments. "It appears to have been substantially compressed. There's a lot of data here. It looks like a schematic of the device Robeson found."

Harper said, "Thompson, go over the specs with Alinari." The engineer had been disappointed by having to redeploy the device without a complete study of its components, so this would make her day. "Make sure we won't be surprised by anything like that again."

With a small nod, Thompson said, "Yes, Captain, right away."

Harper turned back to Robeson. As he stared long and hard at her, Robeson tried to put on her best poker face, but she knew anger and frustration were getting the best of her.

"Cheer up, Corporal. You handled yourself brilliantly today."

"But they all got away, sir." Robeson realized her hands were in tight fists, and she tried to relax. "Three Eyes—Shotiah—got away, and the Combine ship got away, and after attacking without reason."

"I'm sure they had their reasons, just not ones we agree with." Harper folded his arms across his chest. "Listen, there's always a spanner lying about somewhere waiting to get in the works. But we didn't lose anyone, we kept our ship, we gained some intel on a hostile, and perhaps, just perhaps, you developed a resource within the Combine. In my book, that's a good day's work."

Robeson took a deep breath and let it out, feeling her fists unclench at her sides. "You're right, sir."

"Of course I'm right. I'm the captain." He gave her a chuck on the shoulder. "Now go get yourself a nice cuppa and relax. Sleep in tomorrow, that's an order."

"Yes, sir. Thank you, sir." Robeson headed to the gangway, suddenly feeling very tired, and winced at the stiffness in her legs as she descended.

O O O

The door chime pulled Robeson out of bed and to the door before she was fully awake. She suddenly found herself facing the captain and very aware that she had fallen asleep in her filthy PTU. She had no idea what time it was, but she did notice that PFC Bloch, who'd still been unconscious on the deck when she'd returned to her quarters from the bridge yesterday, was no longer there.

"There's just one loose end, isn't there?" Harper said, as if he hadn't noticed she desperately needed a shower and a fresh uniform. "Why were you the only one to wake up?" Then he did look her up and down. "Corporal, I know I told you to sleep in, but, come now, it's after elevenses."

Robeson hesitated although she actually had a pretty good idea of what had happened. "Well, sir, first let me say that security is the purview of the detachment."

Harper tipped his head to one side. "I am aware of the duties of my personnel."

"Yes, Captain. Sorry." She shifted on her feet. "It's just that I've installed some additional countermeasures in my quarters that are not, strictly speaking, regulation." She cleared her throat. "Or approved by engineering. Or medical." She glanced to her side to avoid Harper's piercing gaze. "Some are not entirely one-hundred-percent legal within all of Allied territory." She looked back at the captain. "If you want to be technical. Sir."

"Well, then," Harper said. "Please run your countermeasures past Alinari and Selby, would you? Let's do this by the numbers. Seems you might have come up with a few things we could incorporate shipwide. At least the legal ones."

Robeson squinted up at Harper. He hadn't taken any time at all to think about what she had just confessed. "You already knew, didn't you, Captain?"

Harper's blue eyes seemed to shine even brighter. "I had Thompson scan your quarters this morning. I can't stand a loose end. And I've already discussed the situation with Lieutenant Camp."

"Yes, sir." Camp was Robeson's Marine CO; she'd half expected it had been him when her door chimed. She didn't know if he was going to rip her a new one for not waking him first or commend her on her initiative.

Harper nodded at her and turned to leave. As the door slid shut, he glanced back over his shoulder. "And, Corporal, do change uniforms, will you? This is a ship of the line, not a rugby pitch."

"Yes, sir!" Robeson said with a smile. And from beyond the closed door, she thought she heard the sound of the captain laughing.

Scott Pearson is a freelance writer and editor. He has published humor, poetry, nonfiction, short stories, and novellas, including five *Star Trek* titles for Simon & Schuster. He's also written mystery, science fiction, and urban fantasy stories for various small press anthologies. Since 2014 he's been the freelance copyeditor on many *Star Trek* novels and e-books, and he's also a freelance editor on the new *Star Trek Adventures* role-playing game from Modiphius Entertainment. He cowrote the IMAX documentary *Space Next* and cohosts the podcast *Generations Geek* with his daughter, Ella. Scott lives in personable St. Paul, Minnesota, with his wife, Sandra. When Ella's away from college she's often there as well. You can find Scott on various social media sites; visit his website yeahsure.net for more info.

Granny's Grunts

by Alan L. Lickiss

Introduction to "Granny's Grunts"

I have to admit I was intrigued by this one from the moment I saw the story's title. By the time I'd read the opening line, I knew in my gut that a slot in the Space Grunts anthology was Alan's to lose.

"Granny's Grunts" was absolutely unlike any other submission I received. Like another writer we lost all too soon, Ken Rand, Alan always had a knack for finding an offbeat, quirky way to tell a story that never failed to draw you in, and this tale is no exception. It's fun and funny, relying on the sort of "Been there, done that" perspective you expect from a salty soldier or retired veteran who still carries a bit of their past life close to the surface.

As I was honing the list of stories for the anthology's final table of contents, I'll admit to a few moments of weakness as I considered swapping out this story for another one that was on the bubble and in my "alternate selections" list. In the end, I simply couldn't let this one go. Who was I kidding? Alan had won me over from the jump. He had a knack for that, too.

"You kids go on to bed now. Granny's got to rip an officer a new one."

Gladys watched her two grandchildren walk down the hall to their rooms before heading to her office on the other side of the house. It allowed her the time to transform her face and personality from a loving grandmother of a seven and a nine-year-old into a retired master sergeant with thirty years under her belt. By the time she stabbed the holovid call button with her stiff forefinger her spine was rigid and her manner no-nonsense.

"General Blanders' office, how can I help you ma'am," said the corporal who appeared in the holo.

"Put the old man on, will ya," said Gladys.

"Whom shall I say is calling?" asked the spit and polish soldier who was closer to Gladys's grandson's age than her daughter.

"Tell him it's Gladys Dunckelburg and I said not to keep me waiting."

Gladys enjoyed watching the soldier's face transition from handle-the-old-lady mode to slack-jawed surprise. It was nice to know her name still meant something in the army. The corporal blubbered something incoherent and was replaced by a commercial for joining the army.

Only a few seconds played before the general appeared. "Who is this? What did you say to my aide?"

"Oh drop the bluster, Oscar. Where's my daughter?" Gladys asked.

"Gladys, I should have known. You still enjoy flustering the young ones, don't you," said the general.

"I like to think of it as respect," said Gladys as she stared down into the holovid. "Now tell me what you've found out about my daughter and son-in-law. Have you found them?"

Blanders sighed. "Not exactly. We've found their recon ship, but they were not at the site."

Gladys continued to stare into the face of the general on the holo. She didn't blink, didn't speak. She had known Blanders for years and knew he would soon have to fill the silence.

Blanders cleared his throat. "All four members of the team were missing from the ship. It looks like it was only slightly damaged by the enemy fire they reported, but it landed hard."

Gladys put her hands on either side of the holovid display. "You'd think that when two intelligent species found they had colonized the same planet, but by nature preferred different living conditions, we wouldn't have an on and off war. Well, don't stop now. What else?"

"Damn it, Gladys, this is all classified," said the general, a slight tone of pleading in his voice.

"If you think for two seconds," Gladys said, her words crisp and precise, "you'll recall that this little outpost ranch I live on with my daughter and her family is actually more than it appears, and as such I still have an active clearance more than high enough to hear what you know. The fact that it involves my family makes me need-to-know."

The general looked around himself in the holo. "There was no one on the ship. My team at the site reported that it looks like they were forcibly removed and taken into the jungle."

Gladys stepped back from the table and began to slowly pace back and forth in front of the holo. She stopped after a couple laps and turned to the holo. "How far has your team followed them? Have they any idea how many of the enemy they will be facing?"

"You know we can't pursue," Blanders replied. "Your daughter's team was on a clandestine mission over Thrull territory and barely made it back into ours. They are now back in Thrull territory. We'd be violating the treaty if we send in any troops. You know they'll be watching that section of the border harder than ever just looking for us to make that mistake."

Gladys slammed her fist onto the table, making the holo image shimmer. "Damn the treaty, Oscar. We're talking about my daughter, her husband, and a team that has kept her alive through several tough scrapes. I'm rather fond of all of them."

"I'm sorry, Gladys," the general said. "My hands are tied and I can't do anything more. Times have changed. We try to avoid direct skirmishes and confrontations. You know everything is spying and diplomacy. I've turned everything I have over to the diplomats."

"Yammerheads! After years of service you've left the fate of my family in the hands of a bunch of yammerheads more worried about how many berries are on the centerpieces of a meeting than in actually doing something," Gladys shouted into the general's holovid face.

"It's all I could do," Blanders replied.

"Which was less than nothing," said Gladys as she slammed her palm on the disconnect switch. Gladys continued to lean on the table. She worked to let go of the rage and to calm her breathing. Now was not the time for her to let emotions rule her. She needed to be calm. After a few minutes she placed another call.

A woman appeared in the holo. Her silver hair was pulled back away from her face. The lines in her face were proof that her decades of life had not been easy. "It didn't go well I take it," she said.

"A regular cluster, Jen," said Gladys. "How many were you able to get?"

"Six plus me. I didn't think I'd get that many, but Betty just had her hip replaced and is ready to test it out."

Gladys nodded. "Get everyone out here. We don't have any time to spare."

O O O

Corporal Smithers' feet hurt. He and three others had been posted at the crash site to "secure the site and make sure no damn tourists steal parts from the ship," his sergeant had said. When the order was given at full volume it sounded impressive, but several hours of staring at trees later the order didn't carry the same power.

"It's not like anyone's going to come all the way out here to look at a wreck," said Smithers.

"Yeah, like there'd be any tourists way out here," said the private next to him.

"If you see any, ask them if they have any sandwiches. I'm starving," said the private on the other side of Smithers.

The four had started with a standard formation when they'd first been deployed into position. After a couple of hours of monotony, they'd hunkered down next to the crash, linked up their handhelds, and started playing battle simulation games.

"Did you ever notice that none of the recruiting ads showed soldiers guarding wrecked ground jump ships? They made it look like I'd be piloting some admiral's space yacht," said the private to his right.

"And you believed that? I joined with my eyes wide open. I joined for—"

"Have you seen my doggie?"

Smithers and the others were startled by the old woman standing next to them. She seemed to appear out of nowhere without a sound. She must have been over sixty if her gray hair was any indication. Dressed like she'd walked over from a farm or ranch in work clothes and sturdy boots, Smithers didn't know what to think.

"Ma'am, you shouldn't be here. This is a crash site," said Smithers as he quickly stood, shoving his handheld into his pocket.

"I'm looking for my little doggie," said the old woman, her eyes brimming with tears. "He's a little thing and I'm worried about him."

The woman walked around to the other side of the wreckage. So startled by her presence was Smithers that he found himself running to catch up.

"We haven't seen your dog, Ma'am. Now you'll have to go. This is a government crash site."

The woman stopped looking around the wreckage and looked back at Smithers. She looked like she was going to cry.

"Are they … I mean did they land on my little Snookums? Is he dead? What hospital did they take the people to? Maybe they took Snookums too," said the woman.

Smithers looked over his shoulder at the other soldiers. They had put their handhelds away and come around so they could watch the show. Smithers hated the smirks on their faces, but knew he'd probably be grinning too if it was someone else dealing with the old woman.

"No, Ma'am," he said, trying to reason with her. "They weren't taken to a hospital. I don't mean to alarm you but the people that were in that vehicle were taken by the Thrull back into their territory. You should go home."

The old woman's face twisted with emotion and Smithers couldn't tell if it was anguish or anger. "You're lying," she yelled. "You got him. You stole my Snookums and won't give him back. No one was taken by the Thrull. You made that up."

Making calming motions with his hands, Smithers spoke in a calm voice. "No, no, no. I wouldn't do such a thing. Please believe me."

He looked over his shoulder at the others behind him. Lowering his voice, he continued, "Look, I could get into a lot of trouble telling you this, but I want you to believe me and know this place is dangerous. The Thrull crossed the border and captured the people from the ship and took them back into the woods. We know they have a small outpost on the edge of a swamp only a few kilometers from here. It's not safe; they could be back at any time."

"I don't know," said the old woman. "If it's so dangerous why were you boys hunkered down over your toys? I don't believe you. Prove it or I'm going to call the base and tell them you stole my dog and won't give it back."

Smithers held back a moment of panic. While the commander would probably write off her complaint about the dog as the delusions of an old woman, any mention of them using their handhelds while on guard duty would have all of them on report for a long time.

"All I have is this map," he said. Smithers pulled his handheld out and keyed the map display. A hologram map of the area displayed above his hand. He zoomed the image in tighter until he had a ten-kilometer-wide section displayed. "See, this is where we are, and this is where their outpost is. Not far. Is that proof enough that we're here on military business and didn't steal your dog?"

"Very much, Corporal. Thank you."

Smithers looked up at the change in the old woman's voice. There was something vaguely familiar about her sharp and distinct tone. The eyes were no longer moist, but tight, focused, and very cold.

At that moment Smithers recalled they'd left their weapons stacked on the other side of the ship. The old woman held his forearm in an iron grip. He saw motions in the periphery of his vision. He heard muffled grunts and thuds.

Smithers would later swear the woman's intense stare saw all the way to his soul.

"Corporal, for future reference, you were trained to stand guard a certain way for a reason. Is losing your life worth goofing off when you're bored?"

Smithers tried to pull away from the woman, and then he didn't see, hear, or feel anything for several hours.

O O O

Gladys looked away from the unconscious body of the corporal to survey the others. "Everyone okay?"

"We're all fine," said Jen. "A little slower, but not by much."

Gladys reached down and picked up the corporal's handheld. A few seconds later she had the map transferred to her own handheld. The others gathered around as she called up the topographical version of the map and examined the terrain between them and the enemy base.

"Not too much in the way of hills to cover," she told the others.

Switching to view foliage density the story wasn't quite as pleasant.

"Okay, let's get going. We're going to have to hike in and back out. None of the anti-grav transports we have can make it through the trees."

"That's going to make it a bit more slow going," said Sue.

Gladys looked into the trees as she shouldered her bag. "Can't be helped. It's the only way in."

She turned to the others. "Look, we don't have any recruits along to impress. We'll rest when we need. I hope we can get in and out before dark."

"Should we tie up these boys?" asked Trish.

"No. These boys will have a nice nap, but they'll have a monstrous headache when they wake up. But I'd bet long odds that they'll remember this lesson."

O O O

Motioning for the others to join her on the ridge, Gladys gave them a minute to take in the Thrull camp before signaling everyone to regroup behind the ridge.

"Looks like a standard Thrull outpost to me," said Jen.

"I agree," said Gladys. "Looked to be about twelve to fifteen single story dura-plas buildings surrounding a three story building in the center. If they haven't changed their tactics, that central building will hold their command post, and their prisoners."

The women all nodded in agreement. They had seen enough such posts in their years of service they knew the layout by heart.

"I didn't see a lot of guards," said Betty. "You'd think that if they just grabbed a bunch of humans from the other side and dragged them back that they'd be more worried."

"I noticed that too. My guess is they've got yammerheads on their side too. They probably think all the bluster going back and forth between the diplomats means they're safe," said Gladys.

The women shared a quiet chuckle together.

"It's more likely they've become too reliant on their electronic perimeter sensors," said Sue. "I'll have them redirected away from us so we can approach unnoticed. Then all we'll have to worry about are the actual Thrull sentries."

"Well, we can just teach their young pups a thing or two just like we used to teach 'em on our side," said Jen.

The women again chuckled. All except Gladys. She reached down and picked up a rock and examined it closely for a minute.

"Listen, I've just got to ask again," said Gladys. She looked around the circle, into each woman's eyes. "Up until now we haven't done anything too bad. At least nothing the army would want made public. But none of you need to be here. This is my fight and I don't want any of you to get hurt. This is one time we can't call in air support if things go bad."

Betty spoke up. "I'll admit I'm a little slower, and had to take a couple of breaks on the way here, and I'm going to be sore as hell tomorrow from head to toe, but I'm all in for getting your family back, Gladys."

Gladys looked around the circle again, and all heads were nodding in agreement. She allowed a moment for the glow of camaraderie with her sisters in arms before focusing on the job at hand.

"Okay, like I said we've got no support so we're going to have to go in quiet. Based on the few we saw on guard, and how alert they looked, the Thrull haven't converted completely over from their original nocturnal rhythms. With no war for so long they've gotten sloppy. We've got a couple of hours before nightfall when the Thrulls get really active."

Gladys pulled out her handheld. She sketched out a three-dimensional view of the camp so all could see while she marked assignments as she laid out the plan.

"We go in as three groups. Betty, you and Brittney get the armory. Rig it to blow. If we need a diversion to escape, that will be the biggest one. Can you rig something with their stuff?"

"Oooo, we get the fun job," said Betty, a large grin on her face. "Can do."

"Good. Becky and Maggie, you take out their surface and air ships. I'm not foolish enough to think we'll get out without being seen but I don't want to have to outrace their ships."

The two women looked at Gladys and nodded assent.

"Jen, Trish, and Sue are with me. We're going to take the command center, hopefully without their raising an alarm. After that we find my family and their team and hightail it out of there. Everyone do your jobs and then get back out here where we'll regroup."

"Got it," said Jen. "I just wish you'd let us bring those nice big guns those boys had at the crash site."

"I know, Jen, but we couldn't do that to General Blanders. If this goes wrong there's nothing to say we aren't just a bunch of crazy old women who've been out in the heat too long. That's why I insisted on commercial grade weapons and clothing, nothing that came from the army," said Gladys.

"Still looking out for the officers, huh Gladys," said Sue.

"Someone has to. Lord knows they can't do it themselves," said Gladys. "Let's go. Remember your training and good luck."

Jen chuckled and shook her head. "Always a sergeant."

The women made their way to the edge of the base that wasn't well patrolled. Timing their entries, they slipped in one team at a time. Gladys's team was last, and she hoped this wasn't the last time she would see her friends as she watched them disappear into the camp.

It must have been the Thrull version of a poker game. After an easy trip through the camp Gladys expected to find one or two

Thrull manning the command center. Instead there were five. They were sitting around a table that was covered with stacks of orange, blue, and purple disks. Small pink spheres rotated around a large glowing cube in the middle of the table.

To her advantage there was no one manning the communications station. Gladys reoriented herself before the Thrull at the table did. She rushed into the room and shot her neural disrupter at the Thrull who was just getting up. Jen and the others were right behind her and followed her lead. Unfortunately, the best civilian guns that they could get had lower output and a long recharge period. When they hit a Thrull it would knock them out for several hours, but not kill them. All four shot fast, but only three hit their marks.

With three Thrull out of commission, the remaining two charged the women. Gladys grabbed a chair and hit one of the Thrull over the head. He staggered, but started coming at her again.

The Thrull were humanoid, about a foot shorter than humans, squat with thick dark green leathery skin. Their face was even more different. Their mouth and nose were part of a snout that looked like a cross between a dog and a duck back on earth. They had few vulnerable points to attack in hand to hand, but they did have some. Gladys used the Thrull's delay to get closer and slam her fists against what they had for ears. The Thrull stumbled back, his hands against his ears. A loud cry of pain filled the room.

Gladys heard a body fall. She glanced back fast enough to see it was the fourth Thrull and not one of her team. She turned back to her Thrull in time to see him rushing at her. Reflexes took over and she moved out of the way enough to avoid being hit, but still close enough to grab his arm and swing him around and into a wall. The thing about reflexes is that while the muscles respond, their aim isn't always on target. The Thrull left Gladys's grip, spun toward the wall, and crashed through the door to the outside.

Gladys checked that her disrupter had recharged and fired it at the Thrull before he could get to his knees. He slumped back down into the dirt.

"Damn, I had hoped we could have more time before we got noticed," said Gladys, rubbing the pain in her left shoulder caused by the maneuver.

The door was in shambles. Gladys knew that no matter how hard they tried, the four women would not be able to get the bulk of the unconscious soldier back into the room before the guards passed by again.

"Well, what's done is done. Sue, smash that comm unit. I don't want anyone sending messages about an attack. Trish, cover her and then you two see if there's another way out." Gladys motioned for Jen to follow her as she jogged for the stairs to the next level.

"They used to keep prisoners on the top floor," said Jen.

"That's where I'm heading," said Gladys as she started up the stairs. She was breathing heavy when she reached the third floor. She couldn't remember three flights ever wearing her out before.

The large room had six cells on one side made of thick clear dura-plas. The four humans were standing at the doors of their cells, and the look of relief was mixed with disbelief when they saw her.

"When I say supper is at six, I expect you to be on time," said Gladys.

"Yes, ma'am," said her daughter Cindy.

Gladys turned back to Jen. "Check the desk for a release switch."

"There's a remote in the top drawer," said Steve, her son-in-law.

The sounds of breaking machinery could be heard from the floors below. Gladys looked over the cells while Jen grabbed the remote.

"Cindy, how are you? Is everyone okay? Will you be able to walk?" Gladys asked.

"We're banged up a little from the crash, Mom, but they haven't done anything to us yet. I think we can walk okay. How far to the pickup zone?" asked Cindy.

"All the way back to the crash site. We're on our own here," said Gladys.

Jen handed Gladys a stick with a dozen buttons on it, each button labeled with a Thrull symbol. Gladys wasn't familiar enough with the symbols to understand which would open the cells. She hoped she wasn't setting anything off as she worked through each one until all the cells were open. She paused only a second after getting her daughter's cell open to give her a hug. More noise could be heard from below.

"Uh oh," said Jen. "It looks like we've got some company. Trish and Sue are on the level below, pushing stuff in the way to block the stairs."

Gladys pointed to the plastic storage bins on the other side of the room. "Look in those and see if there's anything we can use to get out of here. If we're lucky, maybe a weapon or two better than what we've got."

Sue and Trish came into the room. "There are six Thrulls down there, and soon to be more," Sue said.

All of the prisoners were free and Gladys turned to the rest of the group. "Block the stairs on this level too. I don't think we're going to be able to get out that way."

Jen and Cindy looked up from the bins they were searching. They each held new Thrull uniforms in their hands. They both shrugged at Gladys.

Everything was pulled out of the desk and bins but nothing useful was available. The sounds they could hear told them the second-floor blockade was still holding. Gladys looked out a window and was surprised to find that there weren't a bunch of Thrull soldiers looking up at her. In fact, the place was still deserted.

Cindy looked up from the box of uniforms she was searching. "I heard a couple of them talking and from the little Thrull I understood it was about some of them wanting to kill us right away to pay for things that had happened in the past. Didn't want to chance the diplomats would turn us over. You know, new recruit bravado talk."

"They may not know it's us yet," said Gladys.

"Now if we only had a rope," said Trish.

"Great idea, Trish. Let's make one," said Gladys.

Gladys had everyone tie the Thrull uniforms together while she watched out the window. "Hurry, we need to be on the ground before the other two teams show their hand."

Cindy brought the bulk of their jury-rigged rope to the window while Steve tied an end to the desk. They fed the length through the window. It was a few feet short, but the sound of the second-floor barricade being breached was enough for them to plan on dropping a few feet to the ground.

"Jen, Trish, and Sue first. Get everyone to the other side of that building on the left," Gladys said and pointed to the building. "After them, the four of you, and I'll bring up the rear."

Jen was sliding down the rope and Trish was ready to go when they heard the Thrull against the third-floor barricade. Gladys listened to what the Thrull were yelling while the others continued to go out the window.

"They are calling to one of their own. The guards downstairs must still be out of it. Just like you said, Cindy, they think some of their own are up here."

Cindy went over to the cell and shouted, "No, leave us alone. We didn't do anything to you. Why are you trying to hurt us?"

Gladys smiled. "That should confuse them for a minute. Now get out there."

When the others were out of sight Gladys got on the window ledge and started down the wall when a loud concussive explosion shook the base. She almost lost her grip, but recovered and scrambled down. A loud horn sounded the Thrull "under attack" signal. She ran for the side of the building to catch up with the others when a second explosion shook the camp and knocked Gladys off her feet.

Gladys crouched and rushed for the building. The others were there looking anxious.

"I'm fine, let's go. The base is about to be full of panicky Thrull and in this place we stand out like humans in a Thrull camp," said Gladys.

Picking a path out of camp away from the armory and the vehicle depot they only ran into one Thrull. Before he could do anything Jen stunned him.

Once outside of camp they were able to meet up with the others. Their missions had gone well as was evident by the magnificent explosions that should have the Thrull scratching their heads for a few days. Gladys took point and led them in a fast march back to human territory. She needed to rest as much as the others, but she wanted to get some distance away from the camp before the adrenalin rush wore off.

O O O

"Gladys, how could you do it? Do you realize you've jeopardized the entire treaty?" General Blanders paced in front of Gladys. No holovid this time, he had come in person.

"What do you mean, Oscar? How could I do such a thing?" said Gladys from her rocking chair. She rocked back and forth at an easy pace while looking up at the general.

"What do I mean?" he said, his voice rising in volume and pitch. He stopped pacing in front of Gladys and turned to face her. "The Thrull do not care for invading armies. Silly of them I know, but that is what the treaty is to prevent."

Gladys stopped rocking. "They took my family from our side to their side and held them prisoner. Then their camp blows up, probably because of some Thrull yahoo doing something stupid, and my family escapes. Who violated the treaty? Not me."

Blanders turned away and began pacing again. "Statements from my men at the crash site put you on the path, Gladys. And our diplomats are hearing some strange tales about soldiers with gray hair from their diplomats."

"Oh stow it, Oscar. I've got my family back and that's the only thing I care about. Let their side tell their wild tales. Remind the stuffed shirts of the explosions and question who was drinking what out there. It'll work. Do you honestly think our people are going to believe the Thrull's wild tales of elderly women kicking their butts and blowing up their camp?"

The general shook his head and sighed. "No, probably not. But then again, none of them had you for a drill sergeant in basic training like I did."

Alan L. Lickiss was raised in the suburbs of Washington, DC, where he met and married his wife Rebecca. He moved to the Front Range in Colorado with his wife, children, and an ever changing variety of pets the children loved. Alan spent his days working as an IT and Logistics Manger and jack of all trades, writing in the evenings and on weekends. He was also an avid photographer. You can learn more about Alan and Rebecca Lickiss at lickiss.net

Part IV: Space Horrors

Edited by David Lee Summers

Last Man Standing

by Danielle Ackley-McPhail

Introduction to "Last Man Standing"

When we were assembling the original Full-Throttle Space Tales, I had written two book series. The first was about a group of space pirates who settled on a distant planet and helped solve the mystery of an alien presence that had invaded the galaxy. The other series was about a group of vampire mercenaries who fought evil. This helps to explain why I edited Space Pirates and why the second book in the Full-Throttle Space tales was originally called Space Vampires.

Soon after I told Danielle Ackley-McPhail about the theme of the second of my anthologies for the series, she pitched a story to me involving an alien twist on the concept of a vampire. Of course, an idea alone does not make for a good story. To do that, Danielle tapped into the essence of horror, which is how people react to the frightening situation. As she shows, that reaction can sometimes be more terrifying than the original horror that inspired it.

We ultimately changed the name of Space Vampires to Space Horrors to allow a greater range of stories. Even so, this tale contains enough grit that you know the vampires won't sparkle and enough science to make you consider the possibilities even through the nightmares.

◁ ▷

If not, we ready are to try our fortunes

To the last man.

—William Shakespeare, *King Henry IV*,
Part II, Act IV Scene 2.

The *Caliphus* landed on the moon MineCorp had designated A-RCK-01 amid a cloud of fine, rust-colored particles. Dust was everywhere, invasive. If not for the high-grade ion field protecting the surface of the ship, and its various venting and intake systems, they would already be in trouble. From an impartial viewpoint, it was a spectacular effect: an aura of red dust limning the ship from ten inches past the buffer. The crew, however, was ill at ease, left to imagine the total encapsulation they could only view in swirling fragments on the monitors.

Tom Henry was beyond concerned. As the mission engineer, he more than anyone else was aware that the ionic drive was not designed to combat such a constant assault. The particles made him uneasy. For lack of a better word, he thought of the matter as dust, but it didn't move right; it appeared slick, almost greased as it slid along the ion field like it was trying to get through. He held back a shudder. This was bad. Their orders were to set up dirtside and stockpile ore until the star-freighter *O'Connor* arrived. Not only was that not currently possible, but every instinct he had screamed at him to lift off immediately, and the contract be damned.

"Your assessment, Mr. Henry?" Captain Jared Troy asked, rising from the chair and coming to stand at his shoulder.

Tom ran a series of computations before responding. The data scrolling across the monitor reinforced his concerns. "The dust storm extends beyond the range of our hull sensors, I can't pinpoint when it will end. We're okay for now, but we have twenty to twenty-five standard hours before the system is overwhelmed if it maintains this density."

Captain Troy straightened and turned toward the rest of the crew. "You heard the man, suit up and get out there, you rock hounds. This has become a hit-and-run extraction."

"Sir," Tom interrupted. "I don't know what this storm will do to their suits, or the equipment." The moon was large, with three-quarters Earth-standard gravity and an oxygen-rich atmosphere, but the chemical composition of the air was not friendly to humans.

Troy's mouth twisted in annoyance. His eyes narrowed and he leaned back over the console. "Planetary evaluation ruled out a corrosive atmosphere and did not register anything over a level-one bacterium, correct?"

"Yes, sir."

"So, the worst we should be facing is some dirt, yes?"

Tom looked away, his expression tight. He focused on the monitor and by sheer will forced his voice neutral. "It would seem so, Captain."

But he didn't believe it.

Troy moved across the deck to the hatch. "Donovan," he called into the crew compartment. The foreman, climbing into her EVA suit, looked up, her expression closed as she continued to slide on and seal her gauntlet. "Sir?"

"Here's where that mech unit of yours proves its worth. Get it out there pounding rock … and double the crew while you're at it. We can't risk the Chomps, so get the extra men running sack relay," he ordered. "I want a constant stream of ore feeding into the cargo bay at all times."

Kate Donovan nodded sharply in acknowledgement as she tugged her helmet into place over her short bristle of dark brown hair, Kate's jaw worked as she toggled her comm active: "Anything else, sir?"

"Check-in is half standard. We don't know how much time we have, so monitor your systems closely. Any sign of malfunction is to be reported immediately."

Two thirds of the mining crew scrambled to comply, the other four remained huddled around the monitors, makeshift markers changing hands as they made book on everything from the time the ion shield would fail to how much ore would end up in the hold before it did.

Tom Henry kept his eyes locked on his station monitor; already sections of shield sensors showed signs of strain. He continued to watch, his lips moving silently in prayer.

O O O

Kate Donovan regularly worked side by side with her crew. In part this was to make sure no one slacked or took unnecessary risk to secure a bonus, but it also allowed her to watch Jean-Paul Marot's back. She had to; no one else would. Not even Jean-Paul Marot. The titanium-plated ass had a death wish.

No one else aboard knew their new mining mech was actually a cybernetic prototype. To them he was just another bit of hardware. Only Kate knew and by contract she couldn't reveal to anyone there was a human soul beneath the chassis. It had been a hard contract to win and though she had wondered at the reason for the odd clause when she'd triumphantly signed the deal, she also hadn't realized how hard it would be to keep silent. Jean-Paul did his best to act the part of inhuman mech, but in a hundred little ways he betrayed his humanity, even if she was the only one to realize it. She had lost count of the thoughtful ways he'd helped her out on shift, both with tricky tasks and unforeseen mishaps. He'd even saved her ass a time or three.

She followed close behind as he passed through the waiting decontamination unit and headed down the ramp to the planet's surface, pickaxe in his right robotic hand, massive jackhammer held casually in the other. Red dust swirled disturbingly around him the moment he was past the ionic shield, adhering to the flexible Kevlar-fabric laminate that sheathed his frame. He unconsciously swiped his optics clear across his arm as no mechanical being would have and headed for rock.

Hey, JP, Kate subvocalized across her comm on his private band, **not too far. There's plenty of surface ore close to the ship. Start with the port-side outcrop there while I organize Troy's bucket brigade.** He didn't acknowledge her command verbally, but set to breaking up the easy-access payload that had placed this moon at the top of MineCorp's A-list. She toggled the comm to the crew frequency and started barking instructions to the rest of the shift workers. In short order, sacks of dust-covered iron ore were being ferried into the hold.

O O O

Everyone earned out their bonus that day. They were beat. Everything was red with dust—right down to the men. Between the mech and the extra men, the ship's holds were full before second shift was halfway through and the crew even managed to set up the steel storage hoppers on the surface and started filling them. Once those were full, they would be shuttled to the *O'Connor* on its arrival. For now, the entire crew called it quits for the day. As the final hold hatch closed, Tom keyed the sequence locking the ship off from the decon unit. When it was secure, he remotely extended the vent shaft until it pushed through the ion shield. A clever one-way valve on the end of the shaft kept the moon's atmosphere from contaminating the ship.

Okay, Donovan, he commed the foreman. **You and your 'hounds are cleared for decon.** He felt his tension ease a bit as the monitor displayed the men and women piling back into the ship with their gear. The mech unit was the last aboard. Once it cleared the walkway, Tom spoke over the crew frequency: **Please stand clear of the closing door, decontamination commencing.**

Directed jets of air dislodged particles of foreign matter from the crew while fans in the duct system sucked the contaminants down the flexible vent shaft and ejected it past the ion shields before retracting back into place. Then, though all of the crew had been through the process before, Tom issued the standard warning for the next stage of decontamination: **Please close your eyes in preparation for low-grade irradiation.** As the final stage completed, Tom Henry ran a scan on the chamber before sounding the all-clear and initiating the release sequence.

Several of the returning crew, including Donovan, were in the process of loosening the seals on their environment suits as they waited for the hatch lock to disengage when a low curse transmitted across the crew frequency. One of the men had dropped his pick. He seemed to sway as he bent to retrieve it, then crumpled to the floor.

Shit! Donovan's startled voice came over the comm. **Do not release your seals!** she ordered the rest of her crew as she moved toward the miner. Tom immediately keyed the interrupt, setting off the automatic alert, and reversing the release. It looked like John Palmer, but it was hard to tell. He wasn't out cold, but he remained flat on the deck as Donovan conducted an eyes-on inspection.

Tom's earlier unease returned as he watched the monitor. There was no sound feed currently active in the chamber, but it was clear from her expression that the foreman reprimanded the crewman. Tom switched on the intercom and the internal recorders. "Donovan, report."

She looked up, her navy blue eyes darkened by the displeasure clearly visible through her faceplate. "Mr. Henry, please send a medtech to the decon quarantine unit, Crewman Palmer apparently sustained a suit breach in the field. Injury appears minimal, but shows signs of dust contamination." Her words propelled Tom's tension to another level all together. Bad enough the potential of some foreign contagion, worse, in Tom's opinion, that Kate Donovan was at risk. He sent the order to medbay and continued to monitor the decon unit.

"Aw come on, boss, it's barely even a scratch!" Palmer interrupted. One hard look from Donovan and he cut off his protest.

"Not a word, Palmer," she growled as she helped the man up. "Safety protocol exists for a reason. You will observe it from here on out or it will be my boot kicking you out the door. Am I understood?"

Tom watched as she turned and scanned the room. Her face tensed, concern overshadowed by anger as she clearly noted those that had breached the seals on their protective suits. With a nod toward quarantine she spoke to her crew in a controlled voice. "Okay, Palmer, Simms, Chou, Colman … pick a bunk and get your butts inside. The rest of you, remain suited." She then turned to face the monitor.

"Mr. Henry, please reinitialize decon procedure," she requested, closing the door behind her as she entered the quarantine cell next to Palmer's.

O O O

Jean-Paul watched as his single link to humanity closed herself in what potentially could be her coffin. That shouldn't matter, but even after the repeat decon completed, he remained facing her cell.

Miners were a superstitious lot; if they ever learned of his past, those standing around him would as likely as not shove him off the ship; out with the bad penny, and all that. If anything happened to Donovan they wouldn't have to. He'd tried to keep distant, but in the silence of his mind he considered her a friend. A dangerous thing, in his experience … for the friend. All too often, people in his proximity ended up dead. One accident after the other had left him the last man standing. The first had landed him in this mobile metal suit. The second landed him in hell as the suit forced him to take another's life to preserve his own … and he could do nothing but comply. That chemical command was the first thing he'd forced the Corporation to deactivate, when he'd sued them to become a free agent, but the damage had been done. In his own mind, it had cost him the last of his humanity. That was one of the reasons he'd become a roamer, taking only short-term contracts before moving on to another crew. Less time for his shitty luck to kick in, less opportunity for people he liked to pay for it.

This time the strategy had failed him. He suspected it was because Donovan reminded him very much of Chloe Kendall, the last friend he'd allowed himself since he realized what kind of monster the Corporation had created in him. His hand unconsciously tightened on the haft of the pickaxe until the sensors in the "fingertips" registered a deformation in the metal.

Go on, JP, Donovan cut into his thoughts. **It's just a precaution. We'll be out of here before the* O'Connor *hits orbit.**

For the first time in almost a year, Jean-Paul spoke, if only over his private frequency: **Quarantine is seventy-two hours, the* O'Connor *arrives in forty-eight.**

So I suck at math! Get out of here, we'll be fine! She waved him away with the gauntlet she'd just removed. **And don't forget to run a systems scan as soon as you hit your bay, I want a full report, even if I am on forced down-time.**

Jean-Paul brought his pick hand up in salute, before slowly turning and leaving the now-empty decontamination unit, passing the harried medtech on his way through the main service corridor that ran the length of the ship. JP silently moved through the crew compartment toward his own bay only to have his preservation mixture flood in chemical-response to the ever-present betting markers transferring from hand to hand.

It took him a lot of effort to resist tightening his grip with the anger and further damaging the equipment.

O O O

Kate heard the chatter over the crew frequency long before she received word from anyone on the command staff.

The *O'Connor* was delayed by a meteor outburst. The trail was far-reaching and heavy with particles, obstructing the entire distance between the star-freighter and the *Caliphus.* Their flight crew were waiting for the shower to pass before continuing on to A-RCK-01, where the star-freighter would take up a geosynchronous orbit above the mining site until its massive cargo holds were full.

It could take many standard days for the route to clear. This delay could cost them every bonus written into the contract. Not to mention the hefty penalties that would be levied against them if they fell behind schedule. Tom Henry had warned her in a private message that Captain Troy had ordered the crews back on shift in between dust storms. The captain hadn't the decency to inform her himself. She was glad they were still making some progress but with her trapped in here, things were running less than smooth.

Rising from her bunk, Kate moved to her computer access, first checking for any messages from Tom or reports from her assistant foreman before checking on Palmer's status. He'd been put through the full spectrum of diagnostic testing, but all results were negative for any identifiable contagion or foreign antibody. The miner mostly slept, complaining about feeling weak and tired. The medtech suspected the onset of anemia and was treating Palmer accordingly, but protocol demanded the four of them remain in quarantine the full seventy-two hours. Time was nearly up.

"Hey, Mac, you have a timer set out there or something?" she called out over the open intercom as she settled back on her bunk.

"It's not like one of us is going to up and keel over in the last ten minutes."

She saw the medtech look up from his most recent batch of tests and cock his head. "Let me see if I remember the phrase properly … safety protocol exists for a reason …"

"Yeah, yeah, talk to my ass, why don't you?" she groused back. Every person on the ship had overheard her comments to Palmer. She was the first to agree, but the only thing she showed symptoms of was boredom and frustration. Outside this ship was a site they'd contracted to mine and in her head a clock counted down to their deadline. Her eyes never left the monitor.

Finally, Mac Taylor punched a few keys on his system and pushed back from his chair. Moments later the lights on the monitoring sensors lining her walls blinked out. Kate was up and waiting at the door to her cell before the hermetic seal parted. As she pushed through into the decon unit proper, the doors to either side of her swung open as well. She turned and scanned her crewmen; Simms, Chou, and Colman looked a little twitchy, much as she herself felt, but otherwise hale. Palmer … he looked like something bit into him hard. Pale and tense, with an odd blue cast to the whites of his eyes. A sideways glance at Mac, who didn't seem fazed, was only marginally reassuring.

"We cleared for duty, then?" she asked.

"Except for your buddy Palmer here, yeah. Need to build up his iron levels a bit before you send him out on shift again."

Kate nodded and turned to her crewman. "You got lucky, John. You go get fixed up, and while you're on medical leave, you be sure to read your procedures manual, am I understood?"

With a disgruntled look at drawing quarter pay, Palmer nodded and followed Mac from the chamber. Kate turned back to the others.

"Well? What are you waiting for? You've just had a three-day vacation … get to work!" The three of them groaned as they preceded her out of the decontamination unit. It was damn good to move further than eight full steps in a row; it was even better to walk out under her own power, with the freedom of the ship and beyond still open to her. Kate headed for the crew compartment to catch up on the status of the operation. There was only so much she could run by wire.

"Hey," she called out as she entered the chamber from the main shaft. "I see an awful lot of loafing going on here."

Her comment was met by laughs and groans and shouts of "Look who's talking!" All of it was good-natured. It was like breathing uncanned air after the isolation of quarantine. She swept a sharp glance around the room, her eyes gleaming. "So, who took the book on me?" More groans, followed by dirty socks and empty meal packs lobbed at Tom Henry, whose cheeks were amusingly flushed at being caught out. Strange, he usually stayed out of the betting. Glancing at Tom, Kate allowed the warmth she felt to show in her eyes as she indulged in a faint smile, her first in three days. "You, sir, can afford to buy me a steak, then." More laughter and the subtle air of tension in the compartment dissipated. Tom looked stunned, though pleased, and slowly nodded, but she'd already moved past, going to check on Jean-Paul.

"It's not there," a voice called from behind her.

"What?" Kate turned and spied Captain Troy standing in the command deck hatchway.

"It's not there," the captain repeated. "I sent it out with the shift. Your crew was falling behind."

Kate ate her response to that criticism, merely nodding in acknowledgement as she pivoted and headed for her equipment locker, all the while expecting Troy to summon her back. She didn't like him or the risks he took with her people, but she was a contractor on this job and he was the boss. That meant she had to play nice; which also meant she stayed as far from his proximity as she could manage. She breathed a little easier with each step she took away from him.

Then she heard the sound of boots behind her, and the clang of another locker opening nearby. She looked over into Troy's reproving gaze and actually had wistful thoughts of quarantine.

O O O

Hey, JP, coming at your back, with company. the subvocal voice coming over his comm, combined with the familiar address triggered a complex chemical response the moment Jean-Paul heard it. Relief, pleasure, warmth; it was hard to focus under the bombardment. He carefully put down the equipment he was using and pivoted around.

It was a mistake on several levels. First, what machine would halt its given task randomly? Second, why should it matter to him that Kate Donovan was well and out of quarantine? Machines did not have friends. JP had to endlessly remind himself of that. He had a practical reason for being glad to see her, though. In her absence, Captain Troy had been running Jean-Paul nonstop like a piece of heavy equipment still under warranty. The chassis could take it, but JP's brain was getting loopy, making it hard to control the servos and gyros that controlled his mobility and balance; more than once he caught himself swaying. No small concern when you were a 400-pound metal behemoth surrounded by frail men of flesh. What was more concerning, he'd started getting a few low-level alerts from his exoskeleton's monitoring system.

Kate came up to him and looked him over before turning to scan the mounds of ore waiting for the rest of the crew to catch up on stowing it. Without a word she walked over to the storage bins and peered inside.

JP, how long have you been out here? she asked across his private frequency.

He remained silent. It wasn't like she really needed an answer to know he'd been out here too long, and talking to her was a bad habit to get into.

You pig-headed ass! she hissed, before turning to Captain Troy. "Thank you, sir, for your diligence on my behalf during the quarantine period." She kept her tone carefully neutral. "Things appear nicely ahead of schedule here. If your inspection is complete, I need to run some *mandatory* maintenance on the JPM unit. We can't have it breaking down, not with the nearest repair facility light-years away."

Jean-Paul had the urge to laugh without the means to do so. Troy's face neared puce in color, but there was no way he could argue. As if there were no question, Kate turned and headed back toward the *Caliphus*. With extreme care, JP followed.

O O O

"What the hell!" Kate's hands clenched and unclenched reflexively as she stared at the diagnostic report spit out by JP's charging and maintenance station. There were half a dozen warnings. Nothing serious, but definitely all of a sudden. Best to start with the simplest issue first. "You've got a problem with your ground wire." Moving to the indicated section, she detached the protective Kevlar skin and opened the access panel so she could eyeball the situation. "Hmmm … must have been a defective batch, looks like some of the copper coating is worn away. The steel core is starting to oxidize." Taking a can of compressed air, she blew away the corrosion to get a better look at the situation. Then she noticed another spot on a nearby o-ring. In fact, anything that wasn't titanium seemed to have sprouted rust. There wasn't much, and it wasn't bad, but it was disturbing. Better to replace it all now before the situation got worse. A trip to the spare parts locker uncovered sufficient replacements. She was even able to swap out most of the corroded bits with titanium, rather than the older steel alloy.

"Okay, pal, I'm going to have to power you down for maintenance." A sound came from JP, short, sharp, and cut off, but she didn't need to hear it to know he was very unhappy with this part. "Don't worry, it shouldn't take long." Maybe it was her imagination, but the silence that met her reassurance seemed thick with displeasure. Couldn't be helped, though; she couldn't do this kind of repair with his system active. With care, she reached in and disconnected the ground wire first. As she extracted it, the intercom squawked an alert.

"Aw, *sh*-it!" Kate swore as the sound startled her, causing her to jerk back. A sharp pain went through her arm as some internal part of the cybernetic unit gouged her hand. This was the very reason she'd deactivated her comm. Fool that she was, she hadn't thought to kill the intercom as well. Her breath hissed out as she gritted her teeth against the pain.

"Donovan, report!"

A few more curses ensued before she managed to extract herself from JP's inner workings. Heading for the intercom, she slapped the toggle active with her uninjured hand as blood dripped from the other. She quickly wrapped it in a clean rag from a pile she had nearby.

"What?" Her tone was less than civil and there was a long pause on the other end.

"You're needed in medbay immediately."

How convenient; thanks to them, she had a need to be there. "Give me ten minutes."

"But . . ." the tech protested. Kate heard the slightest thread of panic in the word. There were some frenzied sounds in the background. Probably some rock hound got a little juiced up. Well, they would have to wait.

"I said ten minutes. It's the best you're getting." She released the toggle and returned to JP, quickly, but carefully replacing the ground wire. She would have taken the book on that one. Finished in Guinness record time, she closed the access panel and powered his system back up.

JP made a sound that was almost a gasp as his sensors and motor functions were restored.

"Sorry," Kate said in a rush. "I'm not done yet, emergency. Didn't want to leave you in limbo. Be back as quick as I can." Not waiting for an answer—it wasn't like he'd talk to her anyway—she flew from the compartment and down the corridor leading to medbay. *It's probably nothing,* she told herself, but as she neared the medics' domain there was an ungodly shriek, followed by several crashes. Cursing and thuds continued to pour down the corridor.

"Aw, crap!" Maybe not quite nothing . . . She picked up her pace until she full-out ran, grabbing the edge of the open hatch and sling-shotting herself into the compartment. Her breath caught in her throat and she stopped short at the sight of Palmer. At first glance he looked like someone had put a dusty shipsuit on one of those terracotta warriors from ancient China and then brought it to life. But when she saw his face it was less serene, than taut and hard like granite, etched in agony. He could barely stand straight as he tore at the med supply cabinet, frantically trying to get it open, as Mac and the other tech fought to restrain him. Each time he moved, a cloud of dust particles swirled in the air around him.

"John!" Kate yelled.

Palmer's thrashing efforts stilled as he turned to look at her, his gaze a curious mix of hatred and terror and pleading. "Make it stop," he groaned. Now that he wasn't flailing around she could see that his body trembled and his teeth had cut through his lip. The blood marking his face was more brown than red, barely visible against the dust permeating his skin. "Please," he begged. Before anyone could move Palmer tensed, his back arching as a high, thin gasp fought its way from his throat. His eyes rolled into his head as he crumpled to the floor.

Kate looked up and met Mac's panicked gaze. "What the *hell* was he doing dirtside without a protective suit?" she asked.

Mac gave a twitching shake of his head, and then another, but managed nothing more. Next to him, looking like she'd been on the losing end of a prize fight, Medtech Eva Sanchez wore a haunted expression as she brushed a bit of dust and blood from her cheek. "He hasn't been outside. He hasn't left medbay."

A tremor shook through Kate Donovan as she looked down at her fallen man. He was as red as the crew that just came off shift, and way too still. Her breath coming just a little quicker, she knelt beside him and started to feel for a pulse. Eva's hand darted out and smacked hers away.

Kate gave her a cutting look. "Like it isn't already too late for that." She reached out again, placing the tip of two fingers against Palmer's throat. It took a lot of effort to leave them there long enough to be sure he was gone, before drawing them back. When she did she couldn't help rubbing at the slick, oily sensation of the dust on her skin as she tongued her comm active to the captain's private frequency.

"Troy," she hailed, "we have a problem."

O O O

Having drawn monitoring duty, Tom Henry was alone on the command deck when the captain hurried through the hatch, clearly a man with a purpose. Clad in a full environmental suit, Troy had a large rucksack over each arm and another on his back. They were jammed full of supplies, with meal packs and other necessities sticking out the top of each of them.

Tom swiveled in his chair and waited expectantly. He could feel the puzzled expression creep across his face.

"Seal off the command deck, Mr. Henry, and prepare to lift off."

Without realizing it, Tom came to his feet. "Sir, there's a double shift crew still dirtside!"

The look on Troy's face burned along Tom's nerves like dry ice on bare skin. "Want to join them?"

"I don't know what's going on, but you are not stranding those men." Tom squared his shoulders and braced himself.

There was a mad glimmer in the captain's eye and there was something off about their color.

In two strides, Jared Troy stood at his side. Before Tom could react, the captain grabbed him by the shipsuit and raised a cutting torch to within an inch of his head. Troy's finger was on the switch. Tom tensed and prayed the frantic working of his jaw would be construed as a nervous response to the situation. He triggered the comm frequency assigned to Donovan and subvocally sent one word across the link: **Help!** Something must have betrayed him, though. Jerking him sharply off balance, the captain shoved him toward the hatch. With the torch still to his head, Tom dared not resist.

"On second thought, I'll cover takeoff myself."

The captain thrust Tom from the compartment with enough force to send him sprawling. Before he could gain his feet, the hatch closed and he heard the locking mechanism slide into place. Tom tried the manual override, but Troy had used his executive code to lock down in siege mode. Already the ship rumbled and groaned as her flight system powered up. There was no way to stop it now. While the designers had factored in the potential for mutiny, none of them had ever considered a scenario where it was the captain hijacking the ship.

A quick roll of his tongue across his lower jaw triggered every frequency aboard ship. "Code Red! All crew return to ship, secure for liftoff! Move it, people, now!" It didn't matter that Troy heard right along with everyone else; the crew had to be warned.

An incoming message across Donovan's frequency: **What the hell's going on, Tom?**

"You tell me! Troy's gone rogue, he's holed up on the command deck … he's initiating immediate launch, without everyone on board."

Silence, thick and heavy.

Palmer's dead.

"What?!"

He's dead … cause unknown.

It was like hitting a wall. That peculiar feeling a person gets when their grip on consciousness or reality slips, like everything is detached, muffled, safely distant; the mind lying to itself. "Oh, shit!" The words were hollow, like they came from the far end of a tunnel, even though the voice was his. A worry for Kate was the only thing crisp and clear to him.

Shake it off, Tom. We have to get those men back on board before it's too late.

There it was: something to focus on. "Yeah, I'm heading for the external hatch."

But it took him too long to get there. As he ran, the *Caliphus* rumbled and shook. At some point ahead of him, a man screamed as the engines engaged, forcing the hatch to close automatically. Tom reached his target moments too late. The first thing he saw was a wide crimson streak running the length of the wall panel that served as the mass-deployment ramp. At the base of that wall, a crewman lay in a crumpled heap and a growing pool of blood. Two others stood close by, frozen in horror at what had just happened.

Cursing, Tom scrambled for a supply locker near the panel, pawing through it until he came up with an extra-long plastic zip tie. He moved to the injured man and looped the strip around the stump where the foot had been severed, yanking it tight until the blood ceased to pump across the floor. Staring in stunned silence at the bloody streak, Tom got the impression the crewman had made a leap for the ramp once it had already begun to close and could not clear his foot in time. It also occurred to him that there were only three miners in the compartment, leaving five men unaccounted for.

"Anyone else make it back on board?" he asked, praying the others had just ignored procedure and left the decontamination unit. But the two men standing shook their heads, guilt shadowing their eyes.

Jared Troy had a lot to answer for. Tom prayed those stranded had been far enough from the blast zone when the engines fired. Their environmental suits contained hydration packs capable of sustaining them for up to a week with strict rationing. They also contained a nutrient solution that would hold them at least as long. Assuming they'd been clear of the liftoff, there was the chance of rescue.

"Okay," Tom said, setting those thoughts aside for now. "We have a situation. You two are to remain suited until cleared by medical. Everything else will be explained when we're safe in orbit. Now help me get your friend strapped into one of those quarantine bunks, then secure yourself for launch." It was difficult to stand, let alone move against the forces of liftoff, but they all managed to strap in.

Donovan, he sent over the foreman's private frequency. **We only got three. One of them needs treatment for a traumatic amputation.**

She cursed quite impressively. **Better than none,** she replied. **Troy can't leave orbit as long as that meteor cloud is in the way … that will give us some time to salvage this situation. Meet me in medbay once the ship reaches apogee. We need to plan.**

O O O

"The unmitigated bastard!" Kate seethed as she paced medbay waiting for the last of the crew to arrive. With her were the four off-shift miners, the two medtechs, and Hal, the third member of the flight crew, in charge of navigation. JP crouched out of the way in the med-chem shower, the only space large enough for him.

Her head whipped around as Tom Henry entered medbay, followed by the rest of the miners on board, the injured man supported in a chair carry between his suited crewmates. The medtechs scrambled to assist, but Kate's attention riveted on Tom. She glanced at the intercom by the hatch before speaking. The activation light remained dark.

"He's diverted all systems control to the command deck and cut us off from the interstellar comm. Can you get us in?"

Tom's brow furrowed as it took him a moment to process what she'd said. As he did, his gaze ran over her, lingering on her bandaged hand, while barely meeting her eye. She saw relief flicker across his expression as he nodded his head. "Yeah, it will take some time, but Troy doesn't know enough to keep me out altogether."

"Good, get on it," she said. "We have to warn the *O'Connor* not to dock with the *Caliphus,* not until we know there's no danger."

Tom had just turned toward the systems substation in the corner when Mac called out from across the room, his words muffled slightly by the mask covering his mouth and nose.

"Donovan! We have trouble!"

Kate, with Tom right behind her, hurried across the bay where the medtechs were working on the injured miner. They'd just started cutting him from his suit, all except the injured leg. Kate grabbed a mask and slipped it on before she rested her hand on Mac's shoulder, leaning around him for a look. She hadn't been able to tell who the injured man was when they'd first brought him in, still suited and slumped over. She saw now that it was Bobby Fletcher, the new man on the crew. *Just a kid, really*, she thought, and she ached for him as she glanced at his mangled ankle. Something struck her as she took in the color of the drying blood, echoing a memory she couldn't place.

And then he looked at her.

His eyes flickered open and he looked right at her. Pain filled his gaze and the whites of his eyes had a decidedly blue cast to them. Kate's breath caught as he shut them again and a rust-tinged tear escaped, leaving a trail in the faint dust she hadn't realized coated his tan skin. Then the memory clicked: just like Palmer, only much faster. His body began to twitch with increasing violence. Seeing that, Mac and Eva scrambled, forcing Kate back as they grabbed the edge of the gurney and shoved it into a quarantine cell similar to the ones down in decon. They then slammed the hatch shut and triggered the lock. From there they moved to their diagnostic stations. Not bothering to sit, their fingers flew over the keys as they darted around the room from system to system.

In Bobby's cell, a nozzle in the wall released a cloud of gas. The man went still, with only his chest rising and falling gently as the power lights flickered on indicating the cell's monitoring sensors had been activated. They did nothing else to care for his wound or make him comfortable.

"What are you doing?" Kate demanded. "You can't just leave him like that!"

She heard the rest of her crew get to their feet and come to stand behind her, grumbling ever louder as the medtechs went about what they were doing without responding. Stalking forward, Kate was about to yank Mac around when Tom intercepted her, laying his hand on her arm. He said nothing, but there was a sad, almost frightened look on his face. She glared at him and pulled away. "Why are you stopping me? It is their duty to take care of that man!" Kate was furious. She didn't know Eva for nothing, but Mac … she'd gotten to know him, to like him. It made no sense that he would ignore Bobby's suffering. "Why?"

Mac spoke over his shoulder, his voice tight and strained, his eyes never leaving his monitor. "There's no more to be done…."

"No more to be done?!"

Eva's head snapped around, her expression livid. "He's already dead, Donovan, all but the dying, just like Palmer, and so are the rest of us if you don't get off our backs and let us try and figure this out. We need to know what's going on in there now, before it's too late.

"Now everyone out of here! Why don't you do something useful, like figure out how to regain control of the fucking ship!"

Tom's arm slid around Kate, and Mac's voice murmured over her private frequency. **He's in no pain, Kate, we made sure he's in no pain.** She recalled the gas that had filled the chamber and nodded, though the medtech couldn't see the motion with his attention still completely on the monitor. Whirling away from Tom—and the sudden, uncharacteristic urge to curl into the protective shelter of his arms—Kate motioned for her people to follow as she left medbay.

JP already waited in the corridor. Not caring if the others would see it as odd, she touched his arm briefly, knowing the sensors there acted much the same as nerve endings. He wouldn't admit to needing the comforting touch, but she did. Jean-Paul was her friend, and though he wasn't in danger of infection the same way the rest of them were, she realized at that moment that he was just as much at risk: stranded and alone, should anything happen to the rest of them, left waiting to die a much slower death.

"Come on," she spoke aloud to those following. On impulse, she reached back, this time taking Tom's hand in hers, pulling him along. "We need a plan."

O O O

So far Tom had regained read-only access to the system via a generic service code, but that was all. And it was all he was likely to get, unless he cracked the captain's command code because Troy had registered a charge of mutiny against each of the crew members with command access, automatically locking them out of the system. None of them had anticipated that. They were currently holed up in one of the storage compartments because everything else was blocked to them.

Tom continued to stare at the monitor, wishing he could accomplish more, particularly as Kate stood with her hand on his shoulder watching everything he did. Sadly, the truth remained; he wasn't a professional hacker. He knew some tricks, but that had only gotten them this far.

"Can you get us a read on what Troy's up to, at least?" Kate asked, pulling Tom from his thoughts. "Maybe slave this monitor to his so we can tell what he's up to?"

"Not … quite … not without him realizing it, but something close." It was brilliant, actually. And he hadn't thought of it. Tom shook his hands loose and rolled his head from side to side, desperately trying to relieve the tension in his neck.

"Okay, here we go …" He punched in the codes for remote diagnostic viewing starting from the time he went on shift to now and there it was, a complete list of the commands Troy had entered since taking over the command deck. As the list scrolled, Tom felt the bile rise from his stomach and creep into his throat. *Kate …* he sent over her private frequency. *Kate …*

What?

He pointed at the screen. *He's preparing to vent the ship.*

Kate sat down hard on a crate beside him. *He's nuts! He'd go right along with us, wouldn't he?*

Tom shook his head, running his finger along several very canny commands the captain had entered. *He's already isolated and sealed the command deck. The only ones sucking vacuum will be us.*

Environmental suits …

Tom shook his head and nodded toward the far end of the storage compartment, where Hal and the miners were looking for any consumables among the stored supplies. *He's locked us out of the crew compartment. The only suits we have are already in use.*

A nearby stack of crates went crashing to the deck as Kate shoved herself to her feet and vented a bit of anger with a well-placed fist. She kicked a few more for good measure. "You done?" he asked out loud.

"It's been a bad day, okay?" she growled through clenched teeth.

He had to smile at her. "Don't worry, it's not over yet." Tom patted the crate for her to sit back down. Apparently she was curious enough to comply.

Now, pay attention here, he told her, going private once more. *We're locked out of the command systems, but it never occurred to Troy to restrict maintenance.* He shot her a smile that had to be just a bit smug as he typed in several commands. *To vent the ship requires the coordination of several interconnected programs, each one responsible for a different stage of the process. This is to prevent accidental venting. It also means that if one of the programs fails to complete its part, none of them can do their job*—with a flourish, he hit the final key—*I've just started the next *system on a self-diagnostic, and scheduled each of the others to begin their own scan, offset by ninety minutes each.**

Done preening? Her words weren't precisely encouraging, but her expression was both relieved and impressed. Tom smiled back at her a bit sheepishly, before he took a chance, leaning closer and murmuring just loud enough for her to hear: "What can I say? Engineers don't often get to show off for the pretty ladies." He watched her flush, but she didn't take the bait … yet.

"How much time did you just buy us?"

"These systems are pretty complex … likely about eighteen hours. Enough time for us to come up with a mechanical workaround."

Kate smiled and for a brief moment all Tom's tension fell away. "My hero," she murmured.

Dare I risk that I'm reading her wrong? Tom reached out to brush a finger lightly across her lips. Kate watched him do it but didn't protest. He was about to lower his mouth to hers when she jerked back and grabbed his hand, holding it up to the light. "Shit …" She whirled away and disappeared out the hatch before Tom even knew what was happening. Puzzled, he looked down at his hand only to notice a faint smudge of red dust on his finger.

"Shit …" Tom slammed his fist into a nearby stack of crates.

It was clearly still a bad day …

… And it wasn't over yet.

O O O

Kate sat on a gurney in medbay staring at the faint tremors running through her hand. Nerves, that was all … so far, anyway. She imagined if she stared hard enough she could see her pores exuding dust. The machinery in the background beeped a bit more vigorously.

"Stop getting yourself all worked up."

The hand Kate had been watching fisted. "Then tell me what we're facing here, Mac. And what you can do about it …"

"Well, you're infected. I suspect we all are, but I can't say to what degree without testing the others. Let's get them down here and see where things stand, then I can brief everyone."

"But …"

"It's in the air, Donovan. We're not talking *if*, we're talking how far along. Getting everyone together isn't going to make a bit of difference."

Kate nodded, but her hand fisted tighter. She accessed the crew frequency and ordered everyone to medbay, then sat back and waited. It wasn't long; Tom was the first through the door. She couldn't meet his eye but was aware, comforted even, as he perched beside her on the gurney, not touching, but close. JP was the last; he moved to the space directly behind her gurney and crouched into his version of sitting. At her back, where no one could see, she briefly felt his robotic hand reach out and lightly touch her shoulder, as a friend would.

"Everyone settle in and listen," Kate raised her voice, sounding steadier than she expected she would. "Mac's got something to say."

They all turned to look at the medtech expectantly. Mac leaned over his keyboard and brought up a view from the external sensors, he then turned and looked each of them in the eye. "It's not dust, it's an airborne organism.

"It doesn't meet any of the organic profiles on record so none of the sensors or diagnostics picked it up. Planetary evaluation didn't catch it because their rovers are made of titanium. The organism feeds on ferrous iron, any source … from raw ore to hemoglobin, it doesn't matter, as long as it's oxidized. Initial warning signs are similar to those for anemia. In the final stages, intense internal pain and what appears to be dust exuding from the skin." He turned and tapped a few more keys, replacing the live feed with a medical slide none of them had the background to identify. He tapped another key and the slide split, the two sides disturbingly similar but for color and some variation in the cellular structures. "The one on the right is a healthy blood sample. The left side is an infected one." When Mac turned to face the group Kate was struck by his somber expression. "Both of these were taken from Fletcher. The first when he was placed in the decon quarantine unit, the second … moments before he died."

There were gasps and curses from the group, and several of the men stood up as if there was something to fight. Kate just went kind of numb. "But, that was just a matter of hours. Palmer took days to even show signs."

She flinched as Mac turned his gaze back to her. There was such sorrow in his eyes. "Eva thought it was a matter of saturation. You breathe it in and there's not much there. Your body can fight it off a while, like you would any airborne infection, until it gets a foothold. If it enters directly through the bloodstream it attacks and multiplies too rapidly for the white blood cells to combat it. The larger the wound and the longer it's open, the more contamination there is, the quicker the body succumbs. Other conditions also affect the rate of decline."

Mac's voice caught as he finished the last statement.

When Kate had first arrived, she'd assumed Eva was resting. Now, she wasn't so sure. Coming off of the gurney, she moved in front of him, where he couldn't avoid her. "Mac, where's Eva?"

The medtech flinched but continued with his briefing as if Kate wasn't there. "In extreme cases where the infected party has a chronic or temporary iron deficiency, such as anemia or rapid blood loss, the organism attacks the iron-rich organs of the body."

"Mac?" Kate tried again.

He continued to ignore her, stepping around her and moving to the pharmaceutical cabinet across the room. Unlocking it, he drew out several large bottles and one smaller one, which he set to the side. Pulling empty prescription pouches from a nearby shelf, he divvyed the bottles among them until he had ten identical bags of large oval brown pills. He tossed one to each of the men.

"Iron pills. Take two now and then one pill twice a day until we find a way out of this. The organism is apparently lazy; it continually goes toward the most easily accessed iron first. This should slow things down."

Kate had enough. She got right in his face and barked: "Mac!"

He stopped still. Didn't look up. When he spoke, she could barely hear him. "She's dead, Donovan … just like Palmer … just like Fletcher … and just like Captain Troy …

"And so are you, unless you start taking these." He handed her the bag of iron pills and the small prescription bottle he'd taken out earlier. She turned it over and read the label, her brow drawing down in confusion. Hormone supplements? Kate looked up and trapped Mac's gaze. And then he spoke, only over her private frequency. **She had her period, Kate … she just … had her period, and now she's dead. She didn't even know.** And then he said aloud, "Take them."

Kate's hand closed reflexively over the prescription bottle. In a woman's normal cycle there was heavy iron loss. Kate shuddered. With a nod she popped the bottle open and took her first dose dry while he watched.

Satisfied, Mac stepped around her and back into the midst of the group.

"Wait …" she called out, spinning around to face him. "Did you say *Troy* is dead?!"

Mac looked over his shoulder and nodded. "He's what broke this, gave us a comparison we needed to isolate what was going on. That's how we found out it will attack the organs. The captain had a history of anemia. He thought he was safe in his suit, but by then it was too late. Because he was in his suit, the medical system automatically tracked his basic biometrics; from nearly start to finish we had a complete profile. Long enough to learn exactly what it does to us … long enough to learn the organism dies very quickly without oxygen.…

"Funny, that," the navigator, Hal, growled out. "So do we!"

If she hadn't been looking in their direction, Kate might have missed the look on Tom Henry's face at Hal's outburst. The look was familiar, just like that little *ah-ha* moment back in the storage compartment. "Tom? Whatcha thinking?"

"I have an idea …" he said. "But first, Mac, how many resuscitation ventilators do you have on board?" Kate thought she saw where he was going with this; ever since the invention of the original Draeger Pulmotor back in 1907, resuscitation ventilators were standard equipment for all mining operations.

A glimmer of hope returned to the medtech's expression as he glanced toward the back of medbay where there was a ward of twelve beds. Each had a ventilator built right into the bulkhead above it. He slowly nodded his head as he answered: "Enough."

"Excellent … is there a master switch capable of activating them all at once?"

Mac nodded, approval clear in the set of his features.

"So," Tom went on, turning back toward the men. "Before the bug got him, Troy initialized a full atmospheric vent on the *Caliphus*…."

Anger kindled in the men's eyes, tightened their jaws. Kate shifted nervously and Tom darted a look in her direction, giving her a bit of a wink.

"Kate and I managed to stall the process, but it's still in place. If we put that process back on track we can purge the organism from the ship."

"What about us?" one of the miners asked. "Mac said we already got it."

"Well …" and here Tom looked nervous, "we'd have to go down with the ship, so to speak…."

The uproar was deafening. As the miners surged forward Tom stood his ground. Kate moved to his side, as did Mac, but the deciding factor was JP, who rose ominously from his crouch.

"Listen to the man," he commanded everyone in the flat, mechanical voice only Kate had heard until now.

Oh my God! You spoke! she sent over JP's private frequency.

Not now! he shushed her, and sheepishly she had to agree. She was just so stunned. "Go on, Tom," JP prompted out loud.

Tom didn't look nearly surprised enough in Kate's opinion, as he continued outlining his plan. "If Mac puts each of us under beforehand, when the ship vents we will suffocate, no pain, no awareness. We program the ventilators to activate two minutes after the ship has been purged. Ventilators come on, we come back … no more bug."

Silence, then Mac cleared his throat. An uncomfortable sound, an unhappy sound.

"Won't work, Tom … the ventilators aren't the type of thing you can program. There is a master button, but it has to be manually operated."

Tom swore softly beneath his breath, only to surge once more as he leaned forward, that gleam back in his gaze. "I'll wear a suit … push the button myself, then when you come around, Mac can do the same for me …"

Mac already shook his head. "There's no way to ensure all the organism is vented that way. You'd just be resetting the clock, eventually we'd reinfect."

"Damn it," Kate said, gripping Tom's arm in support. "There has to be a way to make this work!"

No one said a word. From one face to the other there was some degree of uncertainty, lost looks, and fear. Someone shifted. Someone else coughed, until someone smacked them.

"I can do it."

Everyone turned to look at JP, only they didn't see him; they saw a machine, something Kate was heartily fed up with. **So sue me,** she told Jean-Paul subvocally, before she deliberately violated her contract. "Crew," Kate spoke into the stunned silence, a serene smile on her face, "I'd like you to meet my friend, Jean-Paul Marot, he's a cyborg."

O O O

In the end, they'd cancelled all the diagnostics Tom had scheduled except for the one that had been running. That had allowed them time to get everything set. The crew was strapped in, JP was anchored into place, and in ten minutes the venting process would complete. It was time for him to sedate the crew.

The flashback hit with the force of a comet, leaving Jean-Paul disoriented. He swayed, his consciousness once more doubly trapped: his physical form within a tomb of fallen rock and as a passive observer in his own brain unable to stop the events unfolding against his will. Once more he saw himself reach out, saw the battered and bloody form of his foreman clinging doggedly to life, saw himself slide the end of the umbilical into his friend's neck, stealing Franklin's chance of survival. Saw the blood forever on his own "hand."

For the first time since his encapsulation, Jean-Paul Marot managed a vocal scream. It was pitiful. It came out in a low, constant tone, reminiscent of the ancient time of television and the sound broadcast when a station went off the air.

Not again. Please, God, not again, he thought, the plea held a frantic edge as he felt his mind crumble at the prospect of what he had to do. What if it didn't work? What if some of them … all of them, didn't come back? He was drowning in chemical despair at the risk of being responsible for even more deaths, this time by conscious decision. For God's sake, he'd volunteered! If this did not work, he would well and truly be a murderer. The "scream" increased in volume and intensity until something slapped the side of his brain case.

Tom Henry had extracted himself from his resuscitation ventilator and come up beside him. JP focused on the rage twisting the man's expression. "The longer you take, the more they suffer, the more chance some of them won't survive; either hit the go'damn button or get out of my way."

"But you'll die." His monotone vocals did not convey the anxiety this caused Jean-Paul.

"But *she* won't … not if *I* can help it." Tom's voice was thick with conviction, flavored with disgust at Jean-Paul's hesitation.

And there it was, the real reason JP had volunteered.

"Go back to your bunk, my friend." JP answered. "It's time."

He waited, his titanium hand on the button, as Tom hooked back up.

The last thing Jean-Paul heard as he killed them was Kate's slurred voice over the crew frequency: **You still owe me that steak, Tom Henry.**

Award-winning author and editor **Danielle Ackley-McPhail** has worked both sides of the publishing industry for longer than she cares to admit. In 2014 she joined forces with husband Mike McPhail and friend Greg Schauer to form her own publishing house, eSpec Books (www.especbooks.com).

Her published works include six novels, *Yesterday's Dreams*, *Tomorrow's Memories*, *Today's Promise*, *The Halfling's Court*, *The Redcaps'*

Queen, and *Baba Ali and the Clockwork Djinn*, written with Day Al-Mohamed. She is also the author of the solo collections *A Legacy of Stars*, *Consigned to the Sea*, *Flash in the Can*, and *Transcendence*, the non-fiction writers' guide, *The Literary Handyman,* and is the senior editor of the *Bad-Ass Faeries* anthology series, *Gaslight & Grimm*, *Dragon's Lure*, and *In an Iron Cage*. Her short stories are included in numerous other anthologies and collections.

To learn more about her work, visit sidhenadaire.com.

Into the Abyss

by Dayton Ward

Introduction to "Into the Abyss"

I am a trained scientist and a skeptic, yet ghost stories fascinate me. No doubt part of the fascination comes from the fact my father died when I was quite young. Because of that, I've long questioned what happens to the spark of life in us all when we die, if anything.

As an astronomer, I work in large, mostly empty observatory buildings at night. The buildings are kept dark. It's quiet and the when the wind howls, ventilators rattle. A popular place for tourists and an industrial construction site for 50 years, enough accidents have happened that it's easy to imagine ghosts pressing close to your shoulder when you walk down a darkened corridor. How much creepier must an abandoned space vessel feel with the lack of sound and gravity?

Dayton Ward tapped into both of these primal experiences with his story "Into the Abyss." As a scientist, I hope one day we will understand more about the origins of the universe and humanity, about what gives us the spark of life. Dayton gives us a ghost story with a twist of alien technology and reminds us that there are some things science and experiment might never answer.

Behind you

Casey Flanagan turned, harsh light from the lamps affixed to either side of his suit helmet playing across the dark, cramped day room. The twin beams washed over the octagonal table at the room's center, reflecting off the thin glaze of ice crystals that covered everything. Above and around the table floated assorted utensils and kitchenware, along with a cloud of what Casey figured to be the long-decomposed remnants of partially-consumed meals. Books and magazines, along with loose clothing articles and other debris, drifted about the room and the four passageways leading from the chamber.

Otherwise, the place was empty.

"Jesus," Casey said, hissing the word through gritted teeth and shaking his head.

"You okay, Casey?" said a voice in his helmet speakers. It was Sharon Burnett, pilot of the *Bartleby*, the long-range cargo hauler Casey most definitely wasn't aboard at this moment. As usual, Sharon's tone was one of gentle, almost flirtatious teasing. *"Don't tell me you're scared."*

Casey snorted. "You're damned right, I'm scared. It's creepy as hell in here. Where's Jesse with the power?" Jesse Malone, the *Bartleby*'s engineer, had drawn the undesirable assignment of moving outside the ship in an attempt to connect a power transfer conduit from the hauler to this wreck.

"Maybe fifteen minutes," Sharon replied. *"He's complaining about installing an adapter or something. If you like, I can talk dirty to you to pass the time."*

Her comment had the intended effect, and Casey chuckled despite his unease. Feeling some of his tension drain away, he replied, "Talk's cheap, lady. Save that for when you can make good on it." Something moved to his right, and he angled his head to see what looked like a coffee pot slowly falling toward the floor after having apparently drifted into one of the pipes running along the ceiling. "This place really is eerie, though. Without the gravity, there's crap floating everywhere. It's a real mess."

Only Casey was unaffected by the ship's inactive gravity plating, owing to his suit's magboots. Waving his hand before his helmet's transparasteel faceplate, he watched the glove pass through the haze of food particles and dust floating before him. Though he loathed wearing an EVA suit, Casey was thankful for the helmet and the suit's self-contained oxygen supply, which protected him from what would have to be the foul stench of rotted food.

"That's just nasty," Sharon said, reminding Casey that she, and anyone else on the *Bartleby* who might be accessing the feed from the camera embedded into the front of his helmet, could see whatever was directly in front of him.

"You're telling me," Casey replied. Turning to examine the room's interior again, he made note of the posters affixed to the various bulkheads. Some were of locales like beaches on Earth or one of the colonies on Mars or Titan, while others featured attractive women—and men—in varying states of undress. "Any idea what ship this is, anyway? I haven't found anything like a nameplate or other signage yet."

"It's a mystery, all right," Sharon replied. *"It's got no transponder code, and no hull markings. We'll find out when we power up the onboard computer."*

Casey grunted. "No transponder? Every ship I've ever been on has one, and the batteries they use are supposed to be good for something like fifty years."

Sharon's chuckle made him smile. *"You know as much as I do, sport."*

"Hard to believe it made it all the way out here without anyone ever coming across it," Casey said, maneuvering around the table and heading for the tunnel that according to signage on the day room wall should lead him to the derelict's bridge.

"News flash, kiddo: Space is big. Pass it on."

"I guess," Casey said, conceding the point. With no power and unable to transmit a distress signal, only blind luck had seen to it that the *Bartleby*—on a cargo run to Titan from Mars—had found this wreck at all. Skip Horton, the ship's navigator, had picked up the ship at the extreme range of the hauler's radar systems.

"Find anybody?" Sharon asked, her tone becoming more serious.

Casey shook his head despite there being no one around to see him do it. "Nope. No bodies, no nothing." Glancing to his left, he caught sight of a scuffed brown leather boot, its sole worn and its laces twirling about as it drifted over the table. "There's clothes everywhere, though. It's like everybody shucked their drawers and went skinny dipping or something."

"Now there's an idea I can get behind," Sharon replied, her laugh filling Casey's helmet. He was readying a response—something along the lines of volunteering to get behind *her* during such an excursion—when the pilot said, *"Hang on a sec. The EM field scanner's going nuts."*

Frowning, Casey considered that. The *Bartleby*'s electromagnetic field detection scanners weren't state of the art like those used by the military, but they were still able to sniff out fluctuations and other signs of trouble well enough. "Where's it coming from?"

There was a pause before Sharon replied, *"Somewhere over there. Maybe one of the cargo bays?"*

No sooner had she spoken the words than an abrupt chill coursed down Casey's spine, and a knot of anxiety formed in his gut. If he'd had hair on the back of his neck, he was sure it would've stood on edge.

Help. Us.

"What the …?" It was a woman's voice, but not Sharon's, ringing in Casey's ears and sounding as though it had come from directly behind him. His magboots, heavy and ungainly as they affixed themselves to the deck plating with every step, reverberated through his suit as he tried to re-orient himself. He was aware of an odd blue-white glow coming from just beyond the faceplate's field of vision and turned toward it.

Then something grabbed him.

"Hey!" Casey shouted, his body reacting at the abrupt touch. It took an extra second to realize that was he was sensing was *inside* his EV suit. Inside his *clothes.*

"Casey?" Sharon called out. *"What's going on?"*

Ignoring her, Casey smacked his hands against his torso, searching for whatever was on him. There was an almost electrical tingling sensation now playing across his skin. "Something's inside my suit! Get it off me!"

His feet went out from under him and he cried out in near-panic. He kicked his legs in response, a useless action as he felt himself dragged backwards. Reaching up for whatever gripped him, he found nothing, despite the overwhelming sensation of being pulled into water. The blue light he'd seen now filled his vision, all but blinding him.

"Casey!" Sharon pleaded. *"Damn it, answer me!"*

Terror took hold and his body jerked, muscles racked by spasms as his arms flailed about without his control. An aching tingle flared in his groin and behind his eyes, and his stomach lurched as a wave of nausea washed over him. Casey clawed for any kind of handhold, trying to halt what now felt like a freefall into oblivion. Something cascaded over his body, and when he opened his mouth to scream, it surged past his lips, choking back the words and his breath.

Help! Us!

The woman's pleading voice was the last thing Casey heard.

O O O

"This is all we found."

Erin O'Shea watched Skip Horton drop an armload of clothing and equipment onto the floor of the *Bartleby*'s recreation room before reaching up to wipe sweat from his brow. The navigator was a burly man, at least thirty pounds overweight but still as strong as any man half his age. He wore his long gray hair pulled back in a ponytail, and his beard, also gray, was unkempt, much like Horton himself.

O'Shea studied the components where they lay across the dull, worn deck plates, paying particular attention to the control panel on the front of the suit, which was still active and providing information on the EV suit's status. All of the indicators were green. "It's still sealed?"

"Yep," Horton replied. "It was on the floor of one of the tunnels leading from the day room. Faceplate was still locked down, the gloves were still attached to the sleeves, and seals were all intact." He pointed to the suit's control panel. "There was a system reset. According to the internal clock, it happened right about the same time Sharon lost contact with Casey."

"Any idea what caused the EM spike?" asked O'Shea, reaching up to wipe an errant lock of her black hair from where it had fallen across her left eye.

"Not a clue," Horton said, rising to his feet. "That ship is a dead hulk. Engines are cold, though there's plenty of fuel in the tanks. Their solar collectors were retracted, so it probably just coasted along until the batteries ran dry." He released a tired sigh. "How the hell does that ship drift around out here all these years? They didn't transmit a distress call, at least while the batteries had juice?"

O'Shea shook her head. "Jesse checked the antenna assembly when he was hooking up the power transfer. The circuits for the automated distress beacon are gone, pulled deliberately."

"No transponder, and now no distress beacon?" Horton asked. "Who the hell would do that?"

"Somebody who didn't want this ship tracked," O'Shea replied. "We used to do the same thing when we were running black ops back during the war." Assignments like those were one of the many reasons she'd opted to leave behind military life for a quieter, less dangerous existence. What better way to accomplish that than by shepherding a long-haul freighter between planets?

How's that working out for you now?

Sharon Burnett, who sat with red-rimmed eyes in one of the chairs around the rec room's big circular table, wiped her nose with a handkerchief before asking, "Who cares about any of that? What happened to *Casey*? He said something was inside his suit."

"That's impossible," Malone said, shaking his head and pointing toward the pile of gear on the floor. "It was locked up tight. No way anything got inside."

Everyone looked up as the rec room door opened and Jesse Malone, a muscled man in his late thirties who served as the *Bartleby*'s engineer, stepped inside. "You're not going to believe this," he said without preamble, holding up a portable computer tablet as he crossed to a lone terminal sitting atop a table situated along the far wall. He pulled a chair from the dining table with him and sat down in front of the terminal, inserting his tablet into the workstation's receiver slot. "Check this out."

O'Shea felt her stomach tighten in both anticipation and dread as she moved to stand behind the engineer and look over his shoulder. "What did you find?" she asked, uncertain as to whether she wanted to know the answer.

Swiveling his chair back to face the computer, Malone crossed his arms. "You tell me. This is a frame from the video feed we were getting from Casey's helmet camera. According to its time stamp, it's just after the EM spike, and that's all there was before Casey's suit reset."

Frozen on the screen was a still image from the paused video playback. Leaning closer, O'Shea squinted for a better look at the grainy, low-light footage Casey Flanagan's helmet camera had captured. She recognized the interior of the derelict ship's day room, cloaked as it was in near-total darkness save for Flanagan's suit lights. Neither the room itself nor the debris floating about it in the absence of powered grav plating interested her.

"What is that?" Horton asked, his voice a haunted whisper.

Just visible at the far left of the stilled image and at the edge of the light beam from Flanagan's helmet, was the wraithlike figure of a naked woman.

O O O

It took more than six hours to charge the dead freighter's depleted batteries, after which it was a simple task for Jesse Malone to activate its power systems. An hour after that, the gravity plating and environmental control systems were reactivated.

"According to its onboard computer, it's the Resolute,*"* Sharon Burnett said, her voice filtered into O'Shea's right ear via the wireless headset she wore as she and Skip Horton made their way down one of the ship's narrow, low-ceilinged corridors. *"It's a long-haul freighter owned by McAllister Interplanetary. Listed as missing during a run from Mars to Europa about twelve years ago."*

"Never heard of it," O'Shea said. "Then again, MacInt does a lot of contract work for the military, so it'd make sense for a bucket like this to keep a low profile." McAllister Interplanetary, like the company which owned the *Bartleby*, Okagawa-Gold, had enjoyed profitable relationships with Earth government contracts for decades. Whereas the majority of OG's government work tended toward the various civilian agencies with facilities and ventures throughout the populated solar system, MacInt preferred the more lucrative prospects to be had contracting for the military. It was one of the reasons O'Shea had opted against working for them, instead choosing to accept an offer from its chief competitor.

"That should be the main cargo bay," Horton said, pointing toward a thick hatch at an intersection in the corridor. Wiping his nose, he shook his head. "Damn, but it stinks down here." While EV suits no longer were required for moving about, the lingering stench of rotted food was everywhere.

As bad as the corridor smelled, it was nothing compared to the cargo bay, which O'Shea discovered when Horton pressed the control to open its main access hatch.

"Jesus!" she hissed through gritted teeth as she reached up to cover her nose. The odor emanating from the chamber was all but overwhelming, and O'Shea forced herself to suppress an urge to gag.

"It's like my first apartment," Horton said as he crossed the deck toward a control console. A moment later, lights activated throughout the bay and the sound of massive fans echoed in the chamber. "Main power was off in here. Give it a few minutes to clear the worst of it."

Nodding, O'Shea studied the room's interior, her attention focusing on an oversized crate, open on one side and occupying the center of the cargo bay's deck. "What is that?" she asked. The crate was at least three meters tall, though only half as wide. Walking toward it, she noticed that it bore the logo and other familiar markings of McAllister Interplanetary. Chief among the signage were labels on each of the two sides she could see, which warned in identical text: "TO BE OPENED BY AUTHORIZED PERSONNEL ONLY. M.I. DIRECTIVE 92055."

Moving to stand alongside O'Shea, Horton pointed to the upper right-hand corner of the side nearest to them, which was free of markings. "No package ID."

"I've seen that sort of thing before," O'Shea said, stepping to where the crate's side panel had been pried open. "Sometimes, military shipments get mixed in with civilian freight hauls, when it's something they want kept quiet. Why they thought not marking the crates like all the others was smart camouflage, I'll never know."

She tapped the panel where burn marks around a joint told her it had been cut away. Damage was visible from where something had been forced between the seams to pull away the panel. "Look how thick these walls are," she said, running her hand along the container's smooth side. Scuff marks on the deck beneath the panel testified to the crate's weight and robust construction. "Whatever's inside, they didn't want anybody getting to it."

"You think the crew got curious?" Horton asked, frowning. "It's a long way from Mars to Europa. Maybe they were bored."

Tapping the side of the container where the panel had been pulled open, O'Shea said, "This thing was vacuum-sealed and then welded shut. You ever been bored enough on one of these trips to do that?"

"Nope," Horton replied. "Then again, the stuff we haul is all marked, and we know what's inside." He gestured toward other containers stored in the bay. Everything else appeared to be the typical assortment of tools, equipment, and food stores one would expect to find on a freighter bound for Europa from Mars. "And what's with the 'authorized personnel' crap?" he asked, tapping the label with its angry red lettering. "Who on Europa has to be 'authorized' to open a frappin' shipping container?"

"Good question," O'Shea said as she reached for a small flashlight hooked to her belt. Directing the beam into the container, she got her first look at the crate's contents. "Look at this."

Horton leaned around the open panel to see inside. "Son of a bitch."

To O'Shea's admittedly inexperienced eye, the lone item inside the cargo crate looked like it could be a component from what would have to be a very large engine, larger than anything she'd ever seen or worked on. A gold, cylindrical base supported a column at least twice the size of a normal man and constructed from what might have been glass, though when O'Shea tapped on it, the echo sounded as though it were metal. At the top of the column was another gold end cap, similar in size and shape to the base. Etched into the gold caps were ornate glyphs that O'Shea didn't recognize. "What the hell is this?" When she laid her flat hand against the column's surface, she felt a low reverberation coming from inside the object.

It was at that moment that the voice of Jesse Malone crackled in her ear. *"Erin, Skip,"* the engineer said. *"Where are you guys?"*

"In the cargo bay," O'Shea replied, reaching up to adjust the microphone of her wireless headset so that it was closer to her mouth. "Why? What's going on?"

The engineer replied, *"We're picking up another EM spike. It looks to be coming from in or near. . . ."*

"Erin!"

Startled, O'Shea looked to see Horton backing away from where a ball of bright blue energy had appeared, suspended above a stack of two smaller cargo containers. It expanded outward with each passing second, contorting and elongating until O'Shea realized it now was taking on human form.

"Sweet mother of Jesus," she said, the words catching in her throat. "Is it her?"

"Who gives a shit? Let's get the hell out of here!" Horton shouted, his meaty hand clamping around O'Shea's arm as though to pull her from the cargo bay.

The thing grabbed her other arm.

Help me!

It moved fast, its speed such that O'Shea barely had time to realize it was coming toward her before she felt something cold and clammy close around her bicep. Then her body jerked as though she'd brushed an open flame and she cried out in pain. She lashed out with her other arm and felt resistance, as though punching through some kind of flexible barrier. Pulling back her arm, she looked up to stare into the blue, distorted, pain-racked face of Casey Flanagan.

O'Shea screamed. The bizarre apparition that might once have been Casey held both of her arms now, his eyes wide and his expression twisted with terror and agony. It opened its mouth as if to mimic her cry, but no sound came forth. Instead, Casey's voice sounded in her mind.

Help! Me!

O'Shea felt something cold and hard pelting her skin. Her vision was all but overwhelmed by the blue energy pulsating around her, growing outward from Casey as he gripped her. Then all color drained away and she was looking into absolute, endless blackness.

Make it stop!

Help us!

Voices upon voices, all calling out in staccato fashion, flooded over her. They battered her consciousness with pleas for help and cries of horror and agony, begging for escape from whatever held them in its grasp. They all came too fast, too loud, too powerful for her to decipher. If only she could …

Something yanked at the collar of her jacket. Risking a glance over her shoulder, O'Shea saw that it was Horton, who somehow had secured himself to a nearby support stanchion with a thick rubber cargo strap wrapped around his waist. He now grasped her with both hands, heaving her backward with a groan of exertion that echoed in the cargo bay. O'Shea felt Flanagan's grip break and she stumbled before falling in a disjointed heap to the deck. Rolling over, she was in time to see Casey's body seemingly dissolving as it tumbled end over end away from her. His mouth opened to release a silent scream before he disappeared altogether, leaving O'Shea and Horton alone in the cargo bay.

No, not alone, O'Shea realized, still hearing the plaintive cry of Casey Flanagan echoing in her mind.

Help me.

O O O

"We need to get the hell out of here," Horton said. "Right now."

O'Shea stood in one corner of the day room, arms folded across her chest with her hands pressed against her sides. *Why's it so damned cold in here?*

"Not without Casey," she said, shaking her head. "I don't know what this is about, but until I do, we're not leaving." In another life, one she'd tried to put behind her, she'd been forced to leave behind wounded or dead soldiers. It was one of the things which had made her resign her commission and turn her back on the service.

She wasn't doing that here today.

"What happened to him?" Horton asked, though when O'Shea looked at him she saw that he didn't appear to be posing the question to anyone in particular. "What *the hell* happened to him?"

"It's like the woman we saw on the camera feed," O'Shea said.

"So where *is* he?" asked Sharon, sitting at the dining table with a half-smoked and seemingly forgotten cigarette in her right hand. She had been all but inconsolable after hearing of O'Shea and Horton's encounter with Flanagan.

O'Shea shook her head. "I don't know."

"Guys," Jesse Malone called out from where he was sitting at the computer terminal, breaking O'Shea's reverie. "Check this out." As the rest of the group gathered around him, he said, "I found a personal log on the secondary data server." He tapped a control on the tablet, and the image of a man, perhaps of late middle-age, appeared on the screen. His brown-gray hair was receding and he wore a pair of obsolete wire-rimmed glasses perched on the bridge of his long, narrow nose. Deep lines creased his forehead, and there were dark circles under his eyes.

"My name is Matthew Bendis," the man said, speaking with an English accent. *"I work for the McAllister Interplanetary Corporation. I'm also a passenger on this vessel. I'm sorry to have to be the one speaking to you, but the rest of the* Resolute*'s crew are gone, to where I haven't the faintest clue. If you're watching this, then you need to stop, get as far away from this ship as you're able, find some way to destroy it, and then finish watching."* He leaned closer, his expression turning hard. *"Chances are that if you're watching this, it might already be too late."*

"What the hell?" Sharon asked, and O'Shea turned to see her expression of confusion and even slight panic. She could sympathize, given the knot of uncertainty forming in her own gut.

On the screen, Bendis said, *"The* Resolute *was contracted to transport a piece of classified equipment to our research facility on Europa. If you're watching this, then you've likely already found that item."*

"You ain't lying," Horton said.

"The item in question was but one piece of a large object found by a McAllister Interplanetary construction crew on Mars," Bendis continued, *"while excavating a cavern to serve as an underground storage facility. It was quite an extraordinary find, appearing to be the remnants of a crashed space vessel of indeterminate origin, but almost certainly not belonging to anyone from the planet Earth."*

"Is he serious?" Sharon asked. "Space aliens?"

Bendis said, *"The craft, if that's what it was, hadn't fared well in whatever incident brought it this underground cavern. Indeed, we remain at a loss as to explain how it got there in the first place. We conducted a thorough investigation, and soon determined that the craft was inert, with a single exception."*

"The thing in the cargo bay," Horton said.

"That single component appeared at first to also be without power," Bendis said, *"but a rudimentary EM and radiation scan told us that it has some kind of internal energy source. We soon realized that it was capable of drawing power from any source, no matter how small. Of course, we had no idea what it was supposed to do, other than act as what appeared to be part of the craft's propulsion system. We found no obvious points of access, and so were unable to get a look at its internal composition. Not wishing to take any chances, my superiors ordered it shipped to Europa for further study."*

He paused, flinching as though stung or struck by something off-camera. Grimacing in apparent discomfort, he reached up to massage his temples. *"We packed the item in a special crate containing an electromagnetic dampening field generator, in order to prevent it from drawing power from the* Resolute *while the ship was in transit. However, we were less than halfway to Europa when that generator failed, and Eddie Coburn, the ship's engineer, reported an odd energy spike. It didn't take long to figure out that it was coming from our precious cargo."* When he paused again, it was to shake his head and release a tired sigh. *"I should've had him push the damned thing out the airlock."*

Malone said, "I don't think I like where this is going."

"Eddie opened the box and we detected a power reading from inside, but it was nothing significant, so we thought nothing of it. Then, two days later, the ship's navigator disappeared. The assistant engineer found her clothes in the cockpit, but she was nowhere to be found. We searched the entire ship to no avail."

"I know where she went," Malone said, reaching for the terminal and pausing the playback. He then called up additional information from his computer tablet, and new pictures appeared on the monitor. The first was the video still Malone had captured from Flanagan's helmet camera, whereas the second was an attractive brunette woman, smiling for the photograph included in her McAllister Interplanetary employee file. Beneath the picture was her name and position: Allison Chambers, navigator, CSV *Resolute.*

"Oh my god," she said, feeling her jaw slacken as she realized what she was seeing. "Is this right?"

"As near as I can tell," Malone replied, before resuming the video playback.

"Working with Eddie," Bendis said, *"I determined that the device was generating an all-but undetectable electromagnetic field, which was getting stronger the longer it had energy on which to draw. We cut power to the cargo bay and immediately saw a reduction in the EM readings."* He stopped to swallow, and when he again looked into the camera, his expression had darkened. *"That's when we saw Allison. She … just appeared out of the bloody air, arms and legs flailing like she was fighting to keep from being dragged underwater."* He looked away from the screen for a moment, and O'Shea could see that he was having trouble with whatever memories of the incident he was trying to recall. *"She was naked, and her skin was so pale, as though she was a ghost."*

"Just like Casey," Sharon whispered.

They watched Bendis close his eyes and lean back in his chair, pressing his hands to his chest.

"What's the matter with him?" Sharon asked. "Is he having a heart attack?"

"Maybe," O'Shea replied.

Regaining some of his composure, Bendis continued, *"We tried to grab her, but it was like touching a live wire. She latched onto me and then, just for a moment, I experienced this sensation of standing at the edge of a cliff, looking into nothing. Black, and cold, it was an utter abyss, pressing in on me from all sides. Then, Eddie pulled me free and I let go of Allison, and she … disappeared."* O'Shea watched as tears formed in the corners of the man's eyes.

"Looking into nothing," O'Shea repeated, turning the phrase over in her mind as she recalled her encounter with Flanagan.

On the screen, Bendis leaned closer to the visual pickup. *"Of course, there are no such things as ghosts. There had to be an explanation rooted in science. The electromagnetic field emitted by the device was the key. Once we realized that, it was too late. We'd all been exposed to the electromagnetic radiation it had been emitting for the past three days, and the effects were becoming obvious. Anything living was affected—plants, fruits and vegetables from our perishable stores. All of it was just fading away like it was never there."*

"This is insane," Malone said, shaking his head.

Meanwhile, Bendis said, *"The EM radiation emitted by the device is at a frequency far beyond anything I've ever seen before, possibly owing to whatever power source is at the object's center. It seems to have the effect of altering living matter at a molecular level, shifting it ... out of synch, for lack of a better term, with our natural surroundings. Whether that means some other form of visible spectrum, or another dimension, or something else entirely, I have no idea. The rest of the crew followed in short order. I watched Eddie disappear before my very eyes, and he told me before he shifted that he could feel the effects of the transition taking hold. It's rather like I'm feeling now, actually."*

"Jesus Christ," Horton said, talking more to himself than anyone else. "It's happening to him."

Bendis reached off-screen and his trembling hand came back with a glass of water, some of which he spilled down his shirt as he tried to take a drink. *"Allison and other members of the crew reappearing later supports my theory that the effects might be reversible, if the object's EM field can be disabled or at least altered significantly. However, we found no way of turning it off, with the possible exception of killing all power aboard the ship, which I've done. Now all I can do is wait to see if the crew shifts back, or I join them."* His body convulsed again, and he grunted in obvious distress. *"I don't think I'm going to make it."*

The video playback stopped at that point, and the screen went blank.

"We've got to get out of here," Horton said, shaking his head and making no effort to suppress the panic gripping him. "Obviously, whatever that guy hoped would happen never happened. He shut off all the power, and the thing still ate him, or whatever the hell it did, along with the rest of the *Resolute* crew, and Casey."

"Remember what he said," Sharon countered, gesturing with her hands as though trying to pull from her mouth the words that wouldn't come of their own volition. "He thought it had a battery of some kind. If he's right, that thing was buried on Mars for who knows how long before they found it. What if it's the same thing here, with it just sitting down in the cargo bay, hibernating or whatever, until we show up with new power for it to chew on?"

"And what if he's right about the other thing?" O'Shea asked. "If we can shut it off, the effects might reverse themselves."

"What if he was wrong?" Horton asked, his voice raising an octave. "You want to hang out here long enough to see what happens?"

O'Shea shook her head. "Just long enough to get Casey back."

O O O

It was a simple task for Sharon Burnett to order the *Resolute*'s computer to deactivate the freighter's power systems. With that done, Jesse Malone donned an EV suit and detached the power conduit feeding juice to the derelict's depleted batteries. The only thing tying the two ships together was the flexible docking collar between their respective airlocks, and if it hadn't meant the pain in the ass of getting into EV gear to make the crossing, O'Shea would have severed that, too.

That was the easy part, she reminded herself as she watched Malone setting the explosive charge inside the packing crate which contained the bizarre device. "Almost done?" she asked, standing behind the engineer and aiming a penlight at the explosive so that Malone could see what he was doing. For a moment, she wondered if the strange alien device might be drawing energy even from the light's batteries.

Malone nodded, not looking up from the work he was performing on the squat yellow rectangle he'd affixed to the inside of the packing container. "I just need to set the detonator, and we can close it up." Pausing in his fussing over the device, he looked at her. "You really think this'll work?"

"Only one way to find out," O'Shea replied. Recalling that a consignment of the explosive charges was among the other supplies and equipment the *Bartleby* carried for the Okagawa-Gold mining facility on Titan, she figured the miners awaiting the cargo wouldn't miss one of the devices. Not that she cared, either way.

"Somebody's going to be royally pissed that we blew up their toy," Malone said, keying instructions to the keypad set into the charge's detonator.

O'Shea shrugged. "They can kiss my ass."

"You think that box is enough to contain the explosion?" Horton called out across the darkened cargo bay from where he stood near the reinforced hatch at the room's far end. Except for the bare minimum required to sustain life support and the grav plating, main power was off throughout the *Resolute*, and the navigator was visible thanks only to the portable light affixed to the strap he wore around his head.

"If it doesn't," Malone said, "we'll be the first to know." He pressed another key on the detonator's control pad and O'Shea heard a trio of beeps. "That's it," he said. "Let's close this thing up."

Working together, O'Shea and Malone forced the crate's open side panel closed, and once it was in place the engineer reached into the satchel slung over his left shoulder and extracted a magnetic emergency bulkhead patch. He slapped the patch across the seam connecting the panel to where it had been separated from the crate's corner brace. "That probably won't hold worth a damn."

"Doesn't matter," O'Shea said, slapping him on the shoulder. "Let's go."

They were halfway across the cargo bay, running to where Horton stood in the open doorway, when the voice echoed in her mind.

Help us!

"Did you hear that?" she asked, stopping and casting the penlight's feeble beam into the darkness around them.

"What?" Malone asked, barely visible though he stood less than an arm's length from her.

A blue luminosity was growing out of the gloom, overpowering O'Shea's flashlight, and the same odd sensation played across her exposed skin, just as it had when …

"Casey!"

Seven figures were materializing out of nothingness, with limbs and heads emerging from the amorphous blue globules now drifting within the cargo bay.

The crew of the *Resolute*. And Casey Flanagan.

"Holy Mary, Mother of God," Malone said.

Help! Us!

Flanagan's pleas hammered her mind, feeling as though they might force their way through her skull, and in that moment of intense pain, O'Shea suddenly understood.

Grabbing Malone by the arm, O'Shea yelled, "We've got to blow it right now! Come on!" They sprinted to the exit, with Horton barely managing to step aside as they plunged through the hatch. Turning, she saw the seven figures swimming in the darkness, their bodies radiating an incandescent indigo energy. All of them had formed now: naked, pale, and withering in whatever tortures now consumed them. One of the apparitions turned toward her, and O'Shea saw Casey Flanagan reaching out, his mouth twisting in a silent scream of agony.

"Do it!" she yelled, stabbing the control panel next to the doorway and cycling shut the hatch before throwing herself against the bulkhead and dropping into a protective crouch. Horton followed suit, leaving Malone standing near the hatch and peering through its reinforced transparasteel viewport. He said nothing as he held a remote-control transceiver in his right hand, and his thumb pressed a lone button set into the unit's face.

Everything around them heaved and groaned in protest as the charges detonated, and the bulkhead rang and reverberated with the force of shrapnel pelting it from inside the cargo bay. The flash of the explosion lit up the corridor, and Malone was forced to turn away from the viewport and shield his eyes. The deck heaved beneath O'Shea's feet as the ship absorbed the blast, and she silently counted off the seconds until she expected to feel the rush of air escaping through any hull breaches.

Enough elapsed to reassure her that she probably wasn't going to die from asphyxiation or decompression, at least not today.

"Everybody okay?" asked Sharon Burnett, her voice sounding distant and yet so welcoming in O'Shea's headset. *"Somebody talk to me!"*

Accepting Malone's hand and allowing the engineer to pull her to her feet, O'Shea adjusted her lip mike. "Yeah, we're here. Stand by." She nodded to Horton, who had to use the manual override to open the cargo bay hatch.

"Guys," he said, shining his light into the chamber.

O'Shea moved so that she could peer inside, following the track of Horton's beam. Though the compromised side panel had ruptured and come apart from the force of the explosion, the bulk of the crate had withstood the worst of the blast. As for the mysterious alien device, what little remained of it lay scattered across the deck, shards of gold and glass or crystal reflecting in the flashlight beam.

But there were no bodies.

"Where are they?" Malone asked.

"It didn't work," O'Shea replied. "The explosion must've just pushed them farther back to … wherever."

Only then did O'Shea realize that the voices calling to her from that unending darkness had fallen silent. They no longer pressed against her mind.

She felt nothing.

"What the hell do we do now?" Horton asked.

"Nothing," she said, feeling the sadness wash over her. "They're gone." Whatever had taken Casey Flanagan, Matthew Bendis, and the crew of the *Resolute* from this world had apparently laid final claim to them. Had she killed them, or simply consigned them to eternal torment in some other plane of existence?

I'm sorry, Casey.

At the edge of her consciousness, so faint that she was only just able to sense it, came a small, weak voice—it might have been Flanagan—calling to her from the abyss.

Help me.

Dayton Ward is a New York Times bestselling author or co-author of nearly thirty novels and novellas, often working with his best friend, Kevin Dilmore. His short fiction has appeared in more than twenty anthologies, and he's written for magazines such as *Kansas City Voices*, *Famous Monsters of Filmland*, *Star Trek* and *Star Trek Communicator*, as well as the websites Tor.com, StarTrek.com, and

Syfy.com. Before making the jump to full-time writing, Dayton was a software developer, having discovered the private sector and the perpetual fear of outsourcing after spending eleven years in the US Marine Corps. Though Dayton lives in Kansas City with his wife and daughters, he's a Florida native and maintains a torrid long-distance romance with his beloved Tampa Bay Buccaneers. Visit him on the web at daytonward.com.

LISTENING

by Anna Paradox

Introduction to "Listening"

Have you ever been trapped in a car, an airplane, or a small office with someone you really didn't like? Imagine how much worse it would be to spend three months in such a situation, especially when your life literally depended on the space you were trapped in. That's what it could be like to travel aboard a space vessel. Now imagine that someone aboard the space vessel is a homicidal maniac, then you have the situation Anna Paradox set up in "Listening."

Anna avoids the shocks and scares you might expect from a horror piece, instead treating this as something of a locked room mystery. In doing so, she makes the horror of the situation all the more real and plausible. It becomes easier to imagine yourself getting into this situation and helps feed the urgency of finding a way out … if you can.

My cargo loader called in sick three days before launch.

"Selene, I've been grounded." Neil looked pale on the screen in my cabin. "Health inspection says I have the flu."

"The flu? Where did you pick that up?"

"Probably some tourist who couldn't put off their vacation on Luna just because they had the sniffles. I was down in Luna Mall taking Ivy to dinner a couple weeks ago. Earth inspection must have let another one through."

"Damn, Neil. I hate replacing crew on short notice."

"Don't I know it. Plus, now company regs will keep me grounded at least four weeks without pay."

"Will you be all right?"

"Course I will. I just hate missing the run."

"Have Ivy or the boys caught it?"

"Not so far." He coughed dryly. "I'm on house quarantine. A couple weeks in the bubble on rest and fluids, and I'll be fine."

I frowned. "Neil, make sure you go to the clinic if you feel any worse."

"What can they do that we can't do at home? Just save me a place for the next run. I'll try to get a local temp placement and see you when you get back."

"You know I will, Neil. Get well soon."

"Give the ol' red planet some footprints for me."

I put in the call to Human Resources with misgivings. Our plasma drives would carry us to Mars in forty-one days. We were scheduled for ten days at Deimos Port, then the return trip. The twelve crew of *Copernicus VII* relied on one another. Neil had been a steady and proficient cargo manager for six years. Three months is a long time to spend on a small ship with a stranger. This close to launch, I'd have to take whoever HR had available.

HR promised me a replacement later in the day. I told them to have him meet me at Dock D for an interview. They reminded me that just cause must be demonstrated to turn down a posting.

I suited up and went to give *Copernicus* a walk around.

She was a fine ship of the line, sitting tall and proud on her engines on the Luna plain. We'd attached the crew airlock yesterday. The captain and I boarded first, through the long, airtight corridor from the underground facilities of Dock D. Company security checked us through as usual. Dave, the first engineer, was on board, and the other two engineers would follow later in the day. I'd expected Neil today, too, to begin inspecting and loading cargo through the big tunnel to be attached this afternoon.

The trap door to Dock D for the cargo arm was closed. We'd open the cargo doors to receive the arm after I had a loader. I ducked under the crew walkway. Everything looked good. *Copernicus*'s name stood in bright red letters on her smooth silver skin. The fence was in place and unbroken. Nothing out of place. I leaned my helmet against the ship, taking in her normal buzzes and echoes. Then I gave her a reassuring pat, let myself back in the inspection airlock, desuited, and went to see the captain.

O O O

Captain Aldrin Larssen's door was open. He looked up from his immaculate desk when I knocked, and waved me in. "Complications already," he said.

"You've heard about Neil?"

He shook his head. "Grounded?"

"Regs and flu."

"Bad break. Do the best you can for us with the replacement. Like you always do."

"Thanks."

He tapped the screen on his desk. "No, I meant this. Headquarters is displacing our passengers for a bigwig. They want us to join the suites to accommodate the owner's son. Apparently, he's going to Mars to oversee operations, and we get to give him the ride."

I considered what we'd need for forty days of formality. "So, dinners with the captain every night and butler service for breakfast and lunch?"

He scrolled down. "That's odd—actually, no. Says he is recovering from anti-agathic surgery, and will want his privacy. Plans to bring on his own food and keep to his room."

"I won't rely on that."

"Good plan. Sort it all out." The captain ran a hand through his thinning sandy hair. "I'll send the formal apology to the bumped passengers and a get well note to Neil. Has the third thing gone wrong yet?"

It was an old joke between us: troubles always come in threes, like my ex-husbands or his children. We exchanged small smiles, and I said, "Not yet. I'll keep a watch for it."

I sketched a salute at him, although the company said we were no longer military, and took my leave.

O O O

We had two passenger suites, side by side. Normally, each room held four bunks. Weight matters when accelerating to reach another planet. It was rare someone felt rich enough to pay for an entire room, much less two. We could unbolt all but one of the bunks, open up the door between the rooms, and add a table and a couple of chairs. I wrote out the instructions for the ground crew, and called them in. We'd planned to take precious metals as our discretionary cargo to Mars. I cancelled it, and arranged a ton of canned luxury foods instead.

Then it was time to interview Neil's replacement. I took the crew walkway back through security to Dock D.

I had a few minutes with his file before Timothy Harvey joined me. He'd been with the company for two years, and had done fill-in work on ships for seven months of that. Only one long trip. Born on Earth, came to Luna just before the company hired him, mostly worked in company warehouses. The supervisor comments were all the non-committal generalities that either meant he hadn't stood out or the writers wanted to avoid a lawsuit. They weren't much help.

I stood to shake his hand when he came in. He was younger than I expected, slightly heavy with light green eyes. "Pleased to meet you. What would you like me to call you?"

He slid into the chair across from me. "Tim's fine."

"Thanks, Tim. I'm Selene Terrell, vice-president of *Copernicus VII*. HR offered you to replace an ill crewman of mine for our trip to Mars."

"Yes, ma'am."

"How did you like your last trip to Mars?"

"It was fine." He became more animated for a moment. "The food was a little monotonous near the end."

"It does get a little dull when the fresh foods run out. Why did you decide to come to Luna?"

"I had a friend, said the company was hiring, and it was good pay."

"What was his name?"

"Her name was Mae. Mae Ilahoto."

"It says here you're single. Anyone you are likely to miss while we're in transit?"

He shook his head. "No one in particular. It's only three months and video calls are almost as good."

"I find the lag makes them a bit unsatisfying."

"It won't be a problem."

I clicked the point inside my pen. "Here, catch."

He fumbled a little, but didn't drop it. I remembered Neil's grace and fast reflexes as he caught a falling box, and sighed inwardly. But there was nothing here that I could legitimately object to. I held out my hand for the pen. "Good enough. Welcome to the *Copernicus VII.*"

His hand was a little clammy when he shook mine goodbye. I wiped my palm on my pants after he left, and hoped for the best.

O O O

Back on the ship, more crew had boarded, and I let them know we'd be having a new cargo manager this trip.

"Flu?" asked Kate Heinish. "I hadn't heard of any on Luna."

I frowned. As ship's surgeon, she usually knew of new infections on Luna. We kept close tabs on them—both because they could spread rapidly through our closed air systems and because they were rare. Since we'd built the Lunar ecology from the dirt up, we'd been able to leave most pathogens on Earth. That meant the Luna-born were often more susceptible to the ones that came through. Flu should have been news.

"Do you think Neil might have misdiagnosed?"

She nodded. "But you know they won't change their minds in time for him to join the flight."

"That's true." Health inspection would quarantine him on suspicion at least four days, and we launched in three. I put it out of my mind.

O O O

I checked in on Tim several times a day during loading, and it seemed to go fine. Newton and Mare, who assisted Neil pre-launch, knew how *Copernicus* liked her balance. And if Neil would have packed the holds a little more elegantly and efficiently, it was still good enough.

Invictus Sadad, the owner's son, boarded through security with his face bandaged. His luggage came through the cargo doors, an entire cartload. Tim crashed the cart into the corridor wall while bringing it to our guest's cabin. Later, the captain asked, "Think that was our third trouble?"

"Maybe. If it was, we got off light. Mr. Sadad hasn't complained."

"Good enough," he said.

I called Neil at T minus 2 hours, and he said he was feeling better.

And so we launched.

O O O

Halloween fell one week into our trip. I woke from unsettled dreams, thinking I'd heard something—a scrape and a thump. Those sounds didn't belong on my ship. Was it part of the dream? I dressed quickly, and went to walk the corridors of *Copernicus.*

There was nothing unusual in the hall outside my cabin. We offer what privacy we can, but air must flow throughout the ship, and metal walls ring on impact. We twelve crewmates slept in shifts, four at a time. The steady growl of the engines, the hum of the air pumps, and the talking and moving of the crew make a steady background to our journey. Meals create a bit more sound, and if the engineers need to hammer or a couple fights, we all know it. That bump and scrape—if I'd really heard them—didn't belong.

And my footsteps should echo just so in the corridor. Instead, they were muffled. There was something around the corner.

I spotted the photocell near the floor, tripped it and jumped back. A scarecrow jumped towards me, bouncing into the spot where I would have stood.

I called Dave directly. "Dave Callahan, come to corridor C immediately."

"Ah, Selene, I should have known you would find it. Can't we leave it longer?"

"No. Come."

He arrived rushing. "Selene, it's just a Halloween joke."

"Really? What's that?" I pointed to the blade in the scarecrow's hand, dripping with a black ichor.

"What?! I didn't put that there, Selene, I swear." He reached his hand toward it, and I knocked it away.

"Don't touch it. We'll have Kate analyze it. That blade would have cut me in the stomach."

"Selene, you know I'd never hurt the crew."

"Dave, we've been shipping together for five years, and each year you've done something more elaborate for Halloween. I don't know what to think. Confine yourself to quarters until further notice."

"But—"

"No, I mean it, and now. You don't want to give me any more reasons to be mad at you."

He met my eyes, then nodded and left. I called Kate to examine the evidence.

O O O

Kate sniffed the knife, and frowned. "That's vaguely familiar, but I can't place it. It'll take me a while to analyze this. I'll let you know as soon as I can." We worked together to take the knife out of the scarecrow and drop it into a sterile container without touching it. It had been crudely shoved through the hand of the scarecrow.

The scarecrow was a mechanical marvel. Dave had used some of his own clothes over a wire frame, and would no doubt be able to reuse most of the parts again later. A paper hat and a few tufts of straw completed the illusion. For the moment, we carefully gathered everything and took it to the clinic.

"Will you be able to get fingerprints?"

"I don't know. I don't have any special powder or training for that. It may be easier to get DNA." She set the canister on the spectrograph table and began to open the lid. Before she could finish, an alarm went off, with flashing lights and loud blaring.

"What is it?" I yelled, covering my ears.

Kate went to the readout, pressed a few buttons, and tightened the lid again. The light continued to flash, but the sound stopped. "Ricin! That should never have made it past the security scanners."

"How did it get on my ship?"

"That doesn't make sense. It's one of the substances the security scanners particularly check for. My spectrograph is set for wide scale analysis, so it didn't go off until it detected a dangerous concentration. But the security scanners react to one part in ten million—someone would have to encase it in steel, then scour the exterior, then sterilize what they cleaned it with and do it two or three more times. And then we'd want to know what was hiding in the steel. This should never have made it on the ship."

"Unless someone turned off the scanner. I knew I didn't trust Tim Harvey! I—"

"Ms. Terrell, I need you on the bridge."

"Selene, we have a problem in the galley."

The two voices broke through the intercom at once. "Kate, lock yourself in and guard this. See what else you can find out, and I'll be back as soon as I can."

I heard the bolt slide behind me as I ran for the bridge. Bridge was a fancy name for the room barely bigger than a closet where Captain Larssen and a co-pilot could guide the ship and check her status. "Captain?"

"I've found something odd in our vector. We're behind course, consistent with the ship weighing 600 kilos more than our manifest. It's subtle, but there."

"I have another reason to suspect our new cargo loader. That alarm was Kate discovering ricin, which is on the terror list. He must have shut off the detector to bring it on."

"Take Marco and detain him. Somehow."

I nodded. *Copernicus*'s builders had wasted no space on a prison. I'd find a way.

"And be careful."

"Always."

I began calling up security information. Harvey had to be in his room. We had cameras on multiple independent circuits. We could trace every source of heat on the ship. Nothing human-sized could be out of place.

I listened, too. Nothing out of the ordinary. Until Mare's voice came over the intercom. "Selene, I really think you need to see this in the galley."

It was on the way. I called Marco directly and asked him to arm himself and meet me there.

Marco covered a cough as we met at the door to the galley. I went in first, since his big frame made any space in the ship feel crowded. "Mare, what is it?"

She pointed at a strange mushroom in one of the chilled produce bins. "I know this wasn't here last night. I'd have said something."

"What is it?"

"It's an amanita. It's deadly! That shouldn't be on the ship at all."

Something niggled at me, and behind me, Marco coughed again, harder. I leaned over the drawer.

The amanita called attention to itself with its bright red spotted cap. It would be very hard to miss. It was distractingly out of place. I looked at the rest of the produce. Just barely visible, once I turned my gaze from the deadly mushroom, was a fine powder scattered over the rest of the produce.

I pulled open the next drawer, and saw the powder there, too. "Have you eaten any of this?" I asked Mare.

"No," she said. "I saw the mushroom and worried."

"I did," said Marco. "Randy and I had breakfast an hour ago. And I don't feel so good."

"Marco, go to the clinic, now. Mare, don't let anyone else eat until we check everything. We need to call everyone—except Tim Harvey—and see who has eaten."

I called Kate first. "Kate, we have a possible poisoning situation. Have you eaten since dinner?"

"No, I was on my way when you called me about the scarecrow."

"Good. Don't. Marco's on his way, and we may have more for you."

"What about evidence security?"

"Preserve it if you can. But save lives first!"

"I understand," she said.

"Good. Out."

I called the captain next. He hadn't eaten. Dave hadn't eaten. Randy wasn't answering calls, and neither was Inoko. Quill said she'd had a snack six hours ago, but felt fine. I told her to go to the clinic anyway. Everyone else seemed in the clear.

I hesitated over calling our passenger. True to his word, he hadn't left his cabin since the start of our trip. Why would he have started now?

After a moment, I called him and lied. "Mr. Sadad, this is Vice-President Selene Terrell. We are running a drill. As part of the drill, I need to know if you are in your cabin."

"Why, yes, Ms. Terrell, I am."

"And have you left it for any reason in the last eight hours?"

"No, I have not."

"Thank you. I'm sorry to disturb you."

"Oh, not at all. Not at all."

I closed his line and went to find Randy and Inoko.

Copernicus is a small ship, and I had full security displays running on my specs. It took me only a few minutes to find each of them lying in a pool of vomit, unresponsive. Randy was in hydroponics and Inoko was in his cabin. Newton, and Gottfried, still able-bodied, helped me carry them to Kate's overcrowded clinic.

She had multiple lines running to Marco, who looked pale. She told Quill to stand up and make room for Randy and Inoko. We only have three beds in the clinic.

She began attaching lines to Randy and Inoko.

"What do you know?" I asked.

Kate's eyes slid to Marco. "Not much, yet," she said. "I'll do what I can."

"Tim Harvey has a lot to answer for. Quill, stay here and do what Kate tells you. Gottfried and Newton, you're with me."

O O O

I unlocked the security cabinet, and we took sidearms and body armor. I knew Gottfried could handle himself under fire, so I asked him to lead.

Everything would go so much easier if Tim Harvey would open his door. But I knew he would have heard running in the corridors and Kate's alarm. The question was, was he listening?

At his door, I had Newton stand off to the right, on the hinge side, and Gottfried step to the left. Then I took a breath and knocked on the door. "Tim, I need to talk to you."

"Just a minute."

I stepped back, out of the line of the door, and waved Newton farther away, too. Then we heard the bolt move, and the door swung open.

Harvey's eyes widened when he saw the armor and sidearm. He started to close the door again, and Gottfried rammed it open with his shoulder.

"Just step back, Tim, and let us in."

"What is this? I haven't done anything!" He retreated into the room, hands in front of his chest.

"Haven't done anything?" I advanced on him. "Tim, you're the cargo master. There are things on this ship that shouldn't be here. That means you did it."

"I swear, I didn't think it would cause any harm. He just said …" Then he grabbed for something under his bunk, and Gottfried shot him.

With a Taser. None of us are fools enough to shoot a projectile in the fragile confines of our ship. Tim Harvey stiffened and then slumped. I checked his heartbeat and breathing—both fine.

"Gottfried, restrain him." We had safety ties in our belt kits. "We'll get our answers when he comes to. Don't touch anything. There may be traps or antidotes in here. But we'll need to search very carefully. The two of you take turns watching him. Call me if he wakes up. Otherwise, I'll be back in four hours."

They nodded their acceptance. I left them, with the profoundly uneasy thought that I was overlooking something.

O O O

Back at the clinic, I asked Kate if she could step out for a minute.

"How are they, really?"

"I'm doing everything I can. I've pumped their stomachs, and Marco's bulk seems to have diluted the effect a bit, but I just don't have the tools I need. It's—it's going to be touch and go for a while yet. I haven't even been able to isolate the poison yet."

"Not amanita?"

"No, amanita's effects are different. Flu-like symptoms …" her eyes widened, and the other shoe dropped. "Oh my god. Neil," she said. "Flu-like symptoms, followed by apparent recovery, followed by organ failure. We've got to call him."

"I'll do it." I hesitated a moment. "If the poisoner had an antidote with him, would you be able to recognize it?"

She thought. "Maybe. There's only so much I can do now, so I'll start on the chemical analyses. If we knew, it might help."

"Good. The knife, too—it could be part of the puzzle." There was a scraping sound from the ceiling above us. I cocked my head. "Did you hear that?"

"Hear what?"

I listened a moment more. It wasn't repeated. "I'm not sure. Do what you can, and call me if you need me. I'll call Neil."

I made the call from my cabin, composing myself as best I could through the two minutes of lag to connect to Luna. Ivy answered. "Selene, is that you?"

"Yes, Ivy. Neil needs to go to the hospital right away."

I waited two minutes, and she put her face in her hands. "Selene, it's too late. He died this morning."

"Ivy, I am so sorry. We found amanita on the ship today. Have the coroner check for it."

I waited. She looked up and said, "What does that mean? Is the ship in trouble?"

"Yes, we have some trouble. I'm—"

In a wash of static, the connection went dead. Then I heard the scream.

It's worse when a man screams, somehow. In all the dramas, women scream, high-pitched and frantic until it seems less real. This was real—strangled terror from the front of the ship. I threw open the door and ran to the bridge.

Captain Larssen had fallen half onto the floor. Blood flowed from his chest, and there was a thing perched upon him, stabbing him again and again.

I took careful aim and hit it with the Taser, as short a burst as I could manage.

"Se—Selene," the captain burbled. I moved closer, to hear him. "There's another problem with nav. Check—check the stars. And tell my kids I love them."

There was so much blood around him. I leaned in, to begin first aid.

"Behind you," he breathed.

I twisted, and saw another of the things clinging to the ceiling. It leaped, and I fired, and it fell.

When I turned back, Captain Larssen's eyes were frozen. I saw now that one of the stab wounds had exposed and pierced his heart, and knew it was too late.

Then I saw the hole under the pilot console, with another of the things inside it. Aiming the Taser at it, I began backing away. Three feet, four feet, five … "All crew, stations! We are under attack. Repeat, crew, stations. We are under attack."

The thing made a scraping sound as it leaped for the air duct. I heard it scuttling away.

Then I heard the dry chuckle over the intercom. "That won't help you, you know. This is my ship now."

"What do you want?" I yelled back.

"Oh, you'll know soon enough. You'll all know."

I heard our passenger click off the system. I had blown it. The pattern was there, and I missed it. The obvious scarecrow, and the hidden and poisoned knife. The blatant amanita, and the deadly subtle powder. The clearly guilty cargo master, and the man who had never shown his face. Which meant …

I ran for Harvey's room. I heard thumpings and zapping and yells as I arrived. Then Gottfried opened the door. "There were six of them. They got Harvey and Newton."

I looked in at spattered blood and fallen bodies. Then I took a blanket off Tim's bunk and gingerly gathered up one of the scorched things. "We're not beaten yet. Let's get Dave to take a look at this."

We exchanged our Tasers for fully charged ones at the security locker. Then we went down to Dave's door.

Dave opened at my knock, fully suited and armored. I hoped that our guest wouldn't know that, to *Copernicus*'s crew, "stations" meant suit up, armor up, and stay in place. If he didn't know where to send his pets, we might gain a little time.

"Dave, you're cleared."

"I figured."

"I have something for you to look at." I opened up the blanket. "What are we dealing with here?"

He moved the blanket to a table, and poked at the thing with a long screwdriver. It didn't move. Then he took a knife from a holder on the wall and sliced along the thing's back.

It didn't bleed. The black, glistening skin parted to reveal gears and circuits. Dave peeled the skin away from one of the legs and bent it with the screwdriver.

"It's a highly transformable six-legged robot in a jellied matrix. Looks like smart metal legs—can shrink and extend by a factor of four. Same for the tail, with the integrated blade. These …" he brushed the screwdriver across the mandible-like protrusions at the front "… are fine manipulators, and this is an ocular assembly. Antenna here." He pointed out a globe and a stick above the mandibles. "Quite the elegant piece of engineering, really."

"How does it get its orders?"

He peered at it. "I don't see any sound sensors. So they probably come in through radio."

"So, our guest can't speak its orders?"

"No, he probably can. I'd guess he has a transmitter that takes his commands and resends them as radio. He seems the type."

"How much does it weigh?"

Dave hoisted it experimentally. "About half a kilo."

"The ship's six hundred kilos over manifest. The captain discovered it this morning. So, he could have twelve hundred of these things."

"Probably half that. My guess is they need some support."

"And he had some other materials to smuggle on board," added Gottfried.

"Right. In any case, that's still too many for us to take out one at a time. Dave, would they be susceptible to gas? Ultrasonics?"

He shook his head. "Gas, definitely not. They don't breathe. Ultrasonics—we could get them one at a time with that—not good enough. Nope, what we need for these is a ship-wide EMP."

"Wouldn't an electromagnetic pulse fry the ship systems too?" asked Gottfried.

"Yeah," Dave smirked. "But I can fix it."

I looked him in the eyes. "Are you sure? There's no rescue for us if you're wrong."

He looked more serious for a moment. "I'm sure. Really, Selene, I promise."

"Set it up, then. And keep yourself alive. You just became our most valuable player."

"I'll stay here," said Gottfried.

"What are you going to do?" asked Dave.

"I need to talk to Kate. She has patients, and we don't want to surprise her with her equipment going out. Then I need a button, so I can trigger the EMP at a time of my choosing."

"And then?" asked Dave.

In five years of long hauls, you learn about the people you ship with. I knew what he was asking, and I knew how to tell him.

"And then I'm going to listen to our guest. With extreme prejudice."

O O O

The clinic had gone into quarantine shut down. I suited up before passing through its airlock. With sealed ducts and double doors, it would be the safest place on the ship.

It was a little crowded inside. Mare had joined Quill and Kate, and with all three beds extended, once I came in, it was elbow to elbow.

"The galley's not very defensible," said Mare.

"Good choice," I said. "How are they?"

"All unconscious now," said Kate. "I think—I think an antidote would be our best chance."

"If he has it, I'll get it from him. Kate, I need to understand him. What do we know about this bastard?"

Quill answered. "This might help. His father is 168 years old. He's got the billions to pay for it, and the rejuvenation treatments work great on him. Our boy—he's only sixty-four. And judging by how long he's stayed in his room—I don't think the treatments worked so well for him."

"He likes poisons," said Mare. "The amanita, and the ricin, and whatever was on the food."

"Which I still haven't been able to analyze," said Kate. "But get this—along with the ricin, there was asphalt and formaldehyde in the mixture on the knife. Both used as embalming fluids at various points in history."

The pattern clicked together. "Thank you. That does help." I took a deep breath. "Get ready. In a little while, there will be an electromagnetic pulse. Dave says he can put the ship back together afterwards."

Mare drew in her breath through her teeth. "He'd better. We can't stop this ship without the computer."

"And I'm still hoping …" said Kate.

"Hope, pray, and watch your back," I said. Then I let myself out the airlock.

O O O

"Here's your button," said Dave. "Just push this, and I'll have job security for the next three weeks."

"This is no time for humor," said Gottfried.

"It's always time for humor," said Dave.

"Selene, do you want me at your back?"

"Not this time, Gottfried. It'll be easier to talk my way in alone. You two take care of each other."

"You take care."

"I always do."

Then I took off my suit and put it away. I clipped the button to my chest, underneath my shirt. I put the Taser in the small of my back. I thought briefly of the days when Captain Larssen and I served on a military ship together. Then I walked to the door to the guest quarters, my hands open and in front of me.

"You win, Prince Sadad," I said. "This is your ship. You can have everything you want."

"What do you know about what I want?"

"You said we would know, in time. So, tell me."

That dry laugh came again. "There's nothing that can stop what I want now. My other servants have sabotaged your drives and poisoned your food. You will all die here."

"You are right. You have completely outplayed and outthought us. You hold our lives in your hands."

"Yes! I am like a god to you!"

I pressed my hands together, and bowed to the door. "Do you not want me to bow to you in person? It is right that I should lower myself before my god."

He laughed, harshly. "Why not then? You may enter."

I opened the door, and bowed again, taking in the scene through the corners of my eyes. He'd hung purple velvet curtains along the walls, and dozens of his pets clung to them, pointing their eyes and bladed tails at me. He sat on the edge of his bed, only his face and hands visible, and those wrapped in bandages. He wore the circlet with the rearing cobra on his bandaged brow, and held the scythe and lash.

I bowed again. "It is good to look upon you, Prince Sadad. I am glad to see who I will serve—in this life and the next."

The bandages around his mouth wrinkled horribly. "You know who I am, then?"

"You are the king who rules beyond the veil."

"Yes! I am the ever-living one! Not my father! No matter how he simpers and takes whores to his bed. He let my mother grow old! He let me grow old!"

"All this is nothing to the kingdom beyond the veil."

He quieted. "Yes. I shall rule, and you shall serve me. This ship shall sail forever into the void, and you will serve me forever."

"I bow before you, oh king." I paused. "But mighty king, these ones around me, they cannot die. So, they cannot serve you beyond the veil. And the other humans—they have not yet chosen to serve you. Do you not want servants who follow you by choice? Give me the antidote, and we will serve you of our own free will—this life and the next."

I was close to him now, and I saw his eyes slide, so quickly, towards a box on the table. Then he laughed. "You are a clever one. I shall keep you the longest. When all the others have crossed to await me, you and I shall share this potion of immortality." He put a hand down and caressed a different box at his side. But I knew him now, and I heard the lie.

"You honor me too much," I said, clapping my hand to my chest. All around me his pets fell from the curtains as the pulse spread through the ship. He reached for something, and I grabbed my Taser and shot him.

He fell backwards with a cry. I prodded him with the Taser first, then checked for a pulse. There was none. The treatment must have weakened his heart. "So much for your immortality," I said. Then I took the box on the table to Kate.

"I think this one is the antidote," I said.

"We haven't got a lot to lose," she replied. "And our guest?"

"Heart stopped when I Tasered him."

She nodded, and tested the pearly fluid in the flasks inside the box in vitro first.

Then she gave it to Inoko. After an hour, she gave it to Randy, and the next day to Marco. And in time they woke.

O O O

There was lots of clean up, of course. Dave hadn't been exaggerating when he said three weeks to fix the electronics. We scrubbed where we needed to, and gave Captain Larssen and Newton Barelo and even Timothy Harvey last honors. I found the security video, and watched Harvey turn off the scanner and the scales as Sadad's agents loaded his luggage. He'd done nothing worse than that, and three men had died of it.

At some point, Sadad had tricked the ship into nudging us above the plane of the ecliptic. But we recalculated the fuel use, and Dave and Gottfried made some smart adjustments to the engines, and we limped into Deimos port, two weeks late and heartily sick of the foie gras and caviar from our shipment of luxury foods.

Anna Paradox always wanted one of those science fiction author bios that lists many different occupations. Before she settled into her current work—helping authors complete better books—she collected the titles of mint weeder, combine driver, crew boss, bookkeeper, waitress, tutor, bookseller, telephone support, poker columnist, life coach, and graduate assistant. Her first novel, *The Cracked Bell*, is a young adult fantasy where three young singers face an escalating series of earthquakes. She has edited over thirty books, including Tommy Angelo's *Painless Poker* and Nicholas Graves' *Bound for a Distant Home*. Somewhat surprised to find herself in West Texas, she shares her home with her husband and two quirky cats.

Part V: Space Tramps

Edited by Jennifer Brozek

Backup

by Ivan Ewert

Introduction to "Backup"

Space Tramps is an anthology about the lost, the abandoned, the vagabond. In many stories, these lost people are abused and misused. They are lied to and hurt. They are valued only for what they can provide. In the case of "Backup" by Ivan Ewert, the space tramp once belonged to a wealthy man as a duplicate who abandoned him as he would a suit he no longer liked.

I chose to publish "Backup" for two reasons.

First, the concept of the backup person, a clone treated as royalty until he is abandoned as a soulless vanity, a construct, and nothing more. This, of course is not true. But it is this perception of the backup that makes him valuable to the man who does misuse him.

Second, the ultimate fate of both the backup and the man who tricks him is a good one for some, but, as with most cases when an unfortunate lost person is involved, the backup himself is forgotten.

Guillaume thought the thing looked bad, even for an obsolete backup in the Distrik Armes. Shirtless and emaciated, its head had been shaved with a dull razor and the permatreated hair, frosted white in a style that had been gauche even five years ago, was only growing back in thin patches. Its kilt was crusted along front and back with involuntary night evacuations, and he could smell the musk of the waste combined with the sour tang of its unwashed body from three doors down.

This was always the worst part of his job.

He snapped a tabacapsule beneath his patrician nose and let the scent overwhelm him, permeate the delicate membranes. The backup wouldn't bother him in that regard for at least three hours, more than long enough to handle the transaction. He stripped off a pair of thin Jie designer gloves, thrust them into his tunic, and arranged the carryall across one slim shoulder before moving on.

"Tabac?" He extended a second capsule to the backup, who looked up with eyes brighter than Guillaume had expected. They were a pale blue which must once have gone with the hair color, and rather than drugged or exhausted, they were wary. The memory port behind his left ear blinked in time with its heartbeat, showing the same shade of blue.

Guillaume pasted on a smile, putting equal parts tenderness and pity into it; and relaxed his elbow to make the offer more delicate than before. "Come, friend. I have more than enough."

Furrowed scrapes ran along the thing's scalp, cheeks, and chest; none deep, but hinting at the night troubles so common to backups. It reached out and plucked the capsule from Guillaume's hand and considered it a moment, regarding it with exaggerated attention. Then it brought the capsule to its own broken nose, cracked it and inhaled, those cautious eyes closing in appreciation, ribs thrusting against its skin as its back straightened.

"No God would let this happen," it said, eyes still closed, "so you're wasting time if you're with the Katarici." Its voice was cracked from disuse, but held a pleasant baritone beneath.

"Thank God I am not, then," smiled Guillaume, "and thank the terms of my inheritance that I must offer comfort where I may. Are you hungry?"

"Inheritance?"

"My father was a hard man while he lived, and as so often happens, decided near his passing to soften his memory in charity. I have come into plenty, friend; but by the terms of the inheritance I must show signs of good deeds done in my father's name."

It snorted, looking him up and down. "No backups of his own, then?"

"Only a son. He preferred rejuvenation to such grand and ultimately fickle cautions."

"Good for him."

"Good for you, if you will permit. Now, say what you will of the Katarici, but they run a decent shelter with showers, and you may escape a sermon if you pay them well enough—which I intend to. I've clothes in my bag and there is a place not far from here which serves a passable version of tea."

"And?"

"And, we will have a photo taken together, and a brief mark on my receipts showing what I have done for the deceased, and we shall see what passes in a few hours of conversation." He let the smile widen with a half-shrug which jostled his carryall. "Or, if you prefer, I will move along and find another to trouble with my cares. As they say, there is no shortage of supplicants in a spaceport's shadow."

Its face grew dark, an unwelcome sign of misplaced pride, but only for a moment. Then a self-mocking smile crept into pursed lips, and it placed a hand on the stoop to push itself upright, towering over Guillaume by a full head and a half.

"All right then."

O O O

Hot water streamed across its chest, gray water from the treatment plants turning darker as filth was sloughed from its skin. The temperature was almost unbearable, but it remained beneath the water, allowing itself to revel in the simple joys of warmth and cleanliness.

It remembered the last time it had been in a shower.

That shower had held eight nozzles, arranged to provide the effect of an expert masseuse upon the knotted muscles of its frame. The day had begun with a swim in the marbled pool, under a marvelous sunrise which would prove the last the backup would ever see. It wished, fiercely, it had paid attention to its colors, that it could recall the truth of the sunrise and not a pastiche memory of holovids and photos.

The swim was crucial. Its strength was important. As a backup, its body was the most important—the only important—thing it truly possessed, and in return for being kept in such high style, it held its part of the bargain sacred. Should its original pass, it would be overwritten with the most current memories of its original, and his work and pleasures would continue unabated.

It aged, of course, though rejuvenators retarded the process; and one day it too would die, perhaps to pass on to another backup. Until then, it would remain strong. It would care for itself as it was cared for, and think little more of its place.

The mansion's speakers had crackled to life, interrupting the soothing strains of viola and piano. "Come to the bedroom," his original had called, "now."

It was called, and it came, and it stopped short in the entrance.

Its original stood naked, legs spread and tubes sprouting from the back of his spine. His head had been shaved, the fine mane of carefully frosted hair vanished and swept away by the cleansing servos which crawled across his form like scarabs upon a mummy of Old Sol. At his side stood a small man, wrapped in the blue and silver robes of a Vechii attendant. The backup's stomach sank as its thoughts raced to catch up with the vision.

"Today," said its original, "I am Vech."

He'd been blessed with that voice, that sweet and musical voice which had been so at odds with his bluntness, his inability and unwillingness to dance around an issue. You knew where you stood in his presence, and it saw what was coming.

"I reject the things of this world. I reject the things of this flesh—my rejuvenants, my chemicals, all my man-made sins." His blue eyes flashed earnestly. He was given to such flights, throwing himself fully into the newest fads, but never before had his eyes held such fire.

"I reject all the things of the world. But most of all, the worst of vanities, I reject you."

It had pleaded. It had begged, all to no avail. Those eyes, its own eyes, pierced it as the words dripped from his scornful tongue.

"The law's clear that I can't destroy you. I would, in a heartbeat, but the law's the law." He snapped his fingers, and an attendant glided forward bearing a thick legal file.

"Those papers are clear. You're legally no part of me. You'll be shipped off-world this afternoon. It's Gliese for you."

"Sir," it said, "please. Please, sir. Let me stay a while. Think about it."

"I have. You're out of my life."

"Then not off-world. Not Gliese, please, sir, give me that at least. Send me to a liberty world. Give me some rights. I've done right by you."

"You're a sinful thing, and you'll pay for it," he said. "The liberty worlds are too far. The law's clear. I owe you nothing but a single ride off-world. Tickets to Gliese are cheap. You're flying in cold sleep for less than five hundred."

The attendant opened the file. One ticket. Through the window which overlooked his original's ornamental gardens, gardens where it had been paraded and cajoled before envious friends still too poor or too frugal to afford a backup of their own, it saw the lights of a federal transport.

His original's voice was cool. The priest's smile was icy. "That's the last you'll get of me. Don't even think about coming back."

The water in the Katarici shelter was growing cold.

O O O

As it showered, Guillaume passed an idle half an hour with the cherubic, well-scrubbed attendant, debating the week's racing results, the mission of his sect, the recent arrest of a smuggling vessel out of Old Sol and the church's relationship with nearby medical clinics.

In the process, he learned that the police considered the smugglers' cargo accounted for, that a surprise sweep of the Distrik was unlikely, the location of the street surgeon most despised by the righteous, and, as a pleasant surprise, the odds being given on Nikolai Dzigbode's horses for later in the day.

The backup emerged looking more or less human. The tunic was too short for it, hanging vest-like and open to reveal its hairless chest and sunken frame; but the new kilt Guillaume had provided was both well-pressed and somewhat fashionable, a D'Souza knockoff from last year's collection.

"Bravo, friend, but until you've filled out a bit the scarecrow look fails to suit you. Daniel," he turned to the attendant, "do you have a shirt that might fit him? White, I think, to pick up the trim along the tunic."

"You're in fashion, or something?" The backup asked.

"No. I just appreciate the finer things in life—in food, fashion, and company."

Daniel returned with a well-worn but serviceable shirt, to which Guillaume took a pair of nail clippers, snipping loose threads from hem and collar. The backup shrugged out of the tunic, then allowed Daniel to assist it in donning the shirt. Its eyes had lost some of their wariness, relaxing into a pleasant state of reverie which Guillaume recognized. The original had been accustomed to such attentions as a personal tailor and dresser.

"Better. Yes, I think we might manage a pleasant tea at this point. Thank you, Daniel—for your pains." Guillaume transferred a token amount from his public account into the Katarici's and another, smaller amount marked for the name of Daniel Moorhead, Distrik Armes Shelter, Kepler Port, Gliese. A brief handshake and the two were off, the backup walking now side-by-side with his benefactor.

The teahouse offered intimate private booths, sheltered from the planet's eternal twilight and looming port, as well as an external patio for those who found comfort in the shuddering vibrations of orbital engines or tourists still enamored of the perpetual gloaming. Guillaume gestured, unsurprised that the backup chose a booth for its pleasure.

"Quite enough of the open air, eh?"

"I spend every night in the open air." It was relaxing into the comfortable foam of the chair, its eyes flickering toward the hostess—though not making contact with her own. "You don't know what that's like."

“I am more than willing to try, friend. Tell me.” He motioned the dimmers to shut down, increasing the level of light in the booth at a measured pace. They would continue until they reached capacity, as the smoked glass which separated them from the rest of the teahouse darkened to maintain the romantic level without.

It waved a hand. “That’s one! There’s no proper light, except in the border shuttle stations—the ones on the perimeter of the port. They aren’t manned, so you can steal a few hours. That’s the second thing I noticed after my crash … how much I missed light.”

“I’m sure of that,” smiled Guillaume. “It is a need, a very human need, to feel the light on your face.” It was a practiced speech, one he’d used often. The word *human* was dropped in a casual manner, and he kept his eyes on the screen as he ordered twin bulbs of butter tea. “What was the first?”

“The noise is unbelievable. I thought I knew something about that—before. Here, though, with no proofing and no shelter, no schedule at all? It took me a week before I got more than twenty minutes’ sleep at a time.”

“The mission has some proofing, if little to spend on light.”

“I told you,” it said, “I don’t hold with God. You either make your fate, or … or else it’s made for you.” The bulbs of tea arrived, and they waited in silence as the hostess offered rock salt, which both deferred. She slid the screens closed once more and left them in the stark light. Guillaume raised his own cup to the backup.

“I couldn’t agree more.”

“Thank you,” it said, and raised its cup in return. “To your father.”

“Indeed,” Guillaume nodded.

The conversation was a call-and-response litany, a classic dance in which Guillaume led and the backup followed without its conscious knowledge. Sympathetic questions asked without a trace of pity, the unmentioned empathy in switching on the booth’s cooling unit when sweat appeared on its brow from the heat of the lights, the suggestion that croquettes might go well with the butter tea, the companionable silence in which he allowed it to eat, the sharing of another tabacapsule, the ordering of digestifs with a somewhat higher alcohol content than one might expect for the small amount of food they'd consumed.

"Well, this has been a wonderful, lazy afternoon, my friend." Guillaume stifled a yawn. "Is there anything more you might ask for?"

"You've been … very good to me," it said. "Thanks."

"Nothing else?"

"Only that it never end."

Ah. "And tell me, friend … if I said it didn't have to?"

It would have been too much, earlier in the day. It had been wary, accustomed to living like an animal on the streets of the spaceport. Yet a few hours of catering, some small, flattering attentions, had returned its very basic, very human nature.

"You … might have work for me?"

"I *do* have work for you."

Some backups lost control at this point, breaking down in gratitude. Others returned to their wary state, at which Guillaume often gave them a simple courier's task followed by vouchers for street vendors, pay toilets or unmanned bathhouses.

This one straightened in its chair. "Tell me."

Guillaume took a small drive from the pocket on his shirtsleeve and placed it on the table with care. He had read the backup's tone, its language, its directness and candor. He would now follow suit.

"My employer would like to ride you."

It went rigid, and caution returned. "That's illegal."

"Yes, as you thought the work might be."

"Discorporation's a hard sentence. What did he do?"

"I've no idea," said Guillaume. "I'm a middleman in these affairs. The sentience was given to me along with enough money to come to Gliese, far enough from his or her crimes to make detection less feasible, and find someone willing to play host."

It looked Guillaume in the eye. "I want to get another drink."

"Of course you may." He ordered a third aromatica, and a second tea for himself. "One more, then as far as I'm concerned, you may walk away if you wish. As I say, it's been a pleasant enough way to pass an afternoon."

"You've done this before."

"Certainly I have."

"What about your so-called father?"

"I like to think of my employers as kind old fellows, caught up in the wrong place at the wrong time."

"How often is that the case?"

"Oh, they've all been willing to swear to their innocence once they are hosted, and I am more than willing to believe them." He held up a hand. "Yes, it helps me sleep at night. You don't need to ask."

It snorted as Guillaume palmed the drive, moments before the hostess brought their drinks. Once the screen was closed, he returned it, crouching between them on the cream-colored tablecloth like an expectant and out-of-place insect.

"Tell me what happens to these hosts."

"In most cases, they skulk about for a few weeks, get themselves in order, and decide whether to stay or try to get off-world for their own purposes. It's difficult, of course; since they remain backups in the eyes of the law."

"That's something else. Why come to me?"

"Oh, friend, you were the first I saw. I've spent the past five days looking."

"I mean, why backups? Wouldn't the hosts prefer …"

"Their term is 'fresh meat.' Of course they would. Being a backup, you can't hold a legal account, can't hold a job, and can't travel off-world. Here on Gliese you're not even permitted to leave the port distriks, isn't that correct?"

"Yes."

"I never have understood the law. It would be kinder, I always thought, to have you painlessly destroyed rather than legally abandoned in this nebulous world. Well, to your question: Yes, my employers *would* prefer fresh meat, and they are sometimes less than pleased in my choices. You'd be surprised how few truly unfortunate men are left, though, on the civilized worlds. Some in my trade visit the frontiers, or the liberty worlds, and I suppose they do well enough with addicts or the poor, but here?" He lifted one hand and one eyebrow in a gesture of resignation. "Regulators manage addiction and disease, society manages credit."

"And you don't travel to the frontiers because you like the finer things."

"Guilty as admitted."

It shook its head, lifted the glass, and took a long drink. "Unbelievable. You're a fancy pimp."

"My term remains 'procurer.' I'm old-fashioned enough to find that preferable to abducting the helpless on the frontiers. Have you not had a pleasant meal, a shower, butter tea *and* two drinks for nothing more than entertaining the idea?"

It held up its own hand. "You've been very good, in … every sense of the word. I get it now. So, what happens …?"

It was the standard question. "What happens to *you?* The conscious is supposed to be overwritten by the new one, but I understand that there's some slippage, depending on the skill of the surgeon involved. Those I deal with often don't have the best or most up-to-date equipment. The way I understand it, those first few weeks often see a struggle between the two."

"So I might come out ahead."

"You might come out ahead." Guillaume smiled. "I've seen it."

"And if I don't, it's somebody else's problem."

"Yes, *everything* is his problem. No more sleeping in alleys and doorways, no more eternal twilight and roaring engines. To sum up, either you remain yourself and gain access to a considerable shadow account on which you may draw, or you become part of a gestalt which has access to that account, or your consciousness slips away from the shattered hell which has been your life."

It nodded, and Guillaume fell silent. After this it was important that the target feel the decision was its own. As it turned the bulb of liquor over and over in its hands, he sipped at his tea, scanning the teahouse screen. He'd have time to make a bet on the evening race, one way or the other.

"I'll do it," it said, "and I'll come out on top."

"I wouldn't be a bit surprised," said Guillaume.

As they left the teahouse, he slipped his gloves back on—a signal to the heavyset man in the alley, who faded into the shadows. The target was willing, and there'd be no need to ruin the pleasant afternoon with abduction after all.

O O O

"How do you feel?"

The body lifted its hands, considered them. "Not so bad."

The music was not gone from the voice, but was overlaid with a rough accent. They had spent less than twenty minutes in the gray surgery behind the kebab stand, attended to by a dark-haired Vorsian immigrant with little English and less hygiene. Guillaume found it easier to deal with them as far from the bloodstained steel as possible.

"Would you like to give your name?"

It turned. The blue eyes which had been so wary held something more now. They had seemed the eyes of a starving wolf, desperate but prepared. The light behind them now was harder, somehow less alive than before despite its recent fortunes.

"You've been paid."

"I've received half payment. Now there's half due from your shadow account, to prove you can access it in this body." It nodded, blinked. "Yes. It is in the name of Casphar Milan. You are Guillaume Anoulack?"

"The account is in that name, yes."

"I see. Yes … it is done. Confirm, please."

"That's not the exact amount."

"But it is what you will receive."

"You are in a backup's body, Casphar." Guillaume's smile was almost pleasant as he gestured to the rooftop behind them. "I promise you that I am not alone here, and that nothing would come to me if this fine new body of yours were found in an alley. This game is too familiar, and I am growing bored of routine in this day. Whoever you were—whatever you have done—you are nothing now but castoff meat. So pay me, Milan, and go about your life; or pass out of living memory for the rest of time."

His gaze was uncanny. Guillaume met it, held it, and waited.

"I will pay," Milan said. His face remained neutral as his eyes roamed the rooftops, watching for a glint of streetlight against the barrel of a gun. "Confirm, please."

"That will be fine. Now then, I'm off to watch Dzigbode in the evening races, and you may go to hell in your own merry way. Enjoy a pleasant evening and best of luck to you."

"I will pay," repeated Milan, "and remember."

"Breath is so new to you, Milan," Guillaume called over his shoulder. "Why waste it in empty threats?"

O O O

Dzigbode's horse won that evening, which purchased Guillaume a luxury suite in Kepler Port itself, a dinner of young lamb grilled over authentic Earth fennel and cedar, and two bottles of decent champagne to share with his evening's companion. After every such engagement, he allowed himself a night in such utter luxury to make up for days spent combing the Distrik Armes for hopeless bodies, and cheap butter tea.

Months passed in quieter complacence at his residence in the Distrik Heldr, taking the odd run here and there for luckier smugglers than those who had brought him Milan. There were no more memory jobs—not that he had expected such. Discorporation was an extreme measure, and liberation of a drive extremely difficult; both factors which made the end result so lucrative for the enterprising procurer.

His final job permitted a blend of business and pleasure, bringing a few vials of experimental narcotics to a private box at the racetrack. Clad in a crimson and black ensemble from the House of Ainura, he watched Dzigbode's jockey win with undisguised pleasure, clapping the woman next to him on her bare shoulder with excitement.

"I don't know how he does it," Guillaume said, shaking his head. "Each time the odds run against him, the man pulls an upset victory."

"It is a simple thing," said a voice behind him. Guillaume turned, ready for a sally, and stepped backward in surprise.

Milan's hair had regrown into a leonine mane of frost-white, under which those sharp blue eyes remained suspended between the chill of death and flaring, angry life. The memory port behind his ear was covered now between the length of that hair and the upturned collar on a green tunic, so similar to that which Guillaume had provided months ago. He remembered his concern over the green and white combination.

"Casphar Milan," he said, and forced a smile. "You look well, my friend."

"Yes. I do."

"You're outside the Distrik Armes as well, I see. Your resourcefulness …"

"Do not flatter. Please. We know each other. I am glad to be remembered."

"How could I forget?"

"No. How could *I* forget?"

Milan seized him by the lapels, lifted him off his feet, and brought his body crashing down upon the buffet table. Scallops, ice and steel cutlery flew to the ground in a crash as Guillaume felt the breath driven from his lungs, felt the sharp edge of a knife against his throat. The well-heeled audience, who had welcomed him in, poured him champagne, offered small talk and minor flirtations, were standing in silence or seated in comfort, all regarding the sudden eruption as one might a welcome piece of entertainment.

He remained very still.

"I remember," said Casphar, "a cheat. I remember he has cheated others. He has said so. I remember his name, Guillaume Anoulack. I remember he races the horses. He enjoys the finer things. He has said so."

Casphar had locked his eyes, refused to turn for even a second. Guillaume glanced away, saw the man who held the knife to his throat as Casphar held him down. It was one of dozens of interchangeable, heavyset men, running errands for the criminals of Gliese, doing as he was paid. He'd held the gun on Milan the day they had left the surgeon's.

"And I think. This procurer, with his fancy speech and fine clothes; who else has he cheated? I ask questions. I find work. Work does not bother me. I am more than this, yes? Work has never bothered me.

"Being *cheated*, this bothers me. I think, being cheated, it would bother Mister Dzigbode. I find work with him. I fix some things. I make some things work. I break some things."

Casphar Milan smiled a wicked grin as he whispered, "I break many things."

"Casphar … no, listen to me, *listen* now …"

His right index finger broke under Casphar's grip, and Guillaume screamed.

"I will break some more things, I think, before I am done. And when I am done, I will have what I was promised. I will have, as you said, a *truly* unfortunate man. Yes? I will have fresh meat."

"Why …" the knife pressed harder, but Guillaume gasped, desperate. "No. Why would you break what you want, Casphar? Let me help you. Let me find you that meat."

"I have had bones broken before. The healing, it is not bad. It is the moment of breaking that is bad." The wet crack of a second finger was drowned in Guillaume's shout.

"Enough, Casphar," heavy words rolled from the back of the room. "Trank him now. The next race is starting, and I want to watch. We'll finish this in the surgery later."

The knife was replaced by a syringe, and Guillaume slid into darkness.

O O O

The darkness of the Distrik Armes was terrible, a perpetual twilight in the temperate band of Gliese. It was broken only by streetlights and the red-and-green signals of atmospheric shuttles, which roared and tore at the eardrums, shook the cheap metal shutters which lowered across stores and shelters at the end of their day.

The backup stared at the sky, watched the shuttles and engines and endless night go by beneath the cheap lights of a tenement doorway. The Katarici Mission knew him as heretic, unredeemable; their doors were shut to him. No line of credit, be it shadow or legal, was acceptable to the teahouses, the hophouses, the convenience stores.

It ate what it could find, from locked cans it broke open in agonized frenzies of hunger; from the corpses of birds lying in gutters and under bridges. It wore a kilt out of convenience, with pay toilets unavailable and the tainted streams from the cooling tanks of the Kepler Port.

Far away, in the Distrik Sbelet, the body of Guillaume Anoulack enjoyed its preferred repast of local beer and hearty roast beef in the private box of Nikolai Dzigbode; but here in the Distrik Armes, its mind was tormented by the memories of that wonderful, lost, and fortunate life.

It would have been kinder to be destroyed.

Ivan Ewert was born in Chicago, Illinois, and has never wandered far afield. He has deep roots in the American Midwest, finding a sense of both belonging and terror within the endless suburban labyrinths, deep north woods, tangled city streets and boundless prairie skies. The land and the cycles of the year both speak to him and inform his writing; which revolves around the strange, the beautiful, the delicious and the unseen.

His full-length novels span The Gentleman Ghouls trilogy: *Famished: The Farm, Famished: The Commons,* and *Famished: The Ranch*, published through Apocalypse Ink Productions. A printed omnibus is currently in the works.

In previous lives, he has worked as an audio engineer, a purchasing agent, a songwriter, a tarot reader, a project manager and, for a remarkably short stint, an accountant. In his spare time, Ivan occupies himself with reading, gaming, and assisting with the jewelry design firm Triskele Moon Studios. He currently lives near the Illinois-Wisconsin border with his wife of eighteen years and a rather terrifying collection of condiments and cookbooks.

Ivan can be reached at www.ivanewert.com and on Twitter @IvanEwert.

The Frigate Lieutenant's Woman

by Erik Scott de Bie

Introduction to "The Frigate Lieutenant's Woman"

Not all tramps are unwilling in their life of solitude, of being a nomad, of flying the hidden hyperwaves. "The Frigate Lieutenant's Woman" by Eric Scott de Bie is one such tale. The main character is rich enough to own his ship outright and to carry needed cargo across the stars. But, as with most who seek solitude, his mind is not always his own.

In "The Frigate Lieutenant's Woman," the protagonist meets a woman who needs his help. It's this need, and others, that drives him to bring her onboard his ship. Their conversations are strange. His needs and dreams are explicit. Reality is malleable.

I chose this story for Space Tramps because, in the end, it is up to the reader to determine what was real and what was just fantasy.

Sweat

◁ ▷

The stars glitter in a cold vacuum, but in the captain's quarters it is hot. Flesh hisses upon flesh between sodden sheets, and lungs heave for breath trapped in bodies locked together.

A hand, dark and rough, laces its fingers between those of a smaller, pale hand. He courses in her and she arches her head back into the pillows. Her lips beg for him in nonsense words, while her body pleads in a language all its own.

She gasps and shivers. Her brilliant green eyes open and she is alive in a way that transcends the stars and the unfathomable reaches of the deep.

O O O

The tram shuddered to a halt, rousing the man from where he sat staring down at his hands. Wordless muzak droned around him.

He looked up. The flashing letters on the monitor spelled out station 642-07. Smith had always been good with numbers: seventy-six floors and thirteen boarding gates to go until 718-20 and the waiting *Exeter.* That meant thirteen hours, twenty-four minutes, forty-two seconds.

He had done the calculations in his head, having had little else to do on this train ride.

Smith looked around without hope of seeing anyone. The massive *Artemis V* spaceport with its two thousand floors, each with one hundred gates for one hundred possible docking ships, hadn't hosted more than a dozen occupants in the last decade or so. Smith docked here to unload every few star-years, and rode the tram while the automated system did the work for him. He flew the ship alone, there to provide the five-hundredths percent of non-automated actions the process required. Every time, he set the loading in motion, boarded the same tram—the *Roy Cobb 01*—and sat in the same weight-depressed seat, molded to his body.

As he expected, no one rode the tram with him.

The tram pulled up at gate 642-07, opened its doors briefly, closed them again, then shot away for gate 642-08. A massive military frigate the size of a small moon was docked here, and the tram rushed past it at dizzying speeds. The *Napoleon II*, the ship was called, built in a compensating size.

As always, Smith lost himself in the repetition of the faintly swaying tram. Stop, open, close. Stop, open, close.

He nodded off once more, only to awaken at the 687 dock. From here, the ships were smaller like the *Exeter*, and it would only take four hours, twenty-six minutes, twelve seconds to get to 718-20. The tram never wavered in its pace. Only …

"Wait," he murmured to no one. He checked the time readout on the monitor. It should have read that eight hours, fifty-eight minutes, and thirty seconds had gone by while he slept, but when he did the math, in actuality eight hours, fifty-nine minutes, and eleven seconds had passed. Somehow, they'd picked up forty-one seconds. How was this possible? Had the tram malfunctioned?

He saw her then: the woman who sat across from him and three rows back in the tram, staring out the window at the empty black sky. From the tip of her shoes to the fingers of her gloves, she wore all black—a conservative dress, rather than a flight suit, which he found odd. He stared at her, taking in every inch of her downturned face and curly brown hair. Her cheeks were wet, as though she'd been crying.

Time pressed on. They rode in this way for fifteen minutes, twenty six seconds—she staring out the window, he staring at her—before he spoke. "Hello?" The word sounded forced. Her head rose a fraction and she looked at him sidelong. Then she sniffled and looked out the window once more.

"Are you—are you going somewhere?" he asked, which was a ridiculous question. Why else would she be here? Where had she come from, if she hadn't come by ship?

Her shoulders rose as though to shrug. "Why?" she asked in a tiny voice.

"Sorry," Smith said. "I just—you were crying, and I thought—are you all right?"

She shook her head slightly.

His stomach turned and he felt vaguely ill. "What happened?" he asked.

She finally faced him squarely, and he drew in a sharp breath. Hers was not a beautiful face, not by any stretch of fantasy, but it was striking. He thought the contours of her cheeks and nose would be memorable, sneaking into his thoughts and taking up residence. Her eyes he would remember especially, with their haunted green luminescence. She had a tragic face.

"I am alone," she said. Her voice was soft but not weak. "I was riding on the *Napoleon II*, but no longer. I made a mistake and, well, now they won't take me. No one will."

Smith knew the *Napoleon II*; it was the huge military frigate he'd passed a little over nine hours ago. The commander, according to the data monitor, was one Lieutenant Vargas. He'd never met anyone from the *Napoleon*, but then, he'd never met anyone at *Artemis V* station.

"Why not?" Smith asked. "I mean, why wouldn't the *Napoleon* take you?"

She shrugged. "The Lieutenant's wife. She objects." He understood. He wrote the whole story in his head, in fact. She was the Lieutenant's woman-on-the-side, given berth to warm his bunk on the long, cold trek between stations. Finally, his wife back home—wherever home was—had heard about her husband's whore and put a stop to it.

He felt a wave of compassion mingled with interest. Aside from old, blue-tinted videos, he'd not seen a woman in years, let alone interacted with one. Technically, he was engaged to Tina Freemason, the daughter of family friends back in Alpha, but they'd never met. And Tina lived a dozen light years from *Artemis V*—even farther away from the next stop on his route for that matter—and here was an actual, living, breathing woman.

And she was the Frigate Lieutenant's … *woman*.

"If … if you don't have a berth," he said, "you can come along on my ship, the *Exeter*."

She looked at him dubiously. "Why would I do that?"

"I'm bound for Albion IX. It's a settled planet. There are people there. You could find work or—"

Or you could stay with me, he thought but did not say.

She hesitated. "If that's what you really want."

"It is." He gave her a vigorous nod.

She looked out into the empty darkness around them.

"I'm Smith." He thought about putting out his hand to shake, but that seemed stupid. "Charles Smith."

"Sarah Wellington," she said. "Sarah."

And with that, they said no more.

O O O

In his dream, Lieutenant Vargas is a lumbering ape of a man. He speaks with a nasal whine, like a stuffy foreigner in one of the interminable films he watches to pass the time. He is a graceless, ugly wretch of a human being.

But he has his woman, and that pleases him.

As she stands trembling, wrists cuffed over her head, he tears away her black dress, revealing the soft white flesh beneath. His smile widens as she looks away in disgust.

His fingers drag like blades down her skin, tracing the contours of her breasts and down her ribs toward …

O O O

"Smith?"

He stirred where the swaying tram had lulled him once more to sleep. Sarah stood at his side, her valise clutched to her breast.

He stared at her a moment, blinking as the vision of her body left him, then looked over at the data monitor: 718-18. They had thirty-four seconds before the doors opened to dock 718-20, where the *Exeter* waited. Fortunately, all his bags remained in his bunk on the ship, so he had no luggage to gather up.

The door opened and Smith stepped out. Sarah lingered a moment, staring uncertainly at the cold metal platform outside the tram. The doors beeped, about to close.

"Come on," Smith said. "It's all right."

She stepped through quickly and reached for him. He almost let her touch him, but uncertainty filled him and he withdrew. It would be presumptuous, he thought. An unhappy expression flickered across her face. Smith depressed a lever on the control panel, and the platform ground up the conveyer to the *Exeter*'s loading dock.

"How much do you weigh, exactly?" he asked in the silence.

Sarah looked at him.

Smith flushed. "Sorry, I mean—it's for the fuel. I don't have any other crew, and the mass variance between the cargo I unload here and the cargo I pick up is already taken into account. I've already made the adjustment for the twelve point seven ounces I lost on the train." He coughed. "Restroom."

"One hundred and eight pounds," she said.

He looked at her dubiously. "I have to do the calculations precisely, or we won't have enough fuel to get to Albion. I'd hate to have to blast one of us into space, or possibly blow our legs off."

"Oh." She considered. "Better make it one hundred and twenty."

He did the math in his head and typed the numbers in. From the control panel, he set the *Exeter* to acquire the extra fuel.

"You're very precise," she said.

"I like numbers. Always have," he said. "Watch this."

He punched in commands. For the trip to Albion IX, the reverse nacelles would fire only at the exact moment the fuel ran down to a set level, rather than a set distance. The difference was only a matter of seconds to account for the extra one hundred and twenty pounds, but it was still important. The boggling mathematical skill this required meant he was showing off, certainly, but then, her wide eyes made it worth it.

"Impressive," she said.

He smiled up at the massive ship above them. "We're almost there."

Inside the *Exeter*, he showed her to one of the guest cabins and opened the door for her. He'd picked a room just down the hall from his own cabin. The ship was hardly the size of the frigate *Napoleon II*, but it was still a hovering city. Smith could wander its sterile halls and gargantuan rooms for years and never stand in the same place twice. This ship was his own lonely world, apart from the occasional shore leave on empty spaceports like *Artemis V*.

"If you need anything," he said, "I'm just over there."

Sarah nodded. "I don't have any credits to pay."

"Oh, that isn't necessary," he said, when what he meant was that it was.

A part of him wanted desperately for her to pay for the ride, but not in credits.

They stood another moment, not speaking. Then he shut the door for her and went to the bridge. There, he put in the launch sequence, succumbing once again to the thoughtless monotony of his job. Eventually he fell asleep and when he dreamed, he dreamed of her.

O O O

She joins him on the bridge as he sits in the captain's chair, and he can tell by her wry expression that something is about to happen. She stands right in front of his chair.

"What?" he asks, but she puts a gloved finger to his lips.

"Shh," she says, her mouth just an inch from his mouth. She presses up against him, and he feels the swell of her body melt into his. He trembles.

She says nothing, only slowly creeps down his front and to her knees. Fingers working deftly but slowly, she undoes the buckle of his belt. Beneath, she draws one button free, then another and another, working her way down until they are all undone. She looks up at him and smiles.

"I am what I am," she says.

He starts to speak but she kisses him once—not on the lips—and his words dissolve in a shudder. She puts one hand around the captain's chair to steady herself, and lays one hand splayed out on his stomach. Her satin gloves feel like liquid on his bare skin.

O O O

The first days on the *Exeter*, they didn't speak much. Smith barely saw her, in fact. Much of his time—the time that wasn't devoted to blue movies in his cabin—he spent wandering the corridors, gazing up in indifference at the infinite, unknowable crates stacked to the soaring ceiling in the cargo bays. He could have logged into the data system to find out what he was carrying to Albion, but after years of doing this, he didn't much care. He was more interested in the woman on his ship.

He finally crossed Sarah's path again on the fourth day, at 22:15:13 hours, when he wandered into the uncleaned Sherry bar and found her sitting near one of the huge sheet windows that looked out into space. The dishes of several meals he hadn't bothered to clean up stood on the table. She stared quietly into the stars, chin on her hand.

"Drink?" Smith asked.

She seemed to have been expecting him, though he couldn't explain how. She shook her head.

Smith poured a beaker of synthetic grain alcohol for each of them and sat across from her in the observation booth. He said nothing, as to speak would get in the way of staring.

"I've never seen this before," she said.

"Huh?"

She gestured out the window, to a nebula that turned over itself like a celestial waterfall. It was a wonder he had glimpsed hundreds of times, but never truly *seen* until she pointed it out.

"I've been riding ships since longer than I can remember, looking for new stars," she said. "Coasting from station to planet, taking on a new berth at different ports of call. I just wanted to see things—experience things. You?"

He shook his head. "Space travel lost its lure for me years ago." Though, when he considered it, he as well wanted to see and experience things—they just involved her, not space.

"I thought the *Napoleon* would last forever, but …" She sighed as though that was a great pity, then looked back out the window. Her hand drew close to her drink, but stopped short of actually touching it. Then, at length: "Why aren't you married?"

This question startled him. "What?"

"I read on the data-feed that you're engaged," she said.

"You read up on me?" Smith asked.

"Don't change the subject," Sarah said with a smile that slipped away almost immediately. "But it said you've been engaged for ten years, almost. Why the delay?"

"Tina and I …" He searched for the right words. "We've never met. It's just about her rich uncle, wanting to add the *Exeter* to his fleet. I own this ship, free and clear."

"You must be a rich man."

He shrugged.

"Do you want her or not?" Sarah asked. "When you find something you want, you should pursue it. It shouldn't be any more complicated than that."

Smith thought of lonely, blue-movie nights in his cabin. Absolutely he wanted someone, but … "I don't know her, and I'm not curious about her, you know?" Smith looked down at his fingers tapping on the table. "I'm … I'm curious about you."

Sarah's green eyes were mysterious. She gave him a little smile, then retired to her cabin.

He sat alone in the bar, imagining.

O O O

Sarah finally picks up her drink, downs it in a single swallow, and tosses the beaker aside to shatter on the floor. Shards of glass tinkle like bells across the cold metal bulkheads. She spreads her arms wide and raises her chin, inviting and challenging him with a wicked smile.

He throws back his own drink, then sweeps the table free of accumulated dishes. She surges into his arms and he presses her down on the table. Their lips meet and his hands part her dress like paper. She grasps his wrist and guides his fingers, moaning as he touches her.

He unbuckles his pants, and she sighs in longing.

O O O

They put into Albion IX the next day, an arrival filled with disappointment. Smith may have dreamed about Sarah, but he never told her, and so they never made love in any of the ways he could imagine.

Unexpectedly, Tina is there, waiting for him at Albion IX's station with an entourage of six faceless relatives. As soon as he sets the unloading procedures and debarks the *Exeter*, she throws herself in his arms and covers him with kisses. She is more beautiful than he had thought, and her body pressing against his is distracting.

"What—?" he asks. "What are you doing here?"

"Marrying you, of course," she says. "My uncle wants to secure his company before he retires, and he wants you to be the CEO. It's amazing!"

"It is," he says, and casts a glance back at Sarah. She stares down at her feet.

"Who's this?" Tina asks. "Is this the Frigate Lieutenant's … woman? The one you told me about?"

He doesn't remember telling her this, but he nods anyway. The trek to Albion was a blur in his mind.

Sarah says nothing.

"We're to be married in the morning, at 08:00 hours," Tina says. "Don't be late!"

He goes to his appointed room on the Albion tram, which is larger than the one at *Artemis V*. The train is unexpectedly full of people, Albion IX choked to bursting with the shouts and laughter of a hundred thousand voices. After years of silence, it gives him a terrible headache, which only goes away when he closes the doors of his private cabin behind him.

It is a true passenger car, with a bed, a writing desk, and a restroom. It offers all the comforts of home, lavishly appointed for business travelers of all stripes.

And lying upon the bed, wearing a black robe, is Sarah. Laid out like a woman on a funeral bier, he thinks at first she is dead, but her gaze follows him as he enters the room.

"Wait," Smith says. "What—what are you doing here?"

She sits up, clasping the robe closed. "I'm sorry," she says. "I shouldn't be doing this, I—"

She lets the words fall away and opens her robe. Beneath, she wears lacy black lingerie that arouses him at a look.

"No," he says. "No, I—I'm to be married tomorrow. I can't do this. We can't—"

Sarah rises against him and they kiss, which tastes both of strawberries and dust.

"I couldn't let you go," she says. "After so long together, you did not touch me. I know you wanted to, but you restrained yourself. You're everything I ever wanted, and I cannot let you go. This can't be the end."

Smith tries to argue but can't summon the words. He wants her so badly it aches inside him. When she pulls his shirt over his head and pushes him back onto the bed, he doesn't resist—nor does he try to crawl away when she straddles him and unbuttons his pants. He is hard as a rock and she guides him to the edge.

It is the end of all things.

O O O

Smith awakened from his dream, stuck to his sheetless bed on the *Exeter* with hot sweat.

The vision had seemed more real than any of his previous fantasies about Sarah. For a moment, he couldn't tell if this was truly waking or dreaming, and he sat on his bed shivering. The time display on his readout said 02:47:13. They would arrive at Albion IX in the morning.

He watched as the display ticked off the seconds, then minutes, on a regular time. The reliable numbers soothed him and grounded him.

He heard the clink of metal from somewhere deeper in the ship: something imprecisely secured coming loose from its ties. Or perhaps he heard a door swishing open to admit someone not in his plan. He'd brought chaos onto his ship, in the form of Sarah.

He ached with need for her.

He slid free of the bed and onto the cold floor. Needles pierced his feet from the chill, but he paid it no mind. Instead, he crossed out into the hall and went immediately to Sarah's door. It opened dutifully for him, but inside there was nothing and no one. The bed was neatly made, and the place showed no sign of an occupant. Had she left him, somehow?

He searched the bridge, the Sherry bar, and all the corridors between, finding no sign of her anywhere. His barefoot steps echoed in the soaring passages of the *Exeter*. He rode the lifts to the various levels but found nothing.

Finally, he found her on the observation deck, at the very top of the ship. She stood gazing into the vast reaches of space, her black dress swaying a little in the breeze of the air conditioning units. Out in the blackness, swirls of stars crashed over themselves like ocean waves on a distant planet. It reminded him of encountering her on the tram.

"I want to thank you," she said, before he could speak. Deep sadness gleamed in her tears. "Most men demand payment they can't take in credit. You—you're different."

It sounded so similar to what she had said in the dream that Smith paused, uncertain. He reached out for her shoulder, his fingers wavering just over her. He withdrew his hand.

"You're a good man, Smith," she said. "I don't deserve you, and you don't deserve this life. You deserve so much more, if only you'll take what you want."

How could a woman such as this exist? And yet he could see her heart beating in the hollow of her throat. He felt as much as heard her rapid breath. He wanted to wrap his arms around her and kiss away the salt of her tears.

"I . . ." he said, "I want—"

He reached for her again, but this time she pulled away with a look equally terrified and longing. She turned to run, but tripped over her foot and began to fall.

He caught her in his arms.

He had expected, in that instant, that he would catch nothing—that she was only a fantasy and not real at all. But she fell bodily into his arms, her warm flesh pressed against his in a way that made him dizzy.

All fear suddenly fled, she reached up to kiss him, and he kissed her back. Her lips tasted warm and bitter, like tragedy bound in desperate hope.

They tore at one another's clothes, hands and arms entrapped in restrictive sleeves. The buttons of his flight suit would not come undone, and ultimately Smith tore them free rather than try to open them. He could not wait another moment. Sarah wept in his ear as he crushed her to the floor and lifted her skirts. She cried out and he grunted.

They were together.

From the moment he'd touched her to the moment of release, twenty-six seconds had passed.

"Sorry," he said after they'd lain together a moment. "I—I was hoping it would be longer."

Her expression tight, she shook her head and said nothing. There was a wet stickiness on his midsection, and he realized he was bloody. At first, he did not understand what this meant—it was such a foreign concept to him that he thought it again a dream—but then it made sense.

She had been a virgin.

"You're …" he said as he started to doze, "You're perfect. The virgin whore with the heart of gold." He rests his head on her breast. "The perfect woman."

Sarah received those words with a sad expression.

O O O

After that, Smith throws it all away for Sarah. He retires from cargo freighting and does not marry Tina, no matter how wealthy her uncle might be. In fact, the old CEO takes a new young wife and has no need of an heir to the family business anyway.

Smith and Sarah find a planet to call home and live a simple life, away from space travel, military ships, and loneliness. They are together all the time, and while Smith gets only a little better with regard to his lack of stamina, Sarah never says anything. He is, after all, the one who rescued her from her wretched life.

Or at least, so he tells himself.

Some nights, he finds Sarah out on the deck of their modest house, staring up at the starry sky. Her face wears that same look of tragedy he saw when they first met. He wants to speak to her, but cannot.

He thinks, at these times, that despite everything, they are desperately unhappy.

O O O

Anxious, Smith awakened from his dream to the sound of warning klaxons. The data readout on the observation deck showed a proximity warning to the Albion IX station. The *Exeter* was approaching at too great a speed.

"Sarah," Smith said sleepily. "Sarah—?"

She was gone.

He climbed to his feet, fumbling with his clothing, and hopped to the control panel. He did the calculations of mass, velocity, and acceleration in his head and put in a precise sequence to slow. The reverse nacelles hadn't fired. But why?

"Sarah?" he called. "Sarah?"

No reply.

The computer blinked to indicate the completion of the diagnostic, and he tapped it open to see the cause: extra fuel meant the engine hadn't reached the low level he'd programmed for firing the engines. This was exactly the sort of mistake he needed to be here to correct.

"Sarah?" he asked again.

The word rang through the silent halls and died before it echoed back. He was completely and utterly alone.

He noted the program he'd input back on *Artemis V* to govern the *Exeter*'s flight and saw the discrepancy. He did the calculations: that much fuel would accommodate one hundred and twenty extra pounds of mass.

"No," he said.

He looked down at himself: no blood.

The control panel was blinking. Albion IX was issuing him an automated hailing signal.

"Why would it be a person?" he asked no one.

Of course, there had never been another person. That would have been too perfect.

Smith's shoulders slumped, and he pushed the receive button. Then he adjusted his clothes.

He steered the ship into the dock, got out, and rode the tram.

Erik Scott de Bie is a 30-something speculative fiction author and game designer. He has published ten novels and counting, including tales in the storied Forgotten Realms, Iron Kingdoms, Hellmaw, and his World of Ruin epic fantasy setting (*Mask of the Blood Queen* is the third entry in that series), as well as a pair of forthcoming fantasy and space opera novels from The Ed Greenwood Group. His short work has appeared in numerous anthologies and online, and he is the author of the multimedia superhero project, *Justice/Vengeance*. In his work as a game designer, he has contributed to products from such companies as Wizards of the Coast and Privateer Press, and was a lead creative consultant on Vorpal Games's *Red Aegis*. He lives in Seattle with his wife, sword collection, and entirely too many animals. Check out his website: erikscottdebie.com.

Oh Give Me Land, Lots of Land, Under Starry Skies Above

by Shannon Page and Mark J. Ferrari

Introduction to "Oh Give Me Land, Lots of Land, Under Starry Skies Above"

Refugees from attacked ships allow people who should never have been lost to become vagabonds at the mercy (or not) of their rescuers. I really liked "Oh Give Me Land, Lots of Land, Under Starry Skies Above" by Shannon Page and Mark Ferrari because the protagonist is a woman who should never have been lost in the first place but when she is, she uses her intelligence to make a better place for herself and those around her.

Of course, there's a whole lot more to the story that involves corrupt officials, a corrupt underbelly of the space station she's stuck on, and a reference to Robin Hood that makes me smile. "Oh Give Me Land, Lots of Land, Under Starry Skies Above" doesn't give the protagonist exactly what she wants, but it does give her a victory while she works to make what she has into something more. I really appreciated that about this story. It's one of the main reasons I published it in Space Tramps.

◁ ▷

I shouldered my pack and moved on again, still trying to look like I belonged to someone. Someone important and frightening and powerful.

Who was I fooling?

I'd gone through lots of training before leaving Earth. I'd passed the psych tests with high scores for adaptability, calm demeanor, and flexible attitude. I'd watched virteos about all the possible dangers and side effects and unexpecteds … except for one: being marooned on *Longhorn 6* with no backup, no office, no Principal Broker, and nothing to sell.

Selling was what I had left Earth to do. Selling land, specifically, and structural space, and development tech. I was a real estate broker, trained by Old Rehaus himself. I'd been on my way to help our brokerage develop Astoria Corporation's recently settled planet Greenleaf 43, not to be a stranded vagrant on some space station thousands of light years from nowhere.

Old Rehaus was dead now. I'd been lucky not to perish with him and the rest of the brokerage when our FTL carrier, *Fleetness*, had somehow come apart upon re-entry into system space. Only one small portion of the vessel survived, limping to its end on this unthinkably isolated pit stop.

Ecoballs like *Longhorn 6* are designed to feel like planets. But no matter how big and round it is, how much "wide open space" they've designed, a space station is a space station. You're breathing canned air, hoofing it down tin corridors, and looking up at a "sky" with no sun.

Most problematic for me, there was no private property here. Not to own, not to buy, not to sell.

I'd spent most of the trip from Earth in Rest, a light trance state that makes time pass dreamy-fast. It's far healthier and quicker to get over once one is planet-side than Sleep, where you're put under entirely. It's more expensive too, but being alert for that initial wave of eager buyers had seemed worth the cost to me. I'd imagined those first few turns around Greenleaf's Monopoly board would set up the rest of my career there. Now there would be no Monopoly board—but Rest had saved my life. My colleagues had all decided to economize, sleeping elsewhere on the ship, to their misfortune.

I still didn't know exactly what had happened to *Fleetness*. The Longhorn goons who'd rescued us hadn't said. They'd just brought us down here and dumped us into some huge processing bay.

The station's populace seemed watchful and grim, their dress code inspired by the collision of a circus, thrift store, and military surplus outlet. Their expressions and body language conveyed mute hopelessness. Not the kind of customer I'd been trained to work with. I had no idea how to act here, much less what to do.

Confused and fog-headed, I had obediently taken my place at the end of a long line at first, just grateful to be alive. Soon, however, I began to wonder if I'd have been better off atomized into vacuum along with the rest of my agency. Most of the women ahead of me were being sent elsewhere by rough-looking male handlers with a steady stream of lewd remarks and leering gestures. Soldiers pulled away the larger, fitter men, while older folks and children were sent through a smaller, shabbier exit. As my turn approached, a sudden wave of prickly instinct made me duck from line while none of our handlers was looking.

Longhorn 6 was a busy, crowded place. It was easy to merge with nearby streams of human traffic and just keep going.

O O O

Two days later, I walked down yet another tin corridor, trying to look stern and busy as my eyes flicked about, searching for threats or clues. I'd slept only once, in a deserted construction zone under a pile of refuse, and eaten nothing but the chips and bottled water distributed free of charge at scattered "refreshment stations" sponsored by *Longhorn 6*'s corporate owner, Galactic Enterprises—Astoria's only serious rival in the interstellar real estate business.

If Galactic's patronage translated into any kind of cogent social organization or business model on *Longhorn 6*, however, it was still entirely opaque to me. The place just seemed one endless, rundown, hostile zoo. I knew there must be some system of registration and assignment, but it was clearly unavailable to anyone who hadn't been processed, and I still didn't trust this place or want to be inducted into any of it. I just wanted to get off of *Longhorn 6* and back into a world I understood. I needed honest dirt under my feet, real air in the atmosphere. A desk, colleagues, rules I understood, superiors I knew how to please, and a big old-fashioned data-dump of listings. I'd just have asked someone to help me leave, but I had a growing fear that no one here would do that.

I needed to get hold of Astoria, before someone who mattered figured out I wasn't right, and started making my decisions for me.

But how?

O O O

I collapsed onto a bench in a sort of park on the fourteenth level of the portside residential zone. The greenery was obviously fake, but at least they'd made an effort to provide some restful space. I pulled out a sheaf of papers I'd collected from various recycling bins. Gathered together, I'd hoped they would look enough like a bundle of work orders to fool the casual observer. People were much scarcer here at this hour than they were elsewhere on the station, which was why I'd come. But whenever someone passed, I frowned down at the papers as if I were a harried admin, stealing a quick break on a quiet bench.

I must have dozed off, because the man's words startled me awake.

"What?" I dropped the papers, which fluttered to the ground at my feet.

"I said, interesting work you've got there." He glanced at the papers. The one nearest my foot was obviously a food wrapper. I had no memory of picking it up, and couldn't hide my blush. "You steal the food too, or just the wrapper?"

"How … What makes you think …?" My mouth went dry as I studied his wry expression, trying to suss out how much trouble I was in. He had an assured air that belied his relative youth. He wasn't uniformed, so not enforcement personnel, I hoped. Brown eyes, heavy eyelids, slender shoulders. Cute, if I weren't so terrified.

"Don't sweat it," he said, smiling. "But if you're gonna play these games, be more convincing. Looks bad for the rest of us." He reached into a dark green satchel and pulled out a bundle of papers, tugged the top two sheets off and handed them to me. "Like this."

My hand trembled as I took them. They seemed to be complex schematics with a few inked notes in the margins, arrows pointing to a box in the middle. "Um … thank you," I said. "What are these?"

He laughed. "Just meaningless doodles, but who's to know? Better than what you've got." He bent down to pluck the food wrapper from my pile. His hand brushed mine as he straightened and his expression changed. "How long have you been off-planet?"

"I … How did you know?"

"Your skin. You've lived in real air, and recently too." His eyes narrowed. "You're from *Fleetness*."

Well, this was bound to happen. If I understood him, he was not entirely legitimate either. "What of it?" I said, trying to sound tough.

He glanced around, as if afraid of being seen, then took a step away.

I stood up and put my hand on his arm, babbling almost involuntarily. "Take me with you—help me. You're right: I have no clue—"

He brushed off my hand, looking around more anxiously, though there was no one in the little park to overhear us.

"You weren't processed," he rasped, backing toward the exit corridor.

I followed him, clutching my sheaf of papers and my pack. Everything I owned in the world … any world. "No, I wasn't. I don't belong here."

He laughed, mirthlessly, still moving away. "You don't exist here. And we never met." He turned and ran down the corridor as if I were an imminent hull breach.

I tried to follow him, but he was very good at disappearing. I felt more like a misplaced realtor than ever.

Giving up, I stepped into a personal refresher. As the door hissed shut behind me, I sat down on the closed lid of the commode and rested my head in my hands, fighting off the urge to cry. Crying would accomplish nothing. I had to think.

I had panicked. Stupid. Was he already reporting me to someone? No. "You don't exist," he'd said. "We never met." So why had he approached me? He'd known that I was faking something, and yet had come to—what? Critique my performance? He'd had false papers too … but if he wasn't legit either, why should it have scared him that I was not?

Was my unprocessed status a crime to make even crooks here tremble?

What a terrifying thought.

Would turning myself in now help, or was I already beyond reprieve?

He had mentioned "the rest of us." Was there some larger group that, at least initially, he'd imagined I might belong to? Should I try to find them? Would they treat me any differently than he had?

The commode station gave a warning chime. A small plasma display above the handle invited me to apply for extra minutes by inserting a credit chip in the door. Too bad for me.

Wiping my eyes on the square of rough paper provided, I let myself out of the booth and stepped up to the hand-washing station, thinking to splash some water on my face.

"Follow me at a distance," said a tense but instantly familiar voice from the other side of the thin plio-flex wall above my sink. "Don't stop, and don't speak to anyone until I say to. Lose track of me, and you're on your own. Got it?"

I nodded, then realized he couldn't see me either. "Yes."

"Exit left," the voice commanded quietly.

I started down the ramp to my left and saw him, already fifteen feet away, walking off into the crowd at a calm but businesslike pace. I headed after him.

His route twisted and doubled back repeatedly, passing through crowded public hubs one moment and deserted service corridors the next. I soon stopped trying to make sense of our path. This endless maze without north, south, day or night befuddled me.

Eventually he paused in a narrow, under-street service tube to listen at a closed door. I stood some twenty feet behind him, trying to breathe quietly in the gloom.

Seeming satisfied, he slipped a key into the door's card slot, and it slid open. He finally turned to look at me and said, "What's your name?"

"Mara Sandstrom."

"Come with me, Mara," he said. "And behave."

Wondering what that meant, I followed him through the door into a larger tunnel, blinking and squinting under the light of massive arc fixtures clearly intended for use in much larger spaces. Work stations with ever-shifting data displays cluttered the chamber. The tech here was beat up but sophisticated. Intestinal tangles of heavy pipe and conduit jostled with the gadgetry for space against the tunnel walls, as if someone had tried to jam a whole traffic control hub into a sewer intersection.

People sat at some of the terminals, hard to make out in the glare. I wondered how anyone could see to work in here. Some turned as we came in, but gave us no more than a glance before turning back to their work.

"Stand there," my guide instructed, waving me toward a niche between two unmanned stations as far out of everyone's way as possible in such a crowded space. "Just wait."

I nodded.

My host walked to a second door in the tunnel's side some ways off, pressed his ear to it as well, then entered, closing it behind him. At first, I heard nothing but the sibilant whispers and whirrings of the tech around me, doing whatever it was there to do. Then drifts of animated conversation became audible. A moment later, the yelling started. Everyone turned to look at the door, and then at me with new interest before returning to their tasks as if they wanted nothing more to do with it.

As I began to sweat, the door crashed open against the metal struts around it, making the tunnel boom like a giant bell. A tall, muscular woman with dark, short-cropped hair wearing drab fatigues and a tight tank top strode through, heading straight for me with clenched lips and an angry glare. I managed to hold my ground and keep my mouth shut as she stopped abruptly, pointing at me as if I were a dog who had just peed on the kitchen floor.

"Sit there!" she said, pointing toward the terminal chair left of me. The man who'd done this to me ambled through the door behind her with his hands in his pockets and an expression waffling between defiance and chagrin.

I sat. There.

"Don't move—at all—'til I get back," said the Amazon in the tank top. She started toward the door we had come in by, then turned back and added, "If you so much as scratch your soft white ass before I return," she pointed at my betrayer, "he's going to kill you. If he fails to obey that order, I'll kill him."

To this day, I don't know what possessed me to find my voice at that of all moments. "Am I allowed to speak?"

Two leonine strides put her right in front of me, where she leaned down and said, "Feel free, tiny-tits." She bent even farther, planting her own very aggressive breasts practically in my face. "Just make sure your lips don't move." She straightened, pointing a cocked-gun gesture at my head, then turned and left the chamber like a gust of wind.

None of the terminal jockeys had so much as turned a head through this performance. Even now, they went on working as if nothing had happened. I turned to the man at fault with a look intended to convey ire, but which I suspect communicated nothing but terror.

"She didn't mean it," he said, "about your lips."

"What the hell have you done to me?" I demanded.

"Saved your soft white ass, most likely," he said with infuriating nonchalance. "That's why she's so mad. I've convinced her to do something stupid … I think. We'll know soon enough."

"Something stupid like what, exactly?" I asked, recovering from the rigid dread she'd left me in.

"Like convincing Adam Jones not to sell you straight off to the Cold Ones for sidestepping his authority the other day. Maybe even convincing him to let you join our little band of merry men despite not being vetted first by his boys. I could have been killed too, you know. Just for talking to you. Lexa might still do it, let alone Adam. I hope you're at least a little grateful."

"I'd be even more grateful," I sighed, daring to rub my eyes as well as move my lips, "if you'd fill some of the bigger gaps in all of that before she comes back."

"Gaps?" But then he smiled and said, "Okay. In here, though."

"She told me not to move...." One of the terminal jockeys snickered. Feeling foolish, I stood and followed the man into the room his boss lady had come from.

O O O

As the door shut behind us, I looked around a chamber that seemed part office, part break room, part bunk space. A cluttered desk abutted the left-hand wall, next to a low and shabby couch; a rickety chair and a cooler took up one corner, and a large purple exercise ball sat in the middle of the floor.

Just seeing the bunk's rumpled blanket and thin pillow made my body ache for rest. What I would not have done for a soft, safe space to sleep....

The man sat in the chair and waved me toward the couch, which I sank into wearily. "You got a name?" I asked.

"Robbin."

I nodded, my old training coming back: act confident even if you're not; take the offensive; ask questions; conceal surprise. I sat forward against the couch's undertow. "Who was the charming lady? Lexa, did you say?"

Robbin laughed, a little grimly. "Lexa, yeah. Queen of our resource." He waved a hand around the bleak room. "Master of all this."

"What kind of resource are we talking about?" I asked, wondering if it were something I was qualified to sell.

"Procurement mostly," he replied. "That's our focus. If you need anything you can't get on *Longhorn 6*, you come to us."

His answer baffled me. "Procurement? How is that a resource?"

He looked blank, then suddenly amused. "That's just what we call our ... service guilds here. Resource is a name, not a commodity. There are all kinds. Lexa's resource provides procurement services. Adam's provides immigration services. He decides which resource newcomers get assigned to. Running off without his say-so was a bad idea. He's more or less the top of the food chain around here." He wagged a finger at me. "Not good to piss him off."

"But … doesn't Galactic issue work assignments here?"

"Oh, well, sure, officially." He shrugged. "But who cares? Galactic's little soldiers may stamp their forms and send all the required guff off to their distant corporate bosses, but they take their real orders from Adam or whoever he assigns them to, just like everybody else." Robbin leaned forward soberly. "The first and most important thing to understand now, Mara, is that 'official' channels are empty theater here. Everything on *Longhorn 6* is run by the resources. You work with them, you'll thrive. Try getting all 'official' and you'll lose—badly. Got that?"

"I guess so," I said. "And these Cold Ones Adam Jones was going to sell me to; what are they? The beer resource?"

Robbin didn't smile. If anything, he looked even graver. Before he could answer, though, the door opened and Lexa strode back in.

I tensed, fearing she'd shoot me for moving. But she just tossed a leg over the exercise ball and planted herself on top of it.

"It's fixed," she said, ostensibly to Robbin but watching me. She grabbed two small flex-balls from the desk, and began to squeeze them absently. "Adam's added her to this month's invoice."

"Good," Robbin said, a bit uncertainly.

"Yeah. There's a price. But nothing we can't handle." Her grip on the flex-balls seemed to tighten. "So you're Mara, right?"

I nodded.

"From the *Fleetness*. Their roster lists you as a realtor?"

I nodded again.

"Well, here's the deal, take it or leave it. This tub's got no real estate, and you know nothing about how things function, which means a giant suck on our training and protection before you're of any use. Fronting you the necessary identity and credits to get started will cost us too. We'll do it, but I'll have sole authority to determine the balance of your debt—with interest—at any time. No appeal or recourse. I alone determine how your time is spent, including sleep. We protect you from competing resources, give you bunk, board, and training 'til you have a use here. In return, you work quickly to become a productive member of our resource, with whatever that entails. We don't have much room on *Longhorn 6*. You may have to share a bunk." Her eyes danced with amusement, though she didn't smile. "At least 'til we relocate. You in?"

Alarms were screaming in my brain. *Share a bunk? With whom?* I thought of those other women from *Fleetness*—some as young as twelve—herded off by rough, leering men. *No recourse or appeal? How much interest, and of what kind? All that front room tech hadn't looked like a comfort services operation. But still …*

"Robbin says you do procurement," I said. "What exactly do you procure?"

"Whatever's wanted," she replied. "If it's here, we get our hands on it. If it's not, we find out where it is and how to get it here. Affordably," she added, with a wry look that implied some second meaning.

"Do you procure women?" I asked, seeing no point in delicacy.

She snorted, then laughed. "Whores? You think *that's* what we want you for? You ain't got the tits for it, sweetness, or the spine. That's Chanele's resource anyway." She turned to Robbin. "How do you *find* these stray creatures? Tell her something about life, okay? I've got too much to do." She hoisted herself smoothly off the exercise ball and over to the desk, where she riffled through a pile of papers.

"Mara," Robbin said. "She's giving you a better deal than anyone else here will. I'd take it. Quickly. You owe her already just for saving you from Adam."

My mind continued to race. Take it or leave it, she'd said. In sales of property, personal or real, oral contracts aren't valid. Nor is any agreement made under duress. This could not possibly be legally binding. If I could get hold of Astoria, I could leave without breach. My license would remain clean. Meanwhile, I did need help with basic survival. I didn't have a choice. We all knew that.

"I agree to your terms."

Lexa smiled and came to shake my hand. Her grip was very strong.

O O O

I learned fast. I had to.

Three days later, I was packing up non-essentials in the resource mess in preparation for our relocation, when one of our terminal jockeys, a red-haired woman named Avini, came in and handed me a packet.

Inside I found a key card, skin chip, and bag of stick-on sensors identifying me as one Linda Margress, recently transferred from *Longhorn 4* after unspecified conflict with her supervisor. That rankled me. I'd always gotten along perfectly with my superiors.

"Lexa can help you install that," Avini said, pointing to the skin chip.

"Thanks." I shuddered to think of Lexa near my skin for any reason. It seemed clear by now that the shared bunk she'd threatened was likely her own. Happily, that threat had not been followed up on … yet.

Avini rummaged through the cooler for a drink. "Can't wait for our new digs," she said, glancing at my half-filled boxes. "We got really lucky this time. Or smart." She smirked mysteriously. "Lexa's very resourceful."

"So I've gathered," I said. "I've been wondering, though. If Galactic owns all the space here, who decides how things are allocated?"

"Oh, turf's the biggest game in town," Avini said, opening her beverage. "With more newbies all the time, space keeps getting tighter, so everybody's always scrambling to trade up. There'd have been a Turf resource here ages ago, but no one's willing to hand one group sole authority over something that important."

"I can imagine," I replied. So, real estate wasn't bought or sold per se here … but they were still negotiating deals for structured space—something I knew lots about. Suddenly, I could imagine being much more useful than Lexa supposed.

O O O

As moving day approached, our preparations grew increasingly frenetic. My new identity as Linda Margress enabled Lexa to start sending me on errands elsewhere in the station. I was terrified at first of screwing up and being exposed, but the tech was good. "Linda" passed through doors unchallenged, and I'd learned enough by then inside Lexa's warren to make better sense of what I encountered outside it. Soon I was walking *Longhorn 6*'s corridors with the confidence of a native.

Robbin was a godsend in those first weeks, constantly appearing at my side to answer questions I hadn't known to ask yet, or to help with tasks Lexa had fired at me without sufficient explanation. I quickly came to appreciate and even trust him, but he was so attractive, not to mention so far above me in the pecking order, that I never suspected he might regard me as more than just another of the needy strays he loved to save.

I was often asked to carry messages to members of the Food Services resource with whom we were about to swap locations—a trade down for them. They liked to complain about that, and I took care to be a sympathetic listener, which made them even more forthcoming about the larger "space-trading game" on *Longhorn 6*. I learned tons about who had or was or would be trading which space with whom, and why. As my grasp of which attributes and locations were commonly preferred or avoided increased, I began to see how such preferences might be manipulated even more effectively, and to suspect that Procurement could do better than Food Services' slightly larger but still cramped offering.

I had learned that the Transportation resource was looking not to move but to expand into new equipment and storage space. The Entertainment resource had a very spacious but unneeded warehouse they were tired of maintaining, but Transportation wasn't happy with its location. They wanted something closer to … Procurement's sector, as it happened. A few discreet inquiries convinced me that, with some trifling modifications, Entertainment's warehouse would make luxuriously spacious headquarters for us, if anyone looked beyond the building's current label to see that.

Leery of attracting any more of Lexa's attention, I dropped a few casual remarks about all this to Robbin instead. Two days later our resource was celebrating the announcement that we'd be moving not to Food Service's squalid nest down in the maintenance sector, but into Entertainment's even bigger building three decks up, smack in the station's dining and theater hub. Lexa had convinced Transportation to cover rental on Entertainment's warehouse, but move their excess storage and equipment into our better suited labyrinth of tunnels instead, free of further charge, allowing Food Services, who'd only been strong-armed by Lexa into trading down at all, to stay right where they were. Win, win, win. Everyone agreed that Lexa's cleverness seemed boundless.

Lexa, unfortunately, knew very well whose cleverness lay behind this sudden windfall. Robbin had been scrupulous about giving me credit for the idea. My *reward* was promotion to a desk job in the new hive, right in Lexa's grandly expanded office. I sat all day now at a small terminal to one side of Lexa's desk, where we could consult each other more readily about any other innovative opportunities I might come up with. And about the flatness of my chest and ass, and the cute way I always flinched when Lexa came to look over my shoulder. There were no rules in resource-land about sexual harassment in the workplace, and I soon realized that Lexa expressed interest, even admiration, through taunting and disparagement. My boyish figure might not have suited a whore, but Lexa didn't seem to mind it much.

My yearning to get off of *Longhorn 6* altogether grew steadily. I floated the subject once with Robbin, whose disapproval was instantly palpable. Procurement hadn't taken me in and trained me, he admonished, just to send me off again with best wishes and a sandwich for the journey. I had debts to resolve before I went anywhere. I didn't air the topic again, but they vigilantly denied me any access to off-station communications after that.

I had an even bigger problem here, however, than mere loathing of the predatory Lexa. I simply wasn't formatted for a life of petty criminality. Ironically, it was the very act of recognizing another, much larger "innovative opportunity" for Lexa's resource that brought this fact home to me.

My interest in untapped approaches to *Longhorn 6*'s quasi-real-estate game was now encouraged. Lexa began engineering chance opportunities for me to chat with folks from any resource I wished. She even lured the infamous Adam Jones to her office one evening on some other pretext, just so I could listen in while she salted their conversation with passing queries about his own thoughts on space around the station. He was an older gentleman who, in striking contrast to everyone else I'd seen here, looked and dressed more like a corporate board member than an underworld boss. Interest in the acquisition of place in this inherently spaceless canister was virtually bottomless, as his talk made clear. The upper echelon of underworld bosses here controlled ample wealth to purchase entire prefectures on lots of nice planets. Yet all that wealth was just being endlessly recycled on this dingy interstellar truck stop.

I was baffled by such short-sightedness until I recognized a subtle but important difference between myself and others here. Nearly everyone on *Longhorn 6*—maybe even its extraneous corporate functionaries—had been compelled to come as punishment for something, or been driven here only after exhausting all better options. The very idea of "elsewhere" must have seemed void to them even before arrival. The struggle just to survive here, much less bend this insular network of Darwinian ambitions and imperatives to one's own advantage, was so consuming that perhaps even those who won the game were too shaped by it to retain awareness of any world beyond.

I, however, had not come needing to stand or die here, and thus still thought to look outside the cage we shared. That simple inclination, I realized in a dizzying flash, might constitute a kind of super-power here, if used cleverly.

O O O

That night I fished Procurement's own extensive data banks, then reduced my findings to a single, easily comprehensible page. Next morning, I walked into Lexa's office and asked her to join me at my terminal.

She raised a brow in surprise, and came to lean, too closely as usual, over my shoulder. This time I didn't flinch, and I could tell she noticed.

"What's this, then?" she asked.

"The top list shows price ranges for extensive real-estate holdings on several desirable planets, all of which were available for purchase just prior to my departure from Earth. The middle list contains my conservative guesses at the likely net worth of *Longhorn 6*'s most prosperous resource bosses, including yourself."

"That's any of your business why?" she asked; then, before I could respond, she snorted, "Ridiculously conservative, actually."

"I didn't have access to sufficient data to be more accurate. This longer list down here contains my much more educated estimates of probable return over just five years on any of the investments listed above."

Lexa leaned even harder into my shoulder to scan the bottom list with increasing interest, shoving her breasts against my back. "Impressive, but why should I care about real estate stuck halfway across the galaxy?" she asked, breathing the question into my ear.

"Why shouldn't you care?" I replied, shrugging her off as I stood and turned to face her squarely. "That seems a better question."

She just stared, trying, it seemed, to make sense of my answer, or perhaps of my behavior in general.

"This resource keeps meticulous track of every item on every cargo manifest, and every passenger or crew member aboard any vessel traveling within 40,000 light years of this station," I said. "That's how we locate what we wish to 'procure.' The planetary assets I've listed here are all far closer than that. Why ignore them?"

She just seemed startled by my denseness. "There are lots of ways to steer a slice of cargo from its intended route. We can lure an entire ship here, if needed. But how am I supposed to finesse some big chunk of Elysium 17 over to *Longhorn 6*? If anybody here wanted to purchase planetary real estate, he'd go there to enjoy it. I bring items *here* for people who need to have them *here*."

"Money moves independently of the land that generates it, Lexa. Money's easier to move than any other item in the universe. You of all people know that. Does no one here want to move the kind of money I've listed here as well?"

Lexa grew uncharacteristically silent for the second time in five minutes. I could see gears grinding into reverse behind her eyes.

"Every person on that list could nearly double their hoard within ten years," I said into her silence, "just by going to see a decent realtor."

"There … are no realtors here," she said, half gaping as my point finally pierced her shield of entrenched assumptions.

"There's *one*," I said. "This is what I'm trained to do, Lexa. Remotely, if necessary. Interested in an untapped market for something more lucrative than the occasional case of luxophore vials or taze-guns? Something for the more discriminating customer?"

"Well, well, well," she murmured, gazing inward now.

I had never seen her so off balance, and I grabbed the opportunity. "I know where and how to look for bargains. I can recognize a trap and scam the scammers in this market. I understand the language, the games, the miles of documentation involved, the legal and financial knots and how to cut them. I just need you to start tilling the soil here while I get on the net and troll around."

"Well, well, fucking well," she said, grinning at something other than my tits and ass for once.

O O O

Lexa wasted no time. By the following morning, Procurement's unlikely rising star had an office of her own. Our discriminating customers would, of course, need to feel that they could take me seriously. I even found the nerve to suggest that turning down the sexual brinksmanship a little might crank up my productivity even further. To my quiet amazement, Lexa had just nodded with a wry look of—was that actual respect—or just pragmatic avarice?

Most importantly, my new office contained a terminal with access to unrestricted communications. I could hardly manage complex, mega-real estate transactions, after all, without engaging in research and communication beyond *Longhorn 6*. My plan seemed to be working even better than I'd hoped.

As my fortunes rose, Robbin's "supportiveness" increased. I finally got the picture when he came by one afternoon to ask if I'd have a drink with him at the Blue Muse: a pricey eatery I'd heard about, but never dared to enter, given the debt I was already incurring just by breathing here under Lexa's sponsorship. When I reminded him of my strapped condition, he just looked surprised and said the drinks would be on him, of course. Though he also assured me that, given my amazing progress, I'd surely be settled up with Lexa in record time.

The Lemon Drops we ordered must have cost him dearly in their frosty flutes of real glass. They contained at least a squeeze of real lemon; I found a seed in one of mine. Ignited by the liquor, his charm grew almost incandescent, and I was very flattered—still incredulous, in fact, that a guy this cute would even notice me. A few weeks earlier, I'd probably have lunged at the extra shelter his affection might lend me. But as pretty as he was, and as helpful as he'd been, he was a creature of this place which I now hoped to leave soon. I owed him, yes, but I could not pretend to love him. I laughed at his witticisms, and expressed my gratitude for his many kindnesses, but continued to pretend I didn't understand how much more he wanted.

O O O

Certain that Lexa would carefully monitor my off-station communications, I was perfectly behaved for several weeks. My pursuit of investment opportunities was real and relentless. I even sent a few short missives to Robbin about how exciting it was to have serious work again, and how invested I felt in my future here, hoping that Lexa would see them.

Not until our first big transaction was in motion did I dare hope Lexa might have grown distracted and complacent enough for me to make an attempt at summoning rescue. Having found a credible real estate opportunity in which Astoria was involved, I sent them a complex contractual proposal with an encrypted link to my brief S.O.S. embedded in the yards of fine print at its end. I felt sure their legal sniffers would find it quickly enough, but hoped Lexa would never even read that far. Fine print, after all, was what I was here to spare her.

More than a week passed before Lexa called me to her office to discuss one of our recent proposals. When I arrived, she asked me to close the door and come look at something on her desk display. I walked to her side and looked down:

From Broker Mara Sandstrom, urgent. Fleetness *destroyed on entry into Longhorn space; unknown number of survivors held on* Longhorn 6. *Send rescue. Security here doubtful. Respond to this alias only.*

There wasn't even time to blanch before Lexa's backhand struck me hard enough to rattle teeth. I staggered back, holding my burning cheek and staring at her through watering eyes.

"Traitorous bitch!" she snarled. "How dare you betray me—Robbin—all of us this way, after what we've done for you?"

"How is wanting off this place betrayal?" I demanded. "I can do this work for you from anywhere, but I'll never belong here. That must be as obvious to you as it is to me. Why should you care if I manage your new empire from some place with a real sky?"

"Not just traitorous, but stupid after all," she spat in disgust. "Did you really think anyone here would let someone who knows all you do about this place just flee into the arms of some off-station corporate authority? Hasn't it occurred to you, Ms. Smartypants, what an exposure threat you'd be? If Adam were to discover this little stunt of yours, he'd have you iced yesterday." She shook her head, almost wearily. "Galactic closes its eyes to what goes on here because we make it worth its while to do so. Astoria would have no such motivation. Don't you get that?"

I did now. My stomach was a cold, hard knot of fear. They'd never let me go, however much debt I paid off. They might not even let me live now.

"If you had succeeded at this," Lexa growled, "I would have been held responsible—by anyone here with something to lose—and that's *everyone*! I'd have been fodder for the Cold Ones, and this whole resource would have been stripped of respect or leverage, and reorganized if not dismantled."

I glanced back miserably at the message still on her screen.

"Yes," she said. "That needs fixing. *Now*."

"How?" I asked, no longer able to meet her gaze.

"I don't know or care, but you have three hours to convince me that Astoria has been persuaded to disregard your idiotic message, or I'll march you to the Cold Ones myself." One look at her hard expression told me this threat wasn't empty.

O O O

Back in my office, I tried to compose some credible reversal of my appeal, but there was nothing I could say to Astoria now that would not arouse even greater suspicion. I still had no precise idea of who the Cold Ones were, or what they'd do to me, but with only three hours left before finding out, there was nothing to lose by trying something even more desperate.

I'd heard more than once about a Galactic enforcement official here, a Major Samuel Fisk, whom everyone resented or admired for refusing to be bought. Local lore held him as the only corporate functionary on *Longhorn 6* wholly loyal to Galactic. It seemed time I met him.

O O O

As I hurried to find him, I kept looking over my shoulder, fearful of being overtaken by some henchman of Lexa's, but I saw nobody following. When I arrived at Major Fisk's unassuming complex, claiming urgent need to see him, I was ushered straight into his spartan office.

"How may I help you, Miss …?" he asked, awaiting my name.

"Mara Sandstrom," I said, breathlessly. "I'm told you are the only fully trustworthy man on *Longhorn 6*. Is that true?" Confident of my shrewdly honed "realtor's ability" to read people, I knew I'd be able to parse his response for genuineness if I took him by surprise.

He looked nonplussed. "I pride myself on thinking so. My loyalties are to no one but Galactic, if that is what you mean."

He did seem sincere. I nodded. "Good. I need your help. I was brought here from the *Fleetness*." This drew a startled expression. "Before I could be processed, I was coerced into the service of … a criminal organization here."

"I am well aware of the resources," he said, "and I am in none of their pockets, if that's what you're worried about."

"Yes," I said, deeply relieved. "I have just escaped from one of them after being threatened with execution. I've contacted my previous employer—"

"Astoria Corporation, I assume?" he interjected. At my surprised pause, he spread his hands and said, "You arrived aboard the *Fleetness* ..."

"Of course." Hoping my attachment to a rival company would not dispose him against me, I continued. "I believe Astoria may come to retrieve me, if I live that long. Can you protect me until then?"

"I'm glad you came to me," he said reassuringly. "I do know people who can help you. I'll escort you to them personally."

"I would be so grateful," I said.

He touched his desk display, and a functionary entered. After instructing the man to notify my prospective protectors of our imminent arrival, he turned back to me and said, "Shall we go?"

"I don't know how to thank you."

"No need for thanks," he said. "This is what I'm here for."

O O O

Neither the furtive route we traveled, nor the dark, deserted service tunnel to which he led me aroused my suspicion. We were here to hide me. Of course, it would be done secretively, far from prying eyes. Not until the two forbidding men who met us there grabbed hold of me and clapped my arms into restraints did I understand I'd been betrayed.

"Who are you?" I demanded of my captors, tugging at my bonds to no avail.

"The Cold Ones," one of them replied, with the hint of a smirk. "You haven't guessed?"

"Liar!" I shouted at Fisk, my heart sinking. "Who owns you? Lexa?"

"I am owned by no one here but my employer, Galactic Enterprises."

"Then why?"

"Has no one told you who commissioned the sabotage of your vessel?" he asked. "In all this time? I'm surprised to find so much discretion here."

"Sabotage?" I asked, feeling lightheaded. "Who would want—?"

"My employer did not want yours to gain a foothold on Greenleaf 43." He shrugged apologetically. "Business at this scale requires unpleasant things of us all. Gentlemen," he said, nodding at my captors. Then he turned and walked away as if I were a bundle of celluboard left for the recyclers.

O O O

My captors neither spoke again, nor exhibited any perverse pleasure in their work, but their grip never wavered until I was locked into an unfurnished, corrugated metal holding cell not far from where I'd been delivered. I was soon visited there by a new if equally laconic man who handed me a drab paper jumpsuit and demanded my clothes and few possessions in exchange. I was not allowed privacy, but he kept his hands to himself, showing no sign of prurient interest while I changed. When I'd finished, he gave me a bottle of water and some refreshment stand chips, then turned to go.

"How will I be killed?" I asked as he reached for the door.

"Killed?" he said over his shoulder.

"That's what you do, isn't it?" I said, trying to sound brave for some reason. More reflexive realtor training, I suppose.

"We let people think so." He turned back to face me. "But in fact, little of what you've been told about us is true."

"I've been told nothing," I said in frustration. "People keep mentioning you guys like you're the ultimate nightmare, but they never tell me what you do. You're a resource, I take it?"

He nodded. "A sort of Waste Disposal resource. We dispose of those who prove too useless to merit the space and air they consume here, or too troublesome to those in power. We let the general populace imagine what they will, of course, because that scares them more effectively than anything else, but we don't really salvage organs here, or hoard gold teeth. There's not even any killing, unless we're left no choice. That's up to you, of course."

"Then how do you—?"

"You'll know soon enough," he said, turning away again. "Let your current troubles suffice, Ms. Sandstrom, and rest while you can." He passed through the door, which locked behind him.

I sat down against the wall, seeking some comfortable position on the metal floor, and pondered the long list of mistakes that had landed me here. No wonder Lexa hadn't prevented my flight. She'd known there really wasn't any place for me to run. Now I was to be "disposed of," without being killed?

"This one?" said a voice outside my door.

"Yes, sir. She's in there."

My cell door clicked open once again, and a man I recognized walked in, looking as dapper and respectable as ever.

"Why, Mr. Jones," I said, beyond surprise by now. "I don't suppose you've come to rescue me."

"I rarely offer second chances, Ms. Sandstrom. Never third ones." He closed the door and leaned against the jamb. "What a lot of trouble you have been."

"So what brings a man of your importance here?" I asked.

"I sometimes check on my employees' work, especially when such important guests are involved."

"Your employees? You run this resource too?"

"No one outside our membership is allowed to know that, but yes, I oversee both immigration and emigration here. You slipped past me in one direction, but I really couldn't let it happen twice. It's quite crucial to us all that you be thoroughly misplaced before Astoria's rescue mission arrives."

"They're coming then?" I asked, with less enthusiasm than I might have felt if I had still hoped to be around for their arrival.

"Oh yes," Jones said. "They've been quite stealthy about it, but they're on their way, and with a military escort." He shook his head. "Accidents won't be viable this time, I'm afraid. We must let them dock, and seem quite as appalled as anyone to find you've disappeared. Rest assured, however, that we shall leave no stone unturned in our attempt to discover your abductors. Examples will be made of … well, all kinds of people by the time we're finished finding out what happened to you."

"And what is going to happen to me?"

"As you may know, Ms. Sandstrom, our corporate leaders here on *Longhorn 6* abhor waste of any kind. Merely killing even very undesirable people results in nothing but expense without profit.

On the other hand, there are numerous corporate clients out there desperate to reduce the excessive expense, labyrinthine regulatory burden, and endless documentation associated with any *legitimate* labor force. In places like *Longhorn 6*, Galactic Enterprises has found a way to address these problems quite profitably, by hiring people like me to harvest useless, unproductive individuals and convert them into an astonishingly valuable commodity. As I believe you have been told, Ms. Sandstrom, we're not here to kill you. We are here to offer you a brand new, immensely more productive life on Steele 17, a lovely planet in the—"

"I know very well where Steele 17 is!" I gasped, shooting to my feet. "It's a strip-mine in the Chlorite system! You're selling me into slavery?"

"No, Ms. Sandstrom. Galactic will be doing that. I am just a humble middle man conveying self-selected candidates like yourself for their consideration." He stood away from the wall, and put his hand to the door. "I did give you a second chance, my dear. And for a while I was almost glad I had. What a shame." He shook his head like a disappointed father. "Perhaps they'll need a realtor on Steele 17 as badly as we did."

He left me then, gaping in dismay. I had wanted off of *Longhorn 6*—but not this way.

O O O

Eventually exhaustion prevailed and I slept on my cell floor. Sometime later, a hand on my shoulder nudged me awake. Robbin bent over me, a finger to his lips.

"Come. Quietly," he whispered. "We've only got a minute."

Seemed like I was always following this man. I climbed stiffly to my feet. Whatever he meant to do with me now could hardly be worse than slavery on Steele 17.

I followed him into the corridor and found the two men who'd brought me here sprawled face down on the floor. I looked back up at Robbin in astonishment, but he shook his head and waved me urgently past them. He seemed to know where he was going, stopping only to peer around corners or listen at doors before proceeding. We finally stopped at a floor hatch, where Robbin took something from his pocket, shoved it against a key slot, then pushed the hatch door open and waved me through ahead of him. We climbed down into a poorly illuminated crawl space, through which we hurried in a crouch.

The cramped passage snaked on endlessly. Twice we had to freeze and hold our breaths as running footsteps passed above us. By the time Robbin helped me up into some blessedly taller service corridor, I had an awful crick in my neck.

"Where are we going?" I finally dared to whisper.

He just waved me after him around two more corners to a room lined with wall-lockers full of grimy coveralls and jumbled tools.

"Put this on," said Robbin, handing me a set of coveralls before pulling on his own. Then he rummaged around and produced two welding helmets. "Don't forget to tuck your hair inside," he said, handing me one before donning his.

"What are we doing?" I asked again. "Did Lexa send you?"

"Lexa won't be sending me anywhere but back to the Cold Ones, after this."

I stopped fiddling with my helmet and looked up in surprise. "You did this behind her back?"

"There was some other way?" His voice was muffled by the helmet, but his tone was unambiguously grim. "Astoria's headed here to get you," he said. "ETA five days. Lexa's spitting sparks about it."

"I know," I said. "Adam Jones told me."

Robbin's faceplate snapped around toward me. "How would you have talked to Jones?"

"He came to my cell. He's the Cold Ones' boss."

"No shit!" Robbin exclaimed. "That's info worth a fortune."

"How did you find out where I was?" I asked.

"Called in a lot of favors," he said. "You're not the first stray I've helped, you know. It pays to make friends—even here."

"So, if you're at odds with Lexa, where are we going?"

"I'm not sure yet," he admitted. "I was lucky just to find out where you were before they killed you. Haven't had a chance to think much further. But there are places we can hide until your ship comes in."

"Then what?" I asked. "For you, I mean? Where will you go?"

"With you, of course. I've just crossed Lexa badly, and cold-cocked two Cold Ones. Can't very well stay here now—not breathing anyway."

I shut my eyes, thankful that the helmet hid my face. How would he feel, I wondered, when he learned that even after this, I still didn't love him? "Actually, they weren't going to kill me," I said, half-apologetically.

"Oh, really?" he asked skeptically. "I've never heard of anyone returning from delivery to the Cold Ones."

"They don't," I said. "Adam turns them over to Galactic, who sells them to corporate interests looking for free, unregulated labor. I was slated for sale to Steele 17."

Robbin simply stared at me.

"None of you knew this? Really?" I asked.

"But the stories," Robbin said, sounding stunned. "Everyone's heard—"

"—what everyone else assumes or invents," I finished for him. "The Cold Ones just let you all believe yourselves."

"'Til they're so scary, we don't even want to think about them, much less snoop. It's the perfect curtain." Robbin shook his head. "If people here knew that Adam was selling even the worst of us to Galactic, they'd riot. He'll want us dead now even more than Lexa does. We'd better keep moving." He grabbed a hand torch off the bench beside us and handed it to me. "Just act like you can't wait to weld something."

O O O

For three days we snuck from hidey-hole to hidey-hole. Robbin seemed intimately familiar with every service hatch and ventilation shaft on *Longhorn 6*. He was an accomplished thief as well. We ate better on the run than I had ever eaten at the resource—and for free.

Early on our fourth day, Robbin found us a small, unoccupied living module where we could sit in plush inflatable chairs before a simulated roaring fire on the virteo screen.

"Why do you help people like me?" I asked him. "What's in it for you?"

"There's an ancient myth from Earth about a bandit king named Robbin Hat," he said, sheepishly. "Ever hear it?"

I shook my head.

"My father did," he said. "He loved to tell it to me when I was little. He named me after Robbin Hat, who stole from the rich and gave to the poor." Robbin shrugged. "My dad tried to be that kind of thief, I think. I guess I've always wanted to be too." He stretched out lazily, wiggling his bare toes before the virteo fire as if it were actually warm.

He had never seemed more charming to me than he did at that moment. "Robbin," I said, "I've been thinking about what Adam and Galactic have been doing here, and if we tell Astoria—"

The sound of a keycard in the door brought us both to our feet. We whirled around to find ourselves staring at the barrel of a snub-nosed scrap gun—the kind used by people who don't mind a mess.

"What a cozy place," Lexa said to Robbin, her face a mask of cold fury. "Your realtor find this for you?"

Robbin just looked blank, then dropped his gaze. "How'd you find us?"

"If your network was better than mine," she said contemptuously, "you'd have been my boss, and I'd have been your toady." She glanced at me with even greater disdain. "Her I saw coming, Robbin, but I never thought you'd stab me in the back. You know what Adam thinks of me by now. I've gone from trusted confidante to laughing stock."

"Adam's always thought you were as clueless as everybody else here," I said, recklessly. "He as good as told me so when he dropped by my cell to see how well his Cold Ones were doing their job the other day." Taunting her was suicidal, but Robbin had said that our new information about Adam was worth a fortune. I hoped she'd think so too.

"What crap are you barfing up now?" she growled.

"Adam is the Cold Ones' boss," I said. "Or hadn't he mentioned that? He uses them to harvest slave labor here on *Longhorn 6*, for Galactic to sell off on other planets. That's what really happens to the people they 'dispose of,' but I'm sure Adam's already shared that with you too. He says it's very profitable. Does he kick back any of that wealth to trusted confidantes like you?"

"What an inventive mind you've got in that pretty head," said Lexa. "I almost hate to blow it off."

"It's true!" Robbin insisted. "Jones is in Galactic's pocket, and I'll bet slave labor's not the only way he's sold us out to them. How do you think he's held so much power for so long? He plays both ends."

"Why should I believe you either?" Lexa snapped, pointing her gun back at him.

"Adam said he would be making examples of a lot of people after Astoria comes," I pressed. "Scapegoats to explain my disappearance. How much you wanna bet that you'll be one of them?"

"Shut your fucking mouth!" she yelled, her gun on me again. But I could tell we had her, and began to talk as fast as—well, a realtor.

"Galactic sabotaged the *Fleetness.*"

"What?" Lexa blurted.

I looked her in the eye. "If you don't believe me, ask Major Fisk. I think he arranged it personally." Lexa's jaw went slack, and I decided it was time to bet everything. "Galactic and Astoria are quietly at war, Lexa, and Astoria's been losing. Can you imagine what they'd give for what we know about Galactic? They could destroy their biggest rival overnight. Forget Procurement. Astoria could give us rule of this entire station!"

"Or I could kill you both and let Astoria hand everything to me," she said.

"Your testimony is just secondhand hearsay," I told her. "I'm the only direct or credible witness, and Astoria won't pay for what won't hold up in court."

"None of that'll matter anyway after Adam fingers you for Mara's kidnap, Lexa," Robbin interjected. "Incriminating you discredits your testimony and saves his neck. You can't think he won't see that. I'd be pissed at us too, Lexa, but come on."

"It doesn't matter how we do this," Lexa said. "Adam will—"

"Adam will go down in flames with his partner, Galactic," I cut in. "Help us hide for one more day, get us onto that ship alive tomorrow, and let Astoria set you up for life. Or shoot that thing and go back to your trusted confidante for a pat on the head. That's the deal. Take it or leave it."

O O O

The rest, as they say, is history. Lexa held up her part of the bargain easily enough. Jones was so sure of her that he never thought to look for us under her skirts. Rumor has it he was last seen shortly after Lexa got us aboard Astoria's transport, screaming away from *Longhorn 6* in a small private craft. His Cold Ones have vanished into legend here as well.

Galactic Enterprises is history too. And, as expected, Astoria has rewarded us lavishly enough to make even Lexa blush.

It's been six months now, and I'm finally getting used to my new routine here. Robbin is my second-in-command. Lexa … Well, Lexa works for us. She's our top enforcer now; number-three dog in *Longhorn 6*'s food chain, and damned well paid for what she does. Not all she might have hoped for, but considering that I knew enough to have her clapped in chains for life if I had chosen to share her history with Astoria too, I think she's content.

Am I bummed to find myself still stuck out here on *Longhorn 6*? Not so much. I live in the former Station Master's palace now, and spend my days administering Astoria's new construction project. *Longhorn 6* already orbited a star. It just had no planets, so Astoria has decided to build a very nice one. I can see the work progressing from my window, without even getting out of bed. And when it's done and ready for settlement, its first on-site brokerage will be mine.

Robbin is still trying to convince me to be his Maid Marianne, but I haven't decided. One way or another, he'll be fine.

And so will I.

Shannon Page is a Pacific Northwest author and editor. Her work has appeared in *Clarkesworld*, *Interzone*, *Fantasy*, *Black Static*, Tor.com, and many anthologies, including the Australian Shadows Award-winning *Grants Pass*, and *The Mammoth Book of Dieselpunk*. Books include *Eel River*; the collection *Eastlick and Other Stories*; a collaboration with Karen G. Berry under the pen name Laura Gayle, *Orcas Intrigue*, the first book in the Chameleon Chronicles; and *Our Lady of the Islands*, co-written with the late Jay Lake. *Our Lady* received starred reviews from *Publishers Weekly* and *Library Journal*, was named one of *Publishers Weekly*'s Best Books of 2014, and was a finalist for the Endeavour Award. Edited books include the anthology *Witches, Stitches & Bitches* and essay collection *The Usual Path to Publication.* She practices yoga, gardens, and has no tattoos. Website: shannonpage.net.

Mark J. Ferrari has been a well-known commercial illustrator since 1987. His first fantasy novel, *The Book of Joby*, was published by Tor in 2007, honored as a Booksense Pick, made Booklist's 'Top Ten' for science fiction/fantasy in 2008, and was chosen as a finalist for the Endeavor Award. It was re-released as a mass market paperback in 2012, and has since been published by Science Fiction World in China. He has also published short stories written in collaboration with his wife, Shannon Page, and is currently working on an upcoming illustrated online fantasy serial called TWICE. He resides in Portland, Oregon, and more info on his art and writing can be found at markferrari.com.

Part VI: Space Battles

Edited by Bryan Thomas Schmidt

The Thirteens

by Gene Mederos

Introduction to "The Thirteens"

Space Battles was my first chance to edit an anthology, and I lucked into a subgenre I am a huge fan of and very familiar with: space opera and military science fiction. All the stories center around battles between ships and species and the conflicts and dramatic impacts which arise out of those. Being a series of anthologies, I also picked stories from some series veterans to be sure I captured the feel and style of previous books, and Gene Mederos is one of those veterans.

In "The Thirteens," Captain Andromeda Sax and the crew of La Espada leave their station to investigate a bogey, and come up against Purists, a religious sect dedicated to ridding the galaxy of impurities—like the diverse alien and human species crewing her own ship. Certainly, ideological and interracial/interspecies conflicts have long histories for humans so imagining them shaping our intergalactic relations has a long tradition in science fiction. Mederos accomplishes this with a ton of exciting action and that made "The Thirteens" perfect for Space Battles.

Nestled deeply in the foam mattress of the semi-luxurious hotel suite her rank afforded her, Captain Andromeda Sax was sound asleep when her com went off. The double pulse told her it was something important enough to warrant a secure connection. Even less than half awake her hand automatically flew to the spot on her jaw below her right ear. She pressed the small stud embedded there under her skin.

"Go ahead."

"Captain, a bogey has entered the system," the officer of the watch on board her ship, *La Espada de la Libertad*, informed her.

That could have been anywhere from four to six hours ago, depending on which of the outer system beacons had first detected the incoming ship and transmitted the alert. A bogey was a ship that did not, or could not, transmit a valid ID code. It could be a smuggler, a legitimate freighter with a screwy comp—or it could be the enemy. Sax allowed herself a small smile; after all, there was no one around to see it.

"Recall the crew, *priority one*." That gave the crew ten minutes to get back aboard the ship. She spared one last glance at her room. Aquarii Station was on the frontier, but it still managed to offer most of the comforts of the more cosmopolitan stations of the home-worlds. Accommodations on *La Espada* were much more austere. She smiled again.

Five minutes later she strode onto the bridge. She hadn't really had time to dress, just comb her short-cropped jet-black hair and throw on her officer's greatcoat, but the voluminous garment covered her from neck to ankles. And if anyone noticed she was wearing slippers instead of boots, they wouldn't *dare* comment on it. The guards at the door snapped to attention. The crew on the bridge was all in uniform and seated at their stations. She always kept a full watch on duty while the rest of the crew took liberty.

"Inform the stationmaster we are launching to investigate," she instructed the com officer, then requested the general hail. "Emergency separation from Aquarii station in T-minus four minutes." That was sure to make the stragglers scramble, for anyone left behind would have to fend for themselves out of their own pocket. Stations were notorious for separating crew from their coin, and the community service often imposed to pay off a debt was the most odious of station maintenance work. Some of the crew would not return, for the ship had its own share of odious duties as well as providing a greater chance of getting killed. She'd deal with any of those persons *when* she returned. She never thought "*if.*"

"Release hook-ups," she ordered on the mark.

"Hook-ups released," the officer at conn replied. She heard the usual chorus of clicks as everyone strapped themselves in.

La Espada was now completely on its own power, air and water. Sax strapped herself into her chair.

"Cast off."

The station's magnetic clamps released the ship and she imagined the hiss of air as the powerful propellant tanks pushed them away from the station and felt the familiar tug as the gravity provided by the station's rotation gave way to the gravity generated by the ship's sudden acceleration. She felt the weight ease an instant before the conn announced they were standing clear of the station.

"Full sail," she ordered. The most insane and courageous members of her crew were the riggers. At her command they jetted out in EVA suits along the masts and struts to unfurl the giant micro-thin solar sails. The riggers claimed watching the golden sails catch the rays of the sun was akin to a religious experience. She'd never seen the phenomenon herself, but figured it must be quite a sight if it could induce one to hurl oneself into the void to see it.

Acceleration under sail would increase slowly, but surely.

"Begin rotation," she ordered.

"Beginning rotation," the engineering deck replied on the ship-wide hail, the only warning the crew would get that up and down had to be taken into account again. The sound of the engines that rotated the cylindrical ship within its frame of struts and masts starting up did not need to be imagined. It reverberated and shook throughout the ship. Fortunately, once the ship began to spin at speed, inertia was maintained by magnetic induction and the engines would be almost silent.

The captain felt herself sink ever so slightly into the cushioning. A thought, via implant and wireless transmission, was all it took to make the chair turn slightly on its horizontal axis. She, like the crew, enjoyed the automated, computer guided functions on the ship while she could. During battle, with the comp taken offline, everything had to be done manually. The navigator's station came into view and with it the senior nav officer, Poole. This was the one crewmember she would never leave behind. As she understood it, the ship ran on numbers, and this was the man who crunched them when the comp was down.

Poole raised his head from his displays, as if he could feel her scrutiny like a sensorite. Like all the human beings from his planet, Cygni-I, his skin had a slight blue cast and his hair was colorless. These obvious and innocuous signs of the genetic modifications undertaken by his ancestors to survive on their relatively oxygen-poor world were all that the Purists needed to hate Poole's kind. Sax thought them fools. If anything, the Cygni were far more dangerous for what they had done to their *minds.*

"Have you correlated a course, Mr. Poole?"

"Yes, Captain."

"Let's have it then."

Immediately, a heads-up display appeared before her, *La Espada*'s course outlined against the current layout of the system in a bright certain blue. Lines shaded from yellow to green showed the most probable courses of the bogey, extrapolated second by second as more sensor data came in from the beacons arrayed throughout the system. She was pleased to see that the most probable vectors would intercept with her ship well above the plane of the ecliptic, where there would be plenty of fighting room, *if necessary.* She knew that the universe was more empty space than matter, but to her the Aquarii system had always seemed cluttered with asteroids, comets and other debris.

Debris that could damage her ship.

She willed *La Espada* to go faster, and closed her eyes to imagine the nonexistent creaking of the rigging and masts as light pushed the solar sails out against the star's pull on the ship. She'd been on a sailing ship once, on the oceans of Maravilla, before the Associated Worlds lost the Lalande system to the Purists. Someday, she meant to win that world back. But since the faster-than-light engine could not be used anywhere near a star's gravity well, the ship could go faster only as they got farther from the star. She could order a burn, and kick the ship up to her full speed of a hundred kilometers per second, roughly a third the speed of light. But if she were headed for battle, she would be wise to reserve all the fuel in the tanks for maneuvers.

It would take a little under thirty hours for the ships to meet, and there was much to be done. "Steady as she goes," she ordered Poole as she turned her chair to line up with the exit from the bridge. This brought Augusto Lo into view. His bronze-brown skin was a few shades lighter than the captain's, his eyes and tousled hair darker. He was actually Earth-born, yet had rejected the Purist philosophy and immigrated to an Associate world as a youth. He was slouched at his usual station at the rear of the bridge, his eyes half closed, his head resting on his fist, his other hand fiddling idly with the buckles on his disheveled jumpsuit. To all appearances he was oblivious to what was going on around him. But it was all an act. The captain knew that the "State Liaison Officer" never missed a thing that happened on the ship.

So she wasn't the least bit surprised when he came up behind her in the corridor as she waited for the lift. The guards wouldn't stop him from coming after her like that, after all, they ultimately answered to him.

"Odd, isn't it?"

She raised an eyebrow in reply.

"If I'm not mistaken, that bogey is following the same trajectory as the last Purist ship that attacked this system."

The captain nodded. "Yes, I'd noticed that."

"But that approach gives you, the defender, the weather gauge. The bogey has to expend fuel to fight the same solar wind that *La Espada* has at her back, filling our sails, leaving it less fuel to maneuver. These were decisive factors in our victory against the last incursion."

Again, the captain raised her brow.

"And your superior skill at command and tactics, of course," he amended with a small grin.

Sax smiled in return, more because of his use of the archaic term "weather gauge" than his sardonic compliment.

"Everything means something," he said in return.

"Then figure it out," she said, after pausing for a moment to visualize her deck number.

Lo nodded. "Nice slippers," she heard him say as the lift doors closed.

An hour before intercept, the captain was touring her ship as she was wont to do before a battle. And she had no doubt that there would be a battle—the bogey's course was lining up exactly with the last Purist ship's incursion. A statistical impossibility, Poole had assured her. So, this ship was using the last ship's comp data, possibly retrieved from the latter's logs, which would have been downloaded into a locator beacon before the ship went into battle. It made no sense to her, but then, she thought the whole Purist agenda made little sense. She entered the rigger's loft in the core of the ship. Since the ship rotated around the core, there was no gravity in the long, cold cylinder. It was the perfect place to store cargo, house the ship's engines and, of course, the riggers.

A rigger spotted her and snapped to attention, his elongated prehensile toes grasping a length of cable to steady himself. He was blond and blue-eyed, not too bad looking, with a crooked nose and a wry twist to his mouth that suggested he was always smiling. He was tall and thin, his arms and legs of equal length, with all twenty digits being equally dexterous. His name was Jaller. He'd served on her ship for the past four years and she knew him to be brave, loyal, and kind. And even though the rigger's section of the core was only partially heated, he was naked, as was their wont. Diversity. The idea and the reality that the Purists condemned as unnatural.

She drifted among the riggers, male and females both, for no few minutes, praising their courage, thanking them for their service and exhorting them to battle. Despite her duty uniform and her boots, she still managed to skillfully make her way in Zero G among the giant web of cables that the riggers called home. Their ancestors had destroyed their world in a paroxysm of industrialization that had seen the world laid waste in just six generations after colonization. The riggers had been forced to evacuate onto space stations and ships and had during the centuries of the *sundering*, when all of humanity's worlds had lost contact with each other and faster than light travel had been abandoned, modified themselves to live in micro-gravity.

Members of no fewer than five of the existing seven modified human races served on her ship and of the remaining two, the Aquarii had inadvertently made themselves highly susceptible to space sickness and the folk of Twobit were devout pacifist.

Her last stop on her tour was always the medical deck. Doctor Stures was a sensorite, his people hailed from the dust-cloaked planet of Gliese 876, Umbra. The world was metal poor and had erratic magnetic fields so technology had been difficult to maintain. Without much artificial illumination, the people of that world had modified their other senses to compensate for the gloom. His skin was blue-black with raised oblong bumps that ran from his hairline to his jaw. She knew them to be receptors, allowing the doctor to feel minute changes in temperature, in air pressure and displacement, even vibrations. His eyes were hidden behind a band of dark glass, to protect them from the ship's bright illumination. He greeted her in his usual way.

"Ah, Captain, in excellent health I see." And by see he actually meant by smell, by feeling her body temperature and by hearing her heart beat in her chest. "All is in readiness for the coming battle."

She had expected no less. His people were sensitive by nature and design, but they were also pragmatists. He wasn't one of those medical officers who questioned the need for battle.

"We don't know that the bogey is hostile—" she began to say.

"Pshaw," the doctor interjected. A liberty he could take here, on his deck. "From what I've heard, how could it be anything else?"

"Indeed," the captain said, raising her brow. News travelled fast on a ship. She believed the ancient term was "scuttlebutt." Satisfied that her ship was in order, she headed for the bridge.

As the captain stepped onto the bridge, the ship's executive officer, Commander Ortencia, saluted and left. The XO's station during battle was located close to the core, half the ship's length from the bridge, a hopefully safe distance from anything that might happen to or on the bridge. The commander would monitor all activities on the bridge from there and issue orders in support of the captain's activities during battle. In exchange, Major Drummond, the Captain of the Guard, took a station on the bridge. When ships sailed on oceans, his troops would have been called marines.

"We are coming to transmission and targeting range," Poole said.

"Furl sails, retract masts," she ordered the riggers. "Advise the ship and begin viral transmission," she ordered the com officer.

She waited until all decks had acknowledged.

"Take the computer network offline, Mr. Poole."

A few seconds later she saw the board at the Armscomp station light up.

"Bogey firing missiles!" The officer at the station reported immediately, with more alarm in her voice than the captain had ever heard her use before. She waited for "Scopes," the officer at the primary scan station, to report. She'd never had to wait before.

"Scopes, damn your eyes, how many missiles?" She turned and looked at the man, who appeared flabbergasted.

"Twenty-seven." Poole answered for him, his fingers flying across the board as he entered the intercept coordinates he was simultaneously figuring in his head. On the gun deck the crews would be hastily entering the numbers that flashed on their screen on the missiles' targeting panels.

Twenty-seven? Their entire launch capacity?

"Fire intercepts," she ordered the gun deck.

Poole could calculate firing coordinates in his head faster than his counterpart on the Purist ship, who was baseline human and had to enter data into a calculator. With the efficiency she trained into her gun crews, *La Espada* normally got off three missiles to every two fired from a Purist ship. And just a tad more accurately. Considering the Purists had larger crews and more missiles at their disposal—the Earth and sol system had ten times the resources of the handful of planets humanity had found that were even marginally habitable—the Cygni's superior ability with numbers did much to even the odds.

But all twenty-seven missiles? They'd only been in targeting range for a few seconds. The Purist navigator would have to be twice as fast as Poole to get off even one shot.

"Those missiles can't possibly be targeted …" she said aloud. Poole grunted, and she could tell by the sweat on his brow and the fact that he was still working feverishly; they were indeed targeted at her ship.

"Six, no seven missiles intercepted …" Scopes reported hesitantly.

"Nine," Poole corrected while still entering numbers for the gun crews.

"Twelve seconds to impact," Armscomp reported.

Poole could not intercept them all. She hit the take hold alarm.

"Full burn in ten seconds…." she ordered on ship-wide hail. She didn't dare cut it any closer. All over the ship, the crew would hasten to strap themselves in, brace themselves against padded walls or at the very least hold on to one of the many rungs placed throughout the ship for dear life. Some wouldn't make it.

"Five."

"Four."

"Three."

"Two."

"One."

If the engine room should fail her now … But then she was kicked back almost out of her chair as the ship's engines fired at maximum and the thrust of acceleration hit her like a giant's fist. Of all people she'd forgotten to align her own chair and take-hold. There'd be injuries and no few fatalities all over the ship; not everyone's station was within ten seconds reach of a take-hold.

Explosions against the hull shook the ship. She gritted her teeth and hoped none of the missiles had actually struck the ship. How many had she managed to dodge? How many did the Close-In Defense system installed on the outer hull take out with its pinpoint laser barrages?

Sirens began to wail.

"Detonations astern and off the starboard …"

"Hull breaches on outer decks in sections gamma, epsilon and phi …"

All but three. Three bloody missiles had penetrated her hull in as many seconds. She'd gone through many a battle without even one missile striking her ship. She heard the XO give the necessary orders to assess and repair the damage. Stures would give her the casualty report, in private, when the battle was over. It was a courtesy he'd always extended her.

"Missiles one and two ready," Poole reported calmly.

"Fire!" She ordered the gun crew. The man was a marvel. He'd managed to target two of their own missiles while the ship was under fire and pinned to his seat by acceleration. Another few seconds and they'd have been beyond targeting range.

"Braking thrusters fire," she called down to the engine room. "Prepare to bring us about."

Slowly the press of Gs let up as the rotational gravity reasserted itself. Most of the crew in the engine room was burly, tough-skinned Cancri, their heavy-planet bones could take a hell of a beating. After all, what use was an engine room crew that was beaten unconscious every time the ship maneuvered?

"Missiles one and two intercepted," Armscomp reported.

Sax looked at Poole. "I can come to only one conclusion; their missiles are being targeted by comp," he said.

"Then the viruses we transmitted …"

"Should be working their way through their system as we speak."

"Or, they've found a way to immunize their system against our attack …"

Poole frowned. Sax wondered if he was insulted that his people hadn't been the ones to discover how to counter viral transmissions.

"If that's true," Lo spoke up, "then the Purists have gained a sizeable advantage."

"Incoming," Scopes reported. And then almost immediately, "Twenty-seven missiles heading this way."

They'd fired from every single launch tube again. But at this range …

"Port beam thrusters," Sax ordered. At this range, a garbage scow could sidestep those missiles. Scopes kept his eyes on the screen and she could tell by the way the lines of his face were relaxing that they were going to miss the ship completely.

"Their captain is not right in the head…." Lo drawled, pretending to study his fingernails. "Or he's so woefully inexperienced he has no right being on a bridge. And yet, he hasn't been relieved of command. Possibly, he's not even an officer …"

Lo was telling the captain that the enemy ship was probably in the hands of mutineers. She heard the edge to his voice. One didn't become a State Liaison Officer without a deep-seated dislike for all things mutinous.

"There's only one way to find out. Full speed ahead!" The captain counted down the seconds until they were once again in targeting range. Would the ship launch another twenty-seven missiles as soon as they were in range or would her CO, whoever he or she was, wait until they got closer, like she would do?

"Mr. Poole, target acquisition please."

Poole's eyes scanned his board. The readouts showed him ship's speed, course and velocity, as well as the last recorded position of the enemy ship. In his head was all the pertinent data on the missiles. There was barely a pause or change of expression as he correlated all the data, but suddenly his fingers began to tap out the coordinates for the gunners below.

"Mr. Curzon, fire at will," she ordered.

"Aye, Captain."

"Missile three away … missile four away … missile five away …" Armscomp reported.

Every twenty seconds or so another three missiles were launched. Apparently, someone on the other ship had learned that not even computer accuracy could guarantee a hit at very long range.

"Bogey firing intercepts," Scopes announced.

Sax waited, fighting the urge to chew her lower lip.

"Missile three intercepted."

"Missile four intercepted."

And so it went. Nine missiles intercepted by the computer-guided accuracy of the enemy ship's interceptor missiles.

But the tenth.

"Missile ten on target."

"No further intercepts from the bogey?" the captain asked.

"Nothing on scan," Scopes answered.

"Missile eleven on target."

Missiles ten, eleven and twelve were detonated just shy of the enemy's hull by their CID system, but thirteen and fourteen struck home. Scans showed two impacts and detonations on the starboard midline. And the enemy ship seemed unable to return fire.

"Cease fire," the captain ordered.

"It appears we have infected their comp systems, and shut down all networked operations on the ship."

"We need to investigate and search that ship, find out what is going on." It was a golden opportunity. She'd never heard of a ship neglecting to take its network offline and allow an enemy virus to take over their computers.

"It's been a while since fleetcomp training, but am I right in thinking that you can now transmit orders to their comp system?" Sax asked Poole.

"If we boot up."

Did she dare? If she ordered a reboot, Lo could relieve her of command. She fancied she could feel his eyes upon her but she was no sensorite and turned her head to see him from the corner of her eye. He was indeed studying her intently, all pretense at disinterest gone. Only the most senior officers and, of course, the guard knew how much authority he actually had. His duty was to prevent mutiny and, of course, treason, either intentional or through misguided action on the part of the officers. Even the commanding officer.

"Prepare to boot up," she ordered, turning her eyes to Poole.

"May I ask the captain why she would give such an order?" Lo asked.

"We need to get past their CID system to get any closer."

"It is my understanding that the CID system, while automated, is independently triggered by proximity sensors and is not connected to the network."

The captain returned his direct gaze. "You are correct. However, the CID system is temporarily overridden if the ship launches the escape pods. Which we can order their computer to do."

"To what end?"

"To what end, Mr. Lo?" the captain answered with a wolfish grin. "Why, I intend to board her." She let Lo chew on that for a bit.

"Mr. Poole, am I right in thinking that in the short interval after we boot up but before you can gain control of their computers they will have a chance to hit us with viruses?

Poole arched his brows. “A very slight chance,” he conceded.

“Let’s see if we can’t provide a distraction,” Captain Sax said and hailed the ship’s gunner. “Curzon! Fire the carronades!”

“Aye, Captain,” the gunner responded. The carronades required no targeting, they fired scattershot and were hopelessly inaccurate at long range. But they would blanket the area around the ship with flak. Immediately the enemy ship’s Close-In-Defense system activated. She couldn’t see the lasers on the vid on her heads up display, but she could see the pinpoint flares as lasers struck the flak.

“Boot up.”

Poole entered the codes known only to himself, the captain and Lo, and then bent over his board, his fingers flying over the panel as he sought out the command codes of the enemy ship.

“Fire again, Mr. Curzon.”

Whoever was in control of that ship had completely ignored or been unaware of the protocol against viral transmissions. She doubted they would realize their computer was being taken over, but it only took the press of a button to transmit a virus. Best to keep their minds on other things.

“I have secured their computer,” Poole announced.

“Shut down everything you can over there, including life support, but not rotation, not yet. They’ll have just enough air in the tanks to last until we’re done looking around over there, but it should help take the fight out of them.”

The captain then hailed her XO.

“You’ll be in command. Have all able-bodied riggers suit up and assemble in the portside cargo bay.” She turned to Major Drummond. “I’ll need a squad. Armored.”

The man saluted and left the bridge. She glanced over at Lo as she followed the major off the bridge. He seemed preoccupied with an itch under the collar of his jumpsuit. She figured that meant he wasn’t going to have her arrested. Yet.

Sax arrived at the cargo bay in her combat suit to find everyone else armored and ready to go. Commander Ortencia had given everyone the captain’s instructions while Sax was getting suited up. It was easy to tell the tall spindly riggers apart from the shorter stockier troopers, but even with lighted faceplates, features were hard to make out. There were thirteen riggers and she personally hoped Jaller was among them and hadn't been hurt or lost in the burn, and twelve troopers, their armor marked with insignia. She went up to the major.

"Unit ready for action, Captain," he reported over suitcom.

"Form up," she ordered. At her command, riggers came up behind troopers and used the mast clamps on the front of their suits to attach themselves to the storage struts on the back of the trooper's armor. Sax hailed the bridge.

"Standing by," the XO confirmed.

"Execute instructions," the captain ordered. Over the com she could hear Ortencia order the engineering deck to halt rotation. At the same time, Poole was shutting down rotation on the enemy ship. Slowly, Sax began to shed weight. As they began to float, the rigger at her back expertly slipped his foot into the tethered foothold also rising from the deck. The trooper's suit had propellants to help them maneuver in Zero G, but the riggers were much more at home in weightlessness. She felt much safer crossing the void in their arms.

Rotation came to a complete halt with their cargo bay facing the cargo bay in the midline of the enemy ship. Immediately the bay depressurized. Then the great doors slid open. As one the riggers kicked off into the void like a flock of armored avians. Silently and gracefully they drifted toward the enemy ship, a cylindrical affair nearly a twin to her own. As they neared the range of the CID array Poole began ordering the port side life pods to launch. The riggers fired their jets and hurled themselves toward the enemy ship's starboard cargo bay. The captain watched as the cargo bays door loomed larger and larger. Her trust in the Cygni's timing and accuracy were nearly absolute, yet she had to fight the urge to close her eyes as the unyielding doors drew closer. Poole was supposed to have depressurized the enemy ship's cargo bay before their own so they wouldn't have to wait on the airlock cycle.

Suddenly, at what Sax could swear was the tip of her nose, the cargo bay doors parted. Immediately, her rigger braked and the rest of the flock swerved around her and entered the bay first, taking up defensive positions. Obviously, she mused, a maneuver the good major had worked out with the riggers while she was getting into her armor. She hadn't been expecting any resistance. To repel boarders, you stationed troops in the docking bay, not cargo. As her rigger brought her in, the bay doors began to close. They waited for the bay to re-pressurize so they could enter the ship proper. Poole was under instructions not to restart rotation or the life support, Sax meant to keep her troops in armor.

One of the troopers, a sci-tech badge below his sergeant stripes on his shoulder, was sampling the air through a device attached to his forearm. "Sir," he addressed the major. "The air in here is not breathable."

The air should not have deteriorated so quickly. "Composition?" she asked.

"The ratio of nitrogen to oxygen is almost inversed and the methane levels are too high."

"Remain on full suit support," she ordered as she led the troops into the ship. Two sci-techs immediately detached themselves from the squad to find the Auxiliary Firing Control room and deactivate the CID system. The rest of the squad followed her to secure the docking bay so that the rest of the personnel she needed to secure the ship could come over in skiffs. They hadn't gone far before they encountered the first body floating in a corridor. The woman had apparently suffocated in the poisonous air. They found many others like her, and bodies that had obviously been torn apart by projectile fire. There had been some kind of fight aboard the ship. And once they reached the docking bay, she realized the fighting had been very heavy there. Dead bodies floated everywhere. Strangely, there was no sign of a boarding vessel.

"Captain." Poole hailed her from the ship. "We've been running the ship's internal scans and there is an active life pod not far from your position." He marked the position on her telemetry HUD and within minutes she, the major, and a guard were standing in the airlock outside the life pod hatch. The pods could carry up to twelve evacuees, but there was only a single crew member in this one, curled up in a fetal position. She noted the sci-techs had reported that the CID was deactivated. They would now begin working on securing the rest of the ship's systems.

“Ortencia, send a med team. We’ve found a survivor of whatever calamity befell this vessel.”

Sax waited calmly for the skiff carrying the med team to arrive. In the meantime the major deployed his troops to secure this area of the ship, electronically and physically. The riggers went out on reconnaissance beyond the perimeter. No other survivors were found.

She wasn’t the least bit surprised when Stures himself joined her in the airlock. They cycled the lock and entered the life pod. Stures sampled the air and then removed his helmet. Sax and the guard did likewise. The survivor, a bridge officer by his insignia, was obviously in shock, muttering to himself.

“And the thirteens will be an abomination, the thirteens …”

Sax realized he was quoting Purist scripture. There had been twelve races of humanity, the original three on Earth, and nine self-created races when humanity on other worlds had modified themselves to survive in their new habitats during the sundering. One race had been made extinct when an asteroid struck their planet. Then, when the worlds of humanity once again took up faster-than-light travel and rediscovered each other, the overwhelming diversity triggered the Purist movement. The first act of the Purist regime of earth had been genocide against the shining people of Centauri. And because it wasn’t enough to fear the seven modified races they knew, the Purists created the myth of a thirteenth yet to come.

She lowered a medical bunk and helped Dr. Stures seat the man upright. The doctor gave him an injection, and with a sob, the man came out of his shock. His eyes focused on Sax first. Then they slid over to Stures and widened in fear. As the doctor reached out to take his hand, the captain saw the man recoil in disgust. She bristled at the Purist’s xenophobic reaction and tamped down the urge to throw him out an airlock.

“Stabilize him for questioning,” she ordered. When the man was ready to talk, Stures retreated to the airlock. He was talkative, she could give him that. She learned that the ship had come across a bogey twenty AUs outside the Aquarii system. It had retrieved the log buoy from the previous Purist ship that had attacked the system, and used some of the com codes to lure the Purist ship close. Then dozens of small skiffs had belched forth from the ship and pierced the starboard hull. Strange creatures had emerged from the skiffs and, barely slowed down by decompression, had swarmed the docking bay and opened the ship up to more of their numbers. He had hidden in here and had watched on the pod's HUD as the ship was taken. Then all the creatures left the ship, except for a larger and more hideous one that had ensconced itself on the bridge. The man began sobbing and Sax went to confer with Stures. The doctor was visibly agitated.

"Are you all right?"

"Y-yes, why do you ask?"

"You seem a bit upset...."

"A bit, yes, I suppose I am," he admitted, shaking his head. "I should expect no better from a Purist, but, he's apparently encountered a 'hideous non-human monster' and yet still remains afraid of *my* kind...." He smiled at the captain. "Never mind, I'll be all right. You know, Captain, you're very perceptive for a—"

The doctor caught himself and ducked his head. Sax arched a brow.

"For a commanding officer?" she offered.

"For someone with so much responsibility. Yes," he finished, abashed.

"Poole," she hailed her ship, "the HUD is down in the life pod, could you restore it and give me video of the bridge?"

"Yes, Captain."

Suddenly a screen appeared in the air in the middle of the pod. Sax could see the bridge, very similar to her own, and occupying the captain's chair was an immense being comprised of shiny red and pink globules from which a host of spindly, crystalline appendages sprung in all directions. It immediately reminded her of the sea urchins of Maravilla. The creature was poking around at the unresponsive controls, to her eye, in something like frustration.

The survivor screamed and huddled against the life pod bulkhead. Stures immediately ran over to help him and to the captain's surprise, the man did not even flinch. Obviously, he was much more terrified of the alien, the "Thirteen."

"Poole, vent all the air in this ship except the bridge and slave her helm to ours. We are taking this ship and its occupant back to Earth."

"To Earth?" Ortencia and Lo simultaneously interjected.

"Yes, to Earth," the captain replied. "We are going to give the Purists something new to fear."

And if the Purists and the Associated worlds had to become allies to defeat this new menace, well, then at least there would still be battles and a need for fighting ships.

The captain smiled, and she didn't care if there was anyone around to see it.

Born in Cuba and raised in Brooklyn, **Gene Mederos** obtained his Bachelors of Fine Arts in Theater Arts from the University of Miami. Gene has designed and built sets for theatrical productions and events in Miami, NYC, and Santa Fe. His artwork has been shown in Miami, Tampa, and NYC. Currently Gene is a filmmaker and animator living and working in Santa Fe, New Mexico.

He teaches post production at the Santa Fe Community College and is the Chair of New Mexico Film Resource, a nonprofit dedicated to creating film jobs for film students in New Mexico.

Gene's films have appeared in Film Festivals in New Mexico, L.A., Boston, Toronto and NYC and he recently filmed aboard a submarine, under water! The closest he will probably ever come to being on a spaceship.

Gene is also a published author of Sci-Fi and Fantasy stories. His stories have appeared in six anthologies to date.

The Joystick War

by Jean Johnson

Introduction to "The Joystick War"

A lot of the authors I first worked with on Space Battles have since become friends and collaborators on many other projects. Jean Johnson is one of those and also someone with prior experience in the Full-Throttle series.

This story, like her prior one for Space Grunts, is tied to her Theirs Not to Reason Why military science fiction series which has been a National Bestseller for Ace. She wrote four books based on the characters explored here and then broke off into another trilogy about other characters in the universe as well. It is female-driven military science fiction that asks fascinating questions about the future, the roles of genders, and the role of conflict and war in our societies. "The Joystick War" is just a small taste of what was to come that asks what happens when trainees encounter a live enemy attack: again, lots of fun action and a fight to survive.

Hey, Rrenn, check this out!" From the depths of the huge piles of crates lining the storage bunker, Scott Grayson's bleached tuft of hair popped into view. He curled his arm in a broad wave, beckoning the dark-furred Solarican youth his way, then disappeared back behind the stacks.

"Clann Brrother?" Moving that way, Rrenn F'sauu sniffed the air, trying to get a hint of what his Human friend had found.

"Just wait until you see!" Scott's voice drifted back to him, echoing slightly off the high ceiling.

They were supposed to be checking these crates for salvageable goods. Most of what was stored here in this bunker beneath the rock-and-methane surface of Eris was military surplus, but most of that surplus was from a century and a half ago. His legs, short but muscular, bounded him well over a pile of rummaged goods—they hadn't bothered to turn on the deck plates, leaving them able to move huge loads easily in the dwarf planet's lightworld gravity—and his tail swung to the side, helping him turn corners as he leap-jogged through the maze of discarded matériel.

The extreme cold had acted to both destroy and save most of the goods here. Raw materials like scrap metal were usually salvageable; send it into a foundry unit to remove the oxidized bits, and get paid in cash per resulting ingot. Preserved foodstuffs—which this chamber didn't hold, thankfully—were either reduced to dust, or covered in slow-growing biological contaminants, requiring them to be torched rather than recycled, even as composting material.

Other items might be valuable for historical or informational purposes, but this was just a storage bay for military surplus parts. Most of it was outdated spare parts, age-brittled uniforms, and other odds and ends. All Rrenn could smell was dust, iron oxide, and hints of that distinct, ongoing fart-smell that said they were on a methane-iced planetoid.

The airlocks still worked, small ones for personnel to use and large ones for the crates themselves. As did most of the base's life-support systems. Still, the survey teams had first approached the base fully suited, not ready to trust the airlocks until they had been proven viable from the inside out. That meant methane crystals had been tracked inside. He didn't find the scent as offensive as, say, his sister's version of cooking, but she was back on the ship, matching the salvage inventory to pricing lists on the Nets. Thankfully, it was Scott's father who was doing the cooking for their mixed-species crew these days.

He found the Human toward the back of the cavern, by the great lifts that functioned as oversized airlocks. Scott stood with his hands braced on his knees—a rather unbalanced-looking posture for a race born without tails—while studying a labeling package on a particularly large crate. One of forty or so similar crates, in fact. Each one stood on its own, rather than stacked like all the rest, but then each one was larger than their shared crew-cabin back on board their salvage ship, the *Hunting Party S'kessa.* Rrenn cocked his ears, letting the rings piercing the edges swing and clink in wordless curiosity.

"Look at that, Clan Brother," Scott murmured, lifting his chin at the label. His lips parted in a big grin, revealing his incisors. "A real, honest-to-goodness AITX TarDro … mint condition, in-the-box, packaged with everything you need to launch it and fly."

"Ay-ticks tarrr-droh?" Rrenn asked, peering between the box and his partner. He didn't take offense at the Human's bared teeth; his extended family had worked with Humans for generations, and knew the gesture meant extreme pleasure, not extreme anger. "What is annn AITX TarDro …? Are you actually drroolinng?"

Scott mock-wiped the corners of his mouth as he straightened. Turning his gaze to his salvage partner, he smirked. "I think I *am*, Rrenn my friend … because if anything in these boxes is still good enough to fly, we just hit a bag full of cool-colored credits."

"Explainn," Rrenn said, one ear flicking back in skepticism.

"I'm not completely sure what the TX stood for—I think it was just some product number designation," Scott explained, nodding at the crate. "But the TarDro means Targeting Drone, and the AI means Artificial Intelligence."

Both of the Solarican's ears pulled back at that. He hissed a little, too. "*That* isn't good. Smarrrt machinnery is vital to interstellarr lllife, but artificial intellligences are *trrrrouble*."

"Oh, relax," Scott dismissed, flipping his hand. "This stuff isn't self-aware."

"So you say," Rrenn muttered, skeptical.

"See that inventory list? *Joystick* controlled," his partner pointed out, tapping the relevant line in the fine print posted to the side of the crate. "This sort of stuff's just a real-life vid game. In this case,

AI simply means it's capable of analyzing data, assessing risks, and managing complex flight systems with onboard programming, reducing the operating requirements to simplified control commands. It's passive AI, not active. The *real* question is, does this stuff still function after being locked in its packing crate for a hundred and fifty or so years? *That's* what we need to find out."

Rrenn nodded slowly. "It'd be nnno good trrrying to sell these if we didn't knnow their trrrue value." He nodded more firmly, and lifted his chin at the first crate. "C'mon, let's crrrack one opennn, and see if it's still shipshape."

Scott clasped his hands together and rubbed them in glee, then cast around, looking for where he had left the hoversled loaded with his toolkits. "Let's see … those bolt seals look like they'll need a number seventeen socket drill …"

O O O

It worked. After a century and a half, the machinery inside was still pristine. Still functional. And incredibly simple.

There were only two pieces of equipment in the crate, each one fully assembled and ready to go. The thruster tech was a bit primitive—all of it was a bit primitive, compared to the twenty-fifth century technology they were used to manipulating—but the setup was as easy as pulling them out of their packaging materials, pouring a couple gallons of purified water into the two hydrogenerators, and flicking a set of switches.

The instruction manual was just as simple: It identified the various controls, and showed how to start up the tutorial program. Within minutes, Scott was seated in a semi-spherical seat with restraint harnesses centered in the control cradle, watching an equally curved monitor showing the point-of-view for his drone as it floated and slowly turned. The monitor showed the on-board AI analyzing their crate-lined surroundings and correctly labeling everything, but other than scanning, floating, and analyzing, the drone did nothing but hum.

Watching his partner work the controls, flying the drone around the cavernous underground warehouse, Rrenn noticed the cradle actually moved the seat, simulating vector changes for the controller.

They simulate the moves of the hunt even when they make their machines cull the beasts, he thought, satisfied with the similarities between their species. *Dull-toothed, lacking proper claws, and no tail for balance, these Humans are still a force to be reckoned with.* Rrenn pursed his lips in a smile as Scott sloughed his seat around, sending the drone in a flat spin. *Plus, they know how to have fun. Spiral knows I'd dislike living with a race without a sense of joy …*

"Woo! Oh, man, you gotta try this!" Bringing the drone to a stop, Scott checked the manual and powered down the unit, then unfastened the restraints. He scrambled free and gestured for the Solarican to take his place. "Sitting on your tail during some of those maneuvers might hurt a little, since it's designed for a Human, but the seat's got some decent cushioning in it."

Nodding, Rrenn climbed up into the structure. Tucking his tail between his legs wasn't comfortable, but it wasn't unbearable. The straps fit around his torso in the standard X pattern, suitable for most bipedal sentients in the known galaxy, and the hand controls, while sized for someone a little larger than Rrenn, who had been born on a heavy-gravitied world, leaving him short and stocky for his race, came with an adjustment lever that moved the double-joystick rig into place at a comfortable distance for his shorter arms.

"Gotta love those early-era Space Force design requirements, doncha?" Scott asked rhetorically, helping Rrenn adjust the controls to his height. Stepping back, he nodded at the instruction sheets taped to the center of the dual-joystick bar. "Have at 'er, meioa."

Gripping the controls, Rrenn thumbed the on-switch. Off to one side, the drone lifted off its thin landing strut with a *hummm*, and the cradle-seat moved under him, gliding slightly as it matched the orientation of the re-awakened vehicle. The controls weren't like a modern flight-glove-and-stick, which meant speed was controlled by the right hand and attitude by the left. Instead, the arcs of right and left were controlled by the right joystick, up and down by the left, and both had squeeze-triggers. Two sets per joystick in fact, with the lower ones meant for going forward and one for going backward.

The upper ones, he discovered, were useless. A message flashed across the screen, giving the reason why:

WEAPONS DEACTIVATED IN TRAINING MODE.

There were buttons on the joysticks which rendered them from motion controls to menu controls. Hunting through the options, Rrenn tried to call up the weapons systems. Not to actually use them, but to see what the drones had available. A second message followed the first.

WEAPONS DEACTIVATED IN PROXIMITY TO CONTROL CRADLE.

"Aww," Scott muttered. "But I suppose that's pretty smart. That way we don't blow ourselves up accidentally."

The main view screen was divided by a crosshairs grid marked with faint but discernible degree numbers. By carefully combining the two, he found he could fly the machine in a graceful, spiraling swoop. The training program even politely provided flight coordinates, based on the drone's scan of the room. After flying to the various points around the room, both forwards, backwards, and even upside down, Rrenn was bored. Parking the drone and powering everything down, he sighed.

"What's wrong?" Scott asked him. "Isn't this great?"

Rrenn flicked his ears, the equivalent of a Human shrug. "It's onnly so much fun, fllying arounnd in herrre. This thing should be capable of inn-system flight … and we have no idea what sorrt of armaments it's carrying. How do we know what the *rrrreal* worth is, if we don't knnnow if it can still take potshots at stuff?"

Scott wrinkled his nose. "More to the point, the thought has just occurred to me that if the armaments *are* still live, or capable of being made live … then the military *might* want its equipment back. Even though we have full salvage rights from the Space Force, they might object."

The Solarican nodded. "We're goinng to have to telll the otherrrs what we founnd. This is too big a decisionn for the two of us to make." Rrenn wrinkled his own nose in distaste. "That cuts innnto our personnnal sallvage percentages, but it's the rrright thing to do."

"Sad fact, but there it is," Scott agreed. He flicked his hand, gesturing for Rrenn to climb down. "C'mon, let's unpack a few more."

"Mm?" Rrenn grunted, unbuckling his restraint harness. "Why?"

"Because we don't know if this one was a fluke," the Human reasoned, mouth curved up in amusement, "and we should have several ready for demonstration once the others get over here. Plus, you *know* your cousins are going to want to play with these things, not to mention my uncles—oh, lord, and Aunt Sabina," Scott groaned a moment later, covering his eyes with his hand. "She'll be all over this thing like chocolate on candy, or catnip in tea."

Rrenn sneeze-laughed. "She'llll prrrobably beat your tailless hide to the finnish line, figuring out how to rrrun it better than anyone else—she'll beat *all* our taills. That female is a hunntress bornn!"

O O O

Fourteen mint-condition but no longer in-the-box AITX TarDros swooped and swerved through a cluster of Oort-cloud asteroids trailing in the wake of dwarf planet Eris. A couple million kilometers away, housed in a deep underground bunker, twenty-eight of the thirty-five crewmembers of the *Hunting Party S'kessa* either sat in or clustered around the control cradles for those drones.

Some of those space rocks were now smaller than they had been. Pulverized to dust, in some cases. Each drone came with two retractable laser cannons, capable of firing in a hundred-degree arc, and payload bays with twenty projectile missiles, some of which had now been fired. They weren't overly powerful weapons, and wouldn't make much of a difference in modern warfare terms, but they were enough for small-scale combat.

The main payloads, however, were meant to be the transponder gels each drone carried. Once the lasers took out a small section of shielding panels, the drones automatically fired the egg-packets. Splatting on contact, the gel adhered to whatever it struck. The payload of transceiver chips embedded in that gel then provided exact targeting coordinates for incoming smart missiles … provided one had the missiles. Which they did, in the next storage bay over, but which they hadn't unpacked.

It was one thing to swoop and zap at asteroids with low-powered drones. It was entirely different to fire missiles with payloads capable of blowing apart ship hulls.

As predicted, middle-aged, graying-haired Sabina Grayson was flying rings around the others, Human and Solarican alike. Close on her tail—technically the drone's stern—flew Captain Hrrann S'kessa, grinning ferally with his lips somewhat pursed but his front teeth bared. His fur was equally salted with gray, a commonality both species shared. As was the urge to gloat.

"Haha! Can't catch me, short-tailed slow-poke!" Sabina challenged, double-rolling her ship as she whipped around a chunk of space debris, then dove between two of the others. Their pilots shied away to either side, leaving him plenty of room to cut corners and catch up slightly more.

"You can rrrun, but you cannnnot hide!" he mock-growled, snicker-sneezing. He turned too sharply, however, and was forced to swerve out of the way of another chunk of Oort-cloud rock.

"Scratch the paint, and it comes outta your share!" his "prey" taunted. Again, Sabina started flying circles around him, forcing the others to scatter once more.

Over their headsets, the voice of Rrenn's sister, Parrda, spoke up. *"All rrright, meioas,"* she stated, using the honorific her people had given to the known galaxy. It meant "honored one" and was usually genderless, though the proper suffixes could be added when the speaker was sure of the other person's gender, and was on friendly enough terms to speak that casually. *"I've rreviewed our salvage connntract* and *military sallvage rrregulationns. We* can *keep these if they are arrrmed … but we cannot* selll *anything with live arrmaments. That inncludes the missiles you founnd … and we cannot firre the missiles in this system without Terran perrmission."*

Hrrann cursed in his native tongue and slowed his drone. Switching back to Terranglo, he activated his headset in reply. *"Thenn we will either have to keep them forrr ourselves, or rrruin most of their value."*

Moving away from his aunt's cradle—originally his—Scott shrugged at their captain. "Okay, so it's not a *huge* pile of cool-colored credits, but they're still worth something. We could sell 'em to planetary scouting companies, or maybe to game simulation companies …"

"*I* thinnk we should keep half of them for ourrsellves," Rrenn stated. The others glanced his way. Hrrann flicked his ears, making his dozen rings sway and clink. The younger male tucked his arms over his chest. "Sallvage sometimes carrries risks. Pirrates would think twice if we had a small fleet of fighterr-drrrones to defend our operationnns."

"Most of our salvage is done within the Sol System," Malcom, Scott's uncle, reminded him. "We certainly couldn't keep the missiles. We'd have to strip them for parts, destroy the payloads, the firing mechanisms, and render them inert art objects."

"They'd be worth a lot of money to military paraphernalia collectors," Sabina pointed out.

"And we have to rrregister our ownnership of them," Parrda stated, listening in to their broadcast comments. *"Particularrrly if we wannt to—"*

Proximity klaxons blared through their headsets, quickly followed by collision sirens. Everyone in the storage bay twitched and clapped their hands to their ears. A scream reached them as well, barely audible over the tumult.

"Salik! Salik warships! We're unnder—"

Parrda's shout ended in static. It followed by stunning silence. Rrenn's ears weren't the only ones that had flattened back. Others had pulled their whiskers down, too. Even the Humans stared wide-eyed at each other.

Hrrann stared at the star-filled view on his monitor, eyes so wide, the pinks could be seen. "We … we have to warn everyone …"

"To hell with that!" Sabina growled, clutching the joysticks of her TarDro controls. "We need to *stop* them!"

"We have to warrnn Earrrth! The Salik wouldn't *darrre* attack, unnless they were breaking the Blockade in full!" Hrrann argued. He grabbed at his own controls, orienting his view so that he could see the dwarf planet. "These thinngs have short-range rrradio transmitterrs. There should be a methane minnning station near the equatorrr. . . ."

"We need to know how many, first," Sabina protested, guiding her drone toward the *Hunting Party S'kessa*'s last known position over a third of the way around the planet. "Are they actually Salik, or are they Dlmvla methane raiders? Is it an actual warfleet, or just a lone scout, sent here to spy on us? Does the Space Force need to send just a couple patrol ships, or muster everything we've got? We need to *know*, people!"

"If we expose ourrr positionn," Rrenn's mother worried aloud, "thenn we rrrrisk dying as welll. Is it wise to seek them out? What if they trrrack the trannnsmissions back to our locationn?"

"These things are controlled by constantly operating hyperrelay links," Scott reassured her. "Even if they knew the exact vibrational frequency, the strings would have to be broken and their own transmitter closer to us than the drones for them to pick up the signal when it's re-established. *Then* they'd have to decode it, and this stuff's running on programming from a hundred and fifty years ago."

Mind still numb from the thought of having lost his sister and the others, Rrenn let his mind wander down another path. It followed the path of the golden-haired huntress closing on the last-known coordinates of their lost ship ... and reached a logical conclusion. "We nnneed to set up the rrest of the drones."

Scott glanced his way. A look was all the two salvage partners had to share, before the other young man nodded. "Let's get to it. Come on, people! Eris is on the system's edge, and it has *no* defenses, beyond whatever the mining and salvage crews might bring by ... and *someone* just blew our ship out of the sky! I don't know about you," he challenged the Humans and Solaricans in the storage hall, "but *I* want a little vengeance! Let's get all of them out of their crates."

"Why unnpack all of them?" Rrenn's cousin, Faul, asked, watching Rrenn move to join his salvage partner. "Maybe one forrr each of us, but the rest?"

"The armaments on these things are too small to threaten warships," Sabina said over her shoulder. The screen of her control cradle showed analysis grids as the drone attempted to resolve the difference between black space, white pinpoint stars, and the silvery hulls of starships, if any. "We may have to crash them into the enemy to do any real damage."

"What makes you think they'll even still be there?" Scott's youngest brother, Gregor, asked.

"Lllightwave readinngs," Hrrann answered, still guiding his unmanned ship. The speed of the little drones, a ratio of large field surface to modest mass, was fast enough that the shadowy blue surface was already beginning to fill his viewscreen. "They will wannt to avoid contacting the trrraffic buoys, because all buoys idenntify the ships that query them. Pirates and innvaders do nnot like being idenntified, but they do wannt to know where things arrre. Lightwave rrreadings of Earrth trrrraffic take an hour to annalyze, at this distance."

"Holy *shakk!*" Sabina exclaimed, her screen flashing with the outlines of several lumpy, five-lobed objects. "They *are* Salik warships! Peter, where's the instructions on how to link scanner feeds between these things? I want to relay it through Hrrann's ship to the mining station the moment he finds it."

"I'm on it, Aunt!"

"We arre *nnnot* in the military, you knnow," someone else argued. "Leave thinngs like this to the rrreal soldiers!"

"Don't get too close, Sister," someone else warned Sabina. "The moment they spot you, they'll destroy your ship, too, and maybe go looking for the rest."

"Ahhh … *shakk!*" Hrrann cursed. "I'm on the wrrrong side of the planet!"

More voices joined the tumult. Rrenn flicked one of his ears back in a silent sigh and joined his partner in searching for the tools to open up the next crate.

O O O

"All right, stay in formation," Sabina ordered. "Remember, if your drone gets destroyed, get out and get to the next one as fast as possible. Scott and Rrenn are parking them in the planet's umbra, so run 'em as fast as your thrusters can go."

"Yes, I *knnnow* sending the message lightspeed as well as hyperrrrelay rrruns the risk of your station being discoverrred and attacked," Hrrann argued. His voice was tired, his mane of golden brown headfur rumpled and matted where he had scratched under the band of his headset, and his whiskers drooped. "We're in a worse situationn, Meioa Brriggs. We have no food, no ship, and no trrransport other than shuttles. You'rrre the only other mannned location on Errris at the moment. But *we'rre* doing what we must to defend you Terrranns."

"Okay, children," the woman in control of the lead drone stated. "Get ready. We go on the captain's countdown. Close formation until they fire on us, then scatter and try to find and hit any target you can. Remember, the scanners on these things will pick up the power spikes from the shield panels, so your first strike needs to be a missile. Once you've found a shield panel, target it with the lasers until it's destroyed, then find the next one as close to it as possible."

"We're goinng to rrrun a diversion for you," Hrrann promised. "But you nnneed to start broadcasting the moment just beforrre the enemy nnotices us, so at least some of the message gets out before they try attacking or jamming. Timing is crrrucial."

"If you have to move on to a new target, remember that you only have twenty missiles at most, unless you've fired a few. Make every shot count."

Wiping the sweat from his brow with the damp sleeve of his coveralls, Scott returned from lugging away the last of the odd packing material. A mountain of the stuff had formed off to one side; it was lightweight to begin with, made out of some cross between paper and foam, but the dwarf planet's modest gravity made stacking it even easier. There was just a lot of it to be moved, and move quickly.

Rrenn unscrewed the seals on the last drone's fuel tank. Picking up a jug of purified water—the water purification systems were thankfully among the still-functional parts of the abandoned base—he carefully poured the contents into the tank. Scott moved over to the base of the control cradle and opened its tank, then picked up one of the half-dozen remaining containers from the gallons they had purified earlier, while unpacking most of the machines.

They would need to suit up, go outside, carefully dig up more chunks of methane-water ice outside, and feed it into the base's purification system if they wanted anything to drink. For now, they had more important matters on their minds.

"Hrrann, I'm getting energy spikes. The panels are starting to heat up," Sabina warned Hrrann. "That station needs to transmit *now*."

"You've seenn the data. Trrransmit now!" Hrrann ordered into his headset. He tensed, waiting, then flicked his ears up, whiskers forward. "They'rrre doing it! Go, go, go! Attack nnow!"

"We're on it! Close formation, max thrusters!"

Sealing the tank, Rrenn checked on Scott's progress. The Human finished pouring the second jug into the control cradle's tank, and ratcheted the cap into place with a trio of clicks. Nodding, he stepped back from the final drone and turned, loping toward the controls for the cargo lift. Just as he reached the panel, a hum filled the cavern, coming from the thruster panels. Waiting impatiently, tailtip flicking, he watched Scott drive the drone over to the broad platform, then park it next to the other three.

For a moment, the thrusters vanished, leaving behind quiet. A tap of the controls started a louder hum, almost a rumble. The aging but still functional lift mechanisms ground upward. The great doors built into the storage bay ceiling hissed open, letting in a cold downdraft of methane-scented air. Rrenn sneezed, flapping his hand in front of his face. The base's mechanical life support scrubbers would clear the stench sooner or later, but not for several minutes.

A *thunk* heralded the base of the lift system connecting with the rim of the airlock shaft. A muffled hum followed, signaling the lifting of the upper deck. There were three sets of doors to clear. Rrenn waited until the last one opened; the one functioning camera on the surface showed all four drone ships sitting in the open. They were surrounded by mounds of methane-water snow awkwardly cleared by a flexing of the base shields, before those shields had shorted out.

The remaining crew of the *Hunting Party S'kessa* were truly vulnerable down here, without functional shields. The only upside was that it would take a lot more time for the Salik to detect the meager energy traces being produced by the base, without those shields. More time than they were apparently going to take, here at system's edge. Leaving the control station, Rrenn hurried back to the nearest of the last four cradles.

Scott was already climbing out of the very last one, having set the coordinates for the drone's autopilot program. It would go join the others parked in the shadow of the dwarf planet, awaiting use. It didn't take long for Rrenn to climb into one and set a similar destination himself.

Pausing before he climbed into the next one, Scott looked over at him. "You know, if we slingshot around the far side of Eris … we *could* get these babies up to ramming speed. With their surface panel to mass ratio, they're *way* faster than missile thrusters. They *could* penetrate even a warship's shields."

"That would be a suicide rrrrun … *if* these werrre mannned fighter ships," Rrenn agreed.

"*HA!* Got ya, you *shova v'kask!*" Sabina crowed. The angle of her monitor was a bit awkward, but the golden-white chaff of fire rapidly expanding, then snuffing, proved her words accurate. "Got your attention, too. Didn't expect to need shields up that strongly, eh? Ha!"

"Scott, Rrenn," Captain Hrrann called out. "I've pllotted their trrrajectory. I'm feeding it to the fleet. Move those last two drrones to inntercept."

"Yes, sir!" Scott called back, fastening the straps of his cradle. "Going to try a little ramming speed, Captain?"

"A trrio of half-lightspeed colllisionns just might give them a bad day," he agreed.

"Hell with that," Sabina snorted. "Let's give 'em a *really* bad day. First wave, soften 'em up. Second wave, *ramming speed*!"

Rrenn climbed into the last cradle. Fastening the harness, he gripped the joysticks, toggled the menu options, and restarted the thrusters. Beside him, Scott hovered his own drone.

"The more damage we can do to their warp panels, the less stable their FTL fields are going to be," Sabina reminded the others. "These are warships; they use FTL for in-system thrusters, so if we destabilize them, they'll *really* get thrown off-course."

"Ha! I got one, too, Aunt!"

"I can't get through this one's shields."

"Hey, Rrenn," Scott asked, "race ya to the collision point?"

"You'rrre on, Clan Brrrother," Rrenn agreed, grinning ferally. "Thrrree … two … one!"

Both of them squeezed their thruster triggers at the same time. Rrenn opted for a flatter angle than the steep rise Scott picked. The minimal atmosphere clinging to Eris dragged faintly on the drone ship at best; gravity was more of a factor in his speed, a factor he intended to use to slingshot his ship around the planet's curve.

"Dammit! They blew me up!" Scott's father yanked his harness straps free and scrambled out of the cradle. Bounding to one of the empty ones, he climbed up, strapped in, and grabbed the controls, bringing another waiting drone to life.

He wasn't the only one. Within half a minute, another Human and two of the Solaricans abandoned their cradles. More followed. Even Sabina had to abandon ship, cursing as she wriggled free of the straps.

"Dammit—their shields are too strong to penetrate at these speeds. We're getting shot down before we can open up a large enough hole on their hulls!"

"Hey, no fair, you're getting ahead," Scott joked. "You are *so* not splatting yourself before I do!"

"There are plenty of opportunities to splatter ourselves, children," Sabina chided them from further down the bay. "No bickering. Accelerate and ram these *s'nunn-meioas*."

"Watch yourrr lllanguage, Clann Sister!" Hrrann ordered her. "Battle is nno rreason to speak dishonnorably."

The ships were finally coming into view on Rrenn's screen. They were huge, ugly, and hard to see; their mirror-polished hulls were designed to deflect as much damage from lasers as possible. The slide of starlight over each bend and curve broke occasionally, giving him visual clues to the weapons mounted along the hull.

I am a little g'shek *hunting a* tarrgher, he thought, amused by the very idea. *A Terran fly to a mammoth. I will bring poison in my sting, and stagger the beast with illness … rendering it prime for being hunted down and slaughtered by the Terran military pack.*

Fur fluffing, he increased his speed. Off to the side, four more had to scramble out of their cradles. Scrolling through the menu options, Rrenn found the one that allowed him to receive telemetry from the other ships. An overlay of the local region around Eris showed the Salik vessels as large blobs of dark red, and the drone ships as tiny specks of green.

The four were all Humans, cousins close to Scott's age. One of the females was proposing something to the others.

"There *is* an option in the menu for close-formation flight. I know I saw it," Maurina insisted. "If we can slip a fifth ship between ours, and fly it in an AI-controlled box format, we can accelerate it like a slingshot. Max the thrusters on the fifth ship as we peel off, slip the fields just right, and she goes squirting out at near-Cee speeds, instead of half-Cee."

"Aiming would be a pain," her brother pointed out. "Anything traveling near the speed of light has zero tolerance for a miss—ya know, this would be a whole lot easier if we had a small thermal exhaust port to fire at."

That caused the others to laugh. Rrenn snicker-sneezed. Despite their physiological and cultural differences, Humans and Solaricans shared a distinct love for a good, heroic story. "If we lllive, there will be grrrand tales tolld about us, I think."

"Exactly. What have we got to lose?" Maurina argued, climbing into a cradle near Rrenn's. "They're already on a dead run, trying to get up to FTL speeds to make the jump to the inner system. The only thing holding that fleet back is their mass. We have maybe ten minutes before they hit the half-Cee mark, and start outrunning us—speed is something that *will* overcome those military-grade shields."

"Evenn a tin cann will puncture a warrship, at rrrelativistic speeds," Rrenn agreed, lining up his ship. A squeeze of the upper trigger on his right joystick pulsed the twin lasers on his drone. The bright red light struck the alien battlecruiser, guided by the drone's on-board computers, far more accurate than a biological hand could be at these distances. The tactical overlay showed the attack as a line angled between the two, since Rrenn's TarDro was coming in perpendicular to the movement of the Salik ship.

"Ahh … *shakk* it," Sabina muttered, stalking their way. "Sign me up for the fifth ship in that formation. I lost another one. I *think* I tagged part of their hull with the debris, but it's too hard to tell."

"You did, Cllan Aunnt!" one of the Solaricans called out. "I'm chasing your debrrris-tail now! Impact in five, four, thrrrreeeee … *HA!*"

Warning sensors flared from green to yellow, heading toward the red on the edge of Rrenn's control screen. The lasers were starting to overheat; they weren't designed for continuous fire. Another telltale flared, blinking from yellow to red. A quick twitch of the controls spun his ship, barely dodging the incoming missile. The tactical overlay warned him the even smaller red dot of the missile was already trying to arc around and come back his way.

"You want me to shoot that off your tail?" Scott called out.

Rrenn shook his head, ears perked forward. The tactical display, counting down the seconds to its impact on his tail, was less than a second behind the one counting down his own impact on the ship he had targeted. "No. Lleave it. I wannt it to follow me in, so that it hits its *ownn* side."

"Wise is the warrior who uses one enemy to take out the other," Sabina praised, tugging her straps into place. "Maurina, Marcas, Peter, Aurella … let's move out of the shadow and into the light. And since it's Maurina's idea, let's link to Maurina's ship. Where's that menu option, girl?"

"Ahhh … In-system Combat, submenu Close Quarters … ah, there it is! Group Combat … No, Flight Formations," she recited. "We want the Coordinated Flight menu. I think they'd use that menu for flight exhibitions and sales demonstrations, but we can use it for combat, too."

The enemy ship loomed large. Rrenn squeezed the left-hand upper trigger rapidly. The missiles could only launch so fast, and the speeds at which they traveled were only slightly faster than his drone. He managed to get three ahead of him before the safety systems forced the lasers, swinging around to a near dead-ahead position, to shut off or risk blowing up the missiles prematurely.

Not that they had much chance for survival. A heartbeat and a half after the dark red line vanished, so did the view from his drone's forward-facing sensors. A blip of orange-white static, then empty black as his drone vanished against the hull of the cruiser.

"Good shot!" Scott praised. "You made a hole for—*yeaaah!* Woo!" He flung up his hands from the joysticks in triumph, grinning. "I just drove my ship into the hole you made! Ha, beat *that*, Aunty!"

"As the old expression goes, don't get cocky, kid," his aunt shot back. "They're treating us like gnats and barely even bothering to swat."

Releasing his restraints, Rrenn climbed down from his cradle. A glance at the tactical display on one of the idle drones showed most of the enemy fleet too far away to reach. Moving over to stand by his uncle, he watched Hrrann aiming for the debris-trailed hole made by Sabina's ship. A few moments later, missiles launched just ahead of his drone, Hrrann's screen also went blank.

A glance at the cradle next to his, of a damaged drone doing a tail-chase, not quite fast enough to catch up, gave them a good view of what little they had done. Only three out of the twenty or so warships appeared to have any damage. Hrrann growled. "We haven't donnne much. They'rre not even limpinng!"

"We arrre the poisonous bite of the *g'shek*," Rrenn stated, sharing his thoughts with the others. "It *doesn't* look like we've donne anything. But their scratches may become innnfected, slowing them downn at a crrritical moment in the battles ahead. Spiral grrrant it is so."

"Spirrral grant," Hrrann agreed. "They'rrre nearly at half-Cee nnnow. Cannn anyone else attack?"

"Give us five minutes," Sabina stated. "I think this'll work—Krristh, Barrann, start hitting the biggest ship at the coordinates I'm sending you."

"The one that's the size of a Battle Platforrrm?" Krristh asked. "It's shrrrugged off everythinng we thrrrew at it."

"That's why I want to hit it at near-Cee. Use your lasers; nothing else will catch up with them. Maurina, aim the squirtgun at that same spot. Everyone else, hit somewhere to the left of that spot. I don't want them to know which exact one I'm being aimed at."

Seconds ticked by, turning slowly into minutes. One by one, either missiles took out the trailing, laser-firing drones, or their weapons systems shut down protectively as the cannons overheated. Those who didn't have an actual attack to plan set their ships to return to Eris orbit on autopilot, allowing them to climb out of the cradles and cluster around the five ships still functional.

With a grunted warning, Maurina and the others pulsed their thruster fields one last time as a group, sending Sabina's last ship forward. They peeled off … then reformed again, putting one of the four ships between the other three. It didn't take much to reach maximum speed, either; within thirty seconds of Sabina's launch, Peter's ship followed.

Within thirty more, Sabina's ship slammed into the deadened space scorched by the others' lasers. A minute after that, as the Salik vessels continued to accelerate, Peter's ship hit it as well, his screen going dark. Fifteen seconds after *that*, the impacts showed up on the remaining active monitors.

Or at least, that was when the trailing ships spotted the impacts. Hyperrelays delivered information in realtime, but those relays ended at the moment of impact. The relativistic speeds meant the actual attacks happened several seconds earlier, leaving them dependent upon the lag of light speeding over the millions of kilometers between the enemy and them. It took several more seconds for the onboard AIs to analyze the results of the double attacks, but when the reports scrolled onto the screen, most of the Solarican purr-rumbled in satisfaction.

That satisfaction vanished when the ships did, making the jump to faster-than-light. The after-battle let-down escaped as a group sigh. Some scrubbed at their faces. Others pulled off their defunct headsets. Out of forty unpacked drones, marked by the forty cradle stations set up around them, only nine AITX TarDros remained. Two were barely able to steer, two were scuffed up, and the remaining five hadn't left their parking coordinates in the planet's umbra. Still mint condition, but no longer in-the-box.

An almost respectful silence filled the storage hall for several long seconds. Not only for their brave efforts, but in delayed reaction for the loss of their ship and their loved ones.

Sabina summed it up for all of them. She cleared her throat, then unbuckled her safety harness. Sinking back in her padded seat, she lifted her feet up onto the bar between the two now useless joysticks.

"Well. The others may have died, but that open link gave us time to not only warn the others, but to try and make them pay. For tiny little gnats who could barely make a scratch … I do believe our last two bites will leave some actual scars. They're still capable of FTL," she admitted grimly, "but they're going to have some very obvious wounds for the Space Force to pick at. And if the military has anything in their scanner systems capable of picking up those targeting gels, I know I pegged at least two of the ships with the stuff."

"I know got a few myself," her brother Malcom admitted. Some of the others nodded.

Scott lifted his chin, looking at Rrenn. "I think Parrda and the rest would be proud of that."

"Innndeed," Hrrann agreed.

"Anybody have an idea of what we're going to do now?" Scott asked. "We do have three shuttles on the surface, but they're built for orbital work, not in-system. We can't fly back to civilized space in them, and we don't have anything but air and water in this place."

"I'd rrrreally rather not starrrve to death," someone else muttered.

"We'rre a thirrrd of the way around the plannnet from that mining stationn," Rrenn reminded the others. "The Salik didn't firre a single shot at them, so they owe us forr saving them. We can go take rrrefuge with them."

"We dare nnnot call annnyone for several hours on the shuttles' comms, for fearrr of the Salik turning arounnd and hitting us in rrrevenge," Hrrann stated. "We'lll go to the mining stationn."

"Okay, everyone. You heard the captain," Sabina ordered, sitting up so she could climb out of her cradle-seat. She was his business partner and second-in-command, now that his mate was gone, destroyed with their ship. "Pack up whatever you brought down here, and start heading for the shuttles. The rest of this battle will be up to the Space Force to fight."

"Good job, everrryone," Hrrann added as they followed her orders. "You'd be made into warrr prrinces for this fight, if I had anny say in it. A good day's hunnt. Maybe we can salvage some Salik scrrraps, later onn."

O O O

Most people think the first official shots of the Second Salik War took place when the Salik moved into Earth orbit at FTL speeds and started slinging missiles and lasers at everything they could see. They expected to find the Terrans unprepared for such a bold move, and under normal circumstances, they would've been right. But sometimes Fate deals you a wild card.

You don't have to be a soldier to be a war hero. You just have to be in the wrong place at the wrong time … and do the right thing.

—Ia

With multiple bestsellers ranging anywhere from award-nominated military science fiction to award-winning paranormal romance, **Jean Johnson** may seem hard to pin down, but the answer is obvious: She simply likes to tell a good story. Her military science fiction series, Theirs Not to Reason Why, is dedicated to the hard-working members of the military, in gratitude for their service. Written in that same universe, *The Joystick War* is for those friends, family, and strangers who may not have served, but who honor and support those who are willing to fight to defend our lives and our homes.

If you would like to chat with Jean, she can be reached through her website, www.JeanJohnson.net, via Twitter: @JeanJAuthor, or by just searching for "Fans of Author Jean Johnson" on Facebook. (The publisher is not associated with nor responsible for any of these.)

Guard Dog

by Mike Resnick and Brad R. Torgersen

Introduction to "Guard Dog"

One of my mentors and favorite authors, Mike Resnick, agreed to do a story for Space Battles on the condition he could co-write his story with another writer he was mentoring, Brad R. Torgersen. Together, they wrote one of the more interesting tales in the book and one of my favorites—the story of a long lost father who sacrificed family, life, even humanness to protect his family. To his surprise, and ours, the ensuing journey leads to a confrontation that's totally unexpected with profound consequences. Short, but powerful, publishing "Guard Dog" first is still a career highlight I am very proud of and both authors have continued to appear in numerous anthologies of mine since.

A passive sensor pinged hesitantly and Chang came alert. He felt his way through the familiar diagnostic routine, verifying the status of thousands of different shipboard components. As expected, everything was functioning. The sole minimal change was that his available fuel had decreased.

Chang had never been told exactly how long his fuel would last. In fact, there had never been any mention of refueling, nor rearming. This would have bothered him, prior to being crippled in combat. But now it was simply a fact of life. He knew he was disposable, had known it when he'd blinked twice for *yes* during the Watchfleet accessions interview in the hospital ward. It was still better than the alternative.

Another ping, this time a bit stronger.

Artificial adrenaline began to surge.

The threat. Where was the threat?

Chang's head and spine were plugged into the core of an armored, spherical spacecraft hovering at a nameless set of coordinates that rode directly on the invisible wall between Human Space and Everywhere Else. He'd been on that spot for who knew how long? His cyborg life was composed of a series of extended, dream-filled sleeps in between frenetic, life-or-death battles.

At the time Chang had elected to undergo surgical implant and machine integration, the Watchfleet had been mankind's best defense against the Sortu, a mysteriously aggressive species of xenophobes actively exterminating all "competitor" races in Earth's particular region of the known galaxy. Where it took years to build, arm, and crew an ordinary warship, a Watchfleet monitor took mere weeks, and required only its cyborg pilot. Chang—and thousands of other wounded veterans just like him—had all signed up to establish an interstellar line in the sand: *this far, no father.*

At the time, humanity had been overwhelmed, and the Sortu had almost won.

Chang and his comrades had put a stop to it, but the toll had been high. The Watchfleet had grown thin, to the point that Chang seldom heard the comforting murmur of his fellows—their mental signals broadcast instantaneously through the *gravtrans* buried deep in Chang's armored shell. Once they had formed an intelligent skein, acting and reacting in concert to surround and crush all opponents. Now they were few and far between, like lonely whales hooting forlornly through the ocean's inky depths.

When his sensors did not alert him a third time, Chang set up an automated diagnostic routine and allowed himself to slip back into his dreams.

O O O

Lucy's skin was so pale and freckled that she burned at the merest mention of sunlight. Chang ran a hand appreciatively along his wife's bare hip as they lay together in their bed, heavy rain drumming on the glass of the wall-length window of their tiny high-rise apartment in Hong Kong. One of hundreds of such buildings that dominated the downtown area.

"We should get up soon," Lucy murmured.

"What for?" replied Chang. "I'm on leave through Monday. We used my military ration card to get enough to eat so that we wouldn't have to go anywhere if we didn't want to."

"Yeah, but it's midafternoon. I feel like a slug just hanging out in bed. We should get some exercise."

Chang sighed deeply. "They work the crap out of us in Advanced Crew Training. I get more exercise in a day than you get in a week."

"Oh yeah?" she said defiantly.

"Yeah," Chang said, smiling as he grabbed her shoulder and turned her quickly onto her back, her breasts fluttering pleasantly on her chest. His hands began to mischievously wander up her belly as the two of them kept talking.

"You still haven't told your father about me, have you?" Chang said, his eyes locked onto hers, but his hands possessing a mind all their own.

"No," she said, "I don't want to have to deal with him right now."

"Ashamed of your Chinese husband?"

She smiled roguishly at him. "If I was, would we be doing *this*?"

O O O

Ping! Ping! Ping!

Damn.

It had been a long time since Chang had made love to his wife, even in his memory. He reluctantly returned to wakefulness.

He scanned the diagnostic report on the sensors. As far as his internal maintenance routines could ascertain, everything checked out. So what the hell was going on?

Ping!

Chang slipped his more robust active sensors into the vacuum, their huge domes revolving and twirling beyond the confines of the plated hull—*Hello, anyone there?*

The cold emptiness of interstellar space remained unbroken. Straight out in all directions.

Then … wait. There.

Pong-pong-pong-pong-pong. Not a ghost signature. This was something solid. Several somethings.

Not members of the Watchfleet.

The attack came. From the direction Chang least expected.

Eight small craft appeared like ghosts. Using a breed of engine unknown to Chang's signature recognition software, they moved more quickly than any ships Chang had ever encountered before. Within moments each ship had detached several smaller vessels that were arcing in on Chang's position.

Missiles. Fast ones.

Chang retracted his sensors and slammed his internal drive into action. Treading the fabric of space like an Olympic runner charging across a track, Chang shot out of the path of the incoming projectiles, weaving and dispensing countermeasures in his wake. He used the *gravtrans* to hurl an electronic shout into the universe: *enemy units attacking, grid omega niner niner zero one five niner zero, Watchfleet assistance needed!*

But there was no answer in response.

Worse still, the missiles fired at Chang were different. Smart.

With every twist and curve that Chang threw into his trajectory, the little missiles corrected and accelerated, blowing right through his countermeasures. Like their mothercraft, they moved much faster than Chang would have thought possible. No wonder none of the other Watchfleet units were responding to his calls. They'd probably been destroyed already, leaving him alone to defend himself.

Chang felt tickles of panic running through his organic tissues.

Simultaneously, a memory sprang into his consciousness …

O O O

Lucy's father was a tall, unsmiling man. His cheeks were rosy in the cold October air and his overcoat was speckled with drops of water from the English mist. Chang stood next to him, uncomfortably close. They hadn't said a word to each other since accompanying Lucy to the park with the twins. The park crawled with people, as always.

"Wave to Dad!" Lucy said, propping one of the boys up on a piece of playground equipment. The little toddler, whom Chang had known for all of two days, appeared joyfully bewildered as his head swiveled back and forth, looking for a face he hadn't yet learned to recognize.

Chang waved, half-smiling, and then dropped his hand to his side. His own military issue overcoat was drawn tightly at the waist, collar turned up.

"I'm sorry you had to find out about us the way you did," Chang said finally.

Lucy's father grunted.

"She's just like her mother used to be," the old man said. "Has a mind all her own, and doesn't care to share it with me—except when she really needs something."

"I wanted her to tell you. Especially the last time I was home. She kept evading the issue. When I shipped out to space, I didn't know she was pregnant. I only found out about the boys after they'd been born. And by then she'd moved back here to be closer to you."

Lucy's father sighed, and for the first time turned and looked Chang in the eye.

"It's not your fault," he rumbled, "but know this: You're part of our lot now. Those two sons of yours, they've got some of me in them, and that makes us *both* responsible for them. No matter where you go or how old you are or what you see out there in space, those twins will never, ever stop needing you. It's sealed in blood now, and there's no going back."

Lucy looked at Chang affectionately. Her face became puzzled when he didn't automatically return her smile. He was too busy staring at his sons, and realizing that at age twenty-three his life was now committed to a certain unbreakable trajectory …

O O O

The memory *poofed* away as quickly as it had come.

A missile had closed to within lethal range.

Desperately, he reversed his drive. His ship groaned under the intense stress of the maneuver, but the gravity distortion backwash caught the missile before it could arm itself—leaving a harmlessly dissipating cloud of metal flakes.

Chang experienced short-lived relief. Then, causing another structural groan, Chang reversed direction again.

Moments before impact with the debris from the first missile, he dipped and curved, his path taking him just barely around the expanding ball of metal shards. Kiloton explosions flared and died. Had the remaining missiles proximity fail-safed, or been manually detonated? There was no time to get an answer.

A wedge formation of three mothercraft was coming up fast.

Built like three-sided pyramids, they were very different from anything Chang had ever seen before. His lasers lashed out, their highly-focused beams waving across the enemy like a gardener spraying water from his hose. The pyramidal vehicles disintegrated, then exploded.

Five bogies remained.

The enemy force divided again: two and two and one—and as it did so, Chang picked up the signals from more incoming missiles. He mentally flashed through every detail of every battle he had ever fought as both man and machine, sifting and collating the data until an effective tactic coalesced.

Chang's lasers hit the center of the missile swarm like an eraser, eradicating every projectile they touched. A sizable hole appeared within the swarm and Chang poured every bit of power he could into his own drive.

The missiles were all around Chang, and then they were behind him, their paths curving sharply back on themselves as they all attempted to follow their target. He flashed past the motherships, which also began to turn. A fireworks display of epic proportions erupted directly in his wake. Matter annihilated matter in a fantastically destructive spectacle that lit up the space around it.

The flush of victory again flowed through Chang.

Just three left to go.

Then the enemy touched Chang's skin with their own lasers. He sensed the deadly energy an instant before it hit. There was no use in turning; every part of his armored skin was equally thick. But would it be thick enough?

In a millisecond, a great wound was opened in the hull. An accompanying flow of damage statistics paraded through Chang's brain—the digital equivalent of pain. The *gravtrans* was gone, and the main drive partially damaged, though still functional.

Again, Chang rapid-sorted through his memory banks, seeking alternative courses of action. He had never been damaged like this before. Still, he *had* to survive.

Humanity was depending on him. More to the point, Lucy and the *boys* were depending on him.

O O O

Carter and Eric were five years old when Chang's flotilla was ambushed. He was in his bunk, staring at a digital photo of them on his PDA, when an explosion swept through the deck. If he'd already been in his space armor, the blast wouldn't have done much damage. As it was, Chang had to be carted to emergency triage with third-degree burns. And arms and legs so badly mangled even the months he spent in a liquid regeneration "womb" during the voyage back to Earth couldn't fix them. They were amputated at the veterans' hospital, planetside.

Lucy's father was the one who came to visit.

"I'm sorry Lucy's not here," he explained. "But she's immigrated to the colonies, and there's a ban on space travel now that the war has gotten a little closer."

Chang just stared, his damaged larynx useless. It was true: life on Earth had been no picnic. He was glad she'd made the move while she could. If the residents of Earth lived like sardines in a can, it was only because the Sortu made it so.

The lab men from the Watchfleet showed up a few minutes after Lucy's father did. He had watched Lucy's father's face while the men had explained the program: battle vets, hard-wired into a new breed of super-ship, armed to the teeth, autonomous, yet tied together electronically to form a web the Sortu couldn't penetrate.

The ambush that got Chang hadn't been the only one. Several of the outer colonies had been knocked off. Earth itself was now in danger. The Sortu were tightening the noose. The Watchfleet was going to be humanity's best—and possibly last—answer.

Full pay and benefits, of course, to be delivered directly to family and next of kin—regardless of the duration of the Watchfleet battle tour. Posthumous continuation, guaranteed.

Lucy's father stared at him expectantly, and he remembered their conversation in the park. Unable to nod or make any acknowledging movements, Chang gave the lab men his answer with his eyes.

O O O

The three remaining enemy ships closed in. Chang could feel them poke and prod with their active sensors. He was badly hurt, he had no missiles of his own anymore, and his laser system had been hopelessly damaged.

The only thing he had left to throw at them now was his own fuel.

Antimatter. It could be pumped from the central magnetic holding cell into space by using the emergency flush system.

It could result in victory, but a pyrrhic one.

Using the flush pumps Chang dumped half his available fuel into the black void, the antimatter cloud instantly expanding around his own hull. He could feel it eating away at his ship. But would the enemy notice in time?

To his great relief, they did not.

Two of the three ships flared with white fire as the antimatter ate through their hardened hulls. Bright cataclysms flared and died—the shockwave tossing Chang out of the midst of the cloud.

The third pyramid pulled out in time, if just barely. It began limping along, trailing pieces of itself.

Chang moved in.

Sortu lasers—dramatically weakened—leapt to intercept him, but a secondary explosion wracked the lone pyramidal vessel, and its bombardment ceased.

Chang's sub-light drive pushed him in close to the enemy craft as it tumbled directionless through space. As the distance shrank, he collected data on the make-up of the ship: hardware that had been exposed, the size and type of both known and unknown components, everything he could learn.

At five kilometers, the finer details emerged. Among the floating bits of debris, Chang could identify tiny carbon-based components.

Interesting. He'd never seen the Sortu in the flesh. In fact, he wasn't sure anyone ever had—this would be a first.

He zeroed his remaining sensor equipment in on the lifeless bodies.

After only a few seconds of examination, the truth became clear—the corpses of the aliens … were not alien at all.

There, he could see a little man who had been shredded, his arms and legs curled lifelessly to his chest. Next, a headless human female. Next, a male, his space suit half on, helmet still clutched uselessly in one hand.

Hundreds of human bodies drifted like a school of dead jellyfish brought in on the evening tide.

Chang hung motionless with shock. This simply did not compute. Humans did not fight humans. It was aliens who were the enemy, to be slaughtered with impunity. The Sortu! They were …

He set about slowly collecting the corpses. The uniforms were different from the ones Chang had worn when he'd been a whole man, working in the Service. But the faces were all too familiar—young men and women, as he'd once been, sent to fight and die in the depths of interstellar space. And for what? By who?

Chang stopped cold.

One face in particular caught his electronic eyes.

Carter.

It couldn't be. But the name tape sewn into the breast of the uniform was Chang's last name. The young, dead man bore the same uncannily mixed features. Only now he was grown up: semi-almond eyes, dark hair, freckled skin, and Lucy's fine nose …

Chang set that particular body aside and kept collecting, until a face that was almost identical to the first appeared.

Eric.

Same name tape, same features. Chang put the boys side by side, comparing their faces. They'd been frozen forever, startled at the very end. What was left of Chang—the man joined to the machine—silently began to boil with a sensation of complete and utter betrayal.

Lucy's father had said she—and of course the boys—had moved to the colonies … and the colonies were closer to the enemy. It was the only thing that had motivated Chang, all these years.

He continued to stare at his dead sons for a few more minutes. Then he rummaged through the wreck of the pyramid ship, accessed the computer, and read the records, and suddenly the situation—the *true* situation—became very clear.

It was an entirely different picture from the one Chang had been given when he'd signed up, first as a soldier, then as a Watchfleet pilot.

He hadn't been defending Earth against aliens.

He'd been defending Earth's government against her own children.

A breakaway alliance of human colonies had apparently been fighting the united government's oppression since Chang himself had been a boy.

The Sortu were a lie.

After Chang's internal damage control systems slowly patched up what could be patched, he gathered his sons and all the other dead, and gently set them adrift in the void, along with their ship. The alliance would find them, after he was gone. He left a small message asking that they be given heroes' honors. He left another message, too, about his reasons for what he was about to do.

Chang then set a course for Sol System. For Earth. Maybe the alliance had managed to pick off all his comrades. But there was one watch dog still left.

And before they put him down, he was going to take one hell of a chunk out of his masters.

A native of Chicago, **Mike Resnick** is a graduate of Highland Park High School in Highland Park, Illinois. He attended the University of Chicago from 1959 to 1961 where he met his future wife, Carol. The couple were married 1961. In the 1960s and early 1970s, Resnick wrote more than 200 "adult" novels under pseudonyms, edited seven tabloid newspapers, and edited a trio of men's magazines. He also produced a weekly column on horse racing for more than a decade, and for eleven years wrote a monthly column on purebred collies, which he and his wife bred and exhibited. His wife Carol is also a writer, as is his daughter, Laura Resnick, who is an award-winning science fiction and fantasy author. Resnick's papers, consisting of at least 125 boxes, are in the Special Collections Library of the University of South Florida in Tampa. He was the Guest of Honor at Chicon 7, the 70th World Science Fiction Convention, held in Chicago in 2012. Learn more about Resnick and his body of work at mikeresnick.com.

Brad R. Torgersen is a science fiction and fantasy author who debuted in the 26th volume of *Writers of the Future*, and has since gone on to publish in some of the genre's top venues, such as *Analog Science Fiction & Fact* magazine, Orson Scott Card's *Intergalactic Medicine Show*, and *Galaxy's Edge* magazine. In addition to winning the Writers of the Future award, Brad won the *Analog* Magazine "AnLab" readers' choice award, and was a 2012 triple nominee for science fiction's top three prizes: the Hugo, the Nebula, and the Campbell awards. Brad has also collaborated with bestselling award-winners Mike Resnick and Larry Niven. 2014 saw the debut of Torgersen's first novel—*The Chaplain's War*—from Baen Books. A full-time healthcare tech geek by day, Brad is also a United States Army Reserve Chief Warrant Officer.

Learn more at bradrtorgersen.com.

Additional Copyright Information

"Granny's Grunts" copyright 2009 by Alan L. Lickiss. First published in *Space Grunts: Full-Throttle Space Tales #3*, May 2009

"Last Man Standing" copyright 2010 by Danielle Ackley-McPhail. First published in *Space Horrors: Full-Throttle Space Tales #4*, October 2010

"Into the Abyss" copyright 2010 by Dayton Ward. First published in *Space Horrors: Full-Throttle Space Tales #4*, October 2010

"Listening" copyright 2010 by Anna Paradox. First published in *Space Horrors: Full-Throttle Space Tales #4*, October 2010

"Backup" copyright 2011 by Ivan Ewert. First published in *Space Tramps: Full-Throttle Space Tales #5*, September 2011

"The Frigate Lieutenant's Woman" copyright 2011 by Erik Scott de Bie. First published in *Space Tramps: Full-Throttle Space Tales #5*, September 2011

"Oh Give Me Land, Lots of Land, Under Starry Skies Above" copyright 2011 by Shannon Page and Mark Ferrari. First published in *Space Tramps: Full-Throttle Space Tales #5*, September 2011

"The Thirteens" copyright 2012 by Gene Mederos. First published in *Space Battles: Full-Throttle Space Tales #6*, April 2012

"The Joystick War" copyright 2012 by Jean Johnson. First published in *Space Battles: Full-Throttle Space Tales #6*, April 2012

"Guard Dog" copyright 2012 by Mike Resnick and Brad R. Torgersen. First published in *Space Battles: Full-Throttle Space Tales #6*, April 2012

About the Editors

David Lee Summers is an author, editor, and astronomer living in Southern New Mexico. He edited the science fiction and fantasy magazines *Hadrosaur Tales* and *Tales of the Talisman* for ten years each along with the anthologies *A Kepler's Dozen*, *Space Pirates*, and *Space Horrors*. He's also the author of ten novels including *Owl Dance* and *The Astronomer's Crypt*. His short fiction has appeared in such venues as *Cemetery Dance* and *Realms of Fantasy* Magazines. When not working with the written word, David operates telescopes at Kitt Peak National Observatory. Learn more about David at davidleesummers.com.

A native Texan, **Carol Hightshoe** found her way to her current home in Colorado by way of a five-year detour in The Nederlands—courtesy of her husband Tim and the US Air Force. She has been published in various anthologies and magazines including *Creature Fantastic*, *PanGaia* Magazine, *Stories of Strength*, *Baen's Universe*, *Tales of the Talisman* and *A Kepler's Dozen*. Her novels include: *Call of Chaos*, *Chaos Embraced*, *The Road into Chaos*, and *Chaos Challenged*. In addition to her own writing, she is the editor and publisher of the online e-zines: *The Lorelei Signal* and *Sorcerous Signals* as well as running her own micro-press, WolfSinger Publications.

Dayton Ward is a New York Times bestselling author or co-author of nearly thirty novels and novellas, often working with his best friend, Kevin Dilmore. His short fiction has appeared in more than twenty anthologies, and he's written for magazines such as *Kansas*

City Voices, *Famous Monsters of Filmland*, *Star Trek* and *Star Trek Communicator*, as well as the websites Tor.com, StarTrek.com, and Syfy.com. Before making the jump to full-time writing, Dayton was a software developer, having discovered the private sector and the perpetual fear of outsourcing after spending eleven years in the US Marine Corps. Though Dayton lives in Kansas City with his wife and daughters, he's a Florida native and maintains a torrid long-distance romance with his beloved Tampa Bay Buccaneers. Visit him on the web at daytonward.com.

Jennifer Brozek is a Hugo Award nominated editor and a Bram Stoker nominated author. She has worked in the publishing industry since 2004. With the number of different projects she juggles at one time, Jennifer is often considered a Renaissance woman, but prefers to be known as a wordslinger and optimist. Read more about her at her website: jenniferbrozek.com or follow her on Twitter at @JenniferBrozek.

Bryan Thomas Schmidt is an author and Hugo-nominated editor of adult and children's speculative fiction. His debut novel, *The Worker Prince*, received Honorable Mention in Barnes & Noble Book Club's Year's Best Science Fiction Releases. His short stories have appeared in magazines, anthologies, and online, and include entries in The X-Files and Decipher's WARS, amongst others. As an editor for WordFire Press, he edited books by such luminaries as Alan Dean Foster, Tracy Hickman, Frank Herbert, Mike Resnick, and Jean Rabe. He was also the first editor on Andy Weir's bestseller *The Martian.* His anthologies as editor include *Shattered Shields* with co-editor Jennifer Brozek, *Mission: Tomorrow*, *Galactic Games*, *Little Green Men–Attack!*, *Space Battles: Full-Throttle Space Tales #6*, *Beyond the Sun*, and *Raygun Chronicles: Space Opera for a New Age*. He is also coediting anthologies with Larry Correia and Jonathan Maberry set in their New York Times bestselling Monster Hunter and Joe Ledger universes. Find him online at bryanthomasschmidt.net.

Other WordFire Press Anthologies

Decision Points

Dragon Writers

Five by Five

Our list of other WordFire Press authors and titles is always growing.
To find out more and to see our selection of titles, visit us at:

wordfirepress.com

www.ingramcontent.com/pod-product-compliance
Lightning Source LLC
Chambersburg PA
CBHW050113120726
47904CB00004B/1330

* 9 7 8 1 6 1 4 7 5 5 2 9 6 *